The McQuarrie Sisters

Andrew Bagust

Linellen Press
265 Boomerang Road
Oldbury, Western Australia
www.linellenpress.com.au

Dedication

Did our ancestors' lives look that much different to ours when we read an ancient manuscript? They had more or less the same desires and struggles, right back to Cain and Abel. Years ago, I visited Bath as a tourist in Britain. There, preserved in the bottom of the deep pool for a thousand years, were prayers – cries for help or passioned pleas etched into copper. Translated, they read things like:

'My husband's run off with Bruno, the butcher.'

'I need justice for my son in jail....'

'God help me pay my debts....'

'Please, someone help; my mother is dying.'

I love the ancient writing in Micah 6:8 that says: "*What does God require of us?* A question on our lips as we all wander our way through life. It says three simple things:

To do the right thing, love to be compassionate to others, and walk in humility with God. Has anything changed? I would like to dedicate this book to all those who are silently and invisibly walking through life purposely doing these three things.

Acknowledgements

Mum, without your efforts to track down a thousand photos and faithfully record family history, I would not have taken this next step to bring these characters alive. Your work has left a legacy beyond you.

Thank you to my wife, children and family, who have spent many hours patiently reviewing and listening to ideas in the creation of this story, which is based mainly on fact.

For those who spend thousands of hours searching like detectives through endless scraps of evidence and history to bring this historical fiction to life, I honour you … Well done!

Contents

Preface

Many of us are acutely aware of the highs and lows, joys and sorrows as we journey through this wonderful life. As I have researched endless family stories, listening to them relived round a fire, retold at the dining room table or over a glass of red wine, I became aware that very few people I know share similar tales. It would surprise me when they would behave alarmed or horrified by events out of my family's past, the same way I still react today as I try and place myself in my ancestors' shoes. We all share a history of the family being displaced, downtrodden or suffering, through wars, immigration or the trials of this life. Sometimes they are either running away from something or running to it. I feel privileged to have unearthed and collated some of the incredible pioneering journeys my family experienced as they helped to forge a new colony 150 years ago. Their contribution is still all around in the faces, places and ideals stubbornly held onto in our hope for a better future. I have personally felt some of their journey, sometimes sitting in tears of joy or sorrow as I have endeavoured to reveal a little of their lives. Their hard work, courage and determination are still something I feel proud to be a part of today.

Introduction

Although this is a historical novel, it is based mostly on real characters, places or events from my own family's past. In my first novel, *The McQuarries*, Hector McQuarrie, my great-grandfather, arrives in the new colony in 1856, growing a large family while also building a successful business. Euphemia, one of his daughters, is not only a suffragette but also the first woman in the world to vote. She narrates her story of enduring, despite almost insurmountable odds, while weighing up the duty she feels to her family against society's expectations of taking a lover to complete her life. What must she do with this desire she feels for a gorgeous man, to have a family and settle down or become a successful businesswoman?

This second novel, *The McQuarrie Sisters*, is narrated by her young, charismatic lover, Harry Bagust, whose family are clawing their way out of poverty, grief and disappointment, striving for a better life while at every turn, it appears to be stolen from their grasp. His flamboyance and competitive spirit give him both success and failure in his personal life, business pursuits and sporting prowess. My grandfather is a larger-than-life character, perhaps the person we would simultaneously love and hate to be depending on the day or circumstance.

Some of the most popular tourist attractions today in New Zealand, as you look out the window of a train or a car or come across relics of the past, have Harry's hand of courage, blood, sweat and tears soaked into their core. He was a romantic in every sense, an optimist, passionately always hoping for that pot at the end of the rainbow.

Chapter 1

Eat Humble Pie

The morning had begun ominously, the light peeking momentarily through on the clear horizon soon disappearing again in thick clouds overhead. The chilly breeze from the south matched the dreary expression on James' face, which he did not hide as he reluctantly dropped us both off to, arguably, his favourite place – outside the courthouse. I wanted to serve him a hearty slice of Humble Pie, but, as usual, he did not seem to share the slightest bit of guilt over this whole debacle as he cheerfully tied up the horse. We entered the huge open waiting room already filling with a smattering of onlookers who would also eventually be called by the attendant. The wooden bench seats invited our sorry backsides to linger awhile in the freezing foyer as we found empty spaces amongst the guilty chosen. My heart sank at the sight of our local portly cop 'Stumpy' perched staunchly in his pressed uniform, his heart as black as his helmet.

James blurted out a little too loudly, his voice echoing around the panelled walls, "Bloody Stumpy!" This drew demure scowls from those already seated and smirks from those who knew him only too well. He'd finally caught us as I had stepped in to break up another of James' constant fractious confrontations.

Stumpy, the fat, little, cunning bastard, had been transferred up here to Manuwhatu with a fresh promotion and now had a glistening commendation for cleaning up the rail yards. Then James whispered, "He's more like one of those flea-bitten alley cats found scrounging on the docks. Perhaps his chin strap will choke him one day in a dark wood astride his horse."

Walking into a courtroom always took me back in time. Scents of freshly waxed floors, wet leather boots, camphor and hair cream all seemed to combine to pickle the room like an old farmer's wardrobe. The only sounds were the shuffle of bodies on the hard wooden benches and the occasional smoker's cough. As the smell lingered in my nostrils, almost permeating my soul, I was suddenly fifteen again in Timaru, my awkward, lanky frame standing like a chastised dog while an elderly wigged man with piercing eyes examined me like a specimen in a jar. My guilty heart pounded once more – "Thomas, the accused …"

My fortunate siblings all had nice biblical names, like James, Martha, Mary, John and Joseph, but Thomas was Jesus' ostracised disciple, 'The accused' of unbelief. When I was punished, my name always reverted to 'Thomas Henry' instead of Harry.

Presently the attendant called the room to order, explaining that he would call us in one by one as each case was heard.

We seemed to sit for an age, while other cases were summoned, the events that had beckoned us both here replaying in my mind, a forced distraction from my pending doom.

It all began months earlier when James had lost another large bet that he had no funds to cover. We had agreed to get out of Wellington for a few weeks in the hope of scoring a few plump fares until things settled down a little; planned on cashing in on the weekend game between Manuwhatu and Auckland, hoping for rich pickings from a few inebriated customers splashing their hard-earned wealth about. In truth, it was an all-out war to plunder the most prodigious fare from any innocent passenger before another cabby pirated it first. It seemed like a brilliant plan, even a welcome change to be 250 miles from the dockyard politics on Thorndon Quay. I remembered wandering my way to the rail yards following my usual routine … offered a young lad a halfpenny to watch my cart while I went to solicit a fare. The train had just arrived from Wellington, squealing to a halt amid sparks and magnificent bursts of steam. As the usual porters and passengers off-loaded, I lunged forward to uplift two gold-rimmed leather satchels belonging to a portly gentleman and his wife. Over the hiss of steam, muffled voices and a bustling excited crowd, I heard shouting from a familiar voice. Through the mist, there was the silhouette of James locked in an intense struggle with a fellow gambler. Unfortunately, his usual method of debt recovery was first by force, a first blow followed by a burst of shouting. I dropped the bags and leapt to the man's aid, gripping James' arm before he slugged the poor fellow again. The dumpy little man had reeled back, teetering on the platform's edge, shouting insults above the din and holding his stomach as if stabbed.

I grabbed James' waistcoat. "I cannot afford to be locked up, and you've no crumbs left to settle your immense debts. Mother's depending on me to help feed the children."

He'd pulled away in a desultory manner. "They're not our responsibility! Where was she when little William needed caring for?!"

At that second, I'd glanced along the platform over James' shoulder. There was Stumpy's grimaced face. I had scanned the whole scene as if in slow motion, feeling a touch of muse, imagining the platform as our stage, and we merely actors playing parts in a theatrical performance: the injured man bellowing out, frantically pointing in our direction; bystanders, looking on in horror, taking hold of their children's hands; Stumpy in the lead role, his teeth firmly clenched to his shrill whistle as he now moved towards us.

The screech of his whistle above the cacophony of sounds clearly announced our impending doom. Emboldened and power-hungry, he swathed his way through the crowd with his helmet pushed forward. Using it like a battering ram, he parted the Red Sea while his truncheon slashed away prematurely to crush any perpetrators like bugs. His eyes had become steely as he grinned with evil delight. As he drew nearer, he smacked his truncheon into the palm of his hand and shouted, "Bagusts! Stay right where you are! I'm coming for you."

Stumpy stood to his full five-foot stature and reached up to grab me by the lapels; he shouted in my face, "I've got you this time, Bagust! You're under arrest!" His ruddy face had curled into a grin. "I just can't wait to see you out doing a stretch of hard labour."

James' fists clenched. "Get your hands off my brother!" he screamed in defiance.

Suddenly everything fell to pieces as I released James' arm and instinctively braced my elbow against Stumpy's advancing force in a familiar wrestling block. I caught him across the neck, and he fell backwards off balance, his helmet flying among bystanders' legs and onto the tracks. He'd fumbled helplessly for a moment, like he was in oil, scrambling about on his knees to find his fallen truncheon, his bald head now shining in a beam of sunlight. As he stood, the veins on his neck pulsed, looking about to burst. He puffed his chest out, now fully enraged like a bull ready to charge. Then, as if he was suddenly becalmed like a ship in the eye of a storm, he stood still, closed his eyes to gather himself, and then stared as a wry smile spread across his face.

"I didn't expect Monday to begin so satisfactorily: you've played right into my hands, Harry Bagust."

It did not end well for me, and I was led away in handcuffs. Stumpy's biased assessment of the incident resulted in me landing this seat I now occupied next to an unrepentant brother. Under the new fare rules, they'd taken a pompous delight in cracking down on cabbies. In hindsight, James would have been a patron of the nearest lockup, charged with assault, if I had not stepped in … cold bloody comfort for me. James broke into my thoughts.

"No need to look so serious, Harry!"

I scowled back at him. "You know, James, stepping in for you is becoming bloody tiresome!" As I swore, the lady beside me turned to look unpleasantly at me. I whispered, "I know you've protected me many times while growing up on the farm, but we're not lads in Timaru anymore! This has to stop! I'm not going to keep doing this!"

James looked like he'd sucked on a lemon. "Harry, life's tough; you take what you can get. Don't you remember mother's scoldings? She always knew we would be causing mischief somewhere. It's just how we are!"

Absolutely preposterous! I'm not being lumped in with your stubborn behaviour. I stared back at him in disgust.

She'd call us from the fields, never quite believing our version of the day's events and cuffing us just in case. James smiled, imitating her voice. "James! Thomas! What have you scallywags been up to this time? You'll be the death of me." She had a knack for cleverly exposing any possible disgrace we might have caused in the neighbourhood. "If your father were here, he'd give you a good whipping."

At nine, my simple life had come to an abrupt end. Mother had failed to become both parents. I immediately felt my chest tighten, longing for those carefree summer days as a boy on the farm before 'The Accident'.

"That bloody accident still makes me feel sick. Who would have thought that tiny *Otago Daily* article would change our lives forever?" *The stain of that black ink.*

Like a stunned possum, James tensed in his seat, reciting, "Father James Bagust had been committed to lunacy and LEFT a large family.

"Who left? … not *us*!?" James said, expressing with his hands. "I felt abandoned! He *left* us to fend for ourselves!"

"Rubbish. You're just bitter you copped the brunt!"

"Harry, either way, his ten children were left. He was in the habit of leaving us. Look at Harriet … left on the docks in Plymouth! My oldest sister, only eleven years old. That was eighteen years ago! We were inseparable then. Who leaves a young girl of eleven?!"

I turned my head toward him in surprise. "She was too frail," I repeated the line Mother had always chanted in her defence. "She wouldn't have made the four-month crossing. They did it to save her."

In the hush of the foyer, James raised his voice, spitting out, "No! She was *left* to look after our ageing grandparents, Henry and Martha, who were also *left* behind. Now they're starving in a work camp."

I glared at him, catching sight of Stumpy listening intently. "That's *not* how it was! You've always got some chip on your shoulder like the world's against you!"

"How would you explain it then? We had barely been here ten years before nine hungry children were *left* to fend for themselves. Ellen, myself, Mary, Martha, you, Emma, John, Louisa and Joseph! … all *left* without a father … with barely a hope in the world!"

"It wasn't his bloody fault, James. How can you blame all that on him?" My anger rose, and I turned away from him; noticed people looking in our direction.

The attendant came over to us. "Quieten down please or I will have you out!" he said sternly.

James growled under his breath. "Don't tell me to quieten down."

I grabbed his arm. "James! Calm down, or we'll get thrown in the slammer," I hissed.

He was quiet for a few minutes, enough to calm a little.

"We had nothing! It felt like Mother abandoned us too! Ellen had no choice but to step up and become a second mother to us all. What about her desire to have an education?"

"It's all very well for you to point the finger now! If it wasn't for Mother labouring, we'd have all starved. You never stepped up as the eldest son. The burden of responsibility was yours. Now I'm stepping in for you … again!" I said bitterly.

"I had the right to refuse society's traditional expectation of responsibility to provide for us all. Why should I? They weren't my children?"

"You're impossible … could you have done better? You antagonised Father and considered it a royal calling to butt heads with him over any trivial matter."

"You know nothing" he whispered fiercely. "Father said to me before the accident 'You'll never amount to anything. I never want to see you again.' Who says that to their eldest son?" He stared off into the long corridor.

I stayed silent, thinking, *With James, there's always some dark storm brewing, swirling like a hurricane about to break. How is he ever going to be a father himself?* I glanced at him. *He suddenly looks like a lost child.*

"I was only fourteen. I felt abandoned, like nobody cared."

We had all suffered from all those fathering years lost at such a critical age. I felt some compassion for him as I was in the same boat. How would I ever be a father?

"James, it was probably inevitable that you would take your independence and move out of home."

"You were too young to understand," he said. "I survived some bloody frosty nights in that derelict shed, trying to prove I didn't need him. You don't know what it's like … you're Mother's little boy!"

I scoffed. *You blame everyone for your life.* "You should be grateful. You'd have gone to jail for vagrancy but for Mother pleading your case before the judge."

"Pleading my case?! What about William's death? It was only months later …." His voice trailed off, and he looked away in pain, sighed heavily.

Baby William again! James has never let it go … Mother said he'd casually dropped in to announce that his girlfriend was pregnant and could she help? She was furious.

All we could do was watch it all play out in front of us like some dark satire. As if we were not suffering enough shame already. I remembered Mother's cutting words to James. "What are you going to do now? You're selfish! Have you got employ?'

That was the night I woke to sobbing from her room as she prayed for God's help. Baby William became part of our home as Mother and Ellen took responsibility for him, with James calling occasionally. She pleaded his case, begging the judge for leniency on the promise of his enlistment. The judge allowed James to join the army, hoping he might straighten out. I think it made him more bitter. That same year, '88, two of the girls married. Even now, I wondered if Mother had pressured them to find husbands? Ellen was only married to John Wadsworth for six months before he was tried for stealing and went to prison. Later, it was revealed that he had abandoned another whole family of four only a year prior to their marriage. Martha married at eighteen and moved away down south. Wondering how we had become so burdened with life, I stared at James who at one time had been my champion.

We sat in silence, then James whispered, "Harry, I was surrounded by mothers! ... Women! … I never understood them the way you do. I still don't, I suppose."

I paused, searching for the connection, then nodded towards the pretty girl in a deep blue dress sitting in the row in front. "What's there to get? Your awkwardness with girls has always given me plenty of opportunity to step in." I smirked

An attendant quietly dropped a few more small logs into the cast iron pot belly stove, which seemed a waste of effort as the door kept swinging open, letting in blasts of cold air.

"We've had some happy days together, you and I, haven't we?"

"You'd dare me to follow you to steal fruit from a neighbour's orchard ..."

James looked proud.

"... and leap from a branch onto Nacker's back ...."

"We were strong and fearless!" he said, smiling.

I still felt annoyed with James, but I knew we had shared too many great times together, despite his tyranny. I had no other father figure. Pathetic as it was, there was no one else.

"You were famous for that bloody gimmick."

"I dared my friends to land square on the horse's back."

"Harry, how long did it take you to master – falling on the ground winded all those times?"

"You were a bastard standing over me laughing as I desperately tried to catch my breath. Then you'd throw me on your back saying, 'Come on, you'll be alright, Tommo!"

"Tom, you gotta keep your bloody back straight, I'd say."

"Mother would scold us for being reckless. 'James, you should know better; you can die from a broken leg!'"

James focused on the young man called in by the attendant. The young lad beside James caught my eye, speaking in a broad Irish accent. "'e gut caught tryin' et sell a sack of coal stolen from et docks. He's gut nay kin ... were only lookin' for et feed."

I wasn't sure what to say. For too long we'd been poor ... NOT AGAIN! I'm not going hungry, but I'm wasting my time begging for rides.

"Harry, remember doing the old switch with our names when John, Joe and I marched into the headmaster's office together when he asked for J. Bagust to come to his office after assembly?" James smirked. "Using J. Bagust has always been a source of amusement in prize-givings. Mind you, you took my name!"

"What are you going on about?"

"Henry traditionally should have been passed to me, the eldest son, named after Grandfather."

"I guess it'll be *my* name passed on for generations instead," I said light-heartedly.

"Always the golden boy, Harry!" he muttered darkly.

"Father said that, as they planned to immigrate, he called me Henry knowing he might never see Grandfather Henry again. It means nothing to me – I never knew him at all."

"He was like Father, a blacksmith in Wiltshire for a while, but he'd do anything if it paid a bob or two. He saw opportunities like you do. They did what they could to get by. Harriet told us children how she'd sneak boiled lollies when they were confectioners for the upper class, making sweet cakes and treats. That's when we moved into the warehouse under the rail bridge as 'Chandlers'. When offal or fat is being rendered down, it takes me straight back to the enormous bubbling cauldrons. It was warm in the winter but unbearable in summer. The children worked hard … probably how Harriet's lungs were destroyed. Southwark was a poor community full of sailors, brothels and pubs, beside the putrid waters. Oh god, the stench of the Thames into which all the waste from the abattoirs ran. Cattle were shipped into London, slaughtered, and each part of the dead carcass was processed; butchers trimmed meat and made black pudding. Like I said yesterday, bone merchants, tanners, shoemakers, saddlers. I remember Father saying, 'the flies and maggots could carry you off.' You five children must have felt like birds set free amongst the bush in Timaru."

Chapter 2

Take it with a Grain of Salt

"Birds set free!! Harry, I remember seeing the stars and breathing the fresh air as we sailed away into the ocean. It seemed like the air had no taste, no coal grit between your teeth." James looked content for a moment. "I have a vivid memory of lying in a hammock staring at the magnificent night sky as the ship swayed. Feels like yesterday saying goodbye to Harriet. I was only six when we left Plymouth for Lyttleton. 1874 …" He shook his head. "You remember that chant we'd do while skipping around, the one that came to us on the deck from the shouts of seamen pulling ropes. "Eight hours of work, eight hours of play, eight hours of sleep, and eight bob a day?

"What a complete fable that turned out to be – the new 'land of promise'." He looked around the room. "Promise of what?"

"But don't forget … what promise would our lives have had in Southwark? Things are going to get better."

"Harry, the optimist! For one thing, our wages would be better … Good folks arrived here ill-prepared, holding in their tight fists 'precious titles' not worth the ink that was barely dry on their freshly stamped papers. They imagined a place like Britain with roads and trains, shops, public buildings and botanic gardens, not a jungle to be conquered! All these bloody steep hillsides of scrub and bush needed clearing, stumping and cultivating. Many immigrants, even now after a few years, give up and walk off the land leaving everything they've worked for, totally destitute."

"We've done pretty well for ourselves. You've just chosen to squander yours."

"I'm living life. I could end up like Father. Even now, who makes eight bob a day!? It's still a damn good wage! I've slogged it out with the best of them, but where has it got me? It's only sheer grit, courage and necessity that's transformed this colony, not eight hours of play!"

The attendant came through again, stood to attention. "Bagust!"

We both stood and followed him through.

"Your case will be coming up soon; just take a seat."

James looked around at the serious faces inside the courtroom. "I can't wait to get out of here for a few hours of play!" He thrust his face into mine. "Father would not be in an asylum if it hadn't been so hard! I remember his excitement and hope! Look at us now …" He motioned to the room. "… fighting for a scrap of dignity. Is this the dream Father spoke of?"

"James, I've been holding off telling you something … not here … I'll tell you later."

"What is it?" James said a little too loudly.

"Quieten down, please!" The judge looked our way and banged the gavel down, pointing toward us with the hammer. I whispered a little lower. "I will tell you later – no point getting locked up over it."

James stared quizzically, slightly bothered, before resuming his rant. "My dream is just to be debt free."

"No chance that's happening any time soon with your luck. I always imagined it differently. Father must have been earning eight bob. Every new settler needed horses! He always seemed tired … working late into the night. He must have tried desperately to keep up with shoeing horses for the sale yards.

The poor bugger was probably too tired the night he got kicked."

"He never put anything away for us."

"Nor have you!"

James looked like I had hit him, knowing it was true.

"At least Father fed ten of us while he was alive!" I added. *Bloody selfish bastard, no wonder he's broke.*

The court officials took a break for lunch while we sat waiting together. James seemed more grumpy than usual now and I secretly hoped he felt guilt over his latest outburst. I couldn't wait to get away from him, like he was the only one to suffer! "I felt it too, you know, barely ten when Father was locked away … I would wake in a sweat some nights thinking it was somehow something I did."

"If we'd been in Britain, we'd have had support instead of being stuck here, devoid of family."

"Don't you get it? We would have been destitute either way! Mother took in boarders to make ends meet, doing any work she could. You, as a vagrant, had more rights than her without a husband. Even Ellen toiled as a maid … we were all sucked into that mire of poverty. I made a vow I would never be that poor again."

"There's a few folks sitting here today know something of that."

All this talk is making it worse. There has got to be better opportunities than this. I feel like stale bread just before it turns mouldy and you throw it to the pigs. Somehow, it's time to move on, find something to challenge us, instead of sheer survival.

"James, this bloody seven years of bleak depression has smothered us like black coal smoke hanging over the city in winter."

"Harry, the government's embarrassed, hoping to sweep it all under the carpet, pretend everything's rosy, while the rot's hidden beneath the rug in plain sight to trip on. Now they want the city white-washed, ready for the upcoming elections."

"It has to come right. The districts all a buzz of activity – even the constabulary are out in force to bring about law and order."

"There's everything from thieves to parliamentarians in preparation for these elections. Sometimes I feel like I can't tell them apart.

"We can't expect the government to make things better. We need to look further afield!"

I saw a glimpse of the pain come across James' face telling how he'd suffered.

"Harry, if there were opportunity, don't you think we'd find it? This has happened before: the government's like the grim reaper dragging us into court, loading us with taxes! Emigrants and settlers who'd come for the rush in Gabriel's Gully withdrew in their thousands, you know, despite Dunedin becoming a bustling metropolis. They caught wind of another rush in Australia and America. We should have left while we could."

"Didn't the government offer a considerable reward should gold be discovered in Auckland? Must have helped the battling colony."

"It turned things around, eventually."

His lordship entered the courtroom again, like a vulture out for blood. Disdainfully, he glanced at his colonial subjects, who waited quietly. The tall, crusty man stepped in with his long black flowing robe, sat up on his great chair and viewed his victims. Then he said, "You may be seated!" He wiped his mouth just in case food had been caught in his moustache.

James whispered, "Rock Salt! You'll not get off lightly today, brother. This old retiring judge is as bitter as salt. Looks like you've won the whole nine yards today."

I whispered back, "How do you know?"

"Last I saw him was two years back in Wellington, for driving a carriage round a corner faster than a walk. He asked me if I would care to try another profession."

Court resumed as a young lady was called forward while my memory drifted back to a time when we had a different profession, to a time on the farm when life was happy and carefree days, to times of plenty when I would lead the cows along the Waimate River, the frozen ground crunching under my bare feet as I ran across the frosty white paddocks in the silence of the eerie morning mist. I remembered the cows' breath billowing out smoke like a steam train, their mournful cries like an ancient Celtic wail. There was something special about those still misty mornings when the last of the stars would be out, and I would daydream as I meandered my way along the lush grassland of the riverbank carrying a stick to whack the cows if needed, sometimes standing to thaw my icy toes for a minute in a steaming hot fresh cow paddy, luxuriating as it oozed up through my warming toes. Then it all changed that night I came home to find Father in hospital.

I glanced at James, who was now sitting quietly, paying attention to the young, plainly dressed woman wearing a blue bonnet who was seeking a divorce from her straying husband. My mind returned to happier times with Father and those special moments, like my excitement at finally being off to school. And my most precious memory when Father had said, 'Come on, Harry!' and had taken my hand and proudly smiled as we walked the mile for my inaugural day at Pleasant Point Primary. I had felt like the most endeared member of the family. And I probably was, at least until little Johnny and Lovey arrived. James always said they were spoilt, but that didn't last long either … Everything changed after Father's accident.

At the front of the courtroom, the young woman was granted permission to proceed with a divorce and I noticed James nodding.

"That would have been better for Mother," he said quietly, "rather than what we all went through. Even losing Father would have been easier."

Clearly, the whole incident still haunted him, and I looked down and shook my head. "I can still see Mother's face as we were sworn to secrecy not to tell," I murmured.

"Didn't make any bloody difference. Word still got out within hours of Father's committal."

I nodded. "I remember you crying at night."

"The sadness ran deep, and then there were the fights we endured at school … Why would Mother not let us see him?" The pain was still evident on his face as he looked at me.

"Sparing us the pain, the humiliation of Sunny Side." I shrugged.

"Nothing sunny about that horror house."

I smiled grimly. "Remember the many stories we concocted to conceal Father's absence?"

"Oh yes … Father's away at sea!"

"This was a good one: he's a butler for a wealthy family in Auckland!"

"What about … he's working in the goldfields! Or, he's a representative in His Majesty's service."

"He's been shipwrecked at sea."

James shook his head. "It didn't make any difference … those cruel bastards at school teased us relentlessly. That torturous sing-song voice: 'Your father's a loony, Your father's a loony'."

"At first, I had scores of blood noses, then I learned a thing or two. Hasn't done me any harm – certainly toughened me up fast. It helped having you as protector. You'd wrestle them to the ground in an instant even when they were bigger than you."

"Reckon that's where we learned to fight."

"The year you left, I mastered the art of a few clever words to fend off my attackers, dropping a stick of verbal dynamite at the right moment did wonders, and if not, a few grazed fists."

"We should have called you 'Harry, The Charmer'."

"It didn't work this time, despite all my efforts to twist the truth." I pointed an accusing finger at James. "This was *your* doing, us being here today!"

"Why worry. You look smart in your new shoes, black suit and red tie." He flicked my tie up for emphasis.

The judge was concluding the current case, and I couldn't tell if my stomach was churning with hunger or nerves at the possible outcome.

Then the judge slowly checked his notes and called me forward. I strode to the front of the room, feeling confident as I placed my hand gently on the Bible the attendant held out.

"Do you swear to tell the truth, the whole truth and nothing but the truth, so help you God?"

The attendant looked sternly into my eyes as the room fell into silence.

I stood contemplating the truth, even God for a second. *Does anyone tell the truth? I've not a clue where God is in all this? Today will have to be a version of the truth to save James.* I faced Lordship Rocksalt.

"Yes, I do," I said confidently, making it more a statement of faith rather than fact.

"Please take the stand."

I walked into the booth and stood to my full height, looking at the judge squarely while trying to avoid James' smile.

"Thomas Henry Bagust, what is your defence?

Thomas Henry! My neck bristled on hearing my given name, which seemed to echo off the dark wood panelling in the courtroom. For a split second, I heaved in a breath, looked at the judge and was about to correct his lordship, but his penetrating eyes made me keep my tongue. It could go either way by the look of his salty, weathered face. He appeared in no mood for a cheeky nineteen-year-old.

I stood to my full stature as the judge repeated, "Thomas Henry Bagust! …How do you plead?"

"Not guilty, Your Honour!"

The defence rose; chanted various transport statutes and bylaws while I glanced about the room, deep in my thoughts. I indeed felt some guilt, standing in my new suit while an array of men sat humbly in oversized threadbare clothes, echoing a time when a more substantial, powerful chest filled their now sagging breast pockets. They sat holding dutiful sun-scorched hats as their tired weathered hands protruded from tattered sleeves. This was bureaucracy gone mad when perpetrators were ordinary folk just trying to make ends meet, good men now homeless and begging on the streets. My mind jumped again. *I'm exhausted trying to outsmart Stumpy, running the gauntlet for passengers. There has to be another way to make a bob. Mother still needs support, despite her sending Lovey and Joe to Martinborough. Ellen and John would have made fine parents if they'd born their own.*

Perhaps I will ask young Joe to come and mind our carts at the docks, there's worse things he could do at ten. He's a good lad and has a keen eye to read people. Ellen will not be happy, but he might learn a thing or two about running his own business one day.

I could even ask about part-time work with the local coach builder in Martinborough next time I'm over there, so he can have a few practical skills. Fortune could be just around the corner, but I can't wait to get out of this hustle and bustle.

I could see James nodding off, slouched in the back row. He'd not been sleeping well with Marg almost due, and looked more like thirty-six than twenty-six. I'd always known what a world of trouble he could wade us into, like he was slowly drowning in thick mud … *It's so painful to watch. He toils away at the port making a good name for himself, but what little he makes spills through his fingers like water. Then he squanders twice what he makes gambling, so desperate to drown his cares away in one vicious cycle. Margaret suffers long nights waiting for him, she'll not do it forever.* Then I remembered: he had promised Mother he'd look out for me, but wondered who was looking after whom. *Still, I can't help it, he's my big brother, who else cares? My record's not spotless … back in '88 Mother was wise saying "Just plead not guilty" when old McKenzie arrested me for 'plying for hire without a license'… that had got thrown out.*

Yes, it was the best thing I did skipping school at eleven to do farm work. It wasn't right to sit by and watch the family starve. *Good thing I heard about soliciting fares at the port, it's made me grow up fast. No-one likes a young upstart breaking in on their patch but I've learned a thing or two from a few kind men.*

The first time was an old fella who encouraged me to use Father's old blacksmith cart. It never looked so good, decorated in red with the leftover paint from his shop sign. At the time it seemed perfect … *Poor old bugger, such an irony.*

WELLS AND BAGUST BLACKSMITHS.

HORSES SHOD CAREFULLY

He was careful but it just took one kick. It was times like these I thought of him, wasting away in a mental asylum. And for what? Just like that, it was all over. *Lord Gladstone … thinks he's a Prime Minister … doesn't even know when I saw him last.*

It all seemed so long ago now, convincing the judge I was running errands for Mother – we've all grown up so quick. I had stood nervously to defend myself that day, slightly hunched, trying to make my tall, lanky frame look less than fifteen. None of us could afford shoes, let alone a lawyer. My first dismissal with a warning. Oh! Such a wave of relief when I realised I had not broken my promise to James.

He must have noticed me looking at him as he squinted at me curiously, his fingers mindlessly curling his sturdy black moustache. It was the same look he'd given me the day he left, those eyes looking into my naïve face. I could still feel his hands gripping my shoulders as he'd said, "You're the man now, it's up to you!"

What will my defence be this time?

James and I had gone over this a few times already. Although I felt confident, it did not help my resolve, and I glanced sideways at our surly copper seated for the prosecution. He grinned knowingly, like the alley cat that had just licked up the cream.

Damn it, this is my time to shine. I stared at the impatient face of the judge. *My defence? My bloody defence!*

Rock Salt looked my way sternly, needing an immediate answer.

"Your Honour, I was not soliciting for business. I had returned to pick up a customer's luggage and trunk, tying the wheel of my cart and placing a lad on the seat while I retrieved their goods! I was taken by surprise when the cop grabbed me and I instinctively swung my elbow, knocking him to the ground, for which I am profoundly sorry."

Stumpy rose to his feet, shouting, "Your Honour, I'm certain I saw him soliciting for business on the platform! There was also an altercation with a passenger."

Rock Salt stared directly at me and said, "It appears you have not been here before. I have a feeling there is more to this case, but we are short of time and patience today, so consider this your good fortune!" He slammed down his gavel. "Twenty shillings fine! And next time, you might need a few days in lockup with hard labour, lad, to help you with the truth." He scanned the room, his face stern, and I knew not to utter another word.

As I returned to my seat with a smirk — though I wanted to keep walking out the door — I thought: *Is that it? I'm liberated.* I had gotten off lightly. Twenty shillings. *We can easily make that in a few days and it will come out of James' pocket this time.*

I sat down next to James. "Can you believe that?"

"You lucky bastard. How do you do it?!"

"I'm looking forward to getting out of here."

"There is still another case to go."

James grabbed my elbow excitedly knowing he too had got off lightly. He leaned in close and whispered, "Take it with a grain of salt, brother. I'll chip in!"

I glared at him, annoyed at his flippancy. "Too right you will! It's okay for you; I was the one pulling you out of this scuffle again. There won't be a next time!" I said in a loud whisper. "You're on a first-name basis with most of the black-robed figures in white wigs, but I do not wish to be here again. After four years, I've had enough of standing guard over your coach at night while a throng of cabbies gamble inside and you drown deeper in debt. I need out!"

"You're all talk – we need each other. One day I will win big, brother, you just wait," he said enthusiastically.

"Honestly, I've heard it all before."

"I've stuck my neck out for you too a few times when you've got into hot water teasing the ladies."

"A result of having so many flamboyant sisters."

"*Pah*! Harry, you'll never give up being a cabbie. You hear all the latest tantalising opportunities … gold strikes, bargain horses, land lotteries. You're always in with the slightest sniff of a deal." He looked at me hopefully as if I might just be letting off steam.

The judge's hammer suddenly slammed down in a final verdict with the last case, and we both looked up in surprise. Like puppets, we obediently rose to his bidding, noticing he took a moment to stare sternly at us both, and then he bid his farewell.

James hesitated for only a second then said, "Come on, my shout." He turned on his heels, spurred on by Stumpy's long stare as he passed us in the hallway.

"I'll be seeing you boys another day. Hopefully, next time, it'll be my pleasure to see you locked up with hard labour for a while!"

I grabbed James' arm. "Hold your tongue, brother … another day! Come on!" I loosened my tie as we strode past, giving Stumpy a grim look as we left the sombre chambers behind. *I'll not see you again*, I vowed as I passed him by.

I hastily took out a cigarette to calm my nerves and drew deeply on the first breath, the red glow warming me instantly. *I'll not see another judge for a long while either.*

"Slow down, James. You're like a bloody homing pigeon lost at sea for a week."

"We're off to wash away our sins, brother."

"Your sins, not mine," I said, playfully pushing him into a new telephone pole.

"Watch it! … no respect for your elders …."

We climbed aboard the cart. "Decrepit old bugger, you mean."

Soon we pulled up outside the grand two-storey watering hole. I waved to two ladies smiling back from the balcony that overlooked the street as we tied up the horses. The sounds of raucous laughter billowed out through the windows that stood ajar to free the bar from the cigarette smoke that pickled everyone's clothes.

"I've been told this is the place to come."

An all too familiar sound greeted me as we pushed through the hotel doors to a noisy throng of excited cabbies from all corners of town. Bench seats and slab tables filled the room, randomly surrounded by an enormous horseshoe bar.

"It's like coming to worship at the golden altar. I'm only too ready to drink away my cares today, brother."

Men drench themselves like sheep dip, stumbling home again to whatever family they might possess.

"The Temperance movement wants to put a stop to this,"

James motioned, looking about the room. "Ban liquor altogether!"

"Imagine Margaret's face if you arrived home sober."

"Never! You'll not stop me! They must be mad to think we'll not set up a whiskey still. Wouldn't you create a little moonshine if you had a chance?"

"Depends on how much I could make from it. There are other ways to drown your sorrows, you know."

"You with young ladies."

"On the dance floor!"

"You'll not get me out on a dance floor."

I slumped into a chair while James turned to queue at the bar, where he ordered two jugs from the buxom woman splashing beer about in a feeding frenzy of men.

Chapter 3

Flogging a Dead Horse

I looked out the window to the bustling traffic: a chimney sweep trying to manoeuvre his long pole along the dirt road; two ladies in full-length dresses with small children, squeezed into a trap, out on the town; a huge cart loaded with half a house load of sawn timber, with two young nav's strapping the horses to manoeuvre the heavy load.

James banged the jugs on the table, then poured the liquid gold into our glasses, raising his high. "Here's to outsmarting that cunning bastard!"

"I'll drink to that!" I raised my glass, gulping back the pint in one fell swoop. I poured another, reflecting on Father's plight as I topped up James' glass. "Here's to SIR JAMES GLADSTONE!" I watched my brother squirm a little as he frowned and hesitated. Reluctantly, he lifted his glass. "Why not, poor old bugger!"

"James, you're both so alike."

"*Pahh*! Never! Nothing was ever good enough; why could he not have just told me once, '*I am proud of you, son!?* He was never in the habit of doling out praise?"

"We are not going there again; it's flogging a dead horse. Give it a rest." James, lost for words, looked shocked as I continued. "I remember his calloused hands with big fat sausage fingers. They were always ingrained with charcoal and rusty steel; the hairs burned off his arms."

James motioned with his hand. "He wore that blackened cap."

"Mother still keeps his hat on a hook at the door."

James actually had a small glint in his eyes. "Father sometimes let us drive the bellows. My ears would ring as he struck out on the anvil – like he was at war with it."

"James, for me as a small boy, 'The Smithy' was like stepping into hell … watching Father pound red-hot steel into shape as the sparks flew off. It was mesmerising to watch him stomp on the huge bellows, turning little dancing flames into angry wolves. The glowing red steel would explode as he dipped it into the cooling bucket, hissing like a scolded cat."

"He did teach me a thing or two, but he was not a patient man. I'm not making that mistake with my son."

"Isn't that what everyone says? 'I'll never be like him', and ending up just like him! You'd have to be the most impatient out of us all."

"We can't all be charming like you, Harry … they all tire of your smooth talk and empty promises eventually!"

I've heard that before, so I ignored him. "I think I was about five the first time I tried to drive those bellows down, using all my skinny body weight to force the handles. Father would laugh as I tried desperately to lift the dolly to strike it on the anvil. It was a frightening place. He always warned us: *'It's dangerous to walk behind a horse when it's being shod.'* He must have shod a thousand horses from the yards in those few years."

"Just one skittish old nag, Harry. You've gotta live for the day, brother – you never know when your times up!"

I looked at James in his worn suit jacket and shabby shoes. "Brother, I've seen you looking better. What happened to *you* living the day? Your Margaret is one patient woman … you will get home one day and she'll be gone."

"Harry, it's alright for you. You've got lady luck looking

down. I'd like half your fortunate streak. Even your horse seems to like you."

I laughed silently. "James, in this business, it does help if you actually like horses. Your Coal knows you're a grumpy bugger. It's any wonder she bites you."

"I tell it like it is – no spin, Harry. One day I'll have a fine thoroughbred."

"My Lotti's a good dependable mare with an even temperament. Not easily spooked; perfect for cabbie work. I had her shod last week; she stood so quiet, but I'm ready for a horse with a little more spirit."

"Any Smithy worth his salt would shoe a horse quietly! You have had a few decent horses, I will give you that. Pure luck."

"Is it luck, James… or perhaps a good eye?"

"In your case, luck. As for Father's, a mistake! I always thought I would follow in his shoes, but I got spooked that infamous day … My mistake today was coming to court, seeing that smug bastard Stumpy. I can't believe he had the gall to lecture us in the courtroom afterwards."

"James, he does have a point. It's time to stop gambling inside the coach at night. Like he said, our luck's running out. I'm tired of checking over my shoulder nervously for him. You have a wife and child to think of."

"Ahh, you worry too much, Harry. You've gotta live a little," James said, sloshing his beer on the floor.

"Harry, you said you have something to announce … come on out with it!"

"I have given it a great deal of thought; it wasn't the time to tell you earlier, but I might not be around much longer."

"You thinking of pushing up daisies?" James said with a grin.

"I'm over all this. It's time for me to move on. I'm planning to try my fortune in Thames on the gold fields. If it's anything like the boom in Otago, I could save a bob or two."

"Fool's gold, brother. You'll be just like that roughneck who strayed into the bar a few minutes ago, splashing his money about shouting the bar. Doesn't look like he has two ha'pennys to rub together. I've seen it all before: they come ashore with gold fever from Thames or Otago, bathe themselves in their bloody fortune, and return on the next ship washed up. What makes you any different?"

"I know if I had a crack at it, I could make something of it. Enough to buy a farm!"

"*Pah*! You're full of crud! Why bother dreaming of settling down on a farm. Unless you strike it rich, you'll never have enough to satisfy the bank for a loan. From what I hear, the only poor sods making any serious money up there are the brothels, hotels, and the tax man."

"James, you're a miserable bugger sometimes. At least while you're shouting the beers today, I can strike it rich for one night," I said, smiling at James as I emptied the second jug. "I need to get a few shillings back from the pounds you've robbed off me."

"Might as well cash in on someone else's gold."

James stood up with a stagger before navigating his way to the bar. He grabbed my arm as he sat down again. "You're alright, brother … I'm a hopeless case sometimes."

"You have a good heart, James, but at least when you're drunk you say nice things … really, you're just bitter and miserable; it's eating you up."

"I don't know why I despair."

"Deep down, you want what we all crave … something better … Speaking of that, you know Mother's had to take in a few desperate lodgers. I got a letter yesterday telling a sad tale of her young lodger, Sophia Gray, who she'd taken in. She was depressed over her husband deserting her while she was pregnant. The next minute, Mother found her unconscious on the floor, and desperately tried to revive her. She quickly sent for the doctor, who discovered she'd taken *Rough on Rats*. He managed to bring her round with salts, but when his back was turned, she ran and hid in an abandoned house. The neighbours all helped search, finally unearthing her two hours later, nearly dead. A week later, they appeared in court when she'd recovered enough to stand trial for attempting suicide."

"I hate that impoverished area. Mother is the one who needs to abandon that house and escape that wretched neighbourhood in Pleasant Point!"

"James, they should leave John to board with a family, pack what they can carry and move here … join Ellen in Martinborough." James spoke as he leaned forward slowly, tapping his pipe to empty it out on the floor.

"Next, we'll have the whole family living up here."

"Wairarapa's remote but a nice farming settlement."

"James, you could have a brilliant opportunity over there if you applied for the mail run over that damned hill. You would need a fine team with a sturdy sprung carriage to haul goods over that mountain. It's a bustling community with new settlers. They need goods taken by land instead of that perilous coastal run. You could run a carriage to carry both goods and passengers."

"Where the hell would I get money for that? You're always dreaming, Harry; see every hint of an opportunity. I'll leave it to Joseph; he is a good lad. I can see him doing brave things in the future if his footy is anything to go by."

"I'm told there's some big farms up there. I've heard you can even lease land from the Māori."

"It would take a miracle to own a farm one day … could you ever envisage me owning land?"

"Anyway, I think you're right though. Mother should move up there. By all accounts, the Māori over the hill sound reasonable. I had a customer who told me the Māori there were happy to have the early settlers take up land. His family walked into the valley in the 1840s purchasing a sizeable plot of land off them. They wanted peace from other warring tribes so they embraced new settlers who brought some stability. Apparently, the early whalers taught them how to negotiate market values, being in the area twenty years before anyone else arrived."

"Harry, I can't see you settling down too soon."

"What, till I'm an old man like you?"

"Old man! I've not lived yet! In fact, people are talking of unrest in South Africa. They might even need New Zealand soldiers to enlist against the Boers ... I bet you'll never settle, Harry. You can't decide which girl now. Next, it'll be that girl from the maypole!"

"I'll take that bet, James. How long have I got?"

"You're a charmer; I bet you ten bob you'll not settle before you're thirty!"

I took his hand in a firm grip, looking at him squarely. "You haven't got ten bob! Still, I'm satisfied to hold you to that one – it's a bet. I've got another ten years to shine my shoes."

"That's the easiest ten bob I've ever made."

"We'll see. It could be Alice from the Labour Day celebrations."

"Harry, they're only schoolgirls. You need a strong woman!"

"She's seventeen – looked grown in her new dress. It was a great night and she ...."

Suddenly James interrupted by grabbing my arm. "Look, I've been watching that red-whiskered stranger who just strode through the doors. He looks more like a scarecrow."

The man was dressed in tweed with a bold watch chain hanging out of his waistcoat pocket, a matching tweed hat with three-quarter pants and long sox. He carried an odd-shaped leather case, and already his veins were swimming with alcohol. In no time, he had knocked back a few more rounds, laughing heartily with a few of the lads. He began singing a folk song in one corner then, after a word with the bartender, reached down and opened his case. He pulled out a worn black accordion, slipped his hands under the two straps and began playing, at the same time leaping up to sit on a stool. The room almost exploded into whoops and hollers.

"Harry, look at this. Can he play?!"

"You got to give it to those bloody Irish. They've got something! He has turned this sad room into a festival. Takes a might of courage to pull that off."

"Or stupidity!"

His joy spread like a fire. While feet tapped and hands clapped, he squeezed out one well-known chorus after another. The inebriated roar of men joined in, reminiscing songs of home, washing away their cares. "Can you believe this lad? He's certainly captured an audience."

"You know, Harry, you could do that!! You love to take charge; I could see you up there!"

We both laughed. "Not in those clothes. Perhaps you're right. I do love the dance floor, but to play like that!?"

"Harry, I know where there's a squeezebox. I've seen it over at South Sea Hotel on Lambton. It has been sitting in the luggage room for two years since the dockside strikes of '90. Old Roy hasn't a clue; there's no record of who left it. You should go see him. Pretend it was you who left it; if that doesn't work, give him a few bob."

"I do believe, brother, you are as cunning as old Stumpy. Someone does need to rescue that accordion; I will drop in on Roy when we're back."

"Come on, that train's comin' in early – best we head back." I helped James to his feet, half carrying him out the doors to our carriage.

I was glad for my suit jacket as there was a cold breeze from the south. The night was dark with no moon, but I could hear the flutter of our kerosene lamps dimly lighting up the dark, dusty streets back to our lodgings.

Normally James could drink any man under the table, but tonight, without warning, he vomited violently. It sounded deafening in the evening's silence as he sprayed a white picket fence brown as we passed by.

The melodic sound of horse hooves echoed off the tenement houses, now all dark and quiet without flickering candles.

We staggered up the wooden steps through the door, very much the worse for wear. James still carefully placed his vomit-splashed shoes neatly on a small shelf inside the front door before collapsing on the floor. James is banned from the bedroom if he comes in drunk and there would be trouble if Margaret woke. I delicately picked up his stinking shoes, which made my stomach turn as I placed them on the top step outside, and went back down to untether Coalface.

The tall black mare stood quietly as I fumbled with the straps, trying to get my fingers to release her harness. My head was swimming and I cursed my stupidity for not cutting the night short. I left the cart outside while the mare quietly forced her way through the shed doors into the warm stable beneath the little two-roomed flat. The morning stars shone bright, as the fires had all died by now, and the gentle breeze had wiped away the stench of coal.

I cannot remember a day when I had reflected so much on my life and my childhood. I sat on the steps, lingering for a moment in the peace of a leisurely cigarette while scalding myself out loud: "Thomas, you need a change." … *But what and where?*

Chapter 4

A Change is as Good as a Rest

We spent a few more weeks in the area but decided to head home to Wellington, hoping things had blown over. James and I stood at the docks catching up on local gossip with the other cabbies while anticipating a fare. We finally basked in glimpses of sunlight as our breath made us look more like Puffing Billy's in the cold morning air.

Ordinarily, we'd be warmed up by now, carrying luggage or plying back and forth with customers. Today the ships were all neatly tied up like little soldiers; even their masts stood still in the calm waters of the almost deserted docks. James lounged sideways on his front bench seat while Coalface quietly awaited her next quest. His carriage was big, black and covered in, with four spoked wheels; it seated six inside. I climbed down and took a handful of feed for the horses.

"Harry, did you hear what happened to me last night from the other boys?"

"No. Don't tell me … you are in more trouble again. I'm not running away to Manuatu again."

"Oh, no faith in your older brother?" I did not answer but grinned at him wryly.

"I was out with my friend Tommy last night making our way home. We took a shortcut down a dark laneway behind Custom Street when we heard a man shouting out for help. We hurried down the street toward the noise to discover two voluptuous ladies of the night beating a poor young copper with his own long truncheon. His arms were over his head, his legs tucked up like a hedgehog, trying desperately to protect himself from the savage blows. We leapt into the fray and ripped the baton off the boisterous woman. She would have flattened a man in a scrum or us if she'd 'alf a chance. They'd have been perfect in that tug of war against the Welsh."

"What happened to the copper?" I said, chuckling.

"We took our handkerchiefs to stop the bleeding on his head as he got up limping. He dusted himself off while holding his throbbing head, grateful for us showing up at that moment. We helped him home, as the cut on his head caused the blood running down his face to fill his eyes."

"That's certainly one for the books. Was he alright?"

"A few nasty eggs here and there but otherwise looking very humiliated. We walked him home a few streets away, where he scribbled our names and shook our hands as he thanked us again. He said the ladies were well-known and would be charged."

"James, no wonder you're lying there looking half-shot today. We should get out of here. Will you have to appear in court?"

"Of course ... my favourite place ... verify our actions."

"It makes a change ... you engaged in breaking up a crime instead of being the perpetrator to one." I shook my head. "James, to be honest, I've found myself in the last few days restless, dreaming of ways I can escape the city. I'm sick of the nights and the abuse. I've looked about some days as if expecting a fresh opportunity ... like I'm preparing to move on ..."

"Come on, Harry, I followed *you* here. I know you like being a cabbie."

"Yes, there's things I like about it. I've not got someone breathing down my neck telling me what to do! I can work my own hours. It's heavy work, but with my education, what else could I do?"

"And what about the ladies!"

"I do like the ladies. I've not yet seen an opportunity to make good money doing anything else. I've certainly learned about people out here, but I can't do this forever."

"But you've done all the hard work, banging heads to break into the local patch. It's fortunate we grew up wrestling, but are you really going to quit the last bout?"

"Yes, brother … there's nothing happening here today. I can tell you want to pack it in, and I've lost interest too.

"I can't leave. My fortunes are in the balance."

"James, look at this rare day! No wind! A blue sky! For Wellington, that's a miracle! … Your fortunes can wait for another day. I'm going to head over to see the family for a few days!"

"But it's Sunday, the best pickings of the week!"

"And no one about; it's like a ghost town! It's time you visited the Family as well. How long has it been?! … join me for once or not … either way, I'm off. For once, think of someone else. Come catch up with your sisters and young Joe; they'll be pleased to see you." I swung my cart round, gently flicking the reins while looking over my shoulder for his response.

"It's a day's drive; I'm tired; if anything, I need a rest!"

I shrugged. "All the more reason to leave now! A change is as good as a rest!" All at once, he relented, reluctantly turning his big black carriage in my direction.

"I shouldn't be going off: Margaret is due to have the baby any day. I'm having a telephone fitted on Tuesday morning," he protested.

We were calling out to each other as we drove together.

"We're in the central zone. You must have noticed them setting those poles along the street."

Honestly, James, could you come up with any other excuses! "What telephone! Whatever for? Not a single person I know has one.

Who are you going to telephone?" I said to him in bewildered astonishment.

"It's for the hospital … if she needs help while I'm at work. Anyway, the elections are near – many people have it on. Ninety-six people in the central district so far."

"How will it pay for itself?"

"I thought with the elections coming up, we might get customers wanting early morning pickups or hotel transfers."

"Sounds convincing … Margaret will be alright. Doesn't her mother live up the road? Anyway, you have good neighbours who'll look after her if need be. Where's the problem?"

"I'm not single like you. I can't just drop everything like that."

"Ask her then. We are nearly there."

We soon pulled into Pirie Street again, dropping off the carriage to re-harness with the open sulky. It was only 7 am and James was still a little prickly at the thought of missing a few lucky fares. We checked on Margaret, explaining our sudden flight of fancy. We strapped on our bedrolls, a gun, billy and a little food for the journey and, steering the light cart for the hills, were well on our way before midday. We were soon out of town and passing small farms with smoke rising lazily from the chimneys. Sheep grazed in the warm early sun. Lotti trotted at a good pace as we followed the river to the foothills of the Remutakas. I finally broke the ice, glancing at James' deadpan face.

"I took that girl Alice out the other night; she's light on her feet. Her parents are well off … live in a stately home around Oriental Bay."

"I've seen you with her once or twice. She's very pretty."

"She always looks immaculate as her aunty owns a dress shop that she likes to help in."

James took out his pipe and fiddled about to find his tobacco as the cart bumped about.

"Margaret's looking very pregnant; she must be due any day."

"Could be while we are away! This is madness: I should not leave her in this state!"

I ignored his sour demeanour. "We'll be back before you know it. What will you call him if it's a boy?"

"I like the name 'Ernest James'!"

"Not James Ernest?"

"No. I couldn't bear my firstborn having to take Father's name. It's bad enough *I* have it."

"He's not technically your first, though?" I looked coolly toward James. "What was the *whole* story behind Little William?"

"It seems a long time ago now," he sighed. "Her name was Rosie … You'll remember that when I left school at thirteen to learn the blacksmith trade how Father and I couldn't stand each other most of the time …?"

I glanced at him and raised an eyebrow. "I hadn't noticed … Like two goats butting heads. Too much alike." *It's odd that James and I have worked together all this time and not spoken much of our past.*

"Maybe? …" His tone was scathing. "I was independent at fifteen, the year of Father's accident. Mother was probably grieving … demanding I step into his shoes … 'Show responsibility!'" he said, screwing up his face and throwing his head around like a headmaster scolding a child. "I was angry with him for leaving us destitute … nothing! Not even enough to escape back to Britain and see the last of this wretched colony."

"James, it's not that bad. There's opportunity here if you're looking, even in these tough times."

"Pah! Should have stayed in the old country. I swallowed Father's dream hook, line and sinker of 'Starting Over.' We were sad watching grandfather waving us off in Portsmouth, straining our eyes until they disappeared out of sight.

"I've heard Ellen talk about how much she missed her big sister Harriet."

"We wanted to show our working-class relations we were destined for a 'Glorious new life'. Attaining to 'landowners' status instead of poor peasant farmers! We actually believed it was good riddance to London's smog-ridden city, industrial factories, and huge boiling vats of tallow. Father was always black from the smoke, slaving to make candles.

"I watched the local chandler while waiting for my horse to be shod; it's quite a process."

"They rendered down the animal fat, in the many warehouses under our massive bridge while trains thundered night and day overhead."

"How did he end up a tallow chandler?"

"Grandfather needed help in the candle shop as he'd fallen on hard times, after becoming ill from the terrible fumes. 'Crucifix Lane' was right in the middle of a stinking hell hole of maggots and flies, surrounded with blood and bone merchants, tanners, hide merchants, leather workers, saddlers and cobblers, all making a living off animal carcasses.

"Surely you were happy to get away?"

"Father held us on his knee, telling his naive dream. 'James we are going to abandon our shackles of poverty for a life of abundance!'

"It was cramped on the *Ballochmyle* sailing out just after you were born, with all seven of us bunked down among four hundred. I think the dream grew larger the longer we were on the ship. We truly thought one day, instead of us serving masters, we might have a grand house with our own servants. Four months with just a little sheet up for privacy… still, I can't remember a happier time of freedom and hope in our family."

"There's always stories of that journey. You must have been about seven when you arrived?"

"In 1874 … I think I was. Even at seven, I felt butterflies of excitement as we rounded the point into Governor's Bay to see the little settlement of Lyttleton perched across the steep hillside. But right from the beginning, it was the same bloody back-breaking work! When Mother scolded me the day I turned fifteen for being irresponsible, that was the last straw! I had to get away."

"To me, that was ridiculous, even as the oldest son. Why?"

"It's alright for *you*! I was expected to magically take charge after already carrying the burden of responsibilities my whole life with Father working long hours."

"We were all grieving Father's incarceration."

"Think back, Harry … at fifteen, were *you* in any state to take on anything?"

"Probably not … I did start cabbie work."

"After my vagrancy charge, I took work in a smithy's shop then labouring on a farm. We cleared land digging out the tree roots, burning off, swinging an axe, shovelling till my hands bled and our backs burned from the sun. In London, we at least had family for support. I could have lived with Harriet."

"That's a fantasy. They couldn't have afforded another mouth to feed in the Poor House – at least you had food on the farm."

James looked contemplative, blowing into his pipe to bring the embers back. "That's where I met Rosie; she was a maid working for a wealthy family that had struck gold back in '84 in the rush. But you know all this!"

"No, only some things. Go on! What was she like?"

"She was gorgeous! Two years older than me, but feeling shunned as she toiled to support her family. She was a bright spark in my misery. One night as we sat talking under the stars, we hugged, then we started kissing … things got a little out of hand as we rendezvoused again many times in the barn loft. She soon fell pregnant. I was young and foolish to think we could look after William. Even with Mother's help, we had to give him up for adoption at nineteen months."

"Why?"

"Mother had too many mouths to feed – we almost starved. Mother told me *'I had no right to be so selfish.'* She and Em had tried to look after him but with eight, there just wasn't enough to go round. Rosie's relative, Mrs Garrett, was a widow with no children. She had lost her husband in the war but could offer William a good home. She took custody through the courts, renaming him. He only lived a few months more. They found him dead on the 17th of February, 1889, but they never knew what he died of."

"We were all devastated. I often played with him … Why do you blame Mother?"

"She gave him up! Why wouldn't I blame her? If she'd not given him up, he'd still be alive today."

"You don't know that. He might have died just the same. We all missed little William! He was at that boisterous, precocious age."

"He was a measure of something good … innocent … someone with meaning, purpose … I fell apart after that."

"Do you think you were prepared to be a father?"

"I'm ready to be a father again, but remember, Ellen and I did much of the looking after of you eight children."

"Do you think Mother was right about you being selfish? She had a hard time of it grieving too. Perhaps it's about time you made up with her."

"How would you know! You've not lost someone!?"

"I've had disagreements over the years, even with Ellen, but we always worked things out … That's what family does!"

"Stop the bloody cart! I'm not listening to this rot."

He grabbed the reins off me, and brought Lotti to a sudden halt. Jumping down, he stormed up the river bank beating his hat against his leg saying: "I should never have agreed to this!"

We'd stopped conveniently near a ford over the river to a

farmhouse so I led Lotti gently down the slope to graze and drink. James stood beside a tree for a minute to relieve himself then, standing beside the flowing water, used his hat to toss water onto his already balding head. While I held Lotti's rein, he sat on a boulder to gather himself.

I started to chuckle to myself. *It's almost hilarious the way James gets so wound up.*

He looked startled as he turned towards me a stone's throw away.

"What's so funny?" he shouted.

I waited for him to calm down and draw closer. "We've had a lot happen over the last four years …Remember that day you got upset with the clerk on the Queens Wharf?"

James looked at me gruffly. "What of it?" He looked forlorn as he picked up stones and threw them violently into the stream.

"Just after you arrived up from Timaru, I remember how you'd not yet learned the etiquette on the docks. You were sceptical as to why you should pay a toll for entering the wharf … and refused to relent when accosted."

James took out his pipe again, smirking slightly.

"You pretended to be picking up Mother until the inspector spotted your cabbie license. You were so upset you refused to move your cart!"

I felt laughter rising then and could not hold it in. My eyes began to stream with tears, and my stomach hurt.

James, now smiling, scratched his pipe out with a stick. I could not contain my laughter, reliving the standoff. "You just … you just stood there sternly … while the officer … while he … wrote you an infringement … yelling abuse at you the whole time."

"I was not about to back down – he thought he was God."

"That's what I love about you, James … your Achilles heel. If you think there's been an injustice, you cannot let it pass."

"Some things you can't just lie down over. Give me the reins, I'll take her from here." He snatched the reins and led Lotti back to the main road, mindlessly checking and preening his wild handlebar moustache that he'd become famous for. With one hand, he balanced the reins, while the other took a little tobacco out to make up his pipe, which he held between his knees.

"What about you getting jailed in Feb 91 for that 'saddlery incident?"

"Should never have happened … a week in lock up! Someone needed to harass Faulkner in his saddle shop. Couldn't let him get away with it."

"But three times you and Tommy returned to try and collect your gambling debts."

"He kept making empty promises while still out on the town in his fancy suit with his fancy women. He just needed a little lesson or two."

"I think the law decided *you* needed a lesson too," I said, laughing.

Chapter 5

You Can't Choose Your Family

I checked ahead as we climbed, hoping not to meet another weary traveller as we wound our way in and out of the endless valleys around the tight dark corners. The arduous journey through the fords and over the ranges seemed to pass quickly with all the storytelling.

"James, I'd rather have you on my side in a fight or tug of war!" I said as I climbed up into the little two-seater after a short spell.

"The tug of war! … Aah, that was a great day! Captain William Barry coached our side."

"Watching those giant Scandinavians tug of war against the Welsh – they were bigger than two of us put together. I was optimistic, cheering our boys on … but that was the longest twenty minutes of our lives."

James rubbed his hands like they were in pain. He grinned. "Makes my hands hurt just thinking about it."

"That boisterous crowd at the skating rink were only just warmed up by the time our lads came on."

"The shouting was probably heard at fever pitch from the docks five miles away." I leant back, put my feet out on the front cowling. "Was it your idea to champion the two cabbie teams, Te-Aro and Thornton, to the grudge match?"

"Thought it would settle who was the better side once and for all." James puffed on his pipe, looking smug.

"You were only bloody victorious because my mate James O'Flaherty swung the balance, on your side."

"Can't stand defeat, can yuh little brother – too competitive."

"*Defeat!* You were only rubbing your hands before because you won so much on the bets, if I remember rightly. It was a tidy wee sum."

I took a cigarette from the silver box in my breast pocket, and tapped it contemplatively before lighting a match within cupped hands. *I can't remember the last time James and I laughed so much about old times.*

"It feels somehow refreshing reliving some of these stories."

"You can't choose your family! … Some of them I'd rather forget!"

"Family is one thing but is there any greater rivalry than dock yard cabbies in a stand-off. It's war! Nothing like I've ever seen."

"I don't know. Those Welsh boys up against our football team was a fearsome sight."

James now looked much more relaxed sitting back in the seat, casually holding the reins in his left hand. "I've still got the trophy on the mantel from the prize-giving at the Empire Hotel."

"We were a little worse for wear that night."

"I've never told you this, James, but I really took it to heart at ten when you laid your hands on my shoulders like a priest at dedication saying, 'You are the man of the house now'."

"Harry, I might be the older brother, but we look to you for leadership. You see providence where there isn't any."

"I'm just content to see the family all together."

We had passed the last of the settlements and had started to make our way into the valley, winding back and forth around the hills. We stopped to throw on our woollens as it was well past midday and a gentle breeze had created a chill in the dark, tall, beech forest.

"It can't have been long after that you got caught around April for throwing dice?"

James shook his head. "That bastard 'Constable Black' tried time and again to catch us red-handed with the dice … with the exception of that one, we managed to blow out the lamps and escape. He left quite a few nights fuming and vanquished, after unsuccessfully lying in wait for us for hours," he said, laughing.

"I can see him even now, in bed, lying awake, scheming of ways to catch us."

"Black has made it his goal to apprehend me. He's had me up on a dozen charges, throwing coins, moving faster than a walk, reckless driving, overcharging, soliciting, and gambling in the carriage. It's a game of cat and mouse …."

"Why not surrender before it's too late."

"I've no regard for the law – it only protects the wealthy."

I shrugged. "I'm not wealthy, but I did okay this time."

"Yeah, you were lucky he dismissed the case. I told you the other day you had nothing to worry about."

"I've lost count of the cases you've had dismissed; it makes me wonder if you're bribing the judge."

James threw his head back and laughed. "They didn't all get dismissed."

"Come on. What about that Colonial secretary? Fraser, wasn't it? That case was dismissed."

"I still think five shillings was cheap considering it was late and raining that night. Anyway, how was I to know he was with the government."

"Remember Constable 'Gough' in plain clothes. You tried grabbing his Portmanteaux."

"That scrawny runt … fooled me good and proper. Bastard!"

"Now, now, no profanity – you did fourteen days hard labour for that already!"

"Those days I spent in lockup was my choice. I could have

showed up for the hearing!"

"Brother, I said to look further afield for work in Martinborough, not miss a court hearing for it."

"It was a good fare."

We rounded the corner and stopped again to shovel a small slip blocking our path.

"This rugged road rattles your bones. It leaves my backside numb. The only source of relief is stopping to clear these constant slips and rubble off the track after the heavy rains."

We paused to swing the billy for a mug of black tea, and while we shovelled, Lotti rested again and grazed beside a ford. As we sipped our brew, another traveller on horseback came by in a black rain jacket and canvas hat.

"Morning, you've got the right idea. Where are you boys headed?"

"Martinborough."

"These roads are shocking for a cart, but the road is not so bad from here … it'll be going dusk soon."

"Thanks for that, we'll find a sheltered spot to rest for the night before we end up over the bank."

"You'll find a sheltered spot not far from here on the ridge under the overhang. You'll get first light in the morning, and hopefully you'll miss the rain."

We found the spot beneath an outcrop, just off the track and sheltered under an overhanging rock. We quickly gathered some bracken and firewood in the last light for our beds. Over a generous fire, we boiled a billy of water and prepared a pot of stew with a few onions, carrots, potatoes and hearty chunks of fatty lamb. I recovered a few river rocks from a dry stream to heat beside the fire and bury under our rough bracken beds for warmth. James came back out of the bush with an extra armload of firewood, dumping it on the lee side, and we sat eating in the firelight with glimpses of bright stars flickering through the trees.

"They look so close."

"I forget how magical they are out here. The smoke in the city seems to drown out the glow."

"Glad you came, brother," I sighed. "When was the last time we did this?"

"Gotta be a few years since we tracked that old stag."

We sat in silence mesmerised by the dancing flames and red-hot brilliance lighting up our faces as the embers floated magically into the night sky. The Moreporks were hooting their eerie tune and, as we settled down for the night, I could hear pigs rooting out grubs in a clearing nearby.

We woke surrounded by fog and in the dim morning light I rekindled the fire, and we warmed ourselves with hot tea. We packed up our few things and headed away before the valley mist burned up by the sun rising over the hills in the distance.

"It's a good thing we stopped. You have to keep your wits about you with this steep descent. I will let you take the reins again this time."

I playfully pushed him off the edge of the seat, and he instinctively jumped down, landing in the mud.

"You are getting soft, old man."

"Bloody young upstart. Why did I think I would get any respect as your elder brother. Look at my shoes!" he yelled.

"You should have worn your boots … Don't you love it out here, James. Being surrounded by the bush to clear my head. The birds, the river … they are a welcome balm from the bustle of the city."

"I'll give you balm … I should have stayed home!" he said as he tried to wipe his shoes clean on the grass. "I can't help worrying about Marg. I hope she's alright."

"Don't worry. We'll be back in no time."

"Alright for you to say … you don't have a child on the way."

"Bet the Māoris didn't have to worry about passing through here with muddy shoes," I said with a chuckle. "Actually, James, an old timer told me this track through these hills *was* originally a Māori foot track, and was no bigger than a goat track."

"Wonder what shoes they had?"

"Sandals made of flax in those days. This hill was something the first settlers couldn't penetrate until they paid £150 to cut it through wide enough for one man to carry all his belongings on his back. That's how the Harris family arrived in this fertile valley in the 1840s."

"Most of our roads are cut from Māori trails; they were traversing these hills long before we arrived."

As we made our way over the top and down the other side, with first glimpses of beyond around a few bends, then suddenly sweeping views looked out over the whole valley. The spectacular plains of the Wairarapa stretched out into the distance, framed by soft hills in the far surrounds. The light caught the top of a church steeple far in the distance.

Finally, we made our way from Graytown along Otaraia Road, over the Waihinga Bridge, into the settlement of Martinborough. I loved the little picket fences and tall European trees in this quaint little township.

James spoke up. "I read about John Martin, an early settler who designed this central square. It's in the shape of a Union Jack, and he named things after some of his travels abroad. "It might be a small settlement, but it has all the necessary conveniences.

"Mother would love it here, but don't you think that's extravagant," he said, pointing to the Post Office. "Looks a little too grand for a small town?"

"The idea is for it to grow, along with the convenience store, butcher's shop, two hotels, the bakery, tailor, church and, of course, the school. It is ready for you to move here, James, once the train line's laid."

"We'll see, little brother. Marg likes living near her mother."

We made our way to John and Ellen's humble two-storey pit-sawn cottage, which was a welcome sight. Louisa and Joseph came running out, elated to see us.

Jo immediately took hold of Lotti's halter. "El will be happy to see you. Are you staying long?"

"Just a few days. James needs to get home to Margaret."

Louisa's young face lit up. "Has she had the baby yet?"

James reached into his breast pocket. "No, but it won't be long, lass. I have two red ribbons she sent for you." He lay them gently over her hand, and she squeezed him excitedly then ran into the house, shouting, "Ellen, look what Margaret sent!"

Joe began to undo Lotti's harness to lead her off to feed and water.

"Good boy, Joe. You've filled out since I last saw you. You must have been working hard."

"I've been working on the neighbour's farm after school."

Ellen came to the front door wiping her hands on her apron. She was a commanding presence and took no nonsense from the children, yet she showed a generous spirit and warm hospitality.

"What a pleasant surprise. How on earth did you manage to get Grumpy to come with you," she said, holding a stern gaze that quickly broke into a smile. She hugged us both, then stood for a moment to inspect us, as if we were on parade and she had noticed us for the first time. "You are both handsome men, and I bet you are hungry. You're just in time for lunch, so come inside. James, how is Margaret? She must be nearly full term."

"She is doing very well … and it should be any day now."

"Wasn't it a little reckless to leave her at this time?"

"I'm glad there is another sensible person in our family," he said, pointing at me. "Harry insisted it would only be for a few days."

I changed the subject. "Look at you, Louisa … last time I saw you, you were a stick insect; now you're a young woman."

She beamed up at me. "I am nearly thirteen. Come and look at what I've been making."

Louisa took my hand, talking ninety to the dozen about her school project, which was to design a delicate crochet tablecloth for Ellen's table.

James and Ellen strolled in together, slightly awkwardly as Ellen took his arm. "Will you stay for a few days?"

He shook his head. "No. I must return tomorrow. I'm still nervous about leaving Margaret. Is John about?"

"He's over helping a neighbour, but he should be here any minute for lunch … Lou, can you set a few more places, please?"

Louisa rushed about excitedly, setting the table while Joe prepared the fire for later.

"Did you know Mother has decided to move up here? She is packing up the house as we speak."

"Oh, you received a letter too. I reread the letter to James the other day. Good for her. It's about time she saw sense. What will happen to young John?"

"He has decided to remain there for his final year as he is captain of the footy team this year. He's talking of exploring the goldfields in Thames later, perhaps."

James relit his pipe, puffing on it as he spoke. "Harry is considering the same – perhaps we should all head up there."

Joe came over as Ellen came through from the kitchen, "Joe, could you run over and tell Mary the boys are here." She turned with her hands on her hips. "I thought I could smell tobacco! That wretched pipe! James, if you insist on smoking that thing inside, lift the window a crack and sit near it. Louisa suffers with a cough which seems to be made worse with that damn smoke. That goes for you too, Harry."

"Yes, Mother!" we both chimed in unison.

"I'll have no sarcasm, or you can take them outside. She's your sister too." We both glanced at each other, then burst out laughing.

Ellen froze with a startled face, looking slightly bewildered. "Nellie, now this feels like coming home. It's wonderful to be here, sister."

Ellen blushed and trotted back to the kitchen. "Harry, come and stoke the fire. I'm going to throw a hearty stew on the stove; it will be ready for supper. I want to hear all about what mischief you are creating. Louisa, can you peel some potatoes for me!"

Louisa put down the book she had been pretending to read and poked her tongue out at me playfully on the way past.

"Come on, scallywag, give me a small knife so I can help." Louisa looked up surprised, then pulled out a bowl for the peels and a second paring knife. "Let's do them over here out of the way."

"Nell, where will Mother stay? You are already running out of room!"

"I'm not sure, as I think Emma will end up here too! We will squeeze everyone in somehow. I am thinking we can clear out the attic to create a room upstairs for all the children. You men could build a small wall across the back porch to create a small bedroom while you are here and make yourselves useful for once."

"How does John feel about it all?"

"He never says much, as you know, but he is an angel with the children; he's already trying to come up with ways to accommodate everyone. It will work out."

"I've watched John in the past sitting with the children by the hour to teach them math or listening to them read."

"Harry, how is James doing, do you think?" She lowered her voice.

I did likewise. "Grumpy as usual … He's more like Father

each day."

"I can hear you in there! I'm not deaf!" James shouted while reading the paper we had picked up to bring over for the latest news.

"His debts are bad," I said even more quietly. "I'm not sure what he will do. Perhaps with this baby on the way he might change his ways a little. If this prohibition comes through, he'll have to!"

James called from the lounge. "You'll never bloody stop us drinking by voting against it. You women need to keep right out of politics, if you ask me!"

"James, go back to your paper and mind your language!" Ellen said, rolling her eyes.

"Are you going to vote, Nell?"

"Wild horses couldn't stop us from voting, brother. All the ladies over here are still a little conservative, but we have created a small group of suffrage women who are certainly going to make our mark. I think it's high time we had our say! Without us, the country would come to a standstill."

"Good for you, Nell!"

"Now, what poor ladies are you charming at present, young brother."

"None really, although I have been dropping these girls off for maypole dancing and the other day, I took one to a social dance. It was a nice evening, but she is young."

"When you say young …?"

"Seventeen, I suppose; only two years younger than me, but conservative. She is dressmaking with her aunt after school in their shop. It's her last year in school."

Louisa looked up at me. "What's her name?"

"Alice."

"She will have a pretty dress if she's dressmaking. I'd like to work in a dress shop," Louisa said with a knowing smile.

"You just make sure you treat her right, brother. None of this being out alone. Make sure you have a chaperone."

"Yes, yes. Don't fret. I am the perfect gentleman."

"Well, I'm not so sure about that."

It was a wonderful evening as Mary came round, bringing her pretty young friend Emily to join us. She was petite with blonde hair and striking clear blue eyes. I kept looking at her across the table as we talked about women's movements and endured James going on about prohibition. Ellen came in twice, asking us to quieten down as John was already in bed as he had an early start in the morning. It was always rather raucous when we all got together. Mary kept catching my eye with a hint of intrigue as I flirted a little with her friend. I suddenly felt tired, yawning twice in response to James' yawns every five minutes. He was the first to stand up and give his apologies and we all followed suit saying our goodbyes. I hoped I would get to see Emily again soon. James and I slept like logs after a fun evening, our long ride and a second helping of Ellen's hearty hogget stew. The next morning, I played a few games with the children, running about in the yard. I managed to get James and Joe to help build a rough wall, closing in the back porch to create a room with a curtain over the doorway and we all cleared out the attic before a late morning tea.

It had been a special time and all too soon we bid our farewells with Joe and Louisa riding with us to the edge of town.

"Please come again soon!" Louisa pleaded as she hugged me tightly.

"I will … James will ring the post office when the baby is born to let you know. Perhaps you'll get to hold it, if we can get Margaret to journey over the hill."

James was distracted, thinking about Marg as we silently traipsed our way back up through the valleys.

As we made our way into town, Margaret was looking very round sitting on the steps in the sun. She shouted out as we swung into the driveway. "I had a feeling you might come soon. I've only been out here half an hour."

James leapt off the wagon and gently embraced her as I watered the horse.

Chapter 6

Jumping on the Band Wagon

Even James was light-hearted the next morning as we headed to the docks. Three ships had come in at Queens Wharf, blown in by the south-easterly off the Antarctic. We seemed to thaw out a little more each time the sun shone through the clouds. I stood rubbing my hands while bantering with two cabbies about election musings. I was about to gently accost a couple looking keenly for a ride when a well-dressed man in the latest American-style suit with a matching street hat strode out from Custom Street. He passed the other cabbies, tilting his hat then stopped beside Lotti. He gently took her halter and patted her affectionately on the neck as he looked my way.

"She's a beauty." He took his hat off to the other cabbies again as they looked a little riled that he had not taken the first cab as standard protocol.

"Thank you! Can I take you anywhere, sir?"

There was something about this man, alert, confident, dressed to a fault. He looked at me inquisitively. "Are you Harry Bagust?"

The strong, handsome man of about forty-five carried a brown leather satchel in one hand. He wore snakeskin shoes and a light brown suit with a fine gold watch chain across his waistcoat. It's true what Father would say: 'Clothes make the man.'

"You're too well dressed to be a copper?" I thrust out my

hand. "Yes, I am, Harry." His face broke into a big smile as he shook my hand with one firm movement.

"Lane! Jack Lane, you've got a fine horse. I usually pick my cabbie by his horse." He patted her affectionately.

"Sir, I'm not often lost for words," I said, smiling. "Let me take your bag. Where would you like Lotti and I to take you today, sir?" I pulled out of the waiting line and turned Lotti towards town.

"Where would I like to take *you*, Harry, … is up to you." He looked at me inquisitively as if asking a question. "For today, though, drop me at the hospital then if you bother to wait for me, I've got a little business in town." *I had the feeling this man had a completely different agenda.*

He handed me the black bag and, holding the grab handles, leapt up the steps into the buggy.

"Good then, let's be going."

The roads were busy as I waited to pull out onto the dusty road. We had to speak up above the clatter of many hooves as we entered Custom Street.

"My brain is doing summersaults, sir, as I am desperately trying to work out how you know me. You certainly have me at a disadvantage, which is an odd feeling, I must say."

"I've met James a few times at the station. Your brother is what I would call 'spirited'."

"Yes, James certainly knows a lot of people, some you'd want to know and others you wouldn't. Having said that, you'd definitely want brother James next to you in a fight." We both laughed.

"Harry, I've watched you play rugby a few times against those tough mining boys from Paeroa and a few matches against Canterbury's Otago farmers. For your size, you do not let too many men get in your way on the field. Fast and calculated!"

"I am not ready to play for you Te-Aro boys, if that's what

you are about to ask me. Are you from the NZRFU? What do you make of those twenty-three brave girls off for ten matches against Australia in June. It's got to be an election stunt?"

He laughed heartily. "I think times are changing, and women will end up taking many roles we would not expect them too. I do think they should stick to tennis, but this election will change everything if this government allows them to vote."

I turned to face this stranger sitting slightly to one side now, and, gently pulling the reins, I brought the cab to a standstill on the edge of the road. "Should I know you?" I caught his furtive glance and then it came to me.

"I *do* know! I have heard your name! It's been mentioned a few times in the Gazette with horses. But how did you know it was me?"

"I'm well connected in town … I'm in the Lodge, and I've observed you for a while, how you operate. You have a way with managing people; they feel relaxed with you. You have a flair for business."

"You can tell all that from watching me? Sounds like it was not by accident you chose my fare today. What sort of horse business are you in, Mr Lane?"

"I'm in the livery business. I breed horses, buy and sell 'em. Please call me Jack. … I am off to visit one of my managers, who got thrown off a horse and has a broken leg and collar bone."

"That is nasty. I suppose it goes with the job. Will they be alright?

"I hope so."

"Do I detect a slight Californian accent?"

"Well done, Harry! I'm from Auckland originally, headed out to California a few years back. My parents are ageing. I'm the only son, so I came back as support."

"Are the stories true of Californian gold?"

"I made a little gold over there for a few years," he said again with a knowing smile. "I didn't do too badly."

"What made you give up mining?"

"Diversifying! I had enough of the madness. There's gold amongst the fever, but a smart man can see it in the opportunities without a pick and shovel. I thought I'd try my luck with some different opportunities in the colony."

"Thames is thriving with the gold, Jack."

"Harry, you've got to diversify; don't put all your eggs in one basket. If you drop it, you'll lose the lot. Come by sometime and take a look at a few of my horses."

"I am always interested in an opportunity."

"You strike me as a man with a plan."

"Jack, like so many, I plan on owning land one day. I have been trading my way up with horses till I got Lotti. I've had her a year now; she's a good temperament for around town. I started with Father's Clydesdale on the farm. Strong, dependable, ploughed easy in a straight line but slow and hungry."

"Beautiful horses! Powerful beasts. How did you find this work, Harry?"

"I've been round horses all my life. Father is a smithy and had the opportunity to buy and sell a few horses on the side."

"I have one you would really like. Fast and calculated!" he laughed with a cheeky grin.

"Go on tell me more; we've got a little time."

He got out his pipe and cleaned it, tapping it on the wheel of the cart. "Could we take Riddiford Street? Those sewers they are digging up nearly turn my stomach. I do not know how all the locals get on."

I pulled off again, past a group of men with shovels repairing the road. The smell was still wafting past.

"It was a terrible business, those seventy people dying over that sewerage contamination; the families are probably ecstatic something is finally being done. The land up here was rotten from flooding in '88 when I arrived. I had picked up an old pack horse from this area back then; she was ready for the knackery." We laughed.

"You sound like you're from down south, Harry."

"Grew up on the plains of Timaru – not used to all these treacherous hills. I had to turn down many a fare with these steep tracks; it made me hungry."

"I like to see a man with vision – it's about embracing change."

"Sounds like you might have an opportunity for me then, Jack?"

"You will have to come and see. He is a real beauty, I bought him off some folks leaving town last week – called him 'Black'. He's a two-year-old."

"Sounds interesting. I could come whenever it's convenient to you."

"Good. I was hoping you'd say that. I've got a farm out at Island Bay round the coast. The property goes right down to the water. It's a pretty spot. Why don't you bring a lady friend out on Saturday morning at ten. I've got a few people coming over; I'll show you around."

I dropped Jack off at the hospital. He briskly alighted from the carriage. "I won't be long. Watch my bag; thanks, Harry."

I jumped down and watched him briskly walk off toward the main door then sat leaning on the seat, looking out over the gardens. Three children played chasey in amongst the rose bushes while some elderly folk lounged in night clothes, cardigans and knitted hats under the front porch in the sun.

It's intriguing. Whatever did he mean: where I would like to take you, Harry, is up to you? I paced around the cart, anticipating his return. It seemed an age as I rechecked my watch, then finally pulled out brushes from the little leather storage bag and started brushing Lotti's brown coat.

Jack suddenly appeared, catching me by surprise as I bent over while brushing Lotti's legs.

"Come on, Harry, no time to waste. I have a meeting in twenty minutes on Lambton." I returned the brushes and took the reins.

"How is he doing?"

"*She* is doing quite well, thanks. Took a nasty tumble, leaving her quite bruised. It'll take her a while to heal before she is in the saddle again.

"Oh! I haven't known anyone to have a women manager … how many do you employ?"

"She is brilliant and has an eye for the details. I have eighty employees at present, but we have a few contracts to fill for the government as well as some mining contracts coming up, so I am looking for a few more good men. Perhaps you need to jump on the bandwagon."

Me? Sounds interesting. "Come on, girl." Lotti started to trot as we were out of the bustle of town, beyond where I might get fined for moving faster than a walk.

"I have a friend that might be interested in a little work; should I tell him to call to see you?" We came to a stop outside the impressive government buildings at number 15 on Lambton. Jack jumped down, and I handed him his satchel.

"Bring your friend with you. I look forward to seeing you in a few days." He faced me and shook my hand. "See you on Saturday at ten, Harry."

I couldn't get it off my mind: it was unusual to be invited out by a stranger who seemed to know me, somehow, quite well. *I've been seeing Alice for a few months. I will ask her if she would like to join John and I. She will know the etiquette.*

I was quite distracted as the next few days passed. I quietly asked a few of the cabbies if they knew anything about Jack, but it was pretty much as I thought. He was a shrewd businessman with a number of horses entered in the trots. A few jockeys said he was a good employer who liked a bit of fun.

Chapter 7

Chance is a Fine Thing

Saturday morning seemed brighter than usual as I left early to pick up Alice from her stately family home. Alice looked dainty in her flowing dress as she skipped down the wide steps from her veranda. Her mother waited patiently to wave her off. She wore a matching bold hat, red shoes with a white shawl about her shoulders. She smiled as I helped her up into the cart and waved to her mother.

"You look beautiful, Alice," I said. She was glowing with anticipation.

"You said it was a day out, but I was not quite sure what to wear."

"I don't know, but if it's anything like I've experienced so far, it will be a surprise. Jack seems to hold his cards to his chest."

"Your carriage looks especially shiny this morning. You must have been up early."

"I rose at dawn to clean the cab and polish the leather in a futile attempt to make a silk purse out of a sow's ear. It will probably be covered in salt spray in this breeze as we travel the coast road."

She nodded. "I've been looking forward to this since you invited me. I don't get to go out apart from the dance practice."

"I'm feeling slightly nervous myself, like somehow there's something in the wind other than salt air." We both laughed nervously.

"We are picking Rusty up on our way, I am sorry it might be a little of a squeeze. That's what we call John as he's a big, red-headed Irishman. We'll have to squeeze in like anchovies in a tin." But I didn't mind as Alice sat close while we made our way out of town along the coast in the biting wind.

We finally arrived at the big black gates with LANE forged into the wrought iron. A little bow-legged man wearing a Scottish Tam came from the keeper's cottage directly behind.

"Morn, it's a dreich day!" he said as he opened one of the gates.

He waved us through, and we ambled up the gently sloping drive that bordered many small fields in a beautiful panorama of trees, rose gardens and lush grass. As we came up a rise, the big chimneys on the slate roof appeared beyond the hill. We entered an archway to the circular driveway, surrounded by beds of white roses in full bloom.

A young lad waiting on the stately front steps came over smiling and reached for Lotti's bridle to hold her steady as we alighted.

"Good morning, sir. I will look after your horse. Please, when you are ready, head over to the stables, where you'll find refreshments."

"Thank you. Do you know what awaits us today?"

"I have been told not to say. Hopefully, you'll be pleasantly surprised."

Fidgetting, Alice straightened her crepe dress and removed her linen gloves. "You look ravishing, Alice. Relax. You've worn the perfect dress!"

"I hope so, Harry. I stayed up late last night finishing it off. It's hard if you don't know what to expect."

She took my arm as we made our way over to a group of well-dressed couples gathered outside the long stable buildings. Jack was there, surrounded by boisterous laughter. We caught his eye as we approached.

"Harry!" he said loudly, "glad you could all come. You must be John and Alice. Come and meet everyone."

He took Alice's arm. "You look delightful, Alice!" he said, leading her toward a few ladies. "Come and meet a few friends of mine."

Teacakes and sandwiches were spread out on a big table. Some of the men stood smoking, discussing elections and politics, which I hoped to avoid. A racetrack lay to one side of the stables, and a few jockeys inside the building dressed up, preparing for a race.

I looked at John questioningly. "Looks like a race is about to start?"

John watched the horses warming up as we leaned on the outer white fence rail that ran neatly round the race track.

"Jack, what's happening?" I said with a slight smile, feeling out of my class.

"Harry, are you up for a bit of fun?" Jack smiled, removing his hat and waiting a moment for my response. He looked at me intently while searching his pocket for his pen along with some small pieces of paper.

"Of course … always after a little excitement."

In a loud voice, he called out: "It's time! Everyone chose a number from one to ten along with your name to put in my hat. We are going to have a race. The winner gets to take away ten bob and a bottle of my finest whiskey. The loser gets to entertain us later with a song, recital or some such thing."

There were excited conversations as we took turns to write our names and place them in Jack's hat. As we selected our horse from the list, each had a corresponding number which the jockeys had sewn to their shirts.

My lucky number seven was Run-away. I was hoping it would run away ahead and not run away behind.

Jack had gone over to speak with the jockeys before returning to open a small wooden box on a little round table. Taking out a pistol, he dusted it off affectionately with a handkerchief then shouted: "Is everyone ready? Do you each have a horse?"

Excitement filled the air as people cheered, "Yes!"

We three found a spot and leant on the perimeter fence to see ten horses snorting and pawing the ground as they lined up behind the wooden barrier,

Jack gave a thumbs up to all the riders, then, without delay, called out: "Are you ready?" Then he fired a shot in the air. Instantly, the horses bolted away from the gates. Jack turned to us.

"Alice, which did you choose?"

"Black."

Mmmm, the horse Jack spoke of.

"Well done, my dear!" he said, smiling.

The horse was a tall, spirited black stallion, its only marking a perfect, white, diamond-shaped patch on his forehead.

The oval track curved around a fence line on one edge of the stable buildings, dirt clods flying from its turf as the galloping horses thundered past, spurred on by the small crowd of about thirty as they rounded the track for a second time. The ground vibrated from the pounding of hooves; the air filled with screams of delight as they passed the finish line only yards away. It looked like Black had won, but it was hard to tell as he flew over the line neck and neck with another. To my dismay, Run-away crossed last, having kept up with the pack at first, then slowly lagged behind.

We waited for tense moments to hear the verdict.

"I'm sure it's won! What do you think, Harry?"

"He's a mighty strong horse – there was nothing in it. Did you see him come up the last leg, breaking out so boldly from the pack?"

I was mesmerised by his rippling muscles, evident as his coat glistened in the sunlight. *He's certainly fiery to fight his way through like that.*

Jack had gone off partway through, then over the loud hailer, his voice bellowed out: "Black! The winner today is Black! Congratulations to Alice, who is the sole winner today."

Everyone cheered as Jack made a beeline for us. He kissed Alice with hearty congratulations; slapped me on the back, his face beaming.

"How's that! A winner and loser in the same couple. What do you think of him, Harry? … Do I have an instinct for matching men to horses?"

"He's a fine horse alright!" I turned to watch him cool down, trying to be casual. My heart pounded as I tried to keep a poker face. "What do you plan to do with him?"

Jack caught my arm as he shouted out like an excited schoolboy, "Come on, everyone, let's get inside out of the cold wind."

A doorman stood to take our coats as we entered two huge double doors that led into an entry hall with ornate marble floors. The beautiful curved wooden stairs led to a balcony sparkling with the lights of a huge crystal chandelier.

The room, warmed by a roaring fire at one end, and now filled with excited chatter. I, however, was distracted trying to recall an appropriate poem to recite.

Jack came by and introduced me to three gentlemen in their forties, dressed in fine suits.

"This is Harry, who I was telling you about. You might have seen him on the field or read about him in the Times."

"Hopefully not for my misdemeanours before the judge," I jibbed.

They laughed as I shook hands with each of them. "You picked the wrong horse today, lad! I'm Robert – call me Bob.

Aren't you boys playing against Thames this week? They're a tough bunch."

"Wouldn't miss it, Bob. And yes, they're a burly band of thugs, gold miners, tunnellers, railway gangers, luggers and farm hands, and they've got hands like tree bark with trunks for legs. They're hobbled though on the field like lame horses – too much brawn."

Jack interrupted as he appeared through the side door carrying his Scottish malt high in the air. "Please fill a glass … let's toast the winner!"

While we all took a glass, Jack came over to me. "Now, Harry, I will give you a few minutes to come up with something to share?" He squeezed me on the shoulder sympathetically and then looked about the room. "Has everyone a glass?" He held up his. "So here is to the winner of the 'Prestigious Island Bay Race' … Miss Alice Rutland!" He gently raised the bottle, placing it in Alice's hands with a small envelope attached. She beamed with delight and swung around to show us all her prize.

"Raise your glass for the toast … To Alice!"

Everyone cheered in delight as Jack stood by me with a hand on my shoulder. The room quietened as many of the staff came in to watch the drama unfold. All eyes turned to me. The young man from the door came through in formal attire with another tray of glasses of whiskey and red wine and the young lady with beer. I took a whiskey to calm my nerves. I patted my pocket, looking for my cigarettes, then remembered I had left them in the buggy.

I suddenly had an idea. "Just give me a minute!" I said, putting down my glass and turning towards the door.

Jack called in a loud voice after me in a light-hearted manner, "No good running away, Harry!" The small crowd responded in good-natured laughter. I strode out to the buggy, and slid my case out from under the seat and quickly returned inside.

Although I was not yet proficient, I had been practising with my new accordion.

As I entered the grand ballroom, voices hushed in anticipated silence. The huge room with tall ornate ceilings echoed as I unlatched my case. The long windows revealing picturesque views of the bay let in beams of sunshine along one side of the room, and an elegant formal table extended to a timber dance floor along one side of the room. Beside the table was a lounge area with soft furniture, lavish rugs and the huge roaring fire. Everyone stood awaiting my recital. I flipped open the case, removed the squeeze box then stood up on the hearth of the fireplace and started to play a simple tune: *Sweet Rosie O'Grady.* Faces turned from hesitation to amusement as I played my way badly through the two Irish tunes John had taught me. Then John jumped up with two kindling sticks and beat out a rhythm and suddenly, folk started tapping their feet as the conversation became louder. John stepped out on the dance floor, hands on hips, and started to tap dance about on the wooden floor and was soon joined by two young women who hilariously tried to follow his lead.

Everyone clapped, in high spirits now, with all the comforts of a warm fire, good food, and plenty to drink. It was nearly lunchtime, and the staff started laying out a feast on the long table. I noticed Jack whispering to one of his staff, who then disappeared through a doorway. Shortly after, a young woman returned and sat elegantly at the piano.

"Didn't he do well, everyone! …a man full of surprises. Please help yourself to a drink as we have more frivolity to follow."

Then Jack again put his hand on my shoulder. "Harry, come and sit for a minute." We strolled over to the bar in a private corner, and, taking the fine crystal decanter, Jack topped up both our glasses.

"The other day, I told you about my manager who had an

accident. The reason I came to find you is because I need someone to stand in while she recovers. I think you are the man for the job."

I raised an eyebrow. "What does the job entail?"

"Looking after the stable staff … management of the stables … ordering feed. I run a fairly tight ship, but most of the staff know what I require. The hardest thing is keeping everyone on their toes. It's only for three months. Are you up for it?"

"It is very sudden. When do you need someone?"

"You can start straight away! It'll pay well."

"God knows I need a change?"

"I told you I would let you come and see Black, but I like a bit of fun. I have a deal for you." He looked at me, trying to gauge my response while emptying his pipe out into the ashtray.

A deal! "Alright, what sort of deal have you in mind?"

He tapped his glass with his pipe to get everyone's attention, then said: "I have a proposal: I am about to offer Harry a deal that you can all be witness to. First off, I would like him to come to work for me, filling in while Nora is recuperating?"

What have I got myself into?

"The thing is, I think he could be a little reluctant."

By now, he had everyone's attention.

"Those who know me know I like to have a little fun … so let's play a game of poker.

"I want £30 for 'Black. If you win, you can have him – if you come and work for me for six months."

Everyone murmured with excitement.

Jack waited for quiet again. "I know this will spark your imagination." He turned back to me, looking very serious. "Now, if you lose, you can pay for him outright or come and work for me till he's paid off. Chance is a fine thing, Harry'?" What do you all think?

"Say yes, Harry," John shouted out. "Either way, you'll have work!"

I took a few minutes to look into Jack's cherry face. "Alright, Jack, on one condition."

"Oohhh!" everyone cooed louder.

"… that Rusty can join me as well." I put my hand forward and stared into Jack's stern face.

"You can certainly dance but are you good with horses, lad?" he asked John.

"John looked at me then at him. "You'll have no trouble from me, sir."

Jack shook my hand vigorously, then shook John's amid cheers of appreciation. Then he leaned in; held my arm. "Well done, Harry! I knew you would come to join our Island Bay family."

"Not till we've played that hand, Jack."

Grinning, he motioned to a young man to bring the cards.

"Pretty sure I'm about to be hooked like a fish by one of your many games, Jack." But I had nothing to lose. £30 was still a good price for Black. I just hoped my desperation to try something new didn't put me off my game. *All those nights playing poker with James is about to pay off one way or another.* Everyone had already gathered around the card table, like spectators in a street fight. Jack threw down a handful of red chips and shuffled the cards, flipping them back and forth like a master dealer. I suddenly wished James was here – he would know exactly how this would play out. I had stood too many times guarding James' cart while they played. As I watched the many expressions on Jack's face, I laughed inside as I thought how ridiculous this all was.

"We'll have thirty chips each," he said as he dealt the cards out.

The cards I threw out I should have kept, and I watched my thirty chips slowly disappear, each time to the chiding of onlookers. Then I picked up my next hand, fanned my five cards out slowly. A Queen. Ten and nine of spades ... *What should I do?* I threw out two and could not believe my eyes, fought to stay cool-headed, fought not to show my surprise. *Keep calm, Harry*, I said to myself. I stared at the black Jack and the eight of spades. Suddenly, at that moment, I committed to going all in. I glanced at the eager audience and threw all caution to the wind, cast my last eleven chips with a clatter on the table as I laid my cards out triumphantly.

A sudden gasp went up as everyone held their breath, waiting for Jack's response. Jack slowly laid his cards out for all to see and rose to his feet.

"I do believe, Harry, you're as lucky as you are brave. Well done! Well done!"

I looked at Jack's smiling face and also stood, my hand jutting out towards him. Alice, who had sat quietly, stood up and kissed me on the cheek. Behind Jack, John danced around punching the air with his fists, saying over and over, 'Yes! Yes!'

"He's a strong horse, Harry, and he's yours. I have already entered him in the next local race. This calls for a celebration!" He thrust out his hand and clasped mine. "Alright, we have a deal then. Can you start Monday?"

We shook hands vigorously. "Well, it was a lucky hand, Jack ... it was those last two cards, the black Jack and the eight. That's it! That's perfect – I'll call him 'Blackjack'."

Everyone coo-ed and clapped in agreement. "Yes, Jack. John and I will be here first thing Monday."

"Harry, you'll get a good wage, and there's accommodation on site. It is good to have you aboard. Drink up and enjoy the food, folks. It's Sunday tomorrow ... you can sleep in before church."

The music continued into the late afternoon as people gathered around the piano, singing along in different states of inebriation.

We finally bid everyone farewell and climbed into the buggy for a chilly ride home after lighting the kerosene lanterns.

I peered out over the paddocks in the starlight to catch a glimpse of Blackjack, but he was tucked away for the night in his stable.

Alice glowed as she clutched tightly to her bottle of malt; even John sat in stunned silence from the whiskey. Lotti's hooves melodically clip-clopped her way back along the shore to the city. The cold air had the added benefit of sobering up my foggy head as we wound our way along to the peaceful sounds of waves washing along the shore.

I felt warmly contented as Alice tucked in against my ribs.

I could not tell if it was the drink or at twenty, my life was about to take an interesting turn for the better. What had started almost as a whim in coming out here could well change the course of my life.

Chapter 8

At the Drop of a Hat

"James, I am giving up my daytime cabbie work."

"You're mad. I didn't think you were serious? What are you going to do?"

"I picked up a chap the other day; he is a livery agent with a huge estate out at Island Bay. It's just the break I've been looking for. He invited Alice, John, myself and a group of others for an outrageous evening."

"Doing what?"

"This bizarre day started with a horse race, dancing, drinking, playing poker … all the things you love so much. I thought of you many times as I went up against this chap to win a bet. He proposed that, if I won, he would give me this impressive black stallion on the condition I go and work for him. Apparently, he's been watching us for years. His manager is in hospital, so he sought me out to manage his livery business for three months.

"What happened?"

I couldn't help looking smug. "I was one hand away from losing everything when I picked up the very two cards I needed to complete a flush. I went all in and won!"

James looked away in disgust. "Harry, you are the luckiest son of a bitch! Damn you! I don't want to hear any more." He kicked the ground in a huff.

"I'd like you to come out and see him."

"Where is it?"

"Out at Island Bay. We're getting ready for a race next Saturday."

"I'm not coming all the way out there."

"It's up to you, but it'll be worth your bet!"

"What's he called?"

I laughed. "Blackjack. I called him that after picking up the Jack of Spades."

"I don't know. I'll see how I go."

Really! After all we've been through, you are going to be jealous … how does he not know he is the nearest thing I have to a father. "Up to you, but it would mean a lot to me. I'm starting work for him on Monday. I'll move there tomorrow."

"It's all pretty sudden!"

"I told you I was looking for a change! You'll have to find your own way. If you come, you come." *He's like a cold stone sometimes … why do I bother?*

The following week, I tried to fit into my new role and met all the staff. Most were satisfied to have someone pick up the slack on the reins. Some of the older men, though, were disgruntled with a twenty-year-old in charge but they soon warmed up. Saturday came around quickly. By then, we had the place looking great.

I was shocked to see James turn up in time for the first race. He wasn't in a great mood but placed a few bets after looking Blackjack over.

John, always positive, shook James' hand. "Good to see you, James. I know Harry appreciates you coming," he said when James arrived.

"He's got no experience racing," James replied sharply. "It takes more than a like for horses to win."

John slapped me on the back. "Don't be nervous, Harry! If the jockey's alright, you're a shoe-in!"

"Thanks, John. Your boys have done well to get this event organised …" I turned to James. "Can I get you a beer?"

"If the tip's good, I think I should get them." He wandered off toward the makeshift saloon, leaving me standing, nodding, yet slightly rankled.

James returned, slopping the beers just as quiet descended for the start of the race.

Jack stood tall, his hat held high in one hand and his gun in the other. Looking at the jockeys, he dropped his hat and fired a shot into the air simultaneously. As the gun cracked loudly and the horses plunged forward at the sound, the crowd erupted with cheers of encouragement.

"Go, Blackjack! Go, boy!!" we shouted together! It was like I was strapped in the saddle, feeling the huge muscles straining as every hoof gripped deep into the dirt track as he strode forward. As he rounded the bend for the second lap, I asked to borrow a bystander's eyeglasses. I could see Blackjack's head thrusting vigorously, his nostrils steaming with the effort. With each powerful stride, he surged forward, shoulder to shoulder with the jostling throng. His muscles gleamed in the sunlight. The sounds of hooves beat like drums, the ground vibrating where we stood. *Come on, boy!!*

As if he heard me, Blackjack stretched out with every ounce of vigour. Then, with only half a lap to go, Rusty shouted, "Look, Harry! He's inched his way through the pack! He's only behind by three." Then he leaned over and whispered. "Harry, I've a large bet on Blackjack for a win and a place. If he makes it through, we could win."

"John, shhhh! I'm not getting my hopes up."

The ground shook even harder as the pack of horses thundered past, dirt flying in a shower as they rounded the last bend.

"Come on, boy. Come on!" Rusty screamed.

James looked troubled. I couldn't worry about him now. He'd taken the day off to attend the race, and now we all clenched our hands in trepidation.

"*Yes!* Look at 'em go, Harry!"

We pumped our fists in elation as raucous cheers rose from the crowd as two horses streaked forward and flew across the finish line. We all slapped each other's backs, still unsure of the outcome but knowing it was a brilliant finish. Then we stood, falling silent as we strained to hear the loud hailer.

"Irish wins by a nose. Blackjack second …"

We shouted out of sheer relief, still charged with excitement, and gave each other hearty congratulations – we had actually won a place.

James gripped my hand firmly; looked at me intensely.

"Harry, my little brother, a horse whisperer, to think you made second place and I had a win for once."

Well … that's the nearest thing I'll get to a compliment from James. "Thanks, James, it's unbelievable! Even enough to pay the jockey with hopefully a little left over."

"Harry, it was a lucky day when you picked up Jack for that fare."

As we made our way to the bar, Jack's merry face stood out above the crowd.

"Your first second place, Harry! Well done, lad, well done! This has got to be your infamous brother … nice to meet you!" They shook hands warmly.

"I think you know my older brother, James. We spoke of him when we first met."

"James, you've a smart brother!"

"Smarter still if he'd stayed a cabbie."

I cut across James' comment. "What will you have, Jack?"

"Give me a double, Harry, and remember no one makes you choose anything in life, even if they have a gun to your head.

You still have a choice – *you* chose this! Well done! Next one's on me!"

"How are things on the street, James?"

"It's grim out there. Everyone's holding their coins so tight it cuts their hands. There's an awful lot being said about the elections … I'm over it already. Can't come soon enough; it will be good to have it behind us. Goodness knows who these women will vote for!"

"Well, I am all for it, even though I know it's not a popular stance among the men. Where would we be without a good woman at our side? My manager is the best I've had over the years; she runs a tight ship."

"What do women know about politics, Jack? Let them be school teachers or nurses, but leave the bloody running of the country to us, I say."

"I hear that sort of thing a lot, James, but one day if we don't make room for a woman in the workplace, we'll be sorry. Where are you boys from? Sounds like a southern Canterbury accent."

"We all played for Canterbury, had a spell out at Pleasant Point then moved into Timaru. Been up here for a few years now keeping an eye on my little brother."

"I been watching you boys for a few years throwing that leather around the field – you play a fearsome game." He looked at John and James. "Competitive!"

"Harry's been just what we need here. I will miss him when his time's up but I can see he has goals set that he's determined to achieve. Good on you, son. What about you, James?"

"I've just had a wee, lad. I'd love to settle down with some land, but it's like chasing after the wind from where I stand. Looks like it came easy for you. You've done alright for yourself, Jack!"

"James, I can see you're not a diplomat like your brother. If only you knew … It's not how much you make, James; it's how you care for what you've got. Most of us receive the same opportunities in life, same number of hours in the day, same education, same food; only some live like they are asleep, hard done by, and act like there is a scarcity to everything. Like it's a big pot and the rich are stealing more than their share from the poor."

"I believe that is exactly the case! That is precisely what a rich person would say. Try being poor for a few years. That's why we have the story of David and Goliath, the little guy overcoming the giant."

"Little David is a great example. He used all the *skills* with the weapon he was proficient with to overcome the overwhelming odds. He then put his whole faith in his God, showing blind courage in the face of an impossible outcome. What's even more interesting, Goliath had four other brothers. David picked only five stones for his sling, *expecting* to defeat them all. That's courage, don't you think, James?"

We were all holding our breath, awaiting his response.

"I still think rich people are thieving off the poor."

Bloody James! He's obviously already had too much to drink. But Jack was unfazed.

"Alright, work this out for me, James. I have a large farm I bought for £1,200. I cut it into ten lots and sold each lot for £200. Where did the extra £800 come from?"

"From the poor bugger that sold it?"

"Wasn't it just created out of thin air, a few pieces of paper, a little skill with a slingshot, imagination and courage? You've got to step out in faith. See, I think of it like a river of money, not a pot but an endless supply of wealth, right there for anyone to dip into. It's the person that is awake, looking for opportunity, pushing back against social norms, stepping out, working hard, and taking a few risks that will create wealth."

James, although listening, glared at Jack like an insect. "Easy for you to say when you've already got it all."

I cut across James, feeling completely humiliated, vowing not to invite him again to anything. "Jack, I've not had anyone explain it like that. It makes perfect sense. We grew up poor. My parents used to say, 'Son, money doesn't grow on trees.'"

James drew his shoulders back with pride. "I'm happy with my lot … sounds like rot to me. I don't want to work that hard."

"In that case, I wish you all the best in life. Sounds like you have exactly what you need; can't ask for more than that." He put out his hand to James. "Think about what I said – no doubt we will meet again." James shook his hand reluctantly.

"Can you boys excuse me, I've got a few colleagues to meet." He shook each of our hands warmly and with encouragement.

"James, sometimes I'm ashamed of you. What made you be so rude! I'm not inviting you to the next race."

"I can't stand people that are wealthy. I don't have to respect him."

"James, you didn't respect *me*!" I looked away, disgusted.

"Harry, I'm here, aren't I?"

I almost said it but held my tongue: *I wish you weren't.*

John tried to change the subject to break the tension. "Harry, we won't be around for that meeting. Aren't we headed away to Auckland to play against Parnell?"

"Rusty, your right. I think that is the week we head away. It is the last one of the season! They have billeted us out to a few local folks in the school hall, I think."

Rusty kept the subject moving. "How did that training day go with the military, James? I heard on the grapevine you did fairly well."

"Good thanks, John; it was a close competition."

John picked up our glasses. "Drink up, lads. There's one more race; we can fill up before it starts."

We retired early that night as we both felt shattered after the day's excitement. I saw James off and made straight for the little bunk room, where Rusty and I lay, letting our weary bodies relax.

"Rust, I can't believe I was stupid enough to invite James – it was totally humiliating."

"He's bitter … you said he has immense debts! …I get it: he looks at you with envy. Jack's been around, so don't worry about it."

Rusty's words soothed my heart, and I drifted off to peacefully sleep.

The next morning, still feeling shattered, we dragged our tired bodies out of bed in the dark. Soon we had all the morning chores done as we grabbed a few brushes and talked while we groomed the horses. I heard the faintest whimper in one of the stables further down.

"Shhh, Rusty. Can you hear that?"

I put down my brush and picked up a lantern to follow the minute sound. In the corner of a stable deep in the hay, a tiny black and white pup struggled to free itself from a tangled piece of hemp.

"Come on, little fella. Where are you trying to bolt off to? Where have you come from?"

I untangled his foot and he nuzzled into my woollen sweater, nestled into the crook of my arm, quite content to curl up. Then I gently pulled back the hay to find Bess, the house dog, curled up with five newborns, which were latched on and sucking.

"Rusty, look. The mystery of Bess's disappearance is solved."

He stopped just behind me. "Oh, wait till the girls see them."

I wandered to the kitchen to let them know where Bess was and they were soon fussing over her like mother hens and had a small bed made up for her in the warm woodshed. As I checked on her again later, the little puppy I had rescued earlier came staggering toward me on oversized paws. I crouched down.

"You are an adventurous wee fella. I like your white spot across one eye," I said, stroking him. "You're always nicking off, so I'm gonna call you Bolt." I took off my woollen hat and made a little nest for him against his mother, and he curled up inside it and looked up at me expectantly.

I looked back at Rusty, smiling.

"Harry, don't tell me you are thinking about having a puppy."

The thought sunk in. "Why not? They're not sure what to do with them and the little fella I picked up has taken a shine to me. Sarah said she would look after him for seven weeks until I could wean him. It's a great chance to train a dog here."

"Didn't you have a dog when you were little?"

"Nip." I nodded. "… but he wasn't exactly my dog; he helped round up the cattle and sheep. James took him when he ran away."

"You have a good instinct with animals."

"I admire horses. I never tire of watching them race."

"Harry, if Christmas was not so close, we could easily win a few races with Blackjack."

"I've got no time as Mother is moving up from Timaru. Ellen's been cleaning up the place ready for Mother and my sister Emma – there is nowhere else for them to stay."

"Why not ask Jack for the little summer house down near the beach? It's vacant at present."

"Perhaps I could … I should really suggest they just move up here over Christmas. They need to get away from there. It's ironic … it's really not a pleasant neighbourhood … Pleasant Point. The neighbours' children half live in Mother's house. They're like feral cats as their father just abandons them for a week and when he is home, he beats them. Their clothes are in rags. He locks the food away in the house. Em can't bear to see them so miserable so takes them in. She feeds, clothes and washes them, beds them down at night. They are constantly infested with head lice from the children. She sent a note saying she attended court a few weeks back, as she had witnessed the abuse.

"Would they make the move? They need to be desperate enough."

"Well, last week even young Joseph was caught stealing eight pocket knives with six of his friends. Young Tommy Blanchet was implicated, much to Mother's distress."

"Little Joe! … it's hard to believe!" He stopped and looked at me, demoralised.

"One of his friends broke into the shop through a window at night and smashed a glass cabinet to steal them. By the time the seven boys had given evidence, with a dozen different stories, the judge threw the case out. He was so confused by all their versions of the event and admitted that he knew one of the boys did it.

I joined his laughter. "He couldn't work out whose version was actually true. But that wasn't the last pocketknife incident. A few weeks later, one of the lads used one of the knives to slice a hole in the canvas of a boxing tent to secretly watch a professional fight. The boxer on security spoke to the boys, warning them a number of times to leave, but the boys persisted. When he discovered they had cut a hole in the tent to get a free show, it was the last straw. The seething security guard waited inside the tent next to the slit. As soon as the first boy poked his head through, he smashed him full force in the face, knocked him flying, out cold. Broke all his front teeth and nose. Blood was everywhere. Apparently, he hit him so hard, the kid now talks with a funny lisp."

"Poor little bugger … he will be able to squirt beer further than anyone through the gap in his teeth."

"Joe is a good lad but when he gets with other boys …" I shook my head. "… there's no one to give him a kick up the backside."

"Like a lot of lads, they get in with the wrong crowd, especially at an event like that. We've all been there, haven't we."

"Don't remind me! … Jack was only saying this morning about the Christmas fair: it's the biggest event of the year. He'd like us three to organise this year's picnic festivities for all the staff and special guests."

"*Us!* How could we manage a huge event like that?"

"He asked me to be Master of Ceremonies, liaise with the staff and coordinate everything. It could be fun. I told him as long as I can enter the events."

"I've read reports from other years about his end-of-year carnivals. Can we really pull it off!"

"Well, he's informed me it's to be better than last year, which was by all reports a fairly large affair. There could be as many as 300 people."

"Back home, I helped organise a few events. Plenty of competitions for every age. Tossing the caber, hammer throw, high jump, running races. I could bring my bagpipes to do a Highland Fling."

"Brilliant, Rusty! We could have sack races, toffee apples, candy floss and bring in Alice's friends to do a maypole dance."

"We'll decorate a cart for the children to have special rides."

"I'll speak to the staff who were involved last year – it's a big undertaking. We could use the natural basin in the southern paddocks with a stage to one side."

"Can we bring a number of staff off their usual duties to prepare it all? It will be a great day!"

"I think Jack would be agreeable … Rust, I do love your enthusiasm!"

Chapter 9

The Christmas Spirit

It had been drizzling the morning Jack came by the stables to find me. I was sorting through the canvas horse covers, fishing out those that needed mending for the next season.

"Harry, there's no point being out in the rain today. Gather whatever staff you need for the big picnic and let's get a few things organised. It's only three weeks away."

I nodded. *I know someone who would love to help out.*

"I'll leave it up to you as I think you know what it requires. Bring me a brief outline tomorrow afternoon," Jack continued. "I've got a few busy days ahead. … Actually, I'm off to a Lodge meeting tomorrow night if you want to come. It's always good to have a few contacts."

"Thanks, Jack." I nodded again. "I've never been to a Lodge meeting, but I know a few people who go."

"Good. See you tomorrow."

I found Rusty and asked him to prepare the buggy and a coat for me to go out. I was soon down in the small community of Island Bay, outside a little, white, two-bedroom stone house with colonial windows. It would have been an early settler's cottage. I walked up the path lined on each side with neatly trimmed standard rose bushes and knocked on the sturdy front door. *I hope she's home. I know she will have some program outlines from last year. No point in reinventing the wheel.* A minute passed, and I heard her footsteps on the wooden floor. Then she called out, "I'm coming!" I heard her flick the latch then she stood there with her full leg in plaster and her arm still in a sling. "Good morning!" I said.

She looked at me sternly.

"You must be Nora."

"I am guessing you are Harry by the look of that buggy."

"Nothing gets by you." I grinned. "Can I come in? I need your help a little."

"*If* you must, although next time, let me know in advance."

"It's not the most productive day to be out, so I thought I would drop by."

"You will need a dry towel. Please come in and stand on the doorstep?"

"Thank you!" I went to step into the room

"Stop! Just stand on the mat in case your socks are wet."

"A towel would be lovely, and a rag. Perhaps you can also guess why I am here?"

"Either Jack is out of malt and desperately needs a bottle tonight, or you need help with the Christmas Picnic. I was only thinking this morning what an awful day to be out in the paddocks. I thought you might call, so I prepared. Give me a minute." She turned and hobbled away and returned with a towel and two old rags. "There!" She tossed down the rags and pointed that she wanted me to step onto them to get to the nearest chair.

"Actually, I'm grateful for their company, even yours, as I'm tired of reading books and need something to sink my teeth into. Let me fix the kettle." In the small kitchen, where the little coal range was recessed into an old chimney, she lifted the kettle onto the small range.

Her house had nothing out of place and had lovely views of the water through the double-hung windows to the bay. The curtains and furniture were bright floral fabrics, and a cat squinted suspiciously at me from her warm spot on a lounge chair. I felt awkward and out of place, especially coming in with my slightly damp socks on. *I wouldn't be here if she wasn't so organised. I hope she will be helpful seeing she's annoyed with me for standing in while she's absent.*

We chatted while she prepared a tray and shortbread.

"You have a lovely home. You seem to be managing well under the circumstances."

"My husband bought it when we were first married but he died at sea in a fishing accident about ten years ago. It's just me and Alex, the cat. I always manage things one way or another; it's just this cast that's so itchy; it will be off in a few days, and I can't wait. How is everyone? I need details," she said, smiling for the first time. "It's been two weeks since Bridget called in. Sorry, you can already tell I am climbing the walls for something to do." She tried to look composed while the kettle boiled.

"Well, everyone is doing well at the stables, and I am enjoying working with them all. We would love your help to organise the picnic as you will, no doubt, have all the notes from last year filed away somewhere."

Her face flushed slightly. "Well, I have heard you are charming but not as organised as I. When all is said and done, there is no point …."

We both finished the statement in unison. "… reinventing the wheel!"

"Exactly," I agreed.

She struggled to her feet and opened her beautiful oak writing desk, which dropped down to reveal a file with every piece of paper carefully sorted. "It's filed under Staff Picnics. Yes, here are the lists."

That's where we are different. I would have filed it under 'STAFF PARTY or FUN DAYS OUT. 'I'm not sure what my face is registering but it's probably relief, and I am, of course, in admiration for your wonderful administration skills." I laughed as I darted to the kitchen to catch the kettle that was starting to screech and hiss.

"You will learn, young man, you must be organised. I have four pieces of paper: lists for the kitchen staff, which includes a main course for lunch with dessert treats, toffee apples and cakes to go with afternoon tea. It has a recipe or two attached. Another for the games for children and adults, a third for a skeleton staff to take care of such things as tying and watering the horses for those attending, boiling water, organising the catering staff and then a fourth list of people you can arrange for such things as contacts for the marquee, the Anglican priest, a nurse that lives nearby, a band that usually plays for us, and extra girls to help serve so the staff can get a break. It helps to find a dignitary for the prize giving. You haven't much time to organise having cups engraved. You should have organised those a week ago. You will need a rough mess kitchen set up in one of the stables for boiling water and heating some food. We normally clear out the large stables and clean them thoroughly to be out of the weather, but still on the side of the paddocks used for an entertaining area."

I had been taking notes flat out, as it would not pay to leave anything out. She scowled and lifted one eyebrow, which I ignored.

"Have you ever had rides for the children?"

"Not usually. There are fun things to keep the children busy without special rides."

"I have an idea to take two of the big Clydesdales and fit long chains to a beam, pulling five sacks fitted to steel plates around the paddock. Rusty and I have another idea, to decorate a cart up like a train then fit little blocks on the wheels and short pieces of leather making a chugging noise as it goes along, like a train."

"Who is Rusty? And I do not think that is necessary? It's a great deal to go to just for the children."

"I think it could be fun and perhaps end up being one of the main events. 'Rusty' is what we call John, as there always seems plenty of Johns about."

"Oh, I don't know about that. The main event is the races but it is your head on the block."

Would you be available to help on the day … if you are able?"

"I will see. I will ask Sarah in the kitchen to prepare it. She is likely to just take it on and organise staff to do things when they have time each day. She's a good girl. I will oversee the timing and staff for that."

"That would be wonderful. I have had a little to do with her, she is a bright thing. Bess had puppies the other day and she has been taking care of them. I am hoping she will join me for the Maiden race."

"Oh, I don't think you will be able to compete – there is far too much to do and oversee. You obviously have no experience in these things."

"I will see how we go closer to the time."

"Mr Williams is a friend of Jack's family and will provide all the music for the day. You will need people in different areas of the paddock to coordinate things as you will have different events running simultaneously."

I have John O'Flaherty for the running and sports events."

"Does he know what he's doing?"

"He's the perfect man for the job. He has the Christmas spirit in cartloads."

"Good, then use Frank Buck, who is in charge of sales, and Will Naughton, who manages the racers and jockeys. I am happy to help you further if you need. Next time, get one of the girls to drop a note under my door, and perhaps in a few days, I will be able to walk properly with this wretched cast off my leg. I will come and observe your progress."

"I'm so glad I decided to ask you. It will be a case of looking for the right people to co-ordinate each thing. I hope the weather holds alright or we will be huddled under the big marquee." We talked then about Jack and some of the girls. She had seen many of the girls grow up and have children so it had been quite a loss for her not to be around, as she felt quite motherly towards them, having no children of her own.

I arrived back as Rusty was finishing for the day. "How did it go? he asked.

"Oh boy, talk about a matron! She should be running a hospital ward. We are going to show her a thing or two about organising a *festival*, not a funeral. I need you as my righthand man and will find someone to fill in doing your duties. We have a great deal to organise. Come by the kitchen and we will go over things tonight.

The next day, we lined up those we thought would be perfect for the job, then ran from one area of the property to another, preparing things. We soon had a large group of men running about hammering steel stakes all around the nearby paddock.

"Look at that go up. Since I was a boy, it has fascinated me to watch a circus tent morph into life, like a butterfly hatching. One minute it's a paddock, and a few hours later, there's a huge building standing there."

"I love how they pitch the first two poles then pull everything up on them high into the air. Rust, look over there!" I pointed to the far side of the paddock. "I thought Bull would be annoyed that I asked him to join those four carts together behind the big Clydesdales to create a train, but he's making a great job of it."

"It's going to be fun. I hope this day the children never forget."

"I was talking to Bridget. She has an arty sister who will decorate the canvas pieces on the wheels and sides to look like a train. Pete in the carpenter shop has devised a way to make the blocks and leather to make a sound on the wheels."

"Brilliant, I knew you'd be onto things. What else do we

need?"

"We've got the water trough for the bobbing apples being set up near the marquee; Sarah has taken the list from Nora completely out of our hands and will find people to set up all the tables needed for food and drinks. I have given the list of children's games to Kenneth, who said he has a stack of sacks for racing, and plenty of rope; he's going to get Bill to create a small fenced stall where the children can sit to hold the lambs. Have we forgotten anything?"

"We need to erect a maypole with ribbons and a hoop on top for Alice's dancing group. Nora dropped in today as her cast was off. I asked her to help us organise the cups and prize ribbons. I gave *her* a list!" We laughed. "She is going to ask the Mayor or another dignitary she knows to attend for the prize giving. She also said we could ask for chairs from the local Anglican church, which will need delivering back early on Sunday morning."

"Tom has the young woman making buntings as they have time each day. We will string them up on ropes from the stables to the main public areas. It will look more like a fun carnival by next week."

"Harry, I have found out the back fifteen wine barrels which I thought we could set in a semi-circle and drop flitches of timber onto for a bar. It could fit nicely at one end of the main marque…

"Good thinking … oh, I know … the parking."

"I have asked Kenneth for ropes to cordon off an area in the side paddock – the horses can all run free away from our other stock."

"Brilliant! By this time next week, it will be nearly ready."

Day after day, our yard was a height of activity. I lay awake at night, many times going over each event in my mind. The day before the big event, a crowd of us stood looking around at our creations. We had a sand pit on the field for the long jump, a high jump borrowed from the horse jumps. Chalk lines marked for the running events and races. The brightly coloured train stood waiting to be filled with excited children. Happy buntings flapped back and forth on ropes and draped across a candy floss stand set up on one side, outside the tent, while a large stage made of two big six-wheel hay wagons sat side by side.

"The girls were saying you are entering the competitions, Harry."

"Too right! We have made it so that everyone gets to have fun and be involved. I'm keen to run. We even have a wrestling ring over there for anyone brave enough."

Frank and Will stood with their hands on their hips. "You've no hope of beating us, Harry. We've taken all the prizes other years – won by a country mile."

"Well, I guess tomorrow will prove you right or wrong." I grinned.

Sarah looked at me and winked. "You'll show them what you've got, Harry."

"I'm looking forward to a flutter on the horses. It'll be great to watch Blackjack flex his muscles for a gallop. I cannot miss out on throwing the hammer or tossing the caber, my relatives wouldn't let me live it down. I've been practising me bagpipes too," Rusty said.

"A couple of Alice's girls are coming to do the Highland fling."

"Well done, everyone, a great effort. Looks like it's about as organised as we can get, if half of it comes together, it'll be a brilliant day. Let's go and get a drink and relax … I can't wait till it's all over. I haven't slept well now for weeks."

Tom looked up at the sky. "By the look of those fluffy white clouds, we might be in luck for tomorrow. The last thing we need is howling winds and rain coming in sideways."

The next morning, when it was still dark, Jack came and found me. "Harry, how is it all going? The 8th of December has arrived. Everything looks ready."

"Jack, good to see you. Would you like a morning cuppa? I've just made a pot."

"Not today. It was too late to tell you last night … there is a reporter coming today from the *Evening Post*. It always pays to have a little positive publicity when you're in business. Perhaps you can keep an eye out for him; I told him to find you."

I sipped my tea and took a bite of toast and jam. "Great, thanks for that. If everything comes off, it will be a miracle. It's going to be a carnival out there. We've crossed every 't' and dotted every 'i', so we just have to pull it off now. How's everything your end?"

"I'm working on some good orders from the goldfields at the moment. I hate all the Government bureaucracy, but its looking promising."

He put out his hand. Harry, you've made a fine job of everything so far. It's looking absolutely amazing; you should be proud no matter what happens. I can't wait to hear from a few of our special clients I've invited; they are going to have a ball. It's the most elaborate Christmas party yet and looks like a lot of fun."

"Thanks, Jack. Come back in twelve hours!"

We both laughed.

"I will do just that with a bottle of malt."

Rusty came through, rubbing his face and looking half asleep. I looked outside and in the early morning could already see the silhouettes of people running back and forward from the big house. "People are due to start arriving in about four hours; perhaps we can split up and just check everything is ready. We need to gather everyone at nine, just before guests arrive."

Rusty nodded. "In the marquee? We have young David on the horn, so whenever we wish to bring things to order, he will stand up on that stage and blow it."

Horses and carts started to pour in from the bay in a steady stream and were directed into the parking paddock by attendants. Children ran about in every direction, falling over to get to the brightest thing on the field, the 'Lane Train', which soon started its maiden voyage across the fields and over the farm in a huge loop. Shouts of delight rent the air. The carnival had begun, and pleasant chaos reigned. It felt so good to see the staff having a laugh with their families.

At 11:00, before anyone had eaten too much, the bugle sounded and the train stopped. Everyone gathered, young and old, more than 400 people keen for the races. For the most part, it was playful hilarity, but for Will Naughton and Frank Buck it was war. Will, a big man with a large mop of hair, was quiet and methodical, but burst with energy. Frank was almost the opposite – short, cheeky, and with strong legs, swarthy arms and reddish-brown hair. Between them, they had cleaned up in previous years and weren't about to lose to any outsiders. I had entered for eight events, the first being the 'Maiden' Race for a 150-yard dash. I had already asked Sarah from the kitchen to be my 'maiden' as she was small, light and good fun. It was a hilarious event as all the men lined up with their wives, girlfriends, or sisters on their backs ready to race. Some men staggered under the weight of their voluptuous beauties; others chaffed at the bit like a horse ready to bolt. As the blocks were smacked together, we were off. Countless men charged down the paddock; some fell backwards to the ground, others fell sideways, and others struggled with bow legs just trying to step forward under heavy loads. I could see in the corner of my eye Will straining to catch me as we reached the halfway mark, but

Sarah's weight was perfectly distributed and forward enough for us to run like the wind. We crossed the finish line first, easily beating Will and big mouth Frank. Sarah jumped down and pumped her fists in the air with great excitement.

"We did it, Harry! We won! We won! You beat those two miserable buggers!" Then she whispered, "I can't believe you ran that fast. Take a look at Will's face: that is probably his first loss *ever.*"

Both men half-heartedly came up and congratulated us.

"Lucky win, Harry. Good thing you had Sarah helping you. You'll not win the next round with the Hammer Throw. I'm the champion in these parts."

I shook their hands. "Thanks." I smiled. "I will try my best to beat you, but I'm not much good at the hammer."

Rusty grinned broadly, having come fourth carrying his cousin. He winked at me over the hammer throw comment, knowing my skill.

The huge crowd were now moved into a large circle, leaving plenty of space for wild flying hammers.

"The nurse made me swear we would have no injuries today, Harry."

"Sarah, you have to watch this. Big Rust has thrown this 20-pound hammer his whole life. He's good."

The crowd roared as one person after another swung the large, heavy piece of iron by its handle round and round before letting it go and hoping it went in the right direction. Voices rose in delight, sometimes in disappointment, until Rusty stepped up. Then all the staff fell silent. He'd made good friends here. Round and round, he swung the mighty iron, and when he released it, the hammer flew like a bird. The crowd roared and cheers rang out as the referee called, "The best so far." Some started to call out my name as I hung back to gather my strength again. I walked forward and picked up the familiar handle, glanced over at Will and Frank's sour faces. Then I made my play. Hoisting it and swinging it around and around, on the last powerful thrust, I let it go sailing and watched it soar through the air. The silent crowd murmured then burst into cheers of delight and surprise. The hammer landed beyond Rusty's throw by yards as the crowd called out, "The winner ... Bagust!"

Many people came over and congratulated me, but this time Will and Frank stayed away. Sarah came and gave me a friendly slap on the arm. "Well done, Harry!"

The next event was a favourite for the crowd, and they jostled for a position to watch the contestants lining up. This was the 100-yard dash. More than 100 men lined up across the paddock ready to sprint like crazy for the finish line. The crowd shouted encouragement, women spurring on their husbands, sons, friends and colleagues. Will and Frank lined up only a couple of men away from me.

"Lucky throw, Harry. Beginners luck, hey. You should give up now – I know a few of these young lads will run rings around you."

"Frank, give it a rest ... less words, more action!"

Men now jostled to get their elbows forward and their feet firmly planted. Rusty smiled widely and gave me a wink just as the blocks cracked. We ran together like we had the ball and no one else was on the field. As I crossed the line, I glanced back at Frank with a smile. "Harry Bagust! First ... again."

I went over and shook Frank's hand. "Well done, Frank, third ... I think I am just lucky today."

"That one is easy to win. It's the 220-yard that's difficult."

"My legs are getting tired. Good luck ...win this one," Rusty said and shook my hand. "Could be a lack of sleep on my part ... or perhaps you are bloody hard to beat. How the hell do you do it, Harry? I've tried catching you on the field once or twice in the past, and you just seem to run away."

"It's having eggs for breakfast – it helps you pass wind."

We laughed together.

"I'd rather be on the field with you any day, Rust. You should have won the hammer and the 100-yard. You could be sick."

If James had been there, he would surely have said I had a lucky day. I came second in the 220-yard dash, first in the sack race, first in the hop-step-and-jump and third in the 440-yard. By the time I had come second in the 880-yard run, thrown myself in the high jump and long jump, I was done. Sarah came and brought me a beer as we followed Rusty to watch the horse races. It almost seemed that everyone in the crowd had come and congratulated me; even Nora shook my hand and expressed her delight. It felt great at the end of the day to go home with the *Evening Post* trophy, but I was looking forward to it all being over. It had been the most wonderful experience, and Rusty had an idea to give every person who competed a prize of some sort, leaving most people with smiles. Everything had run like clockwork and, finally, as everything had wound down, Nora came over carrying an apple.

"Are you hungry?"

"I could eat a horse!" We laughed.

"Harry, I must apologise: I was wrong; you pulled a rabbit out of a hat today. On my best day, I could not have achieved what you did today. People love you and are happy to follow your lead."

"Thanks, Nora. I appreciate your praise but obviously you have created a fantastic efficient team of people here. I think everyone respects Jack, and they just wanted to say thank you to him today."

"Well, I think you deserved all those wins today, but the biggest win was seeing the joy on the faces of all those children riding the train. It was a masterstroke of genius on your part. Some of them will remember this for years to come."

I nodded, appreciating her comments, and sighed. "I will certainly sleep well tonight. But now it's your turn to get back on the horse."

"I am a little nervous, but I think I will be ready by the time you leave."

"Jack said when he offered me this job, 'welcome to the family'. It has been like a family … and I will miss everyone.

At that moment, Jack appeared, walking towards us, balancing three glasses on a silver tray, along with a bottle of Malt. "Drink anyone?"

Chapter 10

Busy as Bees

Rusty and I took a break for a hearty sandwich over lunch in the small stable kitchen. We hung about, hoping to see a copy of last night's *Evening Post* with a report on our famous Island Bay Picnic Festival. Sarah promised to drop the paper in after the others had devoured its contents in the kitchen.

Many of the staff looked exhausted after all the sports events, entertainment and frivolity, which continued into the early hours of the morning. Jack was especially pleased with the whole event and said not to expect anything from the staff today. I put the kettle on the little pot belly stove, which normally bubbled away in the background with stewed hot tea, added to throughout the day.

Staff came and went from the communal area, finding a moment to relax at the large wooden table. There were often fresh scones under a cloth on the wooden bench with a bowl of plum jam. The kitchen always provided a plate of cold lamb with fresh butter in the meat safe, to carve a few slices for a hearty sandwich. The Christmas celebration had been a roaring success, creating much chatter about the stables and in the community. It had taken weeks of preparation, which was a relief to have behind us. Rusty sat with his elbows planted firmly on the table, chomping into a huge hunk of meat between two slabs of fresh bread. He could have been mistaken for a Viking out of Dublin, with his wild red hair, big Irish shoulders and the strength of an ox.

We had played our instruments together the previous night, for the dance Jack had organised after we'd knocked back a few whiskeys in the staff kitchen. Even Nora shared a dance before she retired for the evening. Rusty had shown no shame in playing the fiddle, which was always lively and loud. Folk found themselves almost unwillingly on the dance floor in minutes as he whipped up excitement in the crowd. He was also a force of nature on the football field, setting up quick passes with precision, and was as slippery as an eel to catch. We'd played together since we were lads, and I knew he took no nonsense, as a few had learned with black eyes on or off the field.

"Rusty, it's been lively having you here at the stables," I said, to which he nodded and replied:

"Harry, we've never had this treatment anywhere else. I'm just so grateful for the opportunity. It's not easy to find such good employment these days."

"It's a fine spot out here …," I agreed, looking out over the spectacular gardens to the water. "I'll miss it. Jack's a clever businessman, and I've learned a lot from him already; he's picked good people … except you, of course." I bumped him with my shoulder, smiling.

"It was your typical cunning asking Jack to include me in your wager. I might still be stuck in the damp dark hold of a ship lugging coal," Rusty replied.

"For me, it's been a bloody relief to escape from James' cottage in Pirie Street. I didn't realise it had gotten me down so much. It's been a great location for cabbie work and storage, but I am glad to get away from those two squabbling over money. Poor Margaret constantly looks exhausted with the little one – she's had a raw deal, I think."

"Aye, it's no place to bring up a child. She must have some long nights waiting for him to come home from gambling and drinking his fares away."

"All this frenzied talk of prohibition too – I think he's trying to make up for lost time."

"Do you think Seddon's got a chance?" Rusty asked, concerned.

I grinned. "I think if women vote for prohibition, there'll be riots in the streets."

"Harry, it sounds like your brother James would be in the front-line protesting," he said, roaring with laughter.

"It's infuriating. He should be killing the pig, but instead …" I stopped mid-sentence. "What am I saying! It's not my concern. Can I make you a cuppa while I'm up?"

"Thanks," he said, nodding. "I am a little parched. So what do you miss about being on the street, Harry?"

I handed him an enamel mug of tea. "Most folks are easy, but I don't miss taking broken drunks home in the freezing cold or dark rainy nights. I'd rather be tucked up in a warm bed."

"Jack took a chance on us, putting you in charge at twenty. It's worked out, even with the older hands."

"Apart from that surly old stockman, 'Bull', who brings in the feed," I remembered. "What's his story?" I slid the plate of butterscotch biscuits to him, and he took one mindlessly and dipped it into his tea.

"He knew Jack's father. The story goes he was charged by a huge bull while fencing in the far paddock a few years back. As the bull thundered toward him, he grabbed his axe at the last minute, stood his ground, and cracked it squarely over the head with the back of his axe, knocking it out cold at his feet."

"Sounds like he would have been perfect in the picnic tug-of-war." I smiled, visualising the scene. "You know my favourite on that day?" Rusty looked up. "… that wrestling match between those two big Māori boys, who were settling an old score. I couldn't get over how calmly they dressed down to nothing to fight it out. I really thought the old bloke would lose, but he wore young Tupu down till he was humiliated, spent and bloodied."

"I saw that. Then the old bloke quietly went to the watering trough, washed off the blood then put all his clothes back on."

We both shook our heads.

Sarah suddenly appeared at the door with an extra loaf of bread from the kitchen, holding the latest newspaper with a bright face. She was puffing from her rush.

"Sorry, I would have brought it sooner, but we are short-staffed today, and all are so excited to read about the big event, I couldn't get away."

"Thanks, Sarah. Is that the page?"

"Just down on the bottom half there."

"Rusty, here it is!" I threw the *Evening Post* down on the table and flipped it open to see the whole report of our extravagant picnic day.

Looking in with anticipation, Kenneth, Will, Tom and Frank came in as they passed by carrying buckets of oats.

Sarah put her hand on my shoulder. "I was hoping it would be reported today after your illustrious wins."

Frank, still visibly jealous, nonchalantly glanced over — he had come close in many events without a win. "Harry, by next week, it will be old news; sleigh bells and Santa Claus will be on everyone's mind over the next few months." I tried to ignore Frank for being a sore loser, *but I might find a few stinking stables for him to clean out.*

"Listen, it is a good size article, and it mentions you, Rusty!"

Rusty put his scone down and peered over my shoulder.

December 9th 1892

> *"The second annual picnic of the employees of Mr J. Lane, Livery stable keeper, took place yesterday in Mr Lane's paddock, Island Bay. About 80 of the men and their*

A hearty round of clapping went up. "Thanks, everyone, but we all had a great day. It gives all the scores for everyone and just glancing down it looks like Will and Frank were neck and neck." There were a few more hip hips.

"Here it is, Rust: The duties of the handicapper and starter were efficiently carried out by John O'Flaherty. During the day, Mr H. Williams enlivened the proceedings with songs. At the conclusion of the sports, three hearty cheers were given from Mr Lane and the other ladies who looked to the interests of the picnickers. A special vote of thanks was passed to the donors of prizes and the committee who carried out the arrangements and who deserve every credit for the undertaking. Messrs J. O'Flaherty, F. Buck, W. Naughton and H. Bagust.

"The *Evening Post* trophy for the competitor who scored the largest number of points at the meeting fell to H. Bagust. Mr Jack Lane was treasurer. The prize for the driver of the best four-in-hand was carried off by W. Mudgway."

Rusty gave a hearty cheer for Will, Frank and the girls. "And good for you, Harry. You deserved every win!"

"I tried to beat you, Harry ..." Frank's voice showed displeasure, "... but you took first in nearly every bloody event!" His bucket shook in his hand in frustration.

Sarah looked at me. "You were like one of those Greek Olympic athletes, then to dance me off my feet."

Frank spoke up again. "Possibly a stroke of luck. You got first in the 800-yard sprint, Will!"

Rusty looked disgusted. "Only because Harry was limping from the high jump!"

"It was a huge effort and a great job. I'm sure we are all exhausted. Take the day to recover if you need. I'm mighty glad to have it behind me. I even started dreaming about the events in my sleep!" Will said.

We all laughed. Then Sarah whispered in my ear, "You have a few admirers in the kitchen if you want to come by later for some bacon and egg pie!"

I turned to her. "Thanks, Sarah. I might come over later; I'm still sore from the high jump and the hammer throw."

Rusty folded the paper up again. "I noticed James didn't make it, Harry. It would have been a fierce competition between you two if he'd come!"

"He's always too busy…" *Best he didn't come.* "He has been doing a few runs over to Martinborough lately, huge days but he's called a few times to see the family."

I leant over to move my chair. "Aaaw! That pain!"

"Are you alright, Harry? I've got some liniment I could rub into it."

"Thanks, Sarah. That might do the trick actually – I think I pulled a muscle. Every time I twist I get a shooting pain in my side."

"I'll come later when I get off. I must get back to the kitchen. I'll see you boys later, round the fire." Sarah hurried out.

"Serves you right for being so competitive, trying to win every event," Rusty chided.

"Thanks! I see I can count on you for a spot of sympathy."

"You don't need my sympathy, but I wish I had a sore muscle for Sarah to rub."

"Purely medicinal." I grinned.

"It's a competitive business, breeding horses for a living, don't you think?"

"I can see you could make a good living with a few good runners. What did you think about my idea of going half shares in that thoroughbred? She's a beauty."

"She certainly looks like a winner. What would we call it?"

"I think a good name would be *The Wark* because I am in so much pain."

Rusty laughed. "I like it! Alright, then it's settled. *The Wark* it is!" He leaned over and shook my hand lightly.

"We'll register her along with Blackjack for the next club meeting. I think she'll fetch a good handicap."

"She is as fast as the best thoroughbreds out there. She just needs a little more stamina."

"Is that the week after we return from up north? I've been looking forward to getting away from here for a week to Auckland, a chance to come down on those Parnell boys, show them a few of our capital city moves."

"We've been as busy as bees over the last four months. It's even been busy in the city, right before the elections and Christmas."

"Working by day, cabbie by night. I feel tired all the time and always look forward to sleep. I'm going to give it up."

"Probably how you hurt yourself. You'll have to give it up or collapse in a heap. I've seen you look like a dead man walking some days while preparing the picnic.

"Especially those nights we went out to play at the bar."

"It will be a good break away to Auckland for a week, a chance to relax ... think of something else."

I stood, looking searchingly at Rusty. "You are right as always. I kept my foot in the door with the cabbie work as I knew the management role would be short-term until Nora returned. I think when we get back from up north, I will give up the cabbie work ... take a complete break. I only have a few weeks to go, as Nora is already back at work on the books; it will only be weeks before she's back in the saddle."

"Do you really want to go ... do you think Jack will let you go?"

"I made a deal … he would find something for me to do, but in a lot of ways he does not need me now – he's just honouring his word. He knows I'm a free spirit, and I want to be my own boss. Besides, I can see what he likes about her: she is like clockwork, dependable … takes no nonsense and has an eye for detail."

"What will you do?"

"I'm going to have a spell in Martinborough with the family over Christmas, then make a plan after that. I have a little savings, which will give me a break. I will pick up some farming work over there or do some night-time cabbie work. I am still keen to head up to the goldfields to try my luck with a few of those Pairoa boys."

Rusty looked at me intently and put down the plate he was drying. "If you are heading up that way so am I. You are not getting out on the wing or in a scrum without me!"

I laughed. "The two musketeers! I'd be lost on the field without your passes. You're right, Rust; we need to grab it with both hands, run like a man possessed, not turning round till we've scored on the touchline."

"Sounds like a plan: follow our hearts; life can be over so quickly. Look at all the strapping lads we've watched fade away with consumption."

"Everyone's talking of bright futures with the elections coming. I've no vote of confidence in any of them."

"That's an appropriate turn of phrase, 'Vote of confidence!' I'm pretty sure Seddon will get in." I pulled on my boots and started lacing them up. "Who are you voting for Rusty?"

"It's only weeks away, and I'm still not sure. I am sick of hearing about it."

"Try picking customers up all day long. I sometimes just say something controversial to make it interesting. This whole temperance movement is like a red rag to some. People are divided. Nights are the worst around the bars – it's like men can somehow fill their veins with enough alcohol to get them through the next few years of Prohibition."

"I seriously doubt if any of it's going to happen. Everyone is making a mountain out of a molehill."

"By next year, it'll be like one of those fairy seeds, instantly picked up in the wind, then in a moment it's flown out of sight."

"Nothing we can do but vote, Rusty. I'm going to check on some of the stalls before nightfall. Can you finish up here?"

"I'll drop by and bring that bottle of malt once I've locked up the stalls. Don't forget about Sarah."

"Thanks. It will just seem like days and we'll be sailing off to Auckland."

The days passed quickly as we made ourselves busy about the stables. Finally, I did my last late night in the city, and we set sail the next day. It was a very strange feeling to put the cabbie cart away and see James' face. He was speechless.

The time had gone in a blur. Days morphed into one another, like only minutes had passed. Then it seemed we had no sooner set sail for the excitement of Auckland city than we returned in what seemed only minutes, a week later, like some magic trick. I had left fully in charge of my destiny with a solid plan for my life, without a care in the world, returning as if part of me was missing or somehow left behind. I truly felt mentally ill, unable to arrange my thoughts properly. How could a woman completely undo the fabric of my heart, like pulling on a thread of a knitted cardigan, unravelling it one row at a time, leaving one undone. I could not hold back telling my sister Mary of my tales as I relaxed in my room back at the stable house. I still nursed many bruises from our fierce competition in Auckland but there was a warmth in my heart I had not experienced before. I could not concentrate properly on the task at hand. Was I sick?

Sarah said I seemed different.

It was the end of another perfect day with the sun going down over the bay, creating mysterious silvery dark light on the water. I was busting to tell someone other than poor Rusty. Mary was a hopeless romantic who would want to know every detail. I pulled out another crisp piece of paper and began to unburden my heart.

Dearest Mary

It has only been a matter of days and we are back from our trip, exhausted. We gave it our all, pitting our skill against a fine Parnell opposition. As you can imagine we had an eventful time, relieved not to have left anyone in lock up, even bringing back our pride. I am almost certain I will be home for Christmas now as Nora is making steady progress here, which is relaxing for me. I can't wait to see you all for the Festive season. I must tell you of our adventures and how I met a girl who has left me undone.

Once aboard, our sailing was uneventful, except for John who nearly lost the ball overboard, bravely tossing it around with the roll of the ship. I threw down my ruck, found a corner of the ship on a few sacks of flour and made a rough bed. Within moments I fell asleep to the roar of the rumbling steam engines, the sway of the ship, and men's laughter as we made our way into the easterly swell. The departing whistle had blown at midday, but by the time I woke, it was already dusk with red clouds on the horizon. We arrived a day later, to an overcast sky in the Waitemata Harbour, where the steamer pulled up alongside the Queen Street wharf. It was a warmer evening up there, than the constant freezing winds here from the

Antarctic.

While we waited on the front deck for the bow ropes to be tied off, we stood watching a throng of people getting ready to board a steamer bound for Australia. At that moment, a beautiful young woman caught our attention, waving to Rusty, calling out to him. "Duncan!"

She mistook Rusty's red hair from behind for a young shipwright she knew. He turned and leapt in an instant over the rail onto the platform, startling her. She was not amused, having only passed by the docks for a little fresh air to clear her head after a busy day. She was not at all in the mood for his admirations, which I fortunately realised in time to make my own acquaintance, calming her a little. I was immediately mesmerised by her beauty, stubborn spirit, forthright replies, her intelligent answers to our candid advances. I apologised on behalf of Rust as she turned away, taking her leave in frustration.

Despite our plain sailing we were bursting to get off the ship, making for a local bar after two days cramped aboard. We were billeted into a magnificent house, looking out over the harbour. I could watch the ships by the hour. To our consternation, we had no sooner found our way to our lodgings for the night, than Euphemia appeared at the door of our house. Her closest friend, Ruby, turned out to be the daughter of our patrons. Her distress was clearly visible at seeing us again as Ruby introduced us, but to me she somehow seemed even prettier as I again spoke with her. I wish you could meet her, there is something about her. She is mature but striking, and has knowledge of the world. She has strong opinions about the roles of men and the rights of woman. It has caught me off guard, yet it is somehow endearing. You would love her I know, although she is *frightfully vocal, given to clearly speak her mind.*

She is involved in the Women's Christian temperance movement, and is excited to have won the right to vote in a few weeks. My heart was drawn to her family's plight, experiencing some huge financial hardships as they endeavour to shrug off a scandal of no small proportion. Her father, a captain, proposed to a woman half his age in Melbourne, then found out he was being duped … I will tell you more later. They seem an interesting family which I feel drawn to like a bee to a honeycomb … I seem to have lost my head a little, as you know this is a first for me. Consequently, my heart was heavy to leave, sharing feelings I am not sure I have experienced before and not sure how our paths will cross again.

I can hear you saying, "Brother, if it is meant to be it will happen," so I have in my hot hand her address to write to her. I have already sent her a letter and will tell you if I get a reply. I look forward to seeing you all soon, give my love to all the family and Mother too.

Your Harry xxx

I carefully folded the letter and slid it into an envelope to post in the morning.

Chapter 11

Straight from the Horse's Mouth

I wanted to tell James about Euphemia, but there didn't seem an opportune moment. He's like a bullock weighed down with a colossal load of debts, the agony clearly visible on his face. I picked up Bolt out of the little basket I had made for him in the cab. He was growing quickly and was great company to have around. Rusty was good with him, getting him used to the farm but James had no tolerance for 'a stray dog', as he called it.

His countenance grew even darker as he tore open a letter in disgust with a postmark from His Majesty.

I noticed the handwriting on a second letter – a reply from Euphemia – and gently placed Bolt back in his nest. My heart fluttered like a hummingbird, almost taking my breath away. I quickly slipped it off the table, discreetly spiriting it into my jacket pocket. Unfortunately, James saw my sleight of hand, perhaps delighted by a pleasant distraction, as suddenly the deep lines on his forehead disappeared, and his face came out like the sun from behind a cloud.

"What are you hiding, brother? By the look on your face, it's a girl."

How does he do that! Straight from the horse's mouth. "It's none of your business – just a bill for horse feed."

"What! Is that the best you can come up with? It's a love letter, I can tell!"

I slowly took out my cigarette case and offered him one,

holding his gaze. I lit both, then took a deep breath before beginning while he stood with a cigarette in one hand and a nugget brush in the other.

"Remember that three-masted barque in dock when I first arrived from Timaru around '88, the one they fully cut in half and extended?"

James stopped dabbing another lot of black nugget on his brush. "Yeah … you said you'd never seen anything like it. It had some Scottish name."

"The *Gailoch*. The Northern Steamship Company contracted a shipwright from Auckland to transform her from a sailing ship to a steamer with the help of our local lads."

"Didn't you play against them?"

"We played a friendly match against his shipwrights from Auckland on some bare land at the dockyards … only just beat them by two points – they had a few big Māori boys that were pretty hard to flatten."

"I laughed so hard seeing you on the ground trying desperately to catch your breath after one knocked you into next week."

"It's always so wonderful, James, that my suffering brings you such delight."

James tossed his head back and laughed then we both rubbed a little more polish into the black leather harness straps.

"As I recovered off the field, I spoke to Captain McQuarrie, who was boisterously cheering on the sidelines. My curiosity had been sparked by the unusually high regard his men spoke of toward him. I wanted to discover why."

"Wasn't that the ship they completed in record time!"

"Two months! He invited me to call on him for a tour one day while she was in dry dock, so I did. It was meticulous work: only a true craftsman could perform such a thing. He had cut her through, fitted a steam engine, repositioned and added extra ballast tanks, reconstructed the poop deck and lengthened the hull! When he had finished, you couldn't even tell where she'd been cut in half."

"I remember you telling me. It must have sparked something."

"It's always impressive to see a man's craft!"

"Why the history lesson, Harry?"

"Don't you think that sometimes life's puzzle pieces have a way of fitting precisely together?"

"Only for you, Harry!"

Here we go again, poor James.

"Go on. This is interesting."

"Well, as chance would have it, I met Captain McQuarrie's daughter in Auckland. Her name is Euphemia. We met one afternoon on the docks with John O'Flaherty. He was being cheeky to her, and she took offence."

"You're an insufferable flirt, Harry. Why am I not surprised? It's a wonder you've not fathered a child already with some poor young girl."

My jaw tightened. "Do you want to hear the story?"

"Yes, get on with it. I want the whole story."

"Later, when we were barely settled into our fabulous billets property overlooking the harbour, we were bewildered to find her again on the doorstep, conversing with our host. Apparently, she was best friends with Ruby, their daughter, and had just dropped in to visit.

"Soon we were deep in conversation, and the time just vanished. She told of her mother and older sister, who had both passed, only months apart. Feeling responsible for the family, she took over running the house for the Captain. I was captivated."

James interrupted. "That's not surprising!"

"I was surprised! … by her lack of decorum as she just spoke her mind. She conveyed honest opinions on various topics and political views … not at all like other girls I've met."

"What do you see in her then?"

"I'm not sure. I felt captivated by her, unable to determine whether I was annoyed or enchanted. We only met a few times but she challenged me to write to her. James, many women are charmed by me, but she almost did not care. I found myself strangely attracted to her, like an ant to sugar, almost like a test to win her affection."

"She is a smart girl. She should run while she has a chance … and she's too far away anyway."

"Why do I have this feeling you are stabbing me in the back."

"Well, what are your intentions? How will you get see her? You need to find a local girl – you're making it too hard otherwise?"

I pulled the letter out from my pocket; tapped it against the brim of my hat. "That's who this letter is from."

"Harry, come on, read it."

"Why? So you can mock me again? You are like judge and jury all in one!"

"Oh, go on, brother. It will be nice after the news I have just had." James prepared his pipe.

I hesitated to ask what news, but he did not look like he wanted to talk about it.

"If I read my letter, you'll have to tell me if I can help ease the burden of yours."

"If you read your letter first, I might show you."

Dear Harry,

I hope this finds you well and no injuries from your games. I took this opportunity to write, by candlelight, as my days are exhausting … I never seem to have enough hours in the day. I found the time we shared together

"Whoa! Hold your horses, Harry! What was all that about?" James, puffing his pipe, almost choked as he spoke. "Madame Vine. Madame Vine …" he repeated thoughtfully.

"Brother, it's quite a story. Captain McQuarrie stayed in Melbourne for six weeks attending to *The Presto*, a badly damaged ship that had collided with a steamer in the harbour, nearly sinking it. During the intervening days, the burdened captain was heading back from the insurers in Sydney when he became friendly with a delightful lady, a young temptress, who completely beguiled him with her wiles … seduced like a snake out of a charmer's basket."

"I bet he did, the old 'Sea Captain' … Madame Vine was in the papers!? Some scandal in the local times."

"She's conned many a poor soul. The Captain thought she was a wealthy widow coming like an angel from heaven to carry him through his pending bankruptcy. He was hooked like a whale on a harpoon, jollied by her offers to invest in his shipping company."

"Don't tell me!"

"Yes … he proposed marriage."

James laughed heartily. "Probably because her loins had already led him astray."

"I don't know about that but there must have been passion involved as he immediately organised a wedding ceremony. Guests were invited to a large dinner party, ball, and a cake was ordered for the occasion."

"He must have been completely smitten, going all out like that!"

"Fortunately, Lady Luck stepped in. A close friend quietly did a little digging, exhuming her colourful past to expose the betrayal. He urged Hector to run from the betrothal, laying bare the string of elaborate defraudings she'd performed previously. The Captain was horrified and fled to another hotel in the city to hide."

"Good man … did he get away?"

"She soon tracked him down, like a cat playing with a mouse before the kill. He was oblivious to her trap, lured straight into her evil hands."

"Surely not!?"

"The jilted lover charged him a thousand pounds damages for deserting his marriage proposal, which ended in the high court of Victoria."

"Now I feel sorry for him. I hope he sent someone to deal with her! … A thousand pounds! That's more than the whole ship was worth?!! Did he pay!?"

"James, I think the judge knew her well, reducing it to one hundred pounds."

"He got off lightly then."

"Euphemia said it was the straw that broke the camel's back. Like a small infection turning gangrene, they had to cut off the leg."

"Horrible business! Almost seemed like he was cursed. How could you have such a run of bad luck?"

"James, he's a good man! … but this crippled him! …He had no choice but to file for bankruptcy."

"The wiles of a woman, ah? That should be a lesson to you, Harry. Let your charm get away, and look where it leads!" he said in a fatherly tone.

I looked at him disbelievingly, pondering a dozen things to say to that. Then I lowered my voice, as I caught his eye in a school teacher's stare.

"The *lesson* you might like to heed, James, is how a hundred-pound debt could cripple you in bankruptcy! Now do you want to hear the rest of the letter or not?"

James was suddenly quieted, humbly nodding while cleaning with his pipe.

> *Barbara brought back some lovely things for us all and I received a beautiful new dress. We have been going to the new church at St Stephens and although it is adequate, I miss the folk at our old parish. Father has a strong faith in God and has tried to hold his head up through this scandal but, Harry, if God loves us, why is all this happening? I feel angry and disillusioned!*

"She's right, Harry. I already like this girl; we have no need of God. All those do-gooders, never did anything for us! You won't find me praying!"

"James, that's not true! You pray whenever you drop a trunk on your finger or when you lose a bet. … Jesus Christ, you pray!"

"My point exactly. Look how much it's helped!"

"I can't think of a single reason He'd come to your aid. Your goodness is so deep, it's like a well in the desert … it's there, it just can't be reached in the darkness."

"Just continue on, Harry."

I had not realised how well off we've been until we had to stretch our funds. What we spent in the past week we must now make it last a month. It was much easier when we did not have to buy poor cuts of meat or bake our own bread to get by. I have relied more on the children's help as there does not seem enough hours in the day to tend the garden, wash the clothes, prepare meals and keep the house. Perhaps you may meet Father if he brings potatoes up from Canterbury or wheat from the south. He always looks tired, working tirelessly to hold his creditors at bay, shipping coal across from Newcastle and up from Westport.

Father says that 'Steam Power' is like feeding a hungry beast with an insatiable desire for more. There are over 100 stamping batteries running night and day in Thames crushing quartz, trains dragging logs from deep in the bush, traction engines milling timber, and steam ships carrying passengers continuously back and forward from Auckland. You are probably well aware, the papers reported, the population there has well exceeded that of Auckland with nearly 20,000 camped about in the mud. I think you had spoken of perhaps trying your hand there.

I must be missing Father, to quote Nautical terms, but I am grateful to be here helping to steer our ship in the right direction, keeping it afloat and ship-shape for the captain's return. It was a pleasant change to take a morning off and teach a history lesson in Maggie's class. Maggie reported that it had been most interesting and the children were looking forward to my next visit but I climb into bed most nights and sleep like a dead person. Alas, I have spent far

"Hooked, Harry! Who would have guessed, you're smitten too. Your charm has certainly captured her heart."

"James, I keep thinking about her. I have not felt like this before."

"Brother, how old is Euphemia, and who is Maggie?"

"Phee, they call her. She is twenty-three and Maggie is the younger sister. She is probably closer in age to me, perhaps seventeen."

"That only makes you three years apart! What's she like?"

"She is a fine-looking girl, self-confident, funny, quite particular and sings like an angel. I think Maggie has one of those schoolgirl infatuations with me. It's flattering but a little uncomfortable when Euphemia is around."

"Harry, if I didn't know better, I would think you are smitten with her too."

"What a ridiculous notion!" I took a damp cloth and wiped down the leather seat and tried to look nonchalant.

How can I have affection for two completely different women, and they are in a class above me? I cannot reconcile any of these feelings. Euphemia's strong determination, standing on her convictions, but with almost a sense of mystery ... Maggie is flamboyant, playful and warm with a generous spirit ... Both share equal beauty, strength and confidence, which I admire. I will ignore him. It will be my secret.

"James, they are a close family. To watch them banter together, discussing passioned ideas and interesting views on all manner of topics is entertaining. I thought we had suffered, James, but I have not seen another family, who have endured such huge losses in so many ways, show immense courage and support of each other."

"Brother, can you hear yourself? It's not unlike the way we've stood by one another in Father's absence."

"Like coming to court." *Perhaps that's it: I see in them a longing in my heart … A father?*

"Alright, alright … what are you going to do?"

"I'm going to pray … for you too!"

James roared with delight.

Chapter 12

By the Seat of your Pants

The captain struggled to bring the ship into dock as a side wind kept blowing her off course. The coal smoke from the stack was whisked sideways, blinding the waiting crowd.

The docks were a circus of entertainment as passengers waited patiently in the twilight. Children ran about in bare feet, playing tag in and out of the barrels of beer, while a group of mothers in long dresses chatted excitedly. Naves busied themselves about the ship like worker ants, getting ready to tie her off and lower the gangplanks. A well-dressed, elderly gentleman propped up with his walking stick perched on the edge of a large, brown, wooden trunk. A number of miners in hobnail boots stood ready with swags slung over their shoulders. A family bound for abroad sat stealing their last farewells to loved ones. The expectant arrivals, on tippy toes, desperately tried to catch a glimpse of a lover returning, a sister with her new baby, or Father home with gifts from abroad. The tussling local cabbies were already on high alert, their beady eyes searching the crowd for that neatly dressed tourist with a few extra bob to spend. They lined up in orderly chaos, ready to pounce as folk made their way down the wooden plank. The local constabulary did their best to dish out law and order, with hands poised on the long handle of their truncheons.

James and I sometimes sat catching up for a few minutes as he mindlessly preened his moustache, or puffed on his pipe.

"James, I met this politician in charge of transport the other night. I dropped him up to parliament for some late-night meeting. He worked for the Midland rail project down south for years and is here for the elections next week. He told me they are pushing Vogel's plan to carve the main trunk line through to Auckland."

James held his pipe for a moment as it glowed in the fading light. "They will not have an easy job of it. How will they get round all those mountains standing on end. It's tough Māori country up in the interior. Folks' memories are still bloodied from those bitter wars."

"It will be more like war with the land! Conquering it. Huge mountains, rivers, ravines … swamps. Can you imagine how long it will take!"

"Harry, there's no way they will get through without an armload of tunnels."

"He said they imported expert tunnellers from America a few years back. Can you imagine going on a train all the way to Auckland?"

"What, and miss out on the two-day ferry from Wanganui to Taumaranui?" James laughed sarcastically at himself. He'll need deep pockets if he's serious about it."

"They will need to raise more funds for Vogel's ambitious plan … on top of the money they raised off Britain in the seventies."

"Harry, didn't you learn in school about his ambitious vision of 1,000 miles of rail?!"

"This guy was saying they're already well over that through Canterbury."

"Imagine … no more storms at sea, sickness, worrying you'll be held up for days in a calm or choking on coal fumes."

"You will still be choking on coal, Harry, in the tunnels if it is anything like steam transport back in Britain. I suppose it would be a two-day trip."

"They're saying about twenty-four hours. They've got both ends complete; they only need to fill in the middle, up from Taumaranui."

"I know you, Harry. You're curious … always looking for an opportunity."

"Well, Jack has said over and over, 'Diversify'. Don't hold all your eggs in one basket. It's good advice … I finish up with Jack next week, and then I'm off over the hill to graft on a farm in the Wairarapa."

I was indeed looking forward to getting away from all the hustle and bustle. And James being under pressure made it untenable. I felt most for Margaret and wee Ernest caught in the middle. It would only be a matter of time before he had to hand over his cart, and choose a new occupation.

"Can I use your carriage for a few minutes," I asked. "I need to write a letter."

"Sure, relax. They must have a new captain on by the look of his berthing skills."

If I can get a few moments to pen a letter to Euphemia, I can send it away in tomorrow's post. I lit a lamp inside the carriage and began writing.

> *Dear Euphemia,*
>
> *I am sorry I did not get to meet your father again. I am sure you are excited about the elections, which will be soon after you receive my letter. I look forward to seeing you in the beautiful new dress you spoke of.*
>
> *Yes, Wellington is crawling with all the dignitaries in town for the elections. I did play a game against Karangahake last week with no injuries but we lost by one point. I did, however, pull a muscle in my side throwing a hammer at a picnic event, so we called our horse The Wark,*

It was a late night as we ferried passengers to and from their homes. I barely had time to sleep before I was due to clear out my things from Island Bay. I had mixed emotions as I drove round the windy coast again. It had been one of the most curious experiences of my life working for Jack. I packed up my few belongings at the stables, and said goodbye to all the staff that was about.

Jack came out with a bottle of his finest malt and wished me luck.

"Harry, you really helped me out of a difficult spot, and thanks for attending to all the staff as well as our sensational picnic day carnival. I am not sure how anyone will top that off next season; perhaps you will have to join us next year as our events coordinator. Whenever you want to come back to us there is a place for you. I know you are a man with plans – no good standing in your way. I have a reference for you to take with you with a small bonus to show my appreciation."

He shook my hand heartily and looked me squarely in the eyes. "If you need someone to run something by, I'm here; find a job where you are in charge of men. You are a hard worker, but you have a way with people – they like you."

"Jack, thank you, I'd like to take you up on that offer some time. You've been almost like a father to me. You never know where our paths will cross, and this has been a great opportunity for me; I've learned many things. You run a tight ship. Part of me secretly hoped Nora would take on a more domestic roll at home, so I could remain. However, I think you would kick my backside if I didn't get out and follow my heart. Thanks again for the gifts, I will always think fondly of you. I might even drop in for the Christmas celebrations."

Some of the young ladies came out to wave me off, and Nora had come by the nearest paddock astride her thoroughbred. She smiled. Her leg and arm had healed well but this was the first time I had seen her in the saddle.

Rusty came over carrying a bucket and slapped me on the back. "You off to the family in Martinborough? They'll miss you with your squeeze box around here for the Christmas-New year celebrations. Looks like this one's going to be by the seat of your pants. Will I see you in the goldfields in a few months?"

"That's the plan at this stage. Take good care of our horses, John, and wee Bolt. We'll see you for Christmas day if you dare to ride over the hill."

"I will do that. Take care. And don't tease those ladies or Euphemia will discover it from Ruby."

My trap had all my worldly goods on it: my bed roll, canvas clothes bag, leather trunk, my gun, a wooden box of harnesses, boot polish, new dancing shoes and an enamel wash bowl, jug and matching tin mug Mother had given me when I left home.

As I neared the edge of the road, I stopped by a stream to water the horse and feed her a little grass. I was aghast as I cut open the thick envelope Jack had given me and discovered £50 inside a card. The card read: *This is a little extra for your Christmas celebrations. You won first prize competing in every event at the picnic. Lead well, Harry. Yours sincerely, Jack Lane.*

I felt a warmth flow over me, as if from a father's pride, and I thought, *if Father could not be there then by God, I will lead well. It's going to be a grand Christmas of festivities.*

I took a deep breath, preparing again for the notorious Remutaka hill that zigzagged its way over that horrendous mountain range. On a clear day, from the top, I caught glimpses of the plains below, which were becoming more familiar now as I trekked back and forth over to Martinborough. To the left, peaks of the Tararua ranges rose up, while to the right were rolling grasslands of the uplands. I felt weary and stopped to camp in the shelter of the outcrop James and I had slept under for the night and enjoyed the view of the valley below. I awoke to low clouds wrapping everything in wool. Then suddenly, it would clear again with glimpses of blue sky, and birdsong echoed off the rocks. It was chilly as smoke hung from the fire, rising straight up in the still morning. I threw some chunks of bacon in the pan and savoured it between thick slabs of bread. My anticipation at uniting with the family rose the nearer I drew. *Father would be proud to see us all altogether; I'm sure he would have provided a feast if he could.*

Along the way, I searched for treats; called into three stores – Haycock's general store for an order of delicious imported accompaniments, Kwong's for bags of sweets to sneak into the children's stockings and persuade old Grimmers to sell me a fattened turkey, which we would tie up in the yard for the special day and not let into Mother's vegetable garden. My mind wandered to thoughts of Euphemia as I held the reins back on the rough track. *Her campaign in the elections is only a week away now. When will our paths cross again, I wonder?*

Eventually, as I drew closer to town, I could see the smoke rising from chimneys in Waihinga; I saw that familiar tiny tower of the presbyterian church. Ellen's house, on the outskirts of town, had a covered verandah along its front with dormers upstairs. Only young legs could manage climbing those fearful stairs that led to the long attic room where the children slept. It was stuffy in summer but dry in winter and a great space for them all to play in.

The last time James had made the trip over the hill was with me. He was afraid Mother would scold him again over his gambling habits, and she missed seeing her little grandson, Ernest.

Mother must have seen me roll up outside as she had thrown off her pinny and came running and waving. Her wild grey hair caught the sunlight, making her face look even more weathered than before. Her tanned arms looked skinnier than ever from gardening, yet I had never seen her looking so happy, content and healthy.

"Harry, you're here!"

I leapt off the buggy, and we embraced warmly. "Mother, this countryside agrees with you. I can't believe you are finally here to live! And you have so much colour in your cheeks."

"Dear boy, you always say the right thing, but I think it is all the Christmas and wedding preparations ahead that makes me feel needed … Emma's and John Dalton's is progressing well and planned for the first week in February, then Mary's wedding to Jack Gaskin is straight after, set for the 22nd. They will all be rather humble affairs but still need planning."

"I am so happy for them both. Is it your plan to populate the valley? If it is, you'll be in competition with the Martins and Harris families."

"We'll just have to marry you into them."

We both laughed.

"I don't think you need worry about the celebrations being humble … look what Jack gave me!" I handed her the wad of notes. "Take it. Merry Christmas, Mother. You'll make this go a lot further than I would."

She just stood looking bewildered, like I had handed her an unholy thing. "Son, this is a fortune! How?"

"I have just finished up with Jack Lane in Island Bay and he gave us a gift for Christmas, which will afford wedding celebrations, including a fine Christmas for all." I tied Lotti to the fence rail, and pulled down my bedroll.

Mother stood with tears rolling down her face. She came over, took my face in her hands, and spoke into my ear. "God blessed me the day you were born, son. I do not know how we would have managed these years without your support. You have truly done your father proud. God be praised! God be praised! …" Mother took my free arm. "Now, are you hungry? I always seem to be hungry." She talked flat out. "I could not have wished for a better life for us all – the weather here is much warmer. You should see my garden, it's good ground here, it's flourishing. Come inside, we will have tea and the biscuits we baked yesterday."

Mary came running out and, throwing her apron across the front porch, took my bed roll and tossed it aside to free my other arm.

"Brother, you're here! Come tell us all your news! I need to hear all about Euphemia … have you heard from her?" she said excitedly.

I missed Mary. She was a calming influence in the family. As my next oldest sister, I have often shared my heart with her.

"I think it is going to be a grand celebration as most of the family are coming. There will be plenty of mouths to feed."

Joe was delighted to see me and showed me to the small room off the back porch we had created. A curtain was nailed up and weatherboard walls graced one side wall. Its views were over Mother's neat vegetable gardens, set out in regimented rows, and not a weed in sight.

I playfully tossed my bed roll at Joe, saying, "You'll have to put up with me for a few days. I can't believe how tall you've grown."

"I'm nearly as tall as you already!" he said, standing on tip-toe and stretching his head high.

"Doesn't seem long ago I saw you. A couple of months." Joe stood tall, glowing then suddenly remembered something.

"Come. I want to show you what I've made!"

I followed him to the stables and there, standing against the barn wall were two new cart wheels.

"Did you fashion these working at Cameron's coach building shop?" I stood them together comparing their height to one another. "These are fine wheels, Joe!"

"Yes, but I had help."

"Well done." I looked at the joints. "Extraordinary, Joe! Who helped you drop the red-hot hoop iron over the wooden wheel?"

"It took three of us with long tong irons to manage that part but I made the fire round the hoop iron to heat it. I spoke-shaved the spokes, cutting all the timbers in just like they showed me for the frame."

"Did you know Father used to do that sometimes as a blacksmith? I can remember him cutting the steel then rolling it, joining the hoop, then fitting the rim. You were only four or five when Father was sent away."

"I don't remember that, but I remember his big hand bandaged once when I sat on his knee. His hands were hard like tree bark."

"You are very fortunate to be working there. You are a fast learner. When you helped us in the holidays with our cabbie work, you picked things up quickly."

"It's hot work in the summer days, but I discovered a broken cart out back of the Club Hotel." Joe's face lit up with excitement. "They said I could have it if I helped them clean up their stables. I've been going after school. It has broken wheels but a good axle and chassis. I think I could be a carrier like you, transporting produce or wool bales from the farms for Considine's."

"Joe, I can see you have inherited that flair for seeing an opportunity. Splendid, little brother, perhaps I could help you negotiate with them. We could do the repairs then find a reasonable horse and bridle."

"Oh, would you! … oh, but we don't have any Australian hardwood?"

"I've not much else to do. Perhaps we can use some seasoned Matai or heart Rimu to finish it off. You ask around. Someone could be knocking down an old shed."

I lay there that night talking to Joe until he drifted off to sleep. The muffled sounds of voices seemed to bathe my soul in a family magic, and I felt content in a kind of knowing … of alike hearts and minds.

Chapter 13

Straightlaced

Ellen's and John's house was literally bursting at the seams, creaking and groaning as we squeezed into four rooms and the attic for Christmas. Nobody meddled with Ellen's rules as she calmly kept law and nurtured us like a second mother. People described her as straightlaced, yet she joined in our loud frivolity, sitting to retell stories of the past or singing round the piano just the same. It felt like the most joyous occasion we had celebrated together since we were little. We all complained of full stomachs as we sat round the big table in the glow of laughter and conversation.

I caught up with Mary as we returned from the butcher shop together, trotting slowly so as to make the most of the time.

"Harry, is it good that the children will be showered with gifts from Santa Claus? I don't want them to be spoilt."

Harry half smiled at her. "I remember how Father would hide our humble little presents under our beds for the morning. One year I was awake and saw him. I couldn't wait for daybreak to see if any gift had been left … One morning, there was a whole orange, just for me! It smelt wonderful. It will take more than one Christmas to spoil the children, Mary. Anyway, what's the difference between being spoilt or being loved?

"Perhaps it feels like love. Father would be celebrating our extravagance. Don't you ever wonder how he would feel if we could pick him up from Sunny-Side and bring him here. Would he recognise us?"

She stared at me as if I had just revealed a secret. "Harry, I have had the *same* thought! I even asked Mother over the years. Couldn't we at least try?" Then she sighed. "But it's no use; he doesn't even recognise us, especially as the last time he saw the eight of us, we were tiny. I would give anything for him to give me away at the altar instead of James.

"I shouldn't complain, though. It's marvellous to be living so near our kin, despite James testing us all the time."

"His bark's worse than his bite. Ellen sorts him out. Their home is like central station with all the extended family. You will have to find a place to live after the wedding."

"Yes, we are searching now for a small cottage, possibly like that one over there with three rooms or something." She pointed to a typical little cottage like children draw in a picture, with a central door, a room on either side of the hall, a kitchen at the rear, the copper and outhouse near the garden.

"I will keep my ear to the ground."

"After you organised that picnic for Jack Lane, you might have some ideas for the children?"

"I'd be delighted, and I've already given it some thought. I will create fun activities in the yard, like throwing a boot, tossing a broom, and one-legged races. There's rope in the barn to play leap the rope, or skipping. I kept a stack of horseshoes for playing quoits. Rusty is going to show us how and he is the master of fun. He and John can help.

"We could pack a little food and take the cart to the river for a swim in the warm afternoons."

"Brilliant. I will second the boys' help."

"Brother, isn't it like medicine watching Mother's joy over the antics in our home again."

"She honestly looks ten years younger without all that worry. Makes me feel sad, as I'm planning to go north with Johnny and

Rusty once we've ushered in the new year."

"Then once our two weddings are over, make the most of this time here!"

"Mary, I've never seen everyone in such high spirits."

"Anticipating upcoming nuptials always has that romantic effect on people. Oh, by the way, I haven't asked you to help with a specific task but would you just hover around and see what needs doing to lend a hand. You do the best job of getting people involved and drawing a crowd.

"Emily has agreed to help again with both celebrations, I am sure you'll enjoy flirting with her."

"I'll be happy to fill in where I'm needed. As for flirting, you must be thinking of someone else ..." I looked at her, smiling. "How are you feeling?"

"I'm nervous and excited all at once, but it's a while away yet."

We laughed together and talked about what needed to be done as the six girls fussed over details for her and Emma's special days. We were all present apart from Martha, who was expecting another child soon in Southern Canterbury.

Over the next few days, the preparations for Christmas continued. Emily came to help out the day before as we were running about like ants. I teased her like a sister as I intruded into the kitchen carrying water, bringing in the plucked chickens, firewood or stoking the oven. We spoke numerous times while sharing a little to eat or in the buggy as I escorted her home. She was a bright young woman, an only child, and I could not help being taken in by her natural beauty. After meeting her father, I could see her fear when he demanded that she be home by an exact time.

I joined Johnny for a smoke on the long back step in the sun while watching the children running round Mother's garden. He always seemed content in his own space. He was a great sportsman with a natural talent and love of sports. "It's great to have you up from the Deep South, brother."

"It's been a while. I missed being able to pop over to see Mother, although I am happy she finally got away from Timaru. Do you need help with anything?"

"You can give me a hand to create a few games for the children over the next few days. Mary and I have a few ideas but I know you'll have some fun games up your sleeve."

"Of course, I'd love to. Just don't blame me when they come in muddy and exhausted." I slapped him on the back.

"Thanks. I'm sure they will love it. How are you sleeping next to James?"

"Well … if it wasn't for our elderly brother snoring. He's a shocker. Always when he's drunk too much, which is every night.

"I know only too well. I lived with him and Margaret."

"Hey, what's going on with you and Emily?"

"What do you mean?"

"I've watched you flirting with her. You like her, don't you? I know you, don't pull one over me." He looked at me in a way that I knew I was not going to be able to lie and say it was playful banter.

I lowered my voice to a whisper, and talked towards the ground. "John, it's true. As the days pass, I find myself trying desperately to resist her admiration. She likes me, I can see it in her eyes. She's expressed a desire to break away from her draconian parents, longing for the day she can gain employment and secure a little independence…

"Harry, how do you do it? I can't get a girl to look at me."

"It's not like I do it on purpose! I have a girl I'm very keen on in Auckland."

"I'm sure you don't even know you're doing it."

"It's just a bit of fun! Right now, I'm focused on making the most of my time with you all, then I want to get away to the gold fields and try my luck up there."

"I think this will be my last year down south. It's not the same being away. It's hard leaving my team; we play so well together, but I'm very keen to have a look up there too. Let me know how you get on."

"Sure. I will let you know if anything comes up."

"Harry, you are always in where things are happening."

"Speaking of things happening, did you see Joe's cart wheels? Come and have a look."

We made our way to the shed, catching up on so much we had missed in each other's lives in the past four years.

Christmas celebrations went off with a bang, the house packed with laughter and presents for everyone. Rusty was a hit with the children, who hung off his arms or chased him around the yard. Emily happily spent much time with the family, helping prepare food or laughing with the girls. We all ate too much and slept the afternoon away.

Emma became *Mrs* John Dalton three weeks before Mary's and Jack's wedding on the 22 of February. By the time everyone gathered again, we were almost suffering from all the celebrating. It had also rekindled the bond that had been missing for years as we now found ourselves involved in each other's lives once more. This, of course, was good, and bad – living in close quarters added a little more strife over unsolicited offers of advice.

Finally, the bells of Waihenga's cherished little Presbyterian church rang to call folk in for Jack's and Mary's big day of celebration. Mother glowed as she had fussed about fitting all the little bouquets of flowers along the aisle, fluffing up the girls' dresses, and straightening Mary's veil. She joyfully welcomed each person into the chapel as the piano began to play. Emma and Emily stood in their soft pink dresses, warming up in the sunlight as they prepared for the walk, their slim waists accentuated by their full pleated hoops. Suddenly the music changed to the wedding march. It felt surreal watching the girls slowly walk down the aisle to take their places in front of the minister. James looked nervous standing in for Father as the minister asked, 'Who gives this woman?'

Throughout the morning, I kept catching a glimpse of Emily looking my way, always smiling. She looked glorious now, standing there in all her finery, a far cry from peeling potatoes together in the kitchen over the past few weeks.

The robed minister spoke of not entering into this union lightly… *What does that mean? As if you could suddenly end up married, waking up one morning wondering how you got there.*

Mary and Jack finally turned to each other with serious expressions. They held each other's hands and exchanged their vows of Love 'til death do us part.'

Could I really love the same woman for that long? Some old folk celebrate 65 years of marriage … still hold hands … smile warmly, and laugh together. I'm not sure.

A few minutes later, Jack lifted Mary's veil, held her face and kissed her slowly on the lips. Cheers of delight chorused from the congregation. As a crowd gathered outside, Mr and Mrs Dalton were ceremoniously showered in rice amid more gleeful shouts. Mary slowly turned, and all the young women quickly positioned themselves to catch the bouquet as it soared high into the air. It almost fell on Emily's head as she snatched it, her face blushing red. As the congratulations flowed to a new beginning, the only thing left was to enjoy the party before they set off for their honeymoon.

I picked up a few helpers and quickly returned home and get preparations underway for guests to arrive, which included stoking the range and the fire to warm the house as the party was about to go into full swing.

It had already been an enormous day, starting before sunrise to prepare everything and finally, after all the speeches, the last few dessert plates were washed up, and I was free to relax and have a drink.

Mary's Jack had put in a word asking for the small band who played at the Club Hotel to come and play their popular mixture of Irish and folk music. One talented man played the banjo and Irish flute; I played the squeeze box, calling the dances, while two others played the piano and a guitar. The lounge was suddenly cleared to become a dance floor as everyone was in high spirits with fine food, drinks and lively music.

James was already unconscious on a chair in one corner, having started early. Emily had changed into a beautiful light blue dress and occasionally looked in my direction as I played. I was hungry and I finally made my way around to an empty chair to eat my plate of cold roast lamb with vegetables. Jack and Mary came sweeping past, grabbing my arm.

"Come on, little brother, now you're not playing; please ask my friend Emily for a dance!" Mary shouted above the merriment.

I gulped down a few mouthfuls then navigated my way to her through the dancing bodies. *Why is Euphemia so far away? I could be dancing with her, although Emily has been watching me all evening.*

"Emily, would you like a dance?"

"I thought you'd never ask — it's the least you can do after annoying me for the past few weeks," she said, smiling.

She was surprisingly light on her feet, yet each time I thanked her and walked away, she would glance my way again and raise an eyebrow, anticipating another dance, which I reasoned was innocent flirting. *What is the harm in a few dances?* I couldn't remember a time when I danced so much in one night.

"Harry, this is the first time in my life Father has allowed me to stay out till midnight. I told him we had to clean up after the party."

"Really. He sounds very strict." I kept telling myself, *I must resist her charm,* which became less insistent as the night wore on, the beer soon going to my head.

"Emily, I need to cool off. Give me a few minutes, and I will return."

I'm so torn. I must not let my emotions get the better of me, but she's so gorgeous. I picked up a piece of roast meat off a plate in the kitchen as I passed by. Stepping into the cool night air in my sweaty shirt was like stepping into ice-cold water. As I leaned on the garden gate, I felt Emily's hand on my shoulder and turned. She held up the remains of a bottle of malt.

"What does it taste like?"

Emily looked at me, her big eyes wide in the moonlight. *She seems even more beautiful.*

"I have whiskey. I have never been allowed alcohol before. I want to try it."

"Emily, I really don't think you should…" but before I could stop her, she took out the cork and upended the bottle into her mouth. I grabbed her as her face flushed red and she spluttered it back out in a coughing fit, spitting whiskey out over me and the ground.

"Emily! Slow down. You cannot drink that like water – it'll make you drunk or sick!"

"Oh, it's like hot mustard sauce or something. How do people drink this! My throat is burning like fire."

"It's for sipping."

"… makes my insides feel warm … Alright, show me then!"

"Emily, it will go to your head. Have you had anything to eat?"

"No, but I have wine. See?" She sipped on a second glass she had brought out. "I want to try wine too."

"It's been a busy day. We need to eat."

"I can't remember when I ate last. I just wasn't hungry. I am feeling a little dizzy. Father won't allow alcohol because it's forbidden by God. He says, 'Thou shalt not be drunk with wine but filled with the spirit,' so I am trying some spirits.

"I find that hard to understand … Jesus turned water into wine, didn't he!

"But not real wine. It was like juice."

"I don't know anything about that, but how did the wedding guests think they left the best till last. Seems like Jesus turned water into wine, and Christians have been trying to turn it back to water ever since! Come on, let's get you some food."

I took her hand to lead her inside to eat a little. Then we danced well into the night, finally cooling off again as the air became stuffy, filled with hot bodies and cigarette smoke.

The moon was only days off being full, having risen like a sun in the blackness, lighting up the whole valley with its glow.

"I can't remember such a pretty night, Harry. Let's dance in the moonlight. I do not want this night to end. Dance with me like a princess."

Everyone had gone inside as the damp dew was settling down.

"Just one, then I will take you home!" Looking at her radiant, expectant face, I took her hand in the brilliant light and danced slowly around the yard with playful muse.

We rested for a moment, silent except for distant laughter from the house, which was almost as loud as the sound of night crickets. She snuggled in against my ribs as we perched on the chopping block, our breath visible, our perspiration chilled in a soft breeze from the south.

"Harry, these have been the best days of my life, having fun with you. Take me away. I cannot endure this small town any longer. I will choke."

I thought of Euphemia but watched every word on Emily's lips as my heart pounded. I was in a battle against an all-consuming desire to hold her and kiss her. *I need to tell her now about Phee and resist this desire!*

"I have only come back for a few months to be here for Christmas and my sisters' weddings. I need to tell you …."

I hesitated. *Tell her of my love for Euphemia … but, right now, she seems so far away in Auckland.*

"Tell me what, Harry …? Can you hold me. I'm cold!"

I fought to hold back my imprisoned zeal and call reason to my foggy brain as I held her close, but I could restrain myself no longer. Her blue eyes were enchanting as I gently kissed her scarlet lips. They were hot as she responded with passioned pleasure, fixing her eyes on mine as she spoke in a whisper.

"Please kiss me again. I have never kissed anyone before."

She closed her eyes as I gently held her face in my hands. I kissed her face and neck as she slowly turned away in delight. My hands ran free over her pulsating body, down over her breasts.

She was transfixed, holding my gaze as she quietly took my hand and lay down in the long grass, beckoning me to follow. I stood for a moment looking down at her, fighting the demon on my shoulder, torn in two. *No one will know,* I told myself as I lay down and looked up at the luminous sky.

Without a word, she sat up on her knees and leaned over me, grinning nervously but cheekily as she undid the ribbon round her waist. I watched her, wondering what she was doing, then realized and held her wrist to stop her. "Are you sure you want this? We cannot think clearly right now."

"I feel wonderful, Harry! We won the vote – we have a right to choose. Our bodies are our own, and we can choose to do with it whatever we want."

Her words and the wine made it sound so logical so I watched her, wondering at what point she would come to her senses.

When she had shed her dress and chemise, baring her soft, full breasts to the moon, I helped slip off the rest of her garments, any lingering inhibitions set free by the wine as our yearning was set ablaze. Any thread of sound reason fled as I disrobed and lay her on top of me, savouring the slender, ripe body she offered me. For a moment, she winced as we joined, then I rocked her in a motion as old as time until we both reached our highest peak of pleasure. After only minutes, we rolled to our sides and lay back, her white peaked breasts pure in the light as we tried to catch our breath.

As quickly as it had begun, dismay crept into my thoughts, and the demons returned, descending like a black cloud, pouring over me like a flood. I cried out inside, *Euphemia, what have I done!*

Emily stood up, staggering slightly and fumbling to dress again. I picked her up and carried her into the barn, lay her on the clean hay. My head now throbbed, charged with fresh blood that carried sound reason back to my brain, each minute becoming soberer as it started to dawn on me.

"Emily, this was not meant to happen. I am so sorry. I will take you home! Let me get the rest of your things." I ran back to where we had lain; picked up her shoes, ribbons and hat.

"Harry, I have a funny head. Perhaps I could just rest a while.

"Emily, is this your first time?"

"Yes, first drink … alcohol is forbidden! I love you …do you lub me?"

"No … I mean …!" I was suddenly filled with dread as I flicked out my pocket watch to see the time. My heart sank as I stared at the watch hands that had stopped at a quarter past ten. *Damn! My watch has stopped. How could I be so reckless!* I could not deny it. I had suspected it was her first time but now it filled me with dread. I tried to get Emily to stand but she was sleepy, so I swept her up and carried her over to the carriage.

"You have such strong arms," she said, slurring her words.

I gently placed her into the trap, trying to button up her dress and straighten her clothes as best I could in the poor light. I wrapped her shawl around her then harnessed the horse as quickly as my cold fingers would move. "I am taking you home. Emily, you are drunk. You've had too much to drink."

"Whadever you say, Harry, I feel sleepy."

My mind, now ablaze, burned out of control. *What will her parents say? What about Euphemia? What if she finds out … And Maggie. What if she gets pregnant? What shall I tell Mother or Mary?*

The night dew was thick and I suddenly felt cold. Lotti carried our buggy quietly through the streets to Emily's house where there was still a lamp flickering in the sitting room.

I picked her up, carried her to the house where her parents were waiting up for her. I did not need to knock as the door flung open.

I was face to face with Mr Linders. Anger burned red across his face as he tried desperately to contain his rage.

"Good evening, sir. My sincerest apologies for being so late."

"What time do you call this! What has happened to her? We have been worried sick! She should have been home three hours ago. You are Mary's brother? Well, boy, speak up!"

I fumbled for words knowing at any minute they would notice her dress, which I had tried to hide. I handed her hat to Mrs Linders.

"I am Harry Bagust. Yes! I met your daughter tonight at my sister's wedding celebration. We danced together."

"I can smell alcohol on her breath. She is forbidden to drink – did she not say? It is against our belief to have strong drink!"

"I did not realise she had not had alcohol before. She only had two glasses."

Emily's mother helped Emily through the door and disappeared into the darkness of the hall.

"Our daughter has never been allowed out before like this.

You will need to come back in the light of day and explain yourself to my wife and myself. Is that clear! I bid you farewell. See you on the morrow."

He slammed the door and turned the lock. I could just make out the mantel clock over the fireplace, quarter to one. It will soon be daylight. I am not sure what my face registered to Mr Linders but I was not looking forward to that meeting which would come about sooner than I cared to consider.

Lotti's hooves seemed deafening in the early hours as I tried to quietly sneak into the yard. I found a bed of clean hay in the barn and lay down exhausted, waking in the dark to the ear-piecing sound of a rooster atop a post next to the open barn. The sound rang inside my head. The moon was still up in the semi-darkness as I dusted myself off and made my way back into the house. As I entered, the rear door hinges cried out like a tortured bird, but to my relief, all the night-time revellers were quiet in the sleeping house.

Chapter 14

Get Off Your High Horse

What seemed like minutes later, Ellen was shaking me gently.

"Harry! Harry!" She held a note of paper. "You look terrible, brother, and why are you on the floor? You need to get up and have a hearty breakfast: Mr Linders came by to give you this note. He did not look happy. He wants you to go over there at 10am. I wonder what that's about? It's already after nine."

"I caught his front fence when I dropped Emily home. He probably wants me to repair it."

My head pounded as I rose up off the floor, and my heart sank. I hoped somehow this was all just part of an elaborate dream and I would wake with a huge sigh of relief. I could smell bacon and eggs wafting through the room as I put on my waistcoat, dreading the inquisition before I even headed out to Emily's house. I entered the dining room, relieved to discover that everyone had already gone out.

"Where did you go last night? You certainly danced Emily off her feet."

"Can we talk about this later, Ellie. I have a throbbing head, and I need all my thoughts to focus just on the eggs."

"Brother, I have a hunch you may be in some trouble. Believe me, I have lived long enough to know. Did you lay with her?"

I just stared at her blankly. "You have a way of coming right to the point, El." *Oh my god, how does she know?* "No, of course not! I would not do that to Mary. She only had two drinks, then we went out to cool off from dancing. I was missing Euphemia. We lay looking at the stars and we kissed, that's all."

"Harry, what about that girl in Auckland? Perhaps you should forget her. You would be better to be with someone locally, Emily is lovely."

Ellen carried over the steaming plate of food and, standing over me like Mother, looked into my face, her hand on her hip.

"I know when you're lying. You are going to need all your charm today, brother. The last thing we need is another illegitimate child." She walked away and went back to cleaning up the pots. "Can you carry some water up for me before you go? Joe has gone off with the others."

"Sure. I will have a wash at the same time." I adjusted my watch to the mantel clock and cleaned up then set off early to arrive at 9:45. I wore my new suit jacket and tie, and had picked a bunch of roses from Ellen's garden and tied them with a red ribbon she had found.

At Emily's house, I tied Lotti to the gate post. My legs felt like lead as I stepped uneasily up the path to the front door. *If only the sweet scent from these roses could waft away this stench.* I called out through the open door, and stood nervously like a school boy outside the headmaster's office.

Emily's father came to the door and looked me over like I was a dirty rag, then he ushered me inside. "Take a seat. My wife will be out shortly."

Discomforted by his tone, I sat near the door so I could get away if needed. I could hear loud muttering in the hall and presently Mrs Linders came through, her eyes puffy and red from crying. With a faltering voice, she did her best to hold her composure, and cordially put out her hand. She glanced furtively searching for truth in my eyes as we shook. Hers were full of dark disappointment as I handed her the roses, saying. "These are for you, Madam."

"Thank you," she said, and took them momentarily to the kitchen, returning shortly after with a small vase, which she carefully placed on the embroidered side table. She then took her seat next to Mr Linders and placed her hands dutifully in her lap.

Harry, you need to get off your high horse, I thought as I sat down again and spoke up to break the silence. "Mr and Mrs Linders, I am sorry for my behaviour last night. I was so happy to be finally with my family again, to join in such a joyous celebration. I allowed my emotions to get the better of me last night, and feel great remorse this morning. How is Emily today? We had such fun last night dancing?"

I could tell Mr Linders was already choking back fury. "*Emotions got away, did they!!*" He stood, his face red as he blurted out, "Mr Bagust, were you with our daughter alone last night? She is only seventeen. *Did you lay with her? I want a straight answer.* Is it not enough you brought her home drunk when she is forbidden to drink! This morning my wife discovered blood on her dress. My wife informs me it is not her time of the month."

I looked at them both as they pierced me with intense searching eyes. My thoughts were loud in my head. *Seventeen! I have no defence. What am I to say? Is there any point lying?*

"We had been hot after dancing and went out to cool off. It was such a beautiful evening and we lay down beneath the stars and ….

"Mr Bagust, it is yes or no!"

I had come feeling confident my charm would pour forth like a flood at any moment, even though my humiliation gripped me with self-loathing. But it did not come and now the evidence was piling up against me. My head hurt and I was still a little worse for wear. *I have no other choice but to confess … unless perhaps …*

I stood boldly to my full height and threw myself into the part of wounded indignation. "No! I certainly did not. I do not know how her beautiful dress spoiled, but we prepared four chickens in the yard yesterday; it is probably chicken blood!"

Thomas leapt to his feet and faced me, his nostrils flaring. "Come now, Harry, do you take me for a fool! If you have had relations with my daughter, I will expect you to do the honourable thing and wed her."

His wide eyes pierced my soul. Suddenly, Mrs Linders burst out crying and ran from the room.

I decided to take the gamble. Turning to Thomas, I feigned absolute disgust at his allegations. "Sir, as I have already conveyed my apologies, I see no need to continue this pointless banter." I picked up my hat and started toward the door.

"Very well, take your leave, but do not darken this door again unless you can either tell the truth or you are summoned. In time, it will be quite clear what has transpired and then justice will be served. In the meantime, we will consider the matter, and contact you in due course. This is your last chance, Bagust. Do you have anything else to say?"

Feeling completely jaded from the night's adrenalin, I just needed to get out of there. Although my mind felt slow, I thought the meeting had gone about the way I expected, given the circumstances.

I sighed with relief as I stepped over the threshold of the front door. Turning to face Thomas Linders, I put out my hand as if I was contracting business. "There is no more to say. Please give my regards to Emily."

He looked at my hand in disgust, then grabbed it in a vice-like grip, nearly breaking my fingers as he dragged me close enough to smell his garlic breath. "I've known men like you, Harry, full of charm but empty. You had better be looking over your shoulder."

He slammed the front door behind me as I walked away in a daze, looking back for any sign of Emily in a bedroom window.

I do not remember the drive back to Ellen's place, my mind

in a spin as I tried to contemplate what could happen should Emily be pregnant. *It's highly unlikely but if she is, we will face it then. Perhaps there'll be a third wedding this year, only a lot less festive. It might be down at the registry office, with stern faces and bitter stares and I could be stuck here in Martinborough instead of the adventure of the gold fields Rusty and I had planned. What happens next will determine the direction of my life. This sudden fork in the road will mean any hope of being with Euphemia is dashed like a bottle on the bow of a ship. I hope Emily catching the bouquet is not a bad omen. I will speak with Ellen, she has dealt with many crises in our family, although her advice is like taking bitter medicine that makes you gag, but is meant to be good for you. Her motherly advice is seasoned with love, wisdom and a swift cuff across the head.*

I arrived home to Mother busy in the garden, digging in a load of sheep manure ready for planting potatoes in August and roses for the summer. I snuck past her to Ellen in the kitchen. She was folding the children's clothes.

"How did you go, brother?"

I looked around the room to see that no one else was around.

"I think it went rather well."

She walked toward me stretching a warped towel from the ironing pile. "I want the whole story … and do not tell me some cock and bull," she said sternly, raising her voice slightly.

I looked at her insistent face as she stood with her hands on her hips. *There is no point in lying to Ellie. I have to tell her the whole affair.*

"Nell, it is as you suspected. We got a little carried away last night but I did not know the full extent of her only being seventeen, a virgin, forbidden to have alcohol by her religious parents."

"Harry! Could it be any worse! What if she is pregnant …?" She looked out the window in pain, then turned. "We are trying to have some dignity here in this community. What did her parents say?"

"I denied it all. They had discovered her dress. I said we had been preparing chickens for the wedding celebrations."

"We do not need to have another illegitimate child?"

"I will take the gamble, cross that bridge when it comes. I really have no other choice but to marry her. Her father guessed I was lying, holding onto my hand in a vice-like grip, crushing my fingers. His stern warning was to that effect."

"You will know soon enough, brother. In the meantime, prepare yourself one way or the other. It may not just be a crushed hand you get. If she is pregnant then please let Euphemia know. Do not delay – it will only make matters worse. You have dug a hole and there is no way to talk your way out of this one. You might just have to settle here and forget the goldfields."

"Yes, yes, do not worry, I will. Please keep it to yourself for now. I do not wish to spoil Mary's and Jack's special day."

"Of course, you do not have to worry on that front. We are masters when it comes to keeping something quiet."

The days seemed to pass by slowly as I imagined all manner of outcomes. I took the opportunity, busying myself on the neighbour's farm who was happy for someone to plough their fields. It felt good to be out on the land with the huge lumbering Clydesdale tethered to the plough. At first, I had trouble keeping the furrows straight and a few times I was caught by a root or rock, which sent me flying sideways onto the ground. Perhaps I deserved it, one second watching the plough, the next looking up at the sky. It had now been a week since I had seen the whites of Thomas Linders' eyes. At least I slept like a dead man after fighting a plough all day. I figured no news was good news as I popped into town to pick up a bag of flour for Ellen.

As I rode around the central town square, my heart suddenly gripped with fear. There was Emily, arm in arm with her mother, coming out of the Harris's Taylor shop.

I panicked for a moment and stopped the horse, wondering, was she just having a fitting for a new dress or had she grown out of it. All at once I realised how desperate I had been to speak with her, and looked up a few times trying to catch her eye. At last, she glanced up for a second, seeing me secretly beckon to one side. She pretended to crouch down to check a shoe while her mother spoke to a passer-by then she looked directly at me and pointed with one finger, to her chest, her eye and then directly at me. Eye-see-me … I see … you … Oh *"I need to see you."* I nodded and continued on my way with my head down so as not to be noticed. I would devise a plan for us to speak alone, away from the clutches of her obsessive parents. Mary would return from her honeymoon in a week's time; I would ask her to arrange a secret rendezvous somehow. I could even pretend I saw her and she was interested to find out about the honeymoon. Either way, I must know.

It was still another two weeks before Mary and Jack returned as they had gone through to Auckland and were held up in Thames with the weather.

I left it a few days for them to settle in before asking Mary. She was delighted at the thought of catching up on all the local news and asked Emily over the next day.

I made sure to casually drop in an hour after they were to meet for morning tea.

"Yuhoo! Are you home?" I called out.

"In here. Is that my rascal brother? Get in here."

"Mary, you already look different, perhaps even content," I said as I entered the lounge. She whacked me on the shoulder, then linked arms with mine.

"What perfect timing. Emily is here too; she dropped over to fill me in on all the local gossip."

"Of course … I love your new dress, Emily. That colour makes you glow." Mary patted the seat next to her.

"Harry, come sit with us. Would you like tea? I will just hot it up in the kitchen. Give me a few minutes." She went off to the kitchen, giving us just the moment I had anticipated.

Emily's face was bright. "Thank you for your plan. It has worked brilliantly."

"How are your parents? I did not see you after the night I dropped you home. I have thought of you constantly."

"Harry, I am with child. I tried to keep it from my parents until I had spoken to you, but the other day my mother saw me running to the outhouse to vomit, asking me in private if I was unwell or pregnant."

"There was no point lying as she said she would keep it quiet as long as possible from Father. She asked if I wished to go to my aunties in Auckland until I had the baby … I do not know what to do?"

Mary came back into the room carrying a fine china cup and saucer. "You two seem deep in conversation. I saw you the other night dancing like two ballerinas. He does all right for a 'ploughman'."

Emily looked at me and smiled cheekily. Keeping our secret had united us irreversibly. *Can I go on with this charade? I feel compelled to tell her of my love for Euphemia. I'm hoping she knows already.*

I pretended to spill my tea a little and went to the kitchen for a cloth.; stood leaning on the bench over the morning's dishes, feeling slightly sick myself.

"Are you alright? Do you need a towel?"

"No, it's just a little tea. I will come back in a minute, just off to the outhouse." *Think, think! There is no easy solution to this dilemma. Whatever I choose, someone gets hurt. What would Father have said? I can hear him as clear as day in my head. "Do the right thing, son — marry her." Or perhaps that's my conscience. Jack Lane might have said,*

"Take the adventure, Harry. You never know what path it may lead you on! James would say "Let her go to her aunts, keep out of it.' This is when having a father would be great. I wandered around the yard deep in thought, then in a moment decided: *there is no other thing for it, it is my child, I will ask if she will have me.* I returned to the room, and sat for a few minutes, my mind not on the conversation.

"Harry … Harry!" Mary looked at me puzzled. "You are in another world. What is it?"

"Mary, I will explain later but could I have a few minutes to speak with Emily in private?"

Mary stared at me bewildered then slowly rose; she looked at Emily's face, reflecting my sentiment.

"Of course … oh … I have a few pots from the morning dishes to clean up and a hot kettle full of water … if you need anything, let me know." She picked up her cup and saucer and took it with her.

I waited for her to leave then watched Emily's dimples fade along with her smile.

"I have something to tell you. A few months ago, I went to Auckland to play against Parnell. I fell in love with a girl in Auckland called Euphemia. I have been waiting for an opportunity to tell you. I tried to tell you the other night but got distracted. I am not promised to her but we kissed one night before I sailed on my return voyage. I have strong feelings for her."

Stunned, Emily looked directly at me, her eyes piercing my soul. "You did not say … all the dancing the other night. The flirting in the kitchen."

"Emily, my feelings took me completely by surprise too. I did not plan to have relations with you. I did not know how to tell you."

"I just … what will Father …!" Her words trailed off for a moment as she was deep in thought. "Mary had mentioned a girl but I thought you at least had feelings for me! … wanted to be with me!"

"Emily, of course, I was infatuated by you. You are a beautiful girl. We shared such fun together. I am ready to commit to you and to have this baby together."

"I had wanted this more than anything but now I am not sure." She stood and wandered to the window; looked out across the paddocks. "Perhaps you could give me a few days to consider it. I feel suddenly conflicted."

"Emily, I know how much you wanted to get out of home. I will understand if you would rather take your chances by going to your aunt's to start a new life."

"Harry, I realise it was a moment of passion, but do you even love me?"

"It's a huge adjustment for me … perhaps in time … I had plans of going away to the gold fields but I can choose to be with you instead. I love another but I will choose you. It may not be what you need to hear but it is the best I can do right now."

She looked at me blankly for what seemed an eternity. I stepped closer; took her hand

"Emily, we could make this work. I will respect your wishes but give us a chance."

"I cannot think!" She pulled away. "I need to get out of here … need time to think it over for a few days. I'm feeling quite emotional right now and my thoughts are not clear."

She went to the kitchen to find Mary. "I cannot stay, I will come by in a few days." She started sobbing as she moved quickly towards the front door.

"Em! Is everything alright." Mary caught up with her in the doorway.

"It will be." They hugged and glanced my way as Emily put on her gloves. Mary looked at me confused as I stood holding the door, watching her walk off down the road.

"What was all that about Harry? What's going on with you two?"

"Oh, nothing. She just wanted to talk about her parents. I think I will walk home too. Thanks so much for the afternoon tea."

I hugged her and closed the door, my head swimming with conversations — so many things that could have been said.

Chapter 15

Bite the Bullet

The mornings were becoming chilly again as I returned to Mary's the next day. I called out as I went through the front door. There was a wonderful, sweet smell of baked sultana scones filling the house, as I came through to the kitchen. A steaming tray full sat cooling with a freshly made pound of butter sitting on the wooden board.

I looked out the window and could see her hanging heavy linen sheets on a line stretched between two trees in the yard. As I stepped out the back door, she turned.

"There you are. I have everything ready. There's even a bowl of whipped cream and blackcurrant jam in the cooler. You have a lost boy look about you this morning, what's going on?"

"What did Emily say? I thought she might have said."

"Said what? All she said was you had a misunderstanding that needed sorting out, but I could tell she was holding something back."

"What is it, brother? Just bite the bullet and tell me." She stood holding a dripping wet shirt. "I can finish this later; come, I will make tea." She draped the shirt over the line, turning again to me.

"Talk to me. I can tell you're holding something back."

We entered the kitchen and I sat down. "She is pregnant!"

"*What! Who? ...* Emily!?"

Mary's mouth hung open in disbelief as she stood holding the kettle. "*Yours*! … "How!?"

I nodded. "At your wedding party."

"What will you do?"

"There is nothing for it, I will have to marry her."

Mary sat stunned in a chair "And Euphemia?"

"I told her I am in love with Euphemia."

"What did you do that for? Is that really true! It must have broken Emily's heart … Marriage! Do her parents know?"

"Well, yes and no. Her mother discovered her morning sickness, managed to keep it quiet from old man Linders for now."

Mary bent, her head down leaning on her elbows on the table as she gathered her thoughts.

"Ohhh! Now I understand why she was so cagey about the other night. That's why you arranged a meeting. I was being used to get you together in secret." She stood. "Harry, couldn't you have just told me! … Her parents are extremely devout, you are in for a world of trouble, brother."

"I am sorry. I did not want to spoil your homecoming. I tried leaving it a few days."

"I do feel angry with you but … come here!" She wrapped her arms around me, standing up on her toes. "I don't feel like hugging you, but you probably need it right now."

As I held her, a wave of relief flooded my body.

"Come on, get a hot scone." She put milk in our cups, and carefully poured the tea.

"I suppose congratulations are a little too much at this stage. Looks like there'll be another wedding this year."

"I don't know yet. She has gone away to think about it. If she says yes, my life is about to change forever! But what if she says No!"

"Take no notice of that, Harry. She is not about to say no — she has been wanting to be free of her violent father for years.

She could do a lot worse, but you are in for a showdown facing old Linders."

I said goodbye to Mary and busied myself all day about Ellen's house. It was a distraction, fixing two jammed windows and a number of squeaking floorboards she had complained about. The autumn nights were growing colder as the days slowly drew shorter. I felt torn having not heard from Emily, while also feeling an urgency to confess to Euphemia. After everyone had retired, I finally sat in silence with a spitting candle at Mother's writing desk, feeling as tortured as the cracking logs on the fire. My mind was a whirlpool of emotion as I fruitlessly tried, one attempt after another, to convey the insistent ache in my heart. Like a confession of last rites, I watched the sinful black ink try to wash away my pain, creating shapes on crisp virgin paper, of a forbidden dream of a life with Euphemia. I spilled forth my anxious emotions telling of the unfortunate tryst and a wedding looming in the shadows. Then I watched the pages burn bright, unfurling as the flames for a moment lit up the room, turning my words to ash again. I blew out the candle, lay on the rug in the firelight wrapped in a blanket, carrying my thoughts off to a world of peace. I finally rose in the dark to reset a fire in the stove, mesmerised by the glow of red flames through cracks in the cast iron box.

As dawn broke over the hills the next morning a young lad came by the house with a note. I unfolded the paper which read:

I will meet you discreetly at Mary's at 10:40
while her family attend church

I held the sheet for a few moments, rehearsing conversations we might have as I hooked the cast iron plate up to drop the note in the red embers, where I watched it instantly disappear. I soon made hot tea then took the rest of the water to wash. At last, everyone had left the house and I made my way to our secret rendezvous at Mary's. As I unlatched the little gate to the front path, there was Emily, sitting alert on the front porch. Her young face seemed resolute as I made toward the extra cane chair on one side of the doorway. I caught her dark eyes as I climbed the two steps to the porch, suddenly feeling both a sense of anxiety and relief to finally talk to her. It had now been six weeks since that heated moonlit night, and many emotions filled me as she smiled gently.

"How are you, Emily? It's good to finally see you again."

She looked away, controlling her composure, her lips tightly holding back the emotions, yet one tear rolled down her left cheek.

"I am as well as could be expected. Please excuse me looking away, I do not want to be distracted from my resolve by looking directly at you." She looked down; fiddled with a pretty blue ribbon on her dress. She was not showing yet, but had a glow about her I had not noticed before. "I have decided, if your offer is still open, I would like to accept." She clasped her hands tightly in her lap, and spoke in a cold monotone. "I am desperate to get away from my parents, so if you will go through with the wedding, I will not expect you to stay with me."

I rose and crouched beside her chair, to look up into her face.

"So, you … *want* to get married. What have your parents said?"

She looked at me directly, lost, her eyes searching for a way of escape while trying to compose herself,

"Father knows! He took some persuading from Mother to stop him coming to your house with friends to drag you out onto the street for a beating. He has calmed down only slightly over the past two weeks. He has not spoken to me at all except to say. *"You have no other choice – you must marry him."*

She sat upright again. "He is right. This is the sensible thing to do. We must think of the child being fatherless."

"I would provide for you. Many girls have a child without marriage."

"I do not want to end up in court over this illegitimate child."

"Is this truly what you would choose?"

"I am making this decision, not my father! I have no other chance to escape his grip."

"If your parents were not part of this decision, what would you choose?"

"I am not in that position. I have no other choice but this one." She looked into my eyes pleadingly. "I am an unwed mother! I'm seventeen, under my father's roof!" Her hand wrapped around her fist. "You do not cross him."

"Do you remember that night, Emily … you said *women have won the vote, we have the right to choose.*"

"Did I say that? It sounds like something I *would* say. My head was spinning that night. It seems so long ago!" Her voice became stern again. "All that is rubbish now! Despite the election results last year, it appears I can do nothing in society without a husband or my Victorian father." She said this bitterly.

I felt compassion for her and took her cold hand. "You can still choose. If no one was pressuring you, what would *you* choose?"

She looked at me with fear in her eyes, not wanting to say it.

"I can see it in your eyes. Say what it is!"

She took a deep breath and gripped my hand tightly. "I would pack a suitcase, kiss my mother." She looked away and pulled her hand away. "… change my name and purchase a one-way ticket to Australia, never to return."

I slumped back in my chair, shocked by her honesty as I stared at the silhouette of her profile. For an instant I saw her father's strength. I believed her, yet I was still confused at her reasoning.

"You don't mean that! … Are you really that determined to get away from home. From your mother. You are lucky to have a father: my father is in a mental asylum.

She rose abruptly to her feet, started putting on her gloves. "I will not beg you. Perhaps you did not mean what you said?" She turned to face me, eye to eye. "Just tell me straight."

"What has he done to you, to cause this?"

"I have my reasons, but if I do not see him again, I think I will be content. I am afraid of him! If I stay here, I will be under his control forever."

I rose to stand with her; put my hand gently on her arm. "Please sit down," I said quietly.

"I have made my decision. All of that is a fantasy now. These are choices I do not have. Unless you have changed your mind and do not wish to marry me, then I will understand."

I took her other hand, gently sliding off both of her gloves as I dropped to one knee. "Well, we had better make it official."

I looked up into her blushing face, her eyes shining with a wave of emotions about to break. "Emily, will you marry me?"

She collapsed into the chair, her hat held over her face, as she shook with silent sobs. Then in a flood of relief poured out and she wailed, a primal cry from deep in her soul. I stood feeling uncomfortable and awkward, holding a handkerchief out to her. She dried her eyes then stared quietly at me for what seemed an age … then a tiny twinkle touched her eyes and she said, "Yes!" Rising to her feet, she kissed me softly but shyly on the cheek.

I held her in a warm hug as her shoulders pressed in against mine.

Finally, she picked up her gloves while searching my face again. "We must go. I think it must almost be time for them to return!"

I took out my watch "It's actually only ten past eleven. I will call over to your house later this afternoon to ask your father for your hand in marriage. Will you be there?"

"Thank you; I can only apologise in advance for his behaviour." Then she half-smiled. "Thank you again for today," she said while fitting her gloves.

"Hopefully I can see you again in a few days to discuss our plans?"

"That would be wonderful." Emily looked a little more relaxed, smiling at the thought of making plans. "How do I look? She looked up at me, one hand holding my waist.

"Like a beautiful young woman!" I replied, my body warming with desire at the closeness of her.

"Not too young I hope," she said, smiling more warmly. "Hopefully we can pull this off without the authorities finding out my age."

"We will make out you are twenty-one, of legal age. You might need to convince your father on a good day to go through with the ceremony and sign the registry. No-one will question it if he signs the papers."

"Leave him to Mother."

"Why not sit again for a few minutes, it has seemed a long time waiting to see you. We have not talked much." We both sat and turned our attention to each other. "The clerk is a relative of one of the lads I play football with. I will ask him to officiate the marriage to witness it is legitimate."

"I will wear Mother's evening shoes and a mature-looking dress," she said, her face lighting up cheerfully. "Father would rather die than suffer this shame." A flash of determination passed over her face again.

"Harry … he will agree."

"Our family have already suffered the shame of an illegitimate child in court."

"Really? Who with!?"

"James fathered a child a few years back in '88 and Emma

three years ago. Much like us – a romance at Ellen and John's wedding party, letting her hair down a little. She was younger than you ... Mother kept the secret as long as she could."

"How did they conceal the baby?"

"Mother, along with a friend, delivered him at home … after losing James' son William, Mother decided to bring him up this time in the house with the other children. She managed to keep it quiet, but word got out and they ended up in court anyway. The father of the child agreed to pay for support, which was all very well till she met John Dalton last year and they spoke of marriage. He did not want to bring up another man's child, so Ellen has taken him on. She has not managed yet to have a child, but loves caring for everyone else's. She seems strict, but loves them dearly."

"How is it she has not yet had children?" I paused, thinking of practical Ellen, married at just twenty-one to that weasel John Wadsworth.

"It was rather a sad story actually. Her husband was forty-one and concealed the fact that a year before he had skipped to Australia, abandoning his wife and four children. What a cunning …" I held my tongue. "He got justice, being jailed for stealing. Ellen had the perfect opportunity to divorce him, and escaped here to Martinborough where she met and married John Blissett."

Emily looked slightly concerned.

"Goodness, it is complicated … Oh, look at the time, your family will be home any minute."

We stood up as she picked up her things. "It is a lovely day out, I will see you shortly."

I stood holding the gate open as she passed, squeezing my arm on her way, not turning to look back as she disappeared out of sight.

I strolled home and, on entering the lounge, pulled up a chair and stared at the floor rug. I lit one cigarette after another, deep in thought, seeing the face of that surly old man. I found a slice of lamb in the safe; put it between two slabs of fresh bread; felt a little brighter and braced myself at the laughter that announced the family's arrival. Presently, the front door opened as the family poured in from church. Mother looked me up and down.

"Look at you all dressed up. Where are you off to?"

"I am just out for afternoon tea with some friends."

Suddenly everyone was silent. I looked around at their searching faces. "What have I said?"

Ellen went over and threw open two windows. "You could almost give it away by all the smoke in here."

Everyone laughed. "It's alright, little brother, we know. Mary told us about it. How did it go?"

"Really? Am I not entitled to a little privacy? This is the problem, living so close," I said, turning to them all.

"The short answer to that, Harry, is No," Mary said, smiling down at me. Everyone laughed again. "We all love you and support you in the same way you have supported us."

I pulled out my cigarette case and fumbled around for my matches again, but Mother put her hand on my arm and kissed me on the forehead. "Let's sit; we'll have a cup of tea."

"I'm sorry," said Mary, "but I knew that everyone would be sympathetic."

I shifted in my chair while they all sat silently as if waiting for the start of an opera. Mary made up a tray while Mother carefully listened.

"We spoke this morning and I am dressed up to go and ask her father for her hand in marriage. Please do not let this get out before we have settled things, or reveal that I am anything other than happily in love, or to that effect."

Mother looked as though I would say more. "We get on well.

She is lovely. I could do worse."

"Harry, we will make the excuse that we just wanted a small intimate ceremony."

Mary glanced at the mantel clock. "What time do you have to be there?"

I pulled out my pocket watch just to check. "In half an hour."

"Good, it gives us time to have a quick sherry before you go, it might give you a little courage … Mary, leave that, he has to go in a few minutes."

Ellen jumped up and grabbed the decanter, poured eight small glasses, which was even enough for a tiny, sweet taste for young Louisa and Joe. Once Ellen had given out the tray of glasses, Mother took a glass. "At this rate Louisa will be married by the end of the year!"

Everyone laughed, except Louisa, who looked at Mother and blushed indignantly. "Mother!"

"Here is to my dear boy Harry … To Harry and Emily, another family to be … another wedding celebration."

Everyone cheered and lifted their glasses. "To Harry and Emily!"

I looked about at all the smiling faces. "Thank you, everyone. I had not expected your support, it shows me how many things we have struggled through as a family. There is one more toast I wish to make before all the sherry in our glasses has evaporated, and that is to Father. Mr Gladstone."

Everyone laughed affectionately, rose to their feet in respect and lifted up their glasses. "To Mr Gladstone!"

One by one the family came to give me a hug or a kiss of congratulations. We talked for a while then I looked at my watch. Where had the time vanished? As I climbed into my saddle to leave, it felt incredible to see the whole family come out, their faces filled with both delight and concern as they waved me off. By the time I arrived at the little cottage, it was already a quarter past one and I slid my watch away and tied Lotti to the fence. The sherry had calmed my nerves slightly, giving me courage as I went to the solid Kauri door and tapped the cast iron knocker. It was an immaculate little weatherboard cottage with fruit trees on one side and a neat vegetable garden.

Mr Linders opened the door, his square jaw grim as he stood straight and stiff, his big hands braced by his sides.

"You have a nerve showing your face around here."

"Good afternoon, Mr Linders. I would like to speak with you."

"There's nothing good about it. Say what you came to say and leave. I will not invite you into my house again, after lying to my face."

Annie Linders quietly came up, and put her hand on his shoulder to gently entreat him, saying, "Thomas, invite the young man in; this is about our daughter's life!"

"Quiet, woman! Keep out of it!" he said, pushing her away violently.

"I insist on one thing … an apology from you."

I faced Mr Linders and locked eyes with him, as I had as a child facing a stubborn goat. I decided to say what he needed to hear.

"… you are right, sir … I'm sorry for lying to you … both."

He glared at me then reluctantly stepped to one side as Annie said, "Please come in, Harry, and sit down."

"I would rather stand." I remained rooted to the doorstep and looked at her expectant face in the shadow. "I only need a few minutes of your time. You are under no illusion as to my visit. Unfortunately, we didn't get off on the right foot."

"You're right about that."

"Sir, I am here to ask for your daughter's hand in marriage."

"Harry Bagust, but for my daughter's sake, I would cut you out of our lives completely and give you a darn good beating.

This black cloud of shame with your bastard child our daughter is carrying is unforgivable. If not for my wife's constraint, you'd be suffering still. You think that your fancy clothes and smooth talk can wash away what you have done? What sort of man are you? You had two opportunities to tell me the truth, now I have had to ask for an apology."

I looked at Annie as I said "It has not been an easy thing to grapple with. The thought of being married, or becoming a father so soon. I had many plans; it has been quite an adjustment."

I watched his shoulders inflate. "An adjustment for you!" he bellowed. "I have no choice but to allow this union and you follow through immediately with this marriage. Firstly, I have certain demands. That you be married within a week – we are not paying for a ceremony – you will have to register at the marriage office. Also, you will not take our daughter away from here: Annie wishes to be near the child.

I watched as my hand stretched across the divide as my neck bristled with irritation "I will agree to that." He left my hand hanging for what seemed a long time, ignoring it like a dirty rag. Leaning forward, he spat out, "A week from now … It remains to be seen. I will not shake your hand until it is sealed in ink".

I coolly dropped my hand and turned my face away, concentrating on Mrs Linders. "I will arrange a dinner with my mother so we can meet formally."

"That would be most welcome, Harry. Thank you."

"I will inform you when I have the arrangements finalised for the marriage registration," I said matter-of-factly. "Good day!"

Tipping my hat, I turned and walked away to my horse, and had almost climbed into the stirrups when a flurry of steps came bounding toward me, calling. "Harry!"

Emily rushed up, and kissed me on the lips with affection, then, embracing me in a warm hug, whispered in my ear, "We had better make it look authentic."

As I looked over her shoulder, her father turned sour in disgust. Her mother stood behind him smiling contentedly in the half light.

I held Emily's hand. "I will contact you in a few days to go over the details. Would you like to meet me in town so we can make prior arrangements at the registry office together?"

"I would like that. Will you finish early tomorrow?"

"I can do that if old Paddy will let me off the ploughing – he's getting ready to sow. I will come at 12:30. Perhaps we could have lunch?"

To my delight, her face lit up with a warm smile that reminded me of the first time I had taken her hand that night on the dance floor.

"That would be lovely, thank you."

"Emily, get in here now!" her father growled.

Chapter 16

Storm in a Tea Cup

Turning toward the Raumaunga River, I rode away from Emily's house to clear my thoughts beside the flowing water. At the river bank, I tied Lotti to a branch beside the pure clear water; washed my face and cupped my hands to drink then sighed, feeling more refreshed. *How many of life's joys and sorrows, like mine, has this river witnessed flowing down through generations of tumult and upheaval.*

Absently, I selected a handful of smooth flat stones, thinking of Father who, when I was a little boy, had showed us how to make them lightly skip across the surface of the stream. It was always fierce competition with us boys, counting the skips … He was a man of few words, and I wished he was here now. He might have patted me on the back, saying, "Son, it will all work out." I thought of visiting Jack.

I picked up a heavy rock in frustration, almost symbolically hurling it into a deep dark pool on the bend. It caused a high splash that sent ripples across a calm eddy … "How far are these ripples going to go?" I shouted into the bush, then kicked the stones.

It is now so entangled … must I really cast aside my dream? Perhaps Ellen is right: forget Euphemia and settle down without looking back … but I still need to tell her. Euphemia, I will try again to write to you, confess the mess I've caused … How will you ever understand? Young Maggie is almost the same age as Emily …

I sat on a warm rock, desperately searching for another solution.

Emily is determined to be free, yet she said she would not hold me to her. Perhaps in time, there may be a glimmer of hope for Euphemia and me. Perhaps a river will sometimes choose another course ... it may just take a little longer.

A few days later, I met Emily outside the Royal Hotel, dressed in my new jacket. She looked radiant as I escorted her to our lunch table and eased out her chair. Smiling, we sat together.

"How are you? You look very handsome in that suit. I am used to seeing you in that black singlet on the field, battling that dusty plough behind the big old Clydesdale."

"Thank you. I am well. You look lovely too. Have you been well?"

"Not if it includes throwing up two or three times a day out in the freezing outhouse. Look at how much weight I've lost."

"Yes, I can see. I have not had to suffer that. Your cheeks are thin."

"How are the two lots of newlyweds going?"

"Emma and John are doing well and settling into married life at Ellen's. Mary and Jack seem happy even though they are squeezed into his parents. Actually, my brother James is talking of coming this way as well. He has his bankruptcy hearing coming up and has been warned to vacate his flat, which he typically is not taking lying down."

"What is his wife's name?"

"Margaret. She is very patient with him."

"Harry, I know you must get back to work. I have been thinking a lot about our meeting today. I wanted to be very direct with you. Are you sure this is what you want? ... that you want to go ahead with this union. It is not too late to withdraw."

"I will follow my commitment; I have given my word."

"But I know you would rather be with Euphemia in Auckland or in Coromandel digging for gold." She looked at me intently.

I put my tanned hand across Emily's white fingers. "I told you I want to be there for our child. I thought we could rent a little cottage over the hill away from your parents if you like?"

"Couldn't we go to the gold fields together, then we will be right away. I know when the baby is born, Mother and Father will try to control my every move!"

"It is no place for a mother and child. The conditions are shocking, filled with every rat that crawled out of a gutter. Mud up to your arm pits. It's nothing like conditions you have ever seen. Dirt floors, freezing in winter with the wind whistling through cracks in the walls where mice roam freely, dust billows off stampers crashing twenty-four hours a day. If you are serious though, I will take you up there and show you once I settle in. I will send support for you but I will be away for months at a time. It will not be easy as you will be on your own here!"

"That will be bearable. I will meet young mothers in Wellington and have the perfect excuse for you being away. In time, I can follow my dream of moving to Australia in a few years perhaps. Melbourne sounds a thrilling city to be in. They have horse-drawn trams with luxurious hotels. Perhaps you could even visit us there?"

I hesitated. "Let's not get too far ahead of ourselves. One step at a time. Let's see how things go."

Many times, I have wished to write to Euphemia, but the words seem lost in a fog at sea, drifting further away with each new day. I will leave it till things have settled a little. Her sister Barbara must be very ill ... Perhaps she will last till the next match in Parnell.

We talked for hours, finally taking tea before leaving for home. The date had been set for the 5th of July in the registry office, which was as old man Linders had hoped – only days away. I was now ready to face him. Mother had fussed over my suit, pressing my trousers to have them looking sharp. She had made up a special bouquet of flowers with a corsage to take to Emily for the wedding event and had roses for our lapels. She took my arm as we went down the street to the registry office, looking at me with pride, despite our circumstances.

Emily looked lovely in her new pink dress and her hair decorated in a half circle of dried flowers. I took her hand as she stepped down off the carriage, her mother behind her. The ladies chatted outside for a few minutes before the official called us in. Mr Linders stood silently, his hands behind his back, his pursed lips, not uttering a word.

We signed all the papers and the attendant did not query Emily's age. Mother was excited and insisted that we kiss. She had invited everyone over for early drinks, a small celebration to mark the occasion. Mr Linders was as cold as the icy day. I predicated an entire bottle of stiff malt couldn't thaw him out.

After only minutes, we were standing in the sunlight on the street again, this time as husband and wife. I had never imagined being married so young even if it was a sham, but life had a way of throwing a few punches along the way. When there's a fork in the road, there often aren't that many choices on which direction to choose.

I helped Emily up into the carriage alongside Mother before taking the reins and sending the horses into a trot.

The sweet smell of freshly baked cake and biscuits filled the house, and buntings hung from the lamps. There was a small table with a few gifts on it for us and a glorious bunch of red roses.

If it had not been for the girls, who had surprised us and decorated the house to celebrate, it might have been a most formal affair as Mr Linders was as cold as a steel bucket of ice water on a winter's morning.

Mother called out and tapped on a glass, calling everyone to quiet.

"Thank you to both Mr and Mrs Linders for coming today to celebrate the newest members of our family. We look forward to getting to know you a little more in due course, and also to the pitter-patter of little feet soon enough. Harry, James has written a message as he thought he might not be here, but he made it anyway. It reads. "Congratulations, I owe you ten bob." I suppose you know what that means."

"He made me a bet about six months ago."

"Never thought that bet would come in so quickly, little brother. I owe you because I can't pay it right now."

I laughed: *That'd be right.*

"Well, perhaps he is as surprised as I am. It is only July and we have celebrated three weddings already, perhaps there is something in the water here in Martinborough. John could not be here as he is still in Timaru and your sister Martha could not make it either. I am sorry James, my husband, could not be here. He would have welcomed you all into our family. So today on behalf of my husband, I welcome you, Emily, and wish you both all the happiness and good health. Let us raise our glasses to Mr and Mrs Bagust!"

Everyone chorused, "To Mr and Mrs Bagust!" and raised their glasses.

"Please, Mr Linders, would you like to reply?"

He stood rather sternly, looking about the room at all the strangers' bright faces.

"It has been a storm in a teacup for our small family to be here today. We did not expect our Emily to marry at this time in her life so soon out of school. We are content with the outcome and give thanks to everyone who arranged for this small celebration today. I am sure in time, I will accept my daughter's plight and her marriage to your son but, to be honest, it has not been easy for me. If not for my wife, I would not have attended today."

We all stood awkwardly waiting for him to propose a toast which did not come. Luckily, James stepped forward, having already consumed a little beer, shouting, "Drink up, everyone! It is not every day you get free beer and food on Harry's slate." Everyone laughed, almost out of relief. I tapped my glass and the room quieted again.

"If you have something in your glass, I would firstly like to say how beautiful my bride looks today, and Mrs Linders too. Also thank you for allowing us to celebrate in your home, Ellen; and for the decorations the girls have studiously arranged and finding flowers at this time of year. It's a delightful surprise under the circumstances to have brother James here; it's like seeing a Moa, a rare sighting indeed."

Everyone laughed.

James called out, "I wouldn't miss it."

"I would like to raise a toast to the bride and Mrs Linders as well as to my father who would have been here if he could."

We all lifted our glasses and cheered, "Here, here!"

"Thank you also to Mr Linders for giving permission for this wedding to go ahead. Thank you for the gifts, and to all of you for your delight in celebrating this day. Please stay for tea and cake. We will take our leave now, but we will catch up with you all in a few days' time.

We went around talking to and thanking everyone except Thomas, who sat like a stone in an armchair by himself. Annie was having a few laughs with the girls and seemed to enjoy her time with Mother. I took Emily's hand, announcing our departure again before climbing into the carriage and waving goodbye to all on the front veranda as we drove away.

"Well done, Harry. That was wonderful. You speak well in front of people."

"It's not hard. How do you think your father will get on with all the family?"

"I think they will get away quickly. Where are *we* off to?"

"I called on Louie at The Commercial Hotel in Lampton Quay last week to give us a room for a week till we could find lodgings in the city. There is no room for us to stay with Ellen — they have a full house with everyone home. I'm not sure how Mother and James will get on as their relationship has been acrimonious at the best of times. They will have to work it out eventually."

"He has no choice, so he will have to make peace, I suppose."

"James came over for the wedding and to bring a load of things after being forced out of his flat in Pirie Street. He was forced into bankruptcy last month. He has been advertising since the 15th of June trying to find someone to take over the lease."

"Still, it was good that he came."

"He had little choice. Joe took our cart over the hill to Wellington to pick up Margaret with their few personal effects … That reminds me: did you pack a decent bag?"

"Yes, just like you said," she said, smiling. "So have James and Margaret not got anything?"

"The debtors had cleaned him out like ants cleaning off a bone, leaving him angry and completely broken. He had to relinquish his carriage and the two horses so arrived in town with nothing. I managed to secure him a little work on a farm with a flax business with one of the local families here. He says he will get a good dog to try farming for a while, and take young Joe under his wing."

"Joe is a lovely young man. I was so ashamed of Father not doing a toast, but I think it was perfect the way James broke the ice."

"Broke the ice is right. It was a good thing we had the fire roaring or we'd all have been frozen like statues."

Emily giggled and held her hand to her mouth. "Ice

sculptures," she said, then laughed again. We sat laughing out of relief as much as anything.

The time went quickly as, chatting together, we wound our way over the hill. Once we were settled, we went about enquiring about lodgings and in a few days found a small cottage in Te-Aro, renting it from an elderly lady who had moved in with her son. Mrs Gravens needed someone to help look after her house and gardens after having a fall. She was delighted at the thought of having a wee baby with new life in the house again as she told us of her life in the neighbourhood.

Jack heard of our marriage from one of the stable hands, so we received our first package. It was a beautiful vase, matching wash bowl and jug, exquisitely wrapped in a red ribbon with a card.

"Look, Harry, there's a letter. Do you want me to read it?"

"Yes, of course!"

"*Congratulations to you, Harry and Emily. You do not waste any time. Good for you. I wish you all the success you both deserve. I know this gift is very practical. If I remember rightly your jug and wash bowl were looking a little the worse for wear.*

Harry, I heard you were ploughing and wondered if you would like a little employment with a decent wage. I remember you telling me about heading into the gold country. I have a large contract to supply horses up in Coromandel, at Ohinimuri and Kuaotunu – they are the packies from fields nine and ten, along with a few I've acquired.

You might find it interesting in light of moving up that way.

Perhaps you could see what opportunities there are with a report back, killing two birds with one stone."

"The clever bugger! He must have had this partially worked out when I was there. This could be a good opportunity to check things out."

"Harry, after the many stories I have heard, it would be an interesting place to see. I'll read on.

"They are pulling colossal loads into remote areas, feeding the many stampers with huge loads of coal, machinery and supplies from the ports. They haul up over hellish deep mud-filled roads to the mountains. It's not easy work, but it's a good contract as they're using teams of 6, 8 and sometimes 20 horses at a time. I am in the process of supplying coal up there too as they have an insatiable thirst for coal up in the Karangahake and Paeroa mines. There are up to 400 horses in a day sometimes making the perilous journey. The price of everything is through the roof. I had an idea of delivering coal for so much a ton. If you are keen, you could oversee a few teams of men there for a set fee. You'll do well. It will be ongoing if you are interested as the number of steam-driven engines, timber trains and pumps are growing by the day. You are probably aware there are over a hundred coal-fired stamping batteries up there. The ore roasting ovens are hungry beasts, consuming coal 24 hours a day.

You will be surprised by the silence on Sundays when stampers cease, It is almost deafening. They've stripped the bush of Matai, Totara and Kauri to burn but coal is hotter which is needed to soften the quartz by roasting before it's crushed. This is all good for me as I have already bought a ship to run coal from the west coast into Thames – remember, I told you to diversify. I have excellent clients, and I told them I have a good man who could deliver the horses as early as next week. The superintendent at the Martha mine is desperate for his shipment so I will need you to contact me as soon as you can to confirm. I will have another ready to go, just as soon as you can return as I have been advertising far and wide for good packies. You can call me now through the exchange at the post office as I have recently fitted a new telephone at the house. We can work out the details over the telephone, just ask the exchange lady for Jack Lane at Island Bay – they will put you through. Come over for dinner with

176

your new bride before you leave … we will play a few hands.
I look forward to hearing some of your stories and your plans.
Regards,
Jack Lane."

Emily folded up the letter, looking at me warily. I pulled out a cigarette. "I didn't expect this so quickly. It's a lot to take in. Will you go?"

"It's a fine opportunity. The boys could all come up too. How do you feel about it?"

"It's what you wished for! I cannot stand in your way. It seems like the perfect opportunity."

"I would be back before you know it."

"I look forward to meeting him. He sounds like an interesting fellow."

"I will ring him. We could plan to go out this coming Saturday perhaps. Have you used a telephone?"

She nodded. "Yes. I called my aunt in Auckland last week from the exchange."

"James had one fitted at the house. It seemed incredible to talk to someone in a completely different place through an electrical cable."

I suddenly thought of Euphemia in Auckland. *I could telephone her somehow … It seems too long until October when we play the next big match. It must only be half a day to Auckland from the Coromandel … I could visit her directly from there.*

"I will get hold of Jack and find out the details."

Chapter 17

Time to Face the Music

Jack had the steamer booked for our journey to the Coromandel and hoped for a smooth sailing. He sent two of his men to assist us with loading and unloading as it took us a few days to deliver the horses into holding pens at the docks. We loaded the horses onto the steamer and into narrow single stalls in the bow of the ship. A second shipment for Thames was due on our return, giving us a good chance to observe what was happening in the area, before we tried our fortunes. Rusty was excited at the prospect of lady luck coming our way.

"I've heard some rumours about *Try Fluke* mine being a good starting place in Kuaotunu."

"I've heard the same thing. Johnny thinks he will join us up there, so we plan to pick him up from Wellington on our second trip. He is ready to move after he plays his last few games for the season in Timaru."

"It will be good to see Johnny again. He's been playing well by the news articles I've read. How is Emily? Did you get a letter off to Euphemia yet?" Rusty asked.

"I've sat down twice to write to her but I just end up throwing them in the fire. Emily is quite content; we even had a cuddle before I left."

"Oh well, I guess you'll find the words soon enough. I can't believe we are finally bound for the goldfields; it seemed like it would never happen."

"It's going to be a good trip. We will call in to Thames after stopping at the small settlement of Kuaotunu where Jack tells us we might have to swim the horses ashore as the harbour is shallow. If the weather is foul, we may have to take them ashore over the hill in Mercury Bay."

"I don't fancy swimming at this time of year."

"Come on, Rusty. Didn't you grow up walking through the snow in bare feet to school?

"Seems a long time ago now, laddie."

"I was lying in bed last night thinking about what a great opportunity this is. Jack has the horses and coal. Why don't we set ourselves up with a few teams and contract to him? We could get James and Joe running some teams of horses too. With all their cabbie experience, it could be a great business."

"It'd be better than digging holes in the dark. Why did we not think of it earlier!"

"I'm sure Jack would love the idea. I will send him a wire from Thames once we've checked it all out."

Three weeks later, we headed back to Wellington for the next shipment, and were glad when we entered the Cook Strait, and rounded Pencarrow Head into the harbour. Our scouting journey had been a great success, confirming Kuaotunu as a growing settlement with marvellous opportunities. Jack had promised to advertise all over the country for suitable horses.

"Rusty, it will take time for us to team the horses up in groups of six or eight. We'll have to break in the younger horses, harnessing them to work together."

"Do you know how to break them in together?"

"I've watched them on the estate. Once the lead horse is found, they are shackled together hauling increased burdens around the farm to prepare them for hauling colossal loads through the hills and deep mud. Many will be horses from smaller farms used to pulling only a single plow alone. I will let you go ahead to make a start as I need to get back to Emily first. The lads at Island Bay will show you the ropes."

I had been preoccupied with a strange urgency to see Emily, wondering how she had faired in my absence. As we docked, I immediately took a cab to the house, surprised by my anticipation of seeing her. I ran up the steps calling as I entered the front door. I noticed immediately the dark house was filled with a fusty damp smell.

"Emily, I am home!"

She called out faintly from the bedroom and as I opened the door, I could only make out a shape under the covers in the half light. Her face was gaunt, full of utter distress as she wrapped her arms around me; she clung to me tightly as she sobbed in my arms. I could feel by her bony shoulders she had lost a lot of weight.

"What is it? What has happened?"

"I've lost the baby! I woke up last week, discovering a discharge in my night dress. I went to see Doctor Stevens after I had cleaned myself up, and he said I had miscarried."

"Oh, Emily, I am so sorry! Have you told anyone?

"I cannot face anyone. I am just so sad! I've cried myself to sleep for days, waking with a prayer. It is all a terrible nightmare."

"How could you suffer this alone. Do your parents know?"

"No. If only I could speak with Mother alone. He will not let her out of his sight. I know for sure I'm not welcome there. Besides, the thought of going over the hill even to see Mary was too horrid to conceive. It's such a long journey."

I opened the drapes a little as the sunlight emblazoned the room, revealing Emily's pale thin face, dark sunken eyes, which were bloodshot and puffy from crying.

"I didn't know what to do! I have no one to turn to. I just stayed in bed."

"Have you eaten?"

"I didn't feel like making any food. I feel like running away from everything." She threw herself on me again, her head buried in my chest, and sobbed uncontrollably.

"Here, lay down. Try to calm down. You look so pale. I will put some eggs on, maybe you will feel a little better … Let me first make tea."

"We have no eggs. I had not managed to set up the chicken coop, and there's no milk. I could not face going out."

I filled a cup of water. "Here, you must keep up your fluids. I will put on a fire; it's freezing in here. Would you like a hot bath?"

The firebox was empty, and the meat safe, and, except for half a loaf of mouldy bread, the cupboard was bare. *This is shocking. She needs food now!*

"I think I'll go for a walk and pick up a few eggs, fresh bread and butter," I said, grabbing my coat. "I won't be long!"

"No! Please don't leave again. I can't bear to be alone … what if you meet someone? You might tell them about the baby?"

I opened windows and the back door to ventilate the rooms, then tucked her back down under the quilt.

"There is no cut wood. I am just out the back. The door is open."

I went down the back steps, out to the little lean-to where I had stacked logs. I sat on the chopping block trying to gather my thoughts; I lit a cigarette and absently rolled the packet of matches around in my fingers. My mind raced … *What to do. Perhaps she could go to her aunt's in Auckland? I am away for months on end …*

Could she come away with me? It's no place for a woman in a bush hut with mud floors. I cannot believe that, with five sisters, I do not know what to do!

What of our baby? I must banish thoughts of the baby for now! … I feel like I'm in the middle of a paddock in a dense morning fog with no clear path. Ellen would say: Harry, it's time to face the music. Pull yourself together.

I had cut quite a pile of kindling and split an armload of wood before it suddenly came to me. I threw down the axe and gathered enough blocks to hurriedly make a fire. I remembered my sister-in-law Margaret had been staying with her family a few streets away. I could quickly run over there, see if she was still around. *She'll know what to do! She'll be a wonderful support to Emily.*

Within minutes, I had the coal range warming up the room, enough to open a few more windows to invite the fresh air in.

On my way in, I noticed a beautiful spray of the last fresh white blooms on a standard rose in the front yard. Moving briskly, I took a knife and cut a bunch, arranged it badly in Jack's vase by Emily's bed. I stroked her head whispering, "I will just pop to the general store for a few things. I'll be back soon."

She lay in silence.

I walked briskly along the street then over the hill to Margaret's family home, praying she was still there. She had planned to stay with her family for a few weeks after James stayed in Martinborough for work.

The house was built on the high side of the road, giving it a commanding view of the valley. I was a little out of breath by the time I entered the front gate but relieved to see Margaret on the front porch in the sun. She stood up while calling out, "What a pleasant surprise! You're back! What are you doing here?"

She held me by the shoulders at the top of the stairs. "Are you ok?" I kissed her on the cheek. "I cannot stay. Em is not good! We've lost the baby! I came quickly to see if you could help … maybe visit Emily later."

Margaret looked in shock. "No! Dear God! When?" She threw her arms around me. "Harry, I'm so sorry." Looking at my distress, she motioned for me to sit.

"I don't know for sure … a week? She is very thin."

"I would be happy to go and see her. Ernest has his afternoon nap soon, at around twelve. I will get him settled so Mother can mind him."

"I'm not sure what to do? I arrived home this morning to find her inconsolable, in a state of depression. It's a day's ride to Mother. Emily doesn't want to go out or anywhere near her father. She has not been out of the house in a week. She's lost so much weight. I told her I was going out for eggs and bread."

"Harry! I meant to call in … I should have followed my heart. The last time I saw her, she seemed so happy; I had no idea."

"I must get back."

"Wait a minute." She rushed inside and I heard her moving hurriedly about the kitchen; she returned with a paper bag, in it fresh eggs, a piece of loaf, bacon, two tomatoes and a small jar of milk.

"Here, this will save you being away too long. Go, I will come over at about twelve. I will call in at the dairy for a few other bits and pieces."

I found what coins I had on me and put them on the little table.

"Thanks, but you keep those."

"No, I really appreciate your help, thanks!"

She gave me a hug, waiting to see me off down the street. A wave of relief came over me with each step that drew me nearer to home. I had a feeling it was going to be a difficult week. *Perhaps Jack will have delays before we go away again…I may have to take her home.*

I arrived home to find Emily still curled in a ball under the covers, so I quietly closed the door and left her to rest while I made some eggs.

An hour later, Margaret tapped discreetly on the door. "Yoohoo!! Anyone home?" she said in a half whisper. She came in carrying an armload of fresh vegetables with a few small packets of meat, which I took from her.

"I made her some eggs on toast but she didn't eat much even though she was hungry. Go through she is in the bedroom."

As they started to talk, I could hear Emily crying, pouring out her heart while Margaret listened intently.

I listened at the door until the kettle whistled furiously, and sent me running to the stove. The tea tray looked inviting as I carried fresh biscuits and fruit cake from Marg's mother and set it down next to the bed.

Marg had pulled back all the drapes, allowing the afternoon sun to light up the room, revealing the roses shining in the window. The little room had a cast iron fireplace to one side with a small hearth, heavy drapes over the long sash windows, scrim walls with floral paper with a lovely steel-pressed ceiling. There was just enough room for a small armchair, in which Margaret now sat on the edge next to the window.

Margaret had managed to get Emily to sit up, carefully brushing her long hair, which looked golden in the sunlight.

I felt grieved to be so helpless to do anything. "You look lovely, Emily, I will put your cup here on the sideboard."

"Thank you," she said weakly, touching my hand lightly and trying to smile as I came close.

Margaret's face lit up with a flash of inspiration. "Emily, I have just had an idea. Why don't we all go over to visit your family and Mary? I will be going back next week; it would be nice to have your company. We will not tell them about the baby, you could leave that for another time. James is coming to pick us up – I think we will have room, even if Harry has to get off and walk on the steep parts," she said with a smile.

"That's a good plan. We could even stay in the hotel for a few days so you can see your mother. I know the girls would love to catch up; what do you think?"

Emily stared, deep in thought then quietly nodded, not

changing her gaze. It seemed like someone had sucked the life completely out of her.

Margaret talked about her family and a friend of hers who'd recovered from a miscarriage, then eventually rose to her feet. "I'm sorry to leave, but I really must get home. My mother has a bad hip and struggles to pick up Ernest who is getting heavy now. I will come tomorrow, and I will find out if James is due to come over on Tuesday night. I may be able to get a message to him through the post office telephone."

I waited at the door to see her off, feeling grateful for her kindness. I stoked the fire again and washed up the few dishes before going to sit with Emily.

"That was lovely for her to call in. How are you feeling?"

"I would like to see Mary and Mother. I could get a message to her to meet me at Mary's."

The next day, I posted a letter to Jack, asking for a few extra days to prepare things ready to go. Then James called in briefly on Tuesday night. He said he'd pick us up early the next day and we all headed over the hill to the Wairarapa.

We settled in for a few days at the hotel then moved into a room at Mary's. Emily spent days in bed, and even a secret meeting with her mother did not raise her spirits. When calling in one morning to help with a few house repairs, I did my best to cheer her up. Then in the afternoon I quietly crept in to check on Emily when I overheard her and Mary talking in the dining room, and froze when I picked up what Emily was saying.

"… … but the worst thing is, I didn't know when he would come back. I don't know how I will be able to wait for six or eight weeks for him to return from the goldfields, not knowing when or if he will return. The days are so long, I just feel like staying in bed."

"Emily, it is a big adjustment; only last year you were living at home while finishing school, now you are married, thinking of having a … well, you know. Give yourself a little time to adjust. I've heard pregnancy alone can affect your mental state. *I* found it hard to suddenly be married, sick with a child on the way but still expected to look after a house and a husband. Could you get involved in a group or perhaps find a little work to take your mind off it."

"Yes, I suppose I could. But that's not the problem, Mary."

I heard her chair slide out on the floor, and footsteps pacing around the kitchen. "The only reason he married me was for the baby's sake. It's all a lie now the baby's gone! … Perhaps it is for the best! I must admit I had started to like being with him but we are not meant to be together?"

"Emily, you must not think like that. You will have another baby, and will look back on this time in a whole different way."

"He has been a perfect gentleman looking after me, putting up with my parents, but he said it himself, he loves another!"

"There have been sacrifices on all sides, Emily, but he has committed himself to you. I know my brother; he will stand by his decision to be with you."

"It was a struggle to mentally prepare myself to have this baby. I was excited about it but now, there is no point keeping up the charade. My father did things that meant we were living a lie, whatever we chose together. It will be the same. I will always know that he loves another."

"Come, Emily, I think you are feeling depressed. Many women feel like this when they have a baby. It's like waking in the middle of the night, dreading all the terrible things that could happen then, in the light of day, you can hardly recall what those terrible things were."

"Mary, I am not asleep; I am awake. I might be depressed but tell me, in reality, what is my life going to look like? Next month in October, Harry is going to Auckland to play against Parnell. They plan on dropping off the horses in the Coromandel, then heading on up for the big game. Do I deny him the right to be happy? He will visit her … can I live with someone pretending to love me. I want a man who is romantically in love with me. Otherwise, what sort of life are we to live? We already spoke about separating at some point?”

“I had no idea! What would you do? … Will your parents take you back?”

“Never! so help me God! I have realised I am an independent woman. Why can I not choose for myself. I have a little savings put aside especially for this time.”

“I’m truly speechless … I have never seen you like this, it’s almost like I don’t know you.”

“Did you know the terrible things we’ve suffered at Father’s hand?”

“Not really. Even after all these years, you’ve kept them a secret.”

“Perhaps you don’t know me so well after all.”

“Emily, one thing I do know is, you have just suffered a huge loss. Don’t you think this is all a terribly rash decision. Something is going to work out. Please rest and recover. Give yourself time to think it over … By tomorrow, you may feel completely different.”

The kitchen fell silent which was my cue to quickly sneak out of the bedroom where I had been almost holding my breath, hanging on each word. The boards squeaked in the hall as I entered, making out I was coming in from the barn.

“Oh, there you are, Mary. I have just been out in the barn seeing to the horses. Is that tea still hot?” I took a chunk of cake and poured myself a cup of tea. “How are things?”

“Emily was just here. It’s not good, brother.”

“Oh, is she awake?”

“She’s gone for a walk along the river. She is very unhappy.”

I sat down, feigned surprise. “I do not know what to do to

help her get over everything."

She stood apprehensive while wiping down the bench. "Leave her for a few days. It is just going to take time, brother. I will speak to her again tomorrow. Right now, I need to start preparing supper. Could you bring in a little wood for me."

"Yes, sure. I am heading over to Ellen's in the morning before sunrise. James and I are going hunting in the hills for the day. We will be back before nightfall. Do you think I should go?"

"It might be good for you to just get away. I think Emily will be alright."

"Rusty's friend is coming with a couple of hunting dogs; we might come back with some wild pig. I will sleep in the lounge so as not to wake anyone."

"Good for you, brother. I will try to talk with Emily while you're away, hopefully, she is feeling a little better each day. Emotions can be in turmoil after a loss like this."

I went out to the woodshed, feeling stunned, and sat in the dark unable to process all that had been said. *I should feel elated at the possibility of being set free, but I have become fond of Emily. All these weeks believing I would be a father! Was it all a lie? Couldn't it work? We just need a little more time.*

That night, I took a blanket and lay on the lounge rug, mesmerised by the orange flicker of flames in the firelight on the walls. I lay trying to make sense of it all. *Could Emily come to Auckland? Where would we stay in Coromandel? Wouldn't she be even more out of her comfort in a remote town filled with miners, stampers running day and night.* I must have drifted off because when I woke, I counted four strikes on the mantle clock. I jumped up and slipped on my clothes in the dark. Creeping into Emily, I kissed her on the head and grabbed my oil skin coat. She stirred slightly but did not wake. I rode over to Ellen's and found James already sitting on the back step smoking his pipe, waiting for Mark, his neighbour, to arrive.

"Ready, Harry? It will be good to do a spot of hunting, it's a long spell since I tracked anything in the wild. How's Emily? Sounds like she is not too good."

"She will come right I think, but it was lovely to have Margaret call the other day. She's a fine girl."

A slight breeze blew in from the northeast, so we headed up on the south side to throw our scent. The orange sun came up with a little swept cloud as we crept our way through the bush in the half-light. Suddenly, towards late morning, the dogs caught a scent and took off through the dense bush. We ran trying to keep up with the dogs, and passed a clearing of freshly dug ground, busted rotting logs and muddy hoof marks. We followed the trail until we could hear the dogs now excitedly barking at the bailed-up pig. He was a beauty, thrashing about to defend himself with his two long tusks. One dog had locked onto his throat and hung on like a rider on an out-of-control horse as he swung every which way to free himself. As the pig squealed, Mark leapt on his back and, in one movement, ran his knife round its throat, holding its head back while he fought back. Suddenly we noticed one of the dogs had a nasty gash on its cheek, blood spurting out profusely.

"Bugger, it looked like we were going to get away unscathed. Harry, can you pick him up? I will need both of you to hold him still while I try to stitch it up." He pulled out a curved needle with a length of thread, and deftly stitched the wound to slow the loss of blood.

"James, can you clean the pig? I will carry the carcass if you could carry my dog." We cleaned out the carcass and Mark slung it over his back, happy to head for home before darkness set in completely.

"Pork roast, men! Nice for a change. Do you think he'll be alright?"

"Yeah, he'll recover … the other dogs will lick his wound."

"Well done, Mark. Looks like we will be home for supper after all."

We made our way to Ellen's, defying the dusk. On nearing the house, we could just make out in the light, the girls aimed toward us, their expectant faces not a reflection of our prize.

Mary made straight for me through the paddock, her troubled face confirming something was awry. Catching her breath, she was first to voice her fear.

Chapter 18

Going Off Half Cocked

"Mary, what is it? What's happened?"

"Harry … she's gone! Emily's gone."

"What! Where?" I stood stiff with disbelief.

"She's run away!" Mary handed me a note. "Come inside. You can read this note she left on your bed."

I suddenly felt the blood rush to my feet as I held the letter up and tried to read it in the fading light. We slipped off our boots and I sat in the kitchen.

My Dearest Harry

Please forgive me, I have decided to spare us both the pain of a marriage based on commitment only. It's too similar to a life I have already endured. Thank you for all the tenderness you showed me, your little kiss this morning in the dark was sweet. I feel like a caged bird set free, determined in my heart to set us both free. I dispatched a wire for a berth aboard a ship bound for New South Wales this morning. If my coach arrives on time I will sail later tonight. We could have made it work! Who knows, perhaps I am a foolish woman, but as you know, I proposed someday to liberate myself. Making a fresh start now seems as good a time as any.

I beg you not to search for me; I have changed my name.

I will always be grateful to you and your wonderful family

I smashed my fist on the Kauri table repeatedly. "Why? Why! … It could have worked!" I braced myself across the table trying desperately to gather my thoughts. Then I pulled out my watch … *quarter past four.* "James, can I borrow your horse?"

The whole family had stood frozen like statues.

James spoke up. "You're going off halfcocked, lad. You'll *never* make that ship. She's flown the coop, long gone by the time you arrive."

"I have to try!"

"It's a day's journey; you have barely three hours of light, man!"

I shouted at him, as much as at myself. "What if the coach has broken down? What if the ship is held up? What if she changes her mind at the last minute, waiting on the lonely docks." I looked around at everyone. "What if she just needs me to be there?! I could not live with myself if I had not done all I could to save her." Then I thought, *if I had stayed, I could have spent that time with her."*

Ellen suddenly flew into action about the kitchen, wrapping a piece of meat in a cloth with a small loaf of bread.

"Joe, run – get James' horse ready, a blanket, and his saddle bag. Saddle the horse, throw feed into a small bag."

Joe sprinted out the door. She had her boney hand gripped on my neck

"Harry, I agree you must go! Ride like the wind, brother; do all that you propose in your heart. Take a bag with clothes. Stay safe. You must try; there is no other option."

Mother held my arm "She is right, son. You can but try. Be careful."

I hugged them both then ran to the stable where Joe was fitting the last strap. I checked the saddle bags, strapped on the bed roll … packed flint, paper, and billy. I had felt exhausted from the day, but now my body was charged with fire. I tossed water on my face, thrust on my hat, and hurled myself into the saddle.

"Thanks, Joe. I will see you soon."

The afternoon was clear and warm as the breeze had died off. It was going to be a clear night with a good moon. I almost forgot and, swinging the horse around, faced the bewildered faces standing on the porch.

Mary ran out. "Harry, if you see her, tell her, *'You are courageous and beautiful, I will always treasure our close friendship'.*"

"Thanks, everyone. I will see you all soon." I gave them a wave. "Come on, Coal, let's go, boy!"

I felt charged in my body but my mind was ablaze. I tried not to push Coal, but he must have sensed my anxiety, setting a steady pace. As the moon rose, he laboured, traversing the steep track he had routinely crossed. I passed a young bushman who had not seen any carts broken-down and wished me Godspeed. As we came down the hill into the valley, the distant curve of the bay in the morning light stood out clearly and I strained for a glimpse of smoke or lanterns from the steamer mast. At a distance, I searched the harbour full of sailing ships but as we drew nearer, only small steamers were offloading cargo. I finally rode in, immediately tying up the horse and staggering to the nearest gang of men, my legs reviving as I looked in all directions for a lonely lost soul.

"Been any ships leaving for Sydney today?"

"Ah! Is that you, Harry? Don't look so worried, laddie."

"Mac! I didn't recognise you. Have you shaved your beard?"

"Mis's git sick of it, geen er a rash on her fice," he said laughing. Yea 'ad a lass run oat, 'ave yea!"

"Something like that Mac … Sydney!"

"It's well goon, laddie."

I waved and jogged to the tea house, searching frantically for anyone sitting on their luggage, anticipating liberation at any moment. At best, I was holding out hope to find her expectantly standing with her case, quietly awaiting a saviour.

Mounting Coal again, I galloped through the streets to our little cottage, ran up the steps, searched ominously from room to room expecting miraculously to find her just sitting in the dark or asleep. I stared hauntingly at the little white booties Mother had knitted. My heart tore apart like a garment ripped in two. "*Ahhhh!*" I screamed out in frustration. My body filled with such emotion, I felt naked and lost. I kicked off my boots, crawled into our bed in my sweaty clothes to bury my face in her pillow. It was still ablaze with her scent.

It seemed like only a moment later that I woke to a noise, and confused and disorientated in the darkness. I sat up as the dream came flooding back like it was real. I rolled off the bed, expecting somehow for Emily to appear at the door as I opened it, but it was a dog rummaging through a can on the street. I checked my pocket watch, lit a cigarette, *five-thirty*.

I sat on the step and wrestled with the idea of revealing to her parents what had transpired. *I must face them; I will return her few things. And tell them what? I am leaving next week. I will need to clear out the cottage.* I felt numb, not quite sure what to do next. I lit another cigarette, and sat intrigued by the chorusing birds announcing a new day. *It's a new day! It's a new day!* Yet there was no song in my heart. *I need to accept this reality … it is another day, and I can do nothing to change any of it.*

Reluctantly, I filled the kettle, and gratefully downed the bread and meat Ellen had buried in my saddle bag. When I finished it, I spent the rest of the day cleaning up the house ready to hand the keys back to Mrs Graven. Coal needed time to recover before the long haul back over the hill.

We set off at daybreak, slowly making our way over the hill again, arriving in Martinborough in the late afternoon.

I called into Mary's to dispense with my grief. She was in the yard hanging out her washing. She dropped items back in the basket and came over immediately; gave me a hug.

"Harry, how did you go?"

"No sign of her. I checked everywhere: the docks, the cottage, nothing!"

I reflected on it again and again in my mind … If I had thought for a minute she would run off, I would have spent more time talking it over with her. She didn't appear to wake, but she must have been awake when I kissed her at four.

"Harry, we did not go in till about 11:30 thinking she was sleeping in. By the time I finally went in, I found her bed made with a letter on the pillow. By then she'd already had seven hours head start. She must have got a ride somehow. We were desperate to find you, hoping we'd hear a gunshot for a clue of where to look."

"We didn't have to fire our gun; the dogs bailed him up." I slumped down on the step. "Was my love not enough? I did not want to be married at the start, but I thought we were happy."

"You have done all you can. I think she may have come to this point years from now. Isn't it better that it happened now?"

I turned to her in shock. "Mary! How can you say that to me! I was to be a father!"

"Come inside. I'll make tea – you must be famished."

"I'm just tired and confused. I ate breakfast eleven hours ago. I need to face it: Emily was determined to have independence, she might have become unhappy at any time, and chosen to leave. Will we ever know?"

"What are you going to tell her parents? Would you like me to come along for moral support? Old man Linders is likely to take a gun to you."

"I have the perfect remedy for that, sister. Don't worry your head. I have decided to go soon … get it over with. Later I can catch up with Mother at Ellen's and leave for the gold fields from there tomorrow morning. Perhaps you are right. It's no good wallowing in self-pity. Emily chose to put her happiness first, why shouldn't I?

"Harry … in a way, it took her great courage deciding to leave. She also chose to set you free. To me, that was an incredible act of love, her choosing your happiness, just as much as her own."

Mary's husband Jack came in. "Harry, you're here!"

I stood up, nodding. "I will leave Mary to fill you in – we've sat talking for way too long. The washing has suffered but my heart is much less burdened for the chat."

Mary had good advice: "Move on! Each time you think of Emily, remember, she made this choice to be happy.

"Yes, it's good advice under the circumstances," Jack added. "You've set sail on some rough seas these last few months. You could just stay for a week and recover, let the storms pass. We'd love to have you."

"Thanks, Jack … but I need to move forward … Mary, sorry you didn't finish hanging out the clothes? It's overcast now."

She smiled. "They will dry tomorrow; it's going to be fine again. Go, you will need all the courage you can muster to face old Linders. I would love to be a fly on the wall. Will I see you again? Probably not unless you call by for breakfast."

"That sounds nice. I will see you in the morning."

I said goodbye and rode round to the Linders house, hoping they were home. Striding confidently up, I knocked on the door.

Annie answered it and looked surprised to see me. She spoke in a whisper as she slipped through the door and onto the front step. She closed the door softly; looked up at me inquisitively with fear in her eyes.

"Harry, what is it?" She looked out past me for Emily, "I can tell this is not a social call. How is our Emily?"

I whispered back. "Annie, I am so grateful that I can speak to you for a moment alone. You know I mean neither of you any harm; that's why I arranged for you and Emily to meet secretly."

"I've never seen her so out of sorts. It will take her time …."

"I'm sorry, but Emily has run away to Australia."

"No!" She cried out in agony and threw her arms around her tightly. Her face grew pale as she looked into my eyes, searching for an explanation. "I went shooting with my brother two days ago, kissing her before I left at four. By the time I came back in the late afternoon, she was already most of the way to the port bound for New South Wales. I rode all night but her ship had sailed."

"Did you fight with each other?"

"No, not at all. She said she wanted a marriage of love and not commitment only. She wanted to be free! Here, you can read her letter."

I unfolded from my pocket and she sat down on the little bench seat outside the front door, under a Camelia bush, and covered her mouth as she carefully took in each word. Then she looked at me in shock. "Changed her name! How will we ever find her?" Her face became grim. "This is *his* doing, you know. I am too scared to stand up to him, but she is not afraid. Many times, she's taken the brunt of his violence, and was left black and blue. She deserves to be happy but I fear for your life, you must go before …"

"Who are you talking to, woman? I thought I heard …"

Thomas had opened the door. *"What! I thought I told you never to come here unless you are invited. You need a lesson or two, boy!"* he bellowed, clenching his fists and stepping towards me.

"Thomas! Thomas, he has come to tell us about Emily. Come inside, sit down!"

"Be quiet, woman! This is a man's conversation. *What have you done!* Perhaps this is the day you wished you had never met our daughter. *Come on then … out with it, boy.*"

Thomas stood with his strong shoulders back, stretched to his full six-foot height. He stiffened his thick neck and stood like an enormous bull bracing to charge.

Courage charged my body like steel. I learned from an early age never to back down, no matter the odds. I took a step toward him, close enough to feel the breath from his nostrils. Locked eyes with him, almost chin to chin.

"Don't *ever* call me boy! I am not *your* boy, and thank God I never will be. I know now all the things you've done in secret behind these doors. Lay a finger on me and you will wish you hadn't."

"Puhh! Gutless! I'm not listening to this rot." Enraged, he tried shutting the door to escape inside. I jammed my boot in the open door, forcing it open.

"Get off my property!" he yelled. "How dare you! I've a good mind …" His bellowing voice echoed down the street, causing neighbours' curtains tugged aside in their windows.

"Or what …?" I interjected, leaning forward. "… you'll get the Police? Nothing would give me greater delight than to expose your detestable behaviour. Give me an excuse to come this Sunday and divulge in front of your fellowship, Sunday School and friends your shameless acts. The papers, Police or neighbours would happily proclaim them! It takes just one visit to your local lodge to avenge justice. Emily couldn't even stand the smell of you."

Bursting veins on his forehead and neck looked ready to

explode as he grimaced in savage silence. Annie pushed Thomas aside with her chin up, her chest puffed out.

"It's time it was unmasked. Good for you, Harry."

He stared at her in horror, stripped naked with a hint of humility, like a falling leaf in autumn.

"Look at me! Our only daughter considered you loathsome and has courageously liberated herself from your hold over her. She's changed her name to disappear, even escaping to Australia … all so she never had to see you again. She was the only light in my life, the only joy in my heart, now I must exist knowing your abomination and I must live on, knowing I will never see her again."

Stepping through the door, I took my hat off in one hand, with the other took Annie's hand and kissed it. "Annie, I am so sorry! Madam, you deserve better." I hugged her with one arm as she wept on my shoulder.

I thought: *One thing he was right about today: I wish I had never met him, but I will treasure the little time I did have with Emily.*

I turned to Annie, "Madam, please let my sister know if you ever need help. We will testify."

She kissed my cheek. "God bless you, young man. Take care."

I returned to Coal, and handed back the humble bag of Emily's things and her china doll.

Annie took the doll and ran into the house, wailing in deep sorrow.

"I know what you've done to your wife," I said to Thomas as I was about to leave. "I am not afraid to tell the whole community. You asked me what I have done! It's not what I have done, but what you've done. Now you'll have to think about that every time you think of her or look at that doll.

Chapter 19

Green-eyed Monster

It was time for our second football game against Parnell and I was again invited to billet at Ruby's family home. While our boys were eager to splash out on the town, planning a monumental night of revelry, I was impatient to see Euphemia. It seemed an age had passed since we'd seen each other. I could not think how to make the most of the time with her, so Ruby contrived a plan to ask her out for an evening meal with a dance in the city. I wore my suit — it reminded me of the last time I wore it, when I married Emily. Standing in front of the mirror, I heaved a deep sigh. *Harry, it's time to let it go, move on … you look good and you've got a lot of life to live, go and live it!"*

Ruby called outside the door. "Are you alright, Harry? We are ready to go."

Soon we were heading to their house to pick up and surprise Phee. I keenly held in my pocket a small gift that I purchased weeks ago in a jeweller's shop. As the coach pulled up outside their house, I was surprised by the nervous anticipation I felt at seeing both Phee and Maggie. *Perhaps it's the secret I hold to my heart.*

Almost before the driver had rolled to a stop, I was walking up the path to the ten wide steps leading to the front door, having imagined this moment so many times. Ken, Dugald and the twins were playing chasing on the front lawn with a few other boys from the neighbourhood. "Harry what are you doing here?" one of them said.

I held my finger to my lips. "Shhh."

I stepped onto the long verandah that ran the length of the house, and knocked on the heavy iron ring. Maggie opened the door, and stood stunned for a second, motionless, then her face exploded in delight.

I fumbled for words, equally stunned at how beautiful she'd become. "Maggie … ah … is your sister in?" Ruby followed me through the doorway.

"Yes, Hannah is upstairs. Would you like me to get her?"

Hannah! "What? … Oh, ah …"

She looked dead-serious then her face lit with a smile. "It's okay. Eupheeem-i-a! Coo-ome!"

Maggie threw her arms around my neck just as Euphemia appeared. I tried to compose myself, and straightened my waist coat, watching Euphemia, who stood quite still, utterly surprised. Her cheeks instantly flushed red.

"What …? How…? Where have you come from? I did not know you were coming!" She rushed forward and wrapped her arms tightly around me, lay her whole body against mine.

"You're here! How have you been?"

"Well, thank you." I smiled, filled with joy at her response. "We wanted to surprise you as I am here again for the annual match. It was Ruby who suggested it!"

She hugged Ruby a little awkwardly, the tension on her face evident.

"It certainly *is* a surprise. How long are you here?"

"We will stay till Monday. I have taken a week off work and have come straight from the ship to ask if you will join us for dinner tomorrow night. Ruby has arranged for us all to go out."

"Of course, I would love to come. Can you give me a minute and I will be back – I have chicken on my hands. I will be as quick as I can." Excited, she ran off down the hall.

Maggie stayed, watching me closely.

"How are you, Maggie? You are more lovely each time I see you! The last time I saw you, your hair was in braids."

"You can see I'm not at school any longer – I finished up last year. Now I'm helping manage the house as Phee spends more time doing office work."

"It looks like you have the place well organised, like your sisters would. The captain must be grateful to have your help."

"I enjoy being around the house, but the boys are tiresome."

Ruby and I sat down while we waited for Euphemia. "I am looking forward to talking with John again," Ruby said. "Do you see him much?"

"Of course … we are like two Musketeers. He's been looking forward to seeing you."

"Are you still working with horses?"

"It's a long story, but yes. We started a new job together working for a livery agent since our last letter, filling contracts to supply horses for Thames for all the extra works going on in the goldfields."

"How interesting. Does it pay better?"

"We bought a horse that won a race, giving us enough money to have a week off."

I turned to Maggie, who was still smiling at me. "This is a nice house. It looks like you have more space," I said.

"It is a great deal cheaper and we each have a room, except the twins of course."

Euphemia came through looking flushed, and trying to fit her shoes on while walking up the passage.

"There, how do I look, Maggie? What did I miss?"

"I was just about to ask Maggie if she missed the views of the harbour?"

Phee glanced at Ruby. "I miss Eileen and Ruby dropping in, and it's also a long way to the shipyards from here …"

"… and the Queen Street shops!" Maggie butted in, looking

cheeky.

Phee continued, "Perhaps it's good … there's not so many folks to shun us over the scandal … less Highlanders over here in Newton."

Ruby had been listening to Phee, her hands clasped tightly together. She took a few steps towards her. "Phee, I am so sorry I have not called. Life has been hectic. I told Harry on the way here that I have not had anyone extremely sick before, I find it hard visiting. I hoped you did not think it was because of the tuberculosis.

Phee looked at Ruby; placed a hand on her arm. "I understand. It is always awkward to know what to say. I can't believe it has been a year since the last game; it seems like only six months ago we were all together. Now it's nearly Christmas again. You've had a lot going on Harry."

Oh, no, I hope she's not heard of the wedding. I cannot tell her. "This year has really flown by for me. We've had all the family up in Martinborough with two wedding celebrations, now James is living there. We may be a little closer in Coromandel soon!" *How do I tell the girls about Emily? I cannot even imagine how to have the conversation. Phee must be carrying, an immense burden with Hector's bankruptcy, Barbara dying and trying to work. Perhaps an opportunity will present itself in the next few days.*

"Maggie and I have been preparing early this year, squirrelling little things away as we have finances to do it. Father has been working hard all year to pay back some of his debtors, but it is one step forward with two back. Every time it looks like he has a win, there is another repair to do or dockyard fee to pay."

"What goods is he carrying?"

"Just the same. He's been sailing to and from Australia. Barbara keeps an eye on him; she's in a routine of packing and unpacking her bags."

"How is she?"

"Harry," she said in a whisper, so the children could not hear, "the sun is slowly setting on her time with us. I doubt she will sail with Father again once she arrives home. It will be better for her to remain here now and rest."

"At least you will have Maggie to help now. How is the captain?"

"I am not sure. Even with the sale of the house, it is not enough for him to repay all his debts. I am expecting him home next week … the lawyers have said this is it. He has a hearing on December 20th to decide his fate. No man could have done more."

I shook my head. "I struggle to think that he's toiled away all these years, for it to come down to this."

Phee looked at me intently, tears welling in her eyes. *I need to distract her.* I felt in my pocket, for the little gift I had bought. "This is just a little something I saw and thought of you."

She carefully unwrapped the white paper, now smiling at me again. "Oh, it is lovely." Her face flushed red as she carefully held the mother-of-pearl broach. "How wonderful of you to think of me."

Maggie picked it out of her hand. "Here, let me put it on for you …"

"Ouch, you pricked me. I hope you didn't do that on purpose! It's not funny!"

Ruby looked at them both. "Bit of the green-eyed monster, I think."

"Yes, I think so."

"So sorry …," Maggie said. "Oh, it looks lovely on."

"Thank you so much. You did not have to bring me anything," Phee murmured.

"Well, I had your new dress in mind, hoping it would complement it. I will be looking forward to seeing it." I looked at Ruby, forgetting that it was meant to be a quick visit. "I'm sorry, we will have to leave as Ruby's father needs the buggy. Will we see you tomorrow night?"

"Of course, how tantalising."

"We are going out somewhere nice," Ruby said, glancing back at Phee, who called out as we walked down the path. "I will wear my new broach."

I indeed looked forward to tomorrow as we made our way back. I needed to let my hair down, clear out a few cobwebs.

The next afternoon was spent relaxing at Ruby's, sitting in the manicured garden. John swooned over her, relaying all that had transpired since they'd last met, but with no word of my marriage. I lit a cigarette, dwelling on how to tell Euphemia about Emily. It was unusual to see John dressed up in a waistcoat and fine dress shoes. Ruby looked lovely, adorned in a pearl necklace, a bright pink hat with a white ribbon and her light pink dress, its sash matching her hat.

I waited anxiously outside the dining hall for Euphemia to arrive. Eventually, the luxurious black carriage Ruby had sent to pick her up arrived outside the front doors. She stepped down elegantly, dressed in a glorious white evening dress with matching shoes, a blue hat and matching purse. I took her hand, assisted her descent from the carriage and escorted her up the path. "Euphemia, you look ravishing," I whispered.

She smiled coyly, yet looked pleased.

Ruby had secured one of the finest tables in an intimate space beside the fire. Euphemia walked slowly, following the waiter to our table. Chandeliers hung from an ornate ceiling, and a stage at one end of the room held an orchestra playing beautiful dance music. Euphemia's eyes sparkled in the firelight as she looked at me.

"Isn't this fun. I cannot recall the last time I came out like this. I feel a little guilty – this much opulence could feed our family for a month.”

“Phee, tonight please pretend you are not the sister in charge, running a household; tonight, you are a princess. The orchestra awaits your choice of music, and your prince is ready to whisk you off your feet.” Euphemia looked at me in astonishment. “Would you like a dance, my princess?”

She simply smiled and offered me her hand.

We walked between the candlelit tables onto the polished dance floor, our time together disappearing in laughter, articulate conversation, sumptuous food and the finest Scottish malt.

I whispered in Phee’s ear, “I cannot remember a time when I have had so much fun or talked to anyone about my life so much.”

Phee was already very happy, having had two glasses of wine. I took her hand and we stood in the cool night air on the rear balcony overlooking a small pond. Euphemia had never looked so pretty as we held each other close; I gently kissed her red lips.

Then I felt suddenly sick, thinking of Emily, as I was again charged with passion and desire. *This will be different; we must take our time to know each other.*

Euphemia looked at me intuitively. “What is it? It’s like you have something to say, but can’t say it.”

No not here, not now! I want to savour this moment! “No, not at all. I am just thinking how lovely it is to be with you tonight.”

The next few days were full, though our Saturday footy game against Parnell was postponed due to a storm. We played on Sunday on a very wet field to a packed crowd of spectators. Parnell fought desperately to hold their ground, and we only just pulled off a win with the last conversion going over the post two minutes before full time: the final score, 15 to 13. None of us played well due to late night carousing, coupled with early morning training.

I searched to find an appropriate time to tell Phee about Emily, but she was so distracted with the children, Hector and Barbara's arrival home, as well as managing Barbara's sickness. She'd also been collating evidence for Hector's defence in court, only five days before Christmas.

Every time I thought I would get a chance to speak with her, my plan was foiled. I was determined to speak to her before I left the following day. I would go to the house in the morning.

In the early hours, I saw the silhouette of a young lad at the front of Ruby's house. It was Dugald, who had woken the maid, asking if I wished to come to the house. The Captain had unexpectedly arrived in port early. I thanked Ruby's family again for their hospitality, caught a ride over to Newton to meet Hector and Barbara before I made my way back down to our ship. Euphemia met me at the door looking formal and nervous as I took her arm.

"Come, sit down … Father will be out in a minute. He saw you coming, and wanted to put on something a little smarter. I noticed today he is tired, so please excuse him a little."

Euphemia and I sat on the two-seater chair, I could see Maggie's smile from there, but tried not to catch her eye.

"It's nice to have any excuse to see you before I go. Letters seem to take forever to arrive. It is the happiest part of my day, hoping the postman has a special letter for me. By the way, Euphemia, thank you for your letters. In all the excitement I had forgotten to say."

Just then Hector stepped into the room. He was the traditional image of a weathered sea captain, with big strong hands, wiry whiskers, balding head, but eyes that shone with life and vigour.

I stood and shook his hand firmly.

"Harry, thank you for dropping by, my daughter has spoken

of you a few times," he said, winking at me. "I thought it was expedient for us to meet as you will soon be off."

"Thank you, sir. I missed you last year when you were delayed coming home, then again when you had been in Wellington from Lyttleton."

"How are things down there, son?"

"Good, sir. My brother James and I have been busy working nights doing cabbie work, as I've been working for a livery agent during the day. Everything at home is slowly gathering pace, new buildings going up continually." I hesitated for a second not sure if I should be so bold to ask about his bankruptcy hearing. "How are things for you, sir?"

"Well, we will see. I will do all I can to keep our ship afloat, but at the end of the day, as the good book says, 'Let us lay aside every weight, and the sin which so easily besets us… let us run with patience the race that is set before us, and so on … Lad, I have run a good race, lived a lot of life and kept the faith. Our troubles are no one's doing but my own. Your race has only just begun, lad, you must run well."

If only he knew… I had only been a part of this family for a short time, but I was drawn to his fatherly wisdom.

"Where are your parents, son."

"They are in Timaru and Martinborough. Nearly our whole clan is living up there now."

"Are they not together?"

"No. Father was a blacksmith who got kicked in the head by a horse in 1883. I was nine at the time, and he has been in an asylum ever since."

"I am so sorry to hear that. Does he recognise you?"

"No. I have been to visit him a number of times, but he does not recognise me."

"What are your aspirations, son?"

"I would like to own a farm one day. They are surveying some nice land down south but it is inaccessible until they put the road through. There is talk of a road one day joining up to Wellington but why would anyone bother when you can go by ship? It would be a week's journey on a horse."

Murdoch's voice had broken, and he had muscled up from working down at the shipyards. "Father, there is a vehicle that one of the engineers working in the yard spoke to me about. Imagine one day we may not need any horses and carts. We could just drive to Wellington to visit you, Harry."

Hector looked proud of his son, but laughed at the notion. "That'll not happen in our lifetime, lad."

I winked at Murdoch. "It is also convenient to stop and feed your horse on the side of the road."

"Father, how do you think it works?"

"I am not sure, Murdoch, but I suppose it must work much like a steam engine."

Maggie set a large tray with a fine china tea set, hot scones, jam and cream. While carefully pouring the tea, she turned and offered the first scone to me."

I said with as serious a face as I could muster, "Have you got any burnt ones?"

She looked puzzled. Phee just smiled.

"It's alright, Maggie. Last year I burned some scones and Harry kindly took a burnt one from the kitchen to make me feel better."

Quick as a flash, Maggie turned to me with a mischievous look and said, "Would you like me to go and burn one for you?"

Everyone laughed as Maggie continued to pour the tea.

Barbara had been sitting near the open window in the lounge but looked completely exhausted. She held a handkerchief to her mouth and tried her best not to cough.

"I am sorry, Harry, I am very tired; I must take my leave. I would love to give you a hug, but I will not come near just in case. It is so lovely to finally meet you after the children and Euphemia have spoken of you so much. I hope you have a successful journey, and if we do not meet you again soon, please take care."

"Thank you, although I have only known you all a short time, it has been my delight to be in your home. I will certainly do my best. Rest well."

Phee took her arm and helped her up the stairs.

"Harry, I was just thinking, I have been shipping goods through to Thames for the new railway line into Paeroa, which should be open by next year. They are also going to carry that line right through those mountains to Thames and possibly up the peninsula to Kuaotunu. With your energy, you should look at going there or the goldfields, as there are still opportunities to make good money there. Plenty of people are settlers prospecting. With your skills, you could be managing a work crew."

"I can't believe that you have said that, because Jack Lane the livery agent I have been working for, made me promise to diversify, see the opportunities to find work where I could be in charge of men."

"Harry, don't get me wrong … we made some good money in a syndicate I set up, called the Scotia fund. A few of our highlanders had a little business acumen and wanted to get in on the action when gold was discovered back in '67. But with the rail going through, there's enough hungry miners trying their luck in that muddy town. The rail will be going from one end of the country to the other – my money would be in getting involved somehow."

"Jack has asked me to be in charge of coal transport into the mines for him. I might do that for a while."

"It is tough work but you've already had plenty of that if you've been lugging sea trunks for the last four years."

"My brother John is about to move up from Timaru and is searching for the best place for us to go, but a few fellows have mentioned the *Try Fluke* mine up in Kauotunu."

"Yes, it is probably a nicer community too if one was to settle there with a family, but it's a wretched harbour. I have designed a few ships, especially for those harbour conditions, long flat bottom boats that can get into shallow water while still carrying a good load of coal for the battery stampers. The local lads have special carts with big wheels and specially trained horses that pull a cart out into the bay to pick up goods and passengers as they have no wharf."

"I delivered horses up there for Jack Lane a few weeks back. The roads are so muddy, when you make your way up into the second township, it's virtually impossible for a man to walk on foot most of the time. He either sinks up to his knees in mud or falls on his face."

We laughed together over stories from the dockyards and the infamous James. Hector had lived such a full life, so many stories, so many crazy experiences, but I could see he was getting tired, so at last I stood.

"I am sorry, sir, I know you were most gracious to stay up and take the time to meet me. You have a beautiful family but I must get away also as my ship leaves early on the morning light."

I had already said goodbye to Murdoch, Ken, Dugald and Hannah, who had all gone to bed. I shook hands with Hector and promised to keep an eye out for his ship. Maggie came and hugged me tightly, and wished me well for our new venture. I took Phee's hand and walked to the front garden, stood in the dim light of a flickering street lamp; I kissed her passionately, and held her close. The stars shone brightly as we stood and gazed at them, not wanting this moment to end. As I held her, I could see Maggie, in silhouette, watching us through her bedroom window.

"When will I see you again?"

"I do not know. At least I am in the Auckland district now and only a day's sailing. I will have a busy time ahead setting up somewhere to live, especially if the other boys join us for a stint in the gold. I will send you my address as soon as I can." I kissed her one last time and walked backwards toward the street, watching her face as I moved away. "I will write soon."

Chapter 20

Fish Out of Water

"With our second load of horses delivered, we headed back to Martinborough for Christmas. I was excited to be celebrating again with all the family which was growing larger each year. Joe had grown strong, and held an air of confidence about him. I slept again in his little room, talking into the night of his adventures and dreams. Emily was often in my thoughts as I lay down to rest; I wondered about her welfare, and hoped she was content, wherever she was, with whoever she was with. Whenever I thought of her, guilt gripped my heart afresh, as I had not yet confessed to Euphemia, but I must not tell her of my marriage yet as she would be overwhelmed at present. I found a nice Christmas card in town, and inserted in it a letter I had written the night before when everyone had retired to bed.

Dearest Euphemia

Merry Christmas! How are you? You are often on my mind; I find myself wondering what you are doing each day. Have you had your father's hearing yet, I am hoping for a favourable verdict? Your father is a good man, please give him my sincere regards. How did it go facing that evil woman, Madam Vine? I suppose it will revive the scandal you had hoped would be laid to rest?

How is Barbara also? I can only imagine it is a big job

James had been working for two months now cutting and
bundling flax with the Māori boys in the area. They were long
days of hard work, which he was not used to. I went out after
planting one day to visit him in the swamp.

"God, James, look at you, covered in mud; you look more like
one of the Māori boys, except you've got white round your eyes
… you've lost so much weight I hardly recognised you."

"Don't you bloody start! Margaret has tried to fatten me up. Some of these lads are twice my size, so don't you go upsetting them. I've had a gutful. When are we out of here? I feel completely like a fish out of water. You should have a go, you cheeky little bugger."

"What do you do?"

"Cut a bundle, picking only the precise flax leaves, then try strapping it up – the bloody pieces are as slippery as eels."

"It's great to see you so happy; I can't stand seeing people whine."

"Go away, if that is all you came out here to do – mock me!"

"James, you're lucky to have work."

"I've never worked so hard and been so filthy. I throw myself in the Ruamahanga at the end of the day, but the sap sticks on and won't wash off."

"I came to tell you Jack is finalising the last details; we should be able to set sail in a few weeks. I have received a letter yesterday from John, who sent word that he had found lodgings in Kuaotunu. It's a gold miner's cottage in the upper township close to the Mercury stamper and Mariposa."

"Can't come soon enough. Also, I think we should talk to Ellen about Joe. He's fourteen this year … I think he would be a good lad up there. He's asked me if he could come."

"I hope you didn't promise?"

He looked away a little.

"I don't know if it's a place for him!"

"He does have a way with horses. He's strong too, having already worked for the coachbuilders."

"I will speak to Ellen."

"Good. I will get cleaned up tonight, and will arrive at Ellen's about 5:30. What's the time now?"

"It's already half-four.

"See you in an hour." He waved a hand.

With Christmas behind us, we needed to make plans to relocate. Jack was keen for us to take charge of a few teams of his horses carrying goods into the little settlements. With a thousand people in the small settlement, seven stampers, three bakeries needing flour, chaff and oats for hundreds of horses. The most critical supply were the kegs bumping their way up an impassable track from the beach, like camels loaded with barrels on sand hills.

We ate supper, then sat back around the kitchen table while the ladies retired to the living room. James smoked his pipe and Joe leant in with anticipation.

"Joe, can you open that door – Ellen will smell that smoke any minute. Here's the letter John sent. I will read it …

> *I met an old footy player McDevitt from Otago on the Steamer Iona, whose brother had dropped dead in a tunnel, leaving his cottage to him. He went to have a look but couldn't stand the stampers going day and night. He's happy to let it out to us in the meantime and even though it is expensive, I jumped at the opportunity. There are four rooms, with three small bedrooms, enough for all of us including O'Flaherty. It's almost impossible to find lodgings anywhere except the Kuaotunu hotel or Teggart's boarding house. The small town is crawling with new men pouring in each day so we had better take up this windfall. McDevitt said opportunities abound up there but transportation is much needed with one chap running a horse and Bullock as there are no other horses to be had.*

> *I am looking for a field big enough to keep the drafts in, flat land is a premium, but I spoke to a Chinaman growing vegetables who might give us enough for what we need.*

> *The Local Kuaotunu football club is made up of the*

"Joe, could you go bring in a couple of armloads of wood for the wood box and stoke up the fire for the ladies."

"I filled them today already. And I can see the fire roaring from here."

"Doesn't matter, just bring in a little more; it won't hurt." I winked at Joe, who looked at me quizzically, his hands firmly on his hips.

"Oh, I see," he said as he turned and headed for the wood shed.

"That should give us a few minutes to talk about him coming with us. So, what do you think?"

"How does Ellen feel about it?"

"He's going to miss the girls, especially Lovey."

James held his pipe for a moment. "Ellen has her hands full with all the extras in the house. I think she might like the bloody peace and quiet with us away. Lovey is working at the Taylors most days, but you are right; he is going to miss all the mothering from his sisters. It'll do him good!" James tapped his pipe out on the ash bucket.

"He is a great help around here too."

"I worry he might have an accident. It's a long way from any hospital – there's only a local doctor up there and he's rather odd."

Joe's bare feet were sticking out as he'd snuck back to the side door. I raised my voice. "What about your coach building apprenticeship, Joe?"

He came back in and sat down. "I could always come back to it later. We are always going to need horses and carts … I really want to come!" he said insistently.

James put on his gruff voice. "Joe, it's a bloody tough world up there. I don't know what I would do if something happened to you. You would have to promise … what we say goes or else you would be back here on the next ship. Understood?!"

"Yes, James, I promise … don't forget I have helped you now on the docks for a while, and it's no picnic there, especially with you, James!"

James playfully clipped him over the head.

"Besides, they are a tough lot down in the coach yard."

I nudged Joe on the arm. "Joe, you are a good lad. It will be good to have you … better than old Grumpy here … Speaking of coaches, your skills will come in handy. Jack has arranged for three big coaches to go up with the horses. They are all dismantled so we will have to assemble them when we arrive.

"Good, we will need a few extra tools," Joe said.

"You organise what you need, Joe."

James leaned forward after swinging back on the chair legs. "There's something that could put a spanner in the works. I was hoping to get out of it. Yesterday I received a letter from Her Majesty's government, asking if I would consider going to Sydney with the cavalry. It's been a few years since I won that prize for those trials at Trentham, but somehow they have not forgotten. I've been thinking about it all day … what do you think?"

I looked at him thoughtfully; folded my hands behind my head. "It's a great opportunity. What about Margaret and Ernest?"

"I guess if it was going to be for six months, she could come over. I will send finances back to cover her living expenses."

"I know we have been planning on you coming, but I reckon Rusty is as keen as mustard to join us. When are they talking of heading away?"

"I would need to head away almost straight away, as they are getting the men fit for service. They are shipping out in the next two months."

We talked about it till it was dark, till James started yawning. He was slogging it out each day plus with his early starts, the heat of the range next to him, he was nodding off.

"I will let you know how it goes, Harry. Are we done?"

"I will keep you updated. We are a few weeks away yet."

"As long as I can get out of that swamp with that bloody flax. How any man is able to make a living astounds me!"

It was a busy time heading back and forth over the hill to Jack's at Island Bay. I spent a few weeks at a time over there preparing the horses to make up teams. We needed strong teams for those long days when a ship was beached with 200-ton of coal on board to be off loaded before the next high tide. Jack agreed to send more horses as we needed them. The winter rains were well on the way and the days grew shorter. It had all taken a lot longer to prepare than expected, and unfortunately, James had decided to go to Sydney after all, much to Rusty's delight.

It was already late July of '95, and with everything going on, I had not a minute spare to send my condolences to Euphemia over Barbara's death. I also saw in the paper a small article stating that John Reid was to take ownership of the *Frank Guy*. *I wonder how Captain McQuarrie must be feeling, perhaps free at last of all his trials. Phee will be terribly grieved, and I am more determined than ever. I must see her.*

I called in to see Mary on one of my trips over the hill to Martinborough. She looked very pregnant as we sat down for a cup of tea together.

"How are you, sister? Won't be long now."

"Ahh, it's at that uncomfortable stage when I can't sleep and I feel half-drunk from lack of it. Speaking of not sleeping, I don't think I will sleep after reading this in this morning's *Times*. It would give anyone nightmares, especially being a parent."

She spun the paper around to the article. "What is it?"

"You have probably heard about it … all the ladies are in horror down at the Taylors. Minnie Dean … she was seen getting on a train with a small child and a heavy hat box, then someone observed her coming back without either. The little girl Eva had been given into Mrs Dean's care by the girl's grandmother, found a short time later smothered to death.

"They went to Minnie's house to find a three-year-old boy buried in the garden and two other babies. Dorothy, a one-year-old was dosed with Laudanum. They reckon she will be hanged for murder … infanticide they call it."

"Isn't that what they used to do in ancient cultures when they had an unwanted baby or couldn't feed it?"

"Harry, how could any sick culture possibly bring a baby into the world with all its beautiful fingers and toes then kill it?"

"I don't know … I feel sick thinking about it … Emily would have been quite pregnant by now with our little one."

"Brother, I can't begin to tell you what it feels like to have a life growing inside you. I find myself daydreaming about what she will look like, I imagine her playing on the lawn."

"You said her … do you think you will have a girl?"

She laughed. "I am thrilled just to be a mother."

"At first I didn't want to be a father, but as the weeks past, I surprised myself, and had grown quite excited."

"It seems silly but it is exciting to think this person is already part of Jack and I, a little unique Gaskin. They are saying this woman will be the first woman to be hanged in New Zealand."

She drifted back onto Minnie. "She will be tried on the 12th of August."

"I still find myself daydreaming about Emily, wherever she is … thinking about if we'd had the baby. What if we were still together."

"What about Euphemia, Harry? Have you written?"

"The longer it's been the more I'm torn about how to explain to her what happened."

"Harry, you must write. It's not fair to her and I am sure not to you as well. You cannot leave it any longer."

"What am I going to say? I've tried already and failed."

"Be honest. Tell her the whole story; let her decide. Tell her how you feel about her and ask her to forgive you. Perhaps she will understand. Here, I have some fresh writing paper I found a few days ago. There is no one around at the moment, so sit down in the drawing room … do it now and get it over with!"

She stood over me, her hands authoritatively on her hips. I tried to come up with any reason to say no, but Mary was usually right. *It will never be the right time, so why not just do it, then I can stop thinking about it so much.*

I dipped the ink, and held the pen, hoping to get my words together this time … *How do I feel?*

Chapter 21

Pulling Out All the Stops

How can a few letters on a page be so hard to write. I cannot leave it another day. I know the shock she will feel …
I began to write.

Dear Phee

I am so sorry for not writing all these many months. The longer I delayed, the more I agonised as to how I should relate my folly. I know this will come as a shock but three months ago I met a woman at a dance. Her name is Emily Linders. I had been drinking heavily. Much later in the evening I had dropped her home. Unfortunately, one thing had led to another and although I have not seen her again, she arrived one night on my doorstep saying she was pregnant.

Her father, being a devout religious man of strict German descent, was not happy, and urged us to be married immediately. I did the honourable thing, and asked for her hand in marriage.

It was a sad state of affairs as we married in the registry office but within months, she had lost the baby. She was in great distress and I could not console her. I came home to her one evening and she was gone! A note on the table said she would start a new life in Australia. Her bag

I folded the pages and slipped them inside an envelope before
I changed my mind. "Mary, could you post this tomorrow for
me if you are in town?"

She continued to fold the washing in the lounge. "With
pleasure, brother. How did you go?"

"I did what you said … we will see. I must head away now;
we are finalising everything we need to go up north."

"When will I see you again?"

"I am not sure; probably after you have the baby. I am riding
over to Mother's to say farewell to the family. Hopefully, I can
make it back for Christmas. James won't be with us this year as
he is sailing out on the September 4th for New South Wales."

She came over and hugged me, leant her head on my chest.

"Brother, go and see that girl. She deserves to see you face to face even if just to shout at you. You are a good man."

It was well into August '95 before our steamer left port, fully loaded with our horses and cargo. We felt many emotions – anticipation, trepidation at stepping into the unknown, excitement of a new venture. Even Bolt was running around in circles barking at whatever moved, looking for something to round up so we could get on our way. He had picked up our excitement as we boarded the ship, restlessly going from one person to another for a pat. We had pulled out all the stops to get here, throwing all our hats in to make it this far. At least brother John was waiting ahead of us as our welcoming committee. It was worth the delay of an extra two days for fairer weather, passing by the beautiful scenic coastline of Hawkes Bay to the Coromandel. We arrived at the long pier in Mercury Bay where we could easily disembark. It was only a few hours ride over the rugged hills to Kuaotunu. Joe was eager to land ashore, as we pulled in alongside. The *SS Iona* was already tied up and dropping off passengers.

A few unwieldy miners with their burdensome loads had joined us on the sailing from Wellington. One crusty old guy with a sweat-stained hat turned to me as we stood watching our ship berth.

"Iona is our prized wee steamer. Captain Amodeo's been doing this run for years. Mind, you'd not want to go ashore in Kuaotunu. The ship anchors out in the bay, Peterson rows his whale boat or little punt out to meet her three times a week. Then he delivers everyone half way to the beach onto a mighty cart with his specially trained Clydesdale, wading ashore through the ocean to the beach."

"Harry Bagust," I said, thrusting out a hand. We shook.

"Sorry. My name's Bill Foster."

"Bill. Yes, I joined the hilarity a few months back at Kuaotunu. It's quite ridiculous to watch the ladies compose themselves as waves slosh over the big cart, during the transfer. It must be exciting in heavy weather."

"Are you just delivering?"

"No, we plan to stay for a spell."

"Well, you will find out then. The bay's not so bad on fine days, but when there's a northerly, watch out! My favourite thing to watch is the boatmen piggybacking the men ashore. They sweep the ladies up to carry them in their arms to the beach."

"I've only had to do it once. Do you think they will build a wharf there?"

"There's talk of a wharf … there's talk of a train from Coromandel too. They talk about improving the roads, digging out the silt from the creek, upgrading the fire equipment. It's like the last government … they're all talk. What brings you here? Looks like you might be coming in as carriers – you've got some mighty fine Clydesdales there."

"Yes, we're bound for Kuaotunu with a few teamsters, to bolster the carting of coal and goods from the beach."

"Good luck with those roads. Hope you've brought deep boots," he said, laughing. "Since July they have been almost impassable to man or beast with two feet of mud. It's deep enough to swallow you whole, never to be seen again."

"I saw men working on it when I was here."

"Even with a full-time gang working on it, they can't keep up. They have been carrying some huge loads of steel up over that hill for stampers, pipework, steam engines. Hopefully it will get better with finer weather coming in October."

"Couldn't have come at a more opportune time then," I said, smiling.

"They'll be happy to see you! Can't have enough teams with all the cargo coming in. It's got out of control lately; the place is crawling with new folk arriving every day. They say there's a thousand folk up there now."

Once the passengers and small goods were off loaded, we led the horses out, swinging all the tools, timber and heavy wagon wheels ashore. Rusty's strength was necessary in manoeuvring the colossal wheels for the Australian hardwood weighed a ton.

"Joe, we can use the sale yards to pen the horses. There's space to set ourselves up there for assembling the carts. Rust, have you got everything you two need to make a start? I'll go up to the hotel to find food and lodgings."

"We'll get into it right away while the weather's holding. Find out if there are any sale yard auctions this week?"

"They only auction a few cattle here every month. I'll ask, but it should be alright on that side."

"The next few days look fine, so we should make good progress."

I met Thomas Davies at the end of the wharf in the Whitianga Hotel where he assigned us a large room for a few days.

"Looks like you lads have got a little work to do. Those are mighty fine horses coming ashore. Are you lads up from down south?"

"Yes, we are preparing to cart goods to feed the hungry mines," I said.

"Good. Welcome to the Bay. Thomas Davies, good to meet you. By the look of you, you might be related to John Bagust."

I grinned. "I'm Harry, his brother. What's he done now?" I laughed.

"We had a game a few weeks back; he's got some good legs on the field."

"We've all played but it's really in his blood. He captained a team in Timaru before he came up this way. He's got a place for us waiting over the hill."

"Well, this is a spot of luxury for you before you head into hell!"

"We've got a few days' work ahead to assemble our big six wheelers, so I guess we will enjoy the break. Can I get a few ploughman's slabs for the men. We are making the most of the fine weather."

"I will ask the girls to rouse up a few sandwiches to tide you over. Dinner is around six."

"Oh, and are there any sales on? We are using some space in the yard to work."

"Not till next month, so you'll be fine."

Within days we had our two teams heading out of town on our maiden voyage into Kuaotunu. As we wound our way up over the hills, we finally made the top of the saddle with spectacular glimpses of Kuaotunu in the distance. Already the sound of the stampers and a dust cloud rose to meet us. As we rolled into town in the late afternoon, word had already made it ahead of us as men poured out of the hotel onto the porches to watch.

One guy called out: "Clean horses. Are they a special breed? I've not seen any but the colour of mud for a while."

Another beside him: "Welcome to the mud hole, Harry. Fine looking team."

Johnny had lived in town now for two months, and came out immediately, balancing three glasses of beer.

"Well done, lads, very impressive. Here, wet your whistle for a minute. Wash away that dust at least." He took the reins on my lead horse. "I'll lead you to the field we've leased."

"Good boy, Johnny, lead on!" I upended the glass. "I'll need another soon enough, that one didn't even touch the sides."

By nightfall, we had settled into the wee miner's cottage, hardly sleeping a wink for the first few nights with the roar of the stampers shaking the ground night and day. Surprisingly though, within weeks we slept like babies; the purr and tremor of the ground just became a way of life. It could have been that or just that we often crawled into bed shattered after unloading tons of coal. The ships would beach at high tide then we'd have until the next high tide to free its bowels of the black gold. Depending on the tide, we might start in the late afternoon, work all night to offload the precious cargo so desperately needed to feed the hungry crushers. All but Sundays, when we would wake to silence, noticing for the first time that week, the sound of Tuis, Bellbirds and the odd Kaka in the bush. Joe was true to his word: up with the birds each morning to make us all a hearty breakfast, also except Sundays.

Sometimes we would take Sunday morning to sit, but every now and then we would attend the Methodist church. It felt incredible to dust off a suit jacket for one day and to wear shoes that were not wet or stinking of mud.

Most of the entertainment centred around the Royal, Commercial and Kuaotunu Hotels, and often it was a long walk home to our little valley. There was always something happening in town to entertain the grafters, some of us more entertained than others.

"Should I wake Rusty?"

"Let him sleep; he had a hard night last night."

Johnny appeared, and Joe dished him up some fried bread and scrambled eggs. John tried to keep a serious face as he said, "Joe, one of the men told me yesterday that Kuaotunu was originally a Māori settlement. The name means 'Roasted Young'. You know, if you don't behave, Joe, that's what we will do!" He smiled.

Joe quipped back immediately. "I heard it was most likely the roasted baby mutton birds brought back by canoe from Great Barrier Island."

"He's a bright lad, our Joseph, not much gets past him."

Joe joined us at the table with a slight smirk on his face. "Oh, yesterday I heard a story of an old miner riding up the road, who saw a hat down in the mud. He thought to himself, Oh, my lucky day! He found a long stick and as he lifted the hat, a man's head was beneath it., The old timer nearly fell off his horse in fright. The young man said 'Good morning. Can you help me?' The old man gathered himself, saying, 'Take hold of the stick and I will pull you out of the mud.' The young man replied, "Thanks, mister, that would be fantastic, but just give me a minute to get my feet out of the stirrups.'."

We all chorused with laughter.

"Oh, you've got me in tears, boy. Actually, that reminds me, just before you guys arrived the road was completely impassable, the worst it's ever been. True story! A young lady, May Collins, tried to walk the two miles up to the top town with no other hope of getting home before dark. She started through the mud when she slipped and fell in the deep muddy cream. Her shoes were stuck two feet down in the mud, never to be seen again. She tried desperately to free herself but the more she struggled the more her dress stuck fast. It was like quick sand, she couldn't move! In the finish, it swallowed her whole. She cried out for help until her distant cries were heard by Con Murphy, a big burly miner. He managed to get hold of her with his horse and save her."

"John, maybe that's how Con Murphy started his service running the wagon bus back and forth from lower Kuaotunu through the mud to top town."

"Joe, he had so many accolades for saving her, he came up with an ingenious idea to bolt two big bench seats facing each other onto his old cart and charge a shilling each way."

"If it was me, I would have built a platform at each end."

"Harry, it's brilliant having facing seats as the wheels drop violently into deep holes in the mud, throwing passengers often onto the other persons lap on the opposite side. He's making better money than us! That reminds me, I was speaking to Fred Margetts at *Try Fluke*; he said they have just bought out an area that was originally held by *Mariposa*, *Red Mercury* and *Just in Time*. He needs equipment moved from one to the other. I said I would go up to give him a quote for cartage. We can fit it in when we have a lean day."

"John, that sounds good … There's a lot happening right now – looks like *Try Fluke* is fortifying their position."

"They are the largest company here. They must have over a hundred men working for them."

"How much gold do you think they are making to the ton?"

"I heard on average it's about ten ounces. It's said if they could go back and rework the original slurry, this time with the new method of cyanide separation, they would have doubled what they've made."

Rusty came through with his hair standing on end. "What's going on, lads?"

"We're just talking about all the local gossip in the neighbourhood. You don't look too good. Too much stagger juice last night."

"I think Hancock's local beer has got a kick like a mule. And don't even try the local moonshine."

"While we are all here, I just wanted to ask if it's alright for me to go to Auckland, perhaps next week when there is a holiday. I would be away about three or four days."

"Sounds like Euphemia is going to get a visit. Good for you, Harry. I think it should be fine." Rusty looked around at the lads.

"I can always ask Dave to fill in for us."

"Thanks, Johnny, that would be great."

"I should be coming with you to see Ruby."

"Sit down and write her a letter. I'll take it with me. From the sounds of it, she is overdue hearing from you."

Joe looked over with a cheeky grin. "Are you writing to anyone, Johnny?"

"I'm not in a hurry to start writing to anyone except Mother. I think unless we have any big shipments coming in, Harry, it should be fine. Go and sort yourself out, I can tell you are distracted at present."

"Thanks." I smiled. "I didn't realise it showed."

Chapter 22

Flying Off the Handle

The much anticipated holiday had arrived, with a storm expected for a few days. I took the opportunity to go north into the pending storm, but mine was one of turbulent emotions, the one side of Euphemia I had not witnessed personally yet. I decided to take Mary's advice, as I had not heard from Euphemia, so I would take my medicine by seeing her face to face.

I walked up the hill from the port to Ruby's house. Reiwa was hanging out the clothes at the rear of the house. Ruby came round surprised, inviting me for lunch.

"What are you doing here? You've got the courage to show your face."

"Is it that bad?"

"You've stirred up a real hornet's nest with the letter you wrote … Not good timing, Harry."

"I need to see her face to face, even if she flies off the handle and doesn't want to speak to me again, at least I will know."

"I admire your courage. She does not suffer being made a fool of."

"I didn't hear from her, so here I am, for better or worse."

"She only received your letter two weeks ago. The postmark was old so the letter must have gone astray for a time. Why not borrow one of our horses since you are already here. Come, I will take you out to the stables to our stableman."

We walked along the many stable doors till we reached the

last one. "Oh, she's a fine mare. What beautiful markings."

"Take her. It's our secret … Father hardly rides these days, and Belle needs to get out."

I found my way to the house in New North Road, where Ruby had taken me last time I was in town. People stared as I rode Belle past as she was nearly seventeen hands high, with a commanding presence. I tethered her to the front verandah post, feeling apprehensive as I climbed the steps. Ruby's words rang in my head. *'Not good timing'*…

The last time I had walked up those steps I was full of anticipation and excitement at seeing Euphemia, now it was probably going to be more like ripping off a bandage stuck on with blood. *Take a deep breath. Tear it off quickly and bear the pain.*

As I knocked on the door, inside seemed very quiet. Maggie opened the door and suddenly my heart was alive, and I took a moment to gather my thoughts.

"Ahh…" I stuttered.

"Harry! What are you doing here? Come in!" She stood back a little, trying to smile while holding the door open.

"I wrote to Phee … I have not heard from her. I thought I should come and talk to her face to face."

"You are not popular around here, Harry." Her face bore a seriousness I did not like. "Not with one person in particular. We received your letter two weeks ago. Even Father might have had trouble navigating the terrible storms raging in the house. I'm surprised you did not feel them in Martinborough!" she said with a cheeky grin. "Come in. Let me put the kettle on. You will stay for a cup of tea?"

"Yes, I'd like that!" I followed her through to the kitchen. "It's actually been months since I finally found the words to write that letter, it must have gone missing. We are now living in Kuaotunu on the Coromandel Peninsula."

I stood holding my hat as Maggie stoked the fire box on the

stove.

"I've heard Father talk about that harbour … I think he got stuck there once."

"It has a frightful harbour. How is everyone? I think of you all so often, it has been a monumental year for you all. Losing Barbara and the Captain losing his ship."

"Yes, there has not been a great deal of sunlight, but we must create our own cheer, mustn't we, Harry? I think your letter came at a time when Phee was feeling completely overwhelmed. She had been so busy her grief exploded like a volcano."

"Actually, where are they?" I could hear a gramophone playing in the lounge.

"Euphemia is staying with our old neighbour, Eileen, over in Parnell for a week or two. Father has gone up to Matheson Bay to be with friends. The two boys are staying with Aunt Christine, and Hannah is in Kaurihohore, up past Whangarei for a spell."

"Oh, how lovely for you. When was the last time you had the place to yourself?"

"I think this is the first time ever; it has been completely wonderful! I read books, get up late, bake a few biscuits and today I have music playing so I can learn my song for church this Sunday."

"Why don't I hold the music for you so you can sing."

"That's kind of you, but I do feel a little self-conscious with the two of us alone."

"I will pretend I am your audience then."

"Are you sure! It would be lovely to have your company … you can sit there." She pointed to a comfortable armchair on the other side of the room. Perhaps Phee will come over today, you can both be my audience."

"Do you think she will see me?"

"I really do not know. Perhaps she has calmed a little by now."

Maggie did some warm up exercises with her voice then wound the gramophone handle and gently placed the needle. Her voice was breathtaking, clear and strong but as sweet as a bird. I closed my eyes, listening intently, trying desperately not to distract her till she had finished the song. "Maggie, your voice is like an angel. How come have I not heard you sing before now? Where did you learn to sing like that?"

"I loved to sing with Mother; she had been taught by an old aunt that sang in the opera." She picked up another record. "Oh, wait a minute, this is lovely. Would you like another? Let me put this one on."

The recorded music was a favourite waltz, and I could not resist. Immediately I stood and, moving the small table aside, I took her hand. She looked at me a little timidly as I took her moist hand as we danced around the room. Once or twice, I stood on her toe, but by the time we played the waltz again, we had found a rhythm. I'd never seen such delight on her face, and we looked into each other's eyes, not saying a word and yet saying everything. One of those sweet moments in time that felt precious enough to hold onto. As the needle stopped in the middle, we looked for a moment at each other...like time was standing still. She silently wound the gramophone again and gently took my hand again, dancing transfixed, abandoned, oblivious to time.

Suddenly, Maggie's hand tightened and I was aware of a shadow out the corner of my eye. There stood Euphemia, totally aghast, her mouth open in shock, her hands on her hips.

"*What! How could you!*" she shouted.

Maggie quickly took the needle off the record as we stood together like scolded children.

"Is it not enough that you are already *married? Now you dance with my sister in secret. ... I hate you! I never want to see you again!*"

I walked toward her, desperately confused ... *What is going on?*

I've come to see you! "I came up specially to see you. I want to be with you!"

"Get out! Don't even speak to me!"

"Please, Phee. Do not do this!"

"Go! Do not say another word! Just leave!"

I walked toward the door, almost in disbelief and stepped onto the porch. She appeared in the hall and threw my hat at me.

"Take your hat with your fancy words, and don't darken our door again."

I put on my hat; almost stumbled down the steps. My heart filled with pain again. I had held a hope that somehow one day our love would be free to grow and blossom, but now it was like a bucket of sour cream, lumpy and bitter. I felt dazed, not sure what to do next. I took the reins and prepared to mount, when suddenly Maggie was there, grasping my arm.

"Harry, I am so sorry. It was my fault – I got carried away in the moment. Please don't be mad with her; she does love you. She has suffered so much pain lately, too much for one person to carry. If you could wait a day or two for her, I will try to reason with her … she can be stubborn, but I know she wants to be with you. Where are you staying?"

"At the Imperial."

"I will call over at ten o'clock tomorrow, and let you know how I go."

"Thank you. She would not want our pity but I do feel sorry for her."

I rose early the next morning feeling like I'd been in a boxing ring, my sheets twisted round my shoulder. I had to get out and clear my head, so I walked along the dock yards on Queens Wharf. It felt like I was on trial with Euphemia, waiting for the verdict. I kept checking my pocket watch and nervously fiddled with it; mindlessly opened the latch then closed it again. I watched a coal ship being unloaded, the baskets being swung up out of the hold to the Lugger, who walked along the plank with over two hundred pounds on his back. *How do they balance on a ten-inch plank, ten feet above the hold, then throw it into a waiting shoot on the other side. Euphemia must feel like that right now, walking the plank with a heavy load.*

Huge bales of wool were being lowered into another old barque that flew the Australian flag, and was bound for Victoria. It was like being back at work with sweat running down my back. I took out a cigarette and sat watching all the proceedings when my eye caught a young couple about my age, holding hands along the water front. They stopped deep in conversation, embraced, held each other for what seemed an age, then they kissed gently. Then they looked into each other's faces as if searching every crease and line, like time standing still for them alone. They were locking in a safe of memories, sublime images of each other, feelings that would endure beyond fires, war, distance or even time. Unforgettable moments locked safely away, in a vault of the heart.

I sat thinking about the last few months and my shattered dream of seeing Phee. I saw her jealousy of Maggie, though considered it no more than a sister's annoyance.

Perhaps she had detected something in me that I had been unable to identify. Yesterday my secret heart betrayed me, almost standing still at the sight of Maggie in the open door. Did I unknowingly lock that image away to recall it again, to see us so clearly dancing together in sweet abandon, as if it were happening in this moment of time again. Her glistening hair in the sunlight, her shining face, intense eyes, her joyous smile and warm embrace. The things I love about Euphemia are the very things that now make it difficult to love her. Her stubbornness, strong spirit, confident nature, and self-assurance, even her independence.

Maggie had a strength too but is vibrant, even cheery. When she enters the room, it lights up.

I was not sure what Maggie felt towards me, perhaps she was vivacious to everyone! … I feared my head did *not* know … but perhaps my heart was already enthralled, perplexed.

My thoughts were arrested by the young lady, now aboard the steamer, hurrying to the stern of the ship to catch one last glimpse of her lover. As she held the rail, there was no waving, for he has already captured every line of her face, every soft word whispered in his ear, every gentle touch of a warm hand.

I checked my watch again, dusted off my trousers and returned to the hotel. Maybe the evidence had been reviewed, maybe Phee had reached a verdict …I would stand for the judgement to be read …

It was ten to ten when I came through the front doors into the lobby. Passing the bar, I glanced at the whiskey on the shelf and decided, *Why not a little courage.* "Make it a double, Mac," I said, pointing to the bottle of malt.

"Let me guess, you're meeting a lady?"

"How long have you been behind that bar, Mac?"

"Long enough to read people pretty well," he said, laughing. "Looks like her now."

I turned to see Maggie in a beautiful white dress, the sun catching her bright face through the glass of the doors. I quickly knocked back my drink before grabbing the door to welcome her in.

"Maggie, right on time. I have nervously been waiting like a school boy in the headmaster's office. I decided to have a drink – would you like one?"

She smiled but seemed nervous. "No, I have not ever had one. Isn't it a little early?"

"I needed a little courage," I admitted. "How is Euphemia today? I had so many things to ask her … about your father's trial, nursing Barbara. Her work."

"Firstly, she is remorseful for the way she spoke to you. It was such a shock to see you, then with you dancing with me instead of her. She said to apologise."

"Oh, I was not expecting that. Tell her she has nothing to apologise for. I had only hoped to see her face to face to explain about Emily."

"If you wish to tell me, I could relay the story to her."

I asked the young waitress to bring tea service and directed Maggie to a table. "Where do I start …?" I said with a deep sigh. "The thing I wanted to explain to her is, I think Emily was not so much in love with me as she saw it a way to get away from her father. I told her I was in love with another woman in Auckland. She said if I would just allow her to be married, she would be able to free herself from the abuse her father had subjected her to all those years. She lived in fear. She said she would probably change her name and move to Australia at some point in the future, which I agreed to, hoping that one day things would work out with Euphemia. I do not know what to say now."

"We spent the whole morning talking about you," Maggie replied. "She loves you very much and has never felt about anyone the way she feels about you. She has thought it over many times since your letter came, wanting on the one hand to pursue a relationship, while on the other she is content to have her independence as a free woman, not constrained by the values of society to have a husband, a home and children. She already has many responsibilities with children to look after with Father needing her support. She just does not have time or the emotion to commit to another person at this time in her life."

I looked at Maggie's sincere face, thinking how lovely she was to show such compassion towards her sister. "I suppose in a strange way, that is the resolution I came up here for. I had hoped somehow she would forgive me. Do you think she might see me one last time?"

"I think so … but … oh, I feel hot. Give me a minute." Maggie stood and went out to the parlour, and I bent my head in consternation. *What am I doing here? I know if I could just see Euphemia and explain to her.*

When Maggie returned, her hair was down, and she carried her shawl across her arm.

"Oh, you look so different, like a young woman I saw this morning when I went for a walk along the docks. In the midst of men working everywhere, two people about our age were oblivious to anything going on around them. They were each locked in a moment of time, focused only on each other, fully present there at that moment, wanting desperately to be together and yet separated in their love."

"Harry, that is beautiful. It's one of my favourite things over the years as I have waited at the docks for Father, to see all the raw emotion of final goodbyes or those returning. I long for that one day! Unlike my sister, I would like to settle down and have a family. I have never pursued an education or wanted to be a businesswoman. I love looking after a home, looking after the children. I want to meet a good man who will love me."

She blushed for a moment, then looked away as she took a sip of her tea. "And you, Harry?" she said, turning back to me with a serious look.

I pulled out a cigarette and lit it, drew in a deep breath. I looked at her. "That was my exact thought as I stood there. I want that! I have never realised it before. The point is, they didn't even wave! Their hearts were so filled with love for each other, they knew it would keep them till they were together again. That's what I want.

"I want to love someone like that, have children, a home, a farm of our own. I had dreamed of that with Euphemia."

"You just said *our* own. Don't you mean a farm of *your* own?"

"Well, you know what I mean. It's my dream to settle one day with a farm." *Why did I say* our *own? ...*

"I am hoping that if I work a few years in Kuaotunu, I might save enough to buy a small farm. I have been trying to support Mother for the last few years, so I have not saved any. I think now with James, Joe, Louisa, Mary and Ellen all there in Martinborough, we can all share the load a little."

Maggie bowed her head. "It has been a very difficult time for us with all Father's debts, but we have scraped by now for the past few years. Father is a good Scotsman; he never spends any money unnecessarily ... Why don't you come over to see him before you go. He is in at present as he is waiting for a ship to return to sail through to Victoria"

"Do you think that will be alright with Euphemia?"

"I don't really think she does *not* want to see you; she is just going to take time to let you go."

"That would be wonderful. Let me take you home. We can get a cab."

As we stood waiting for the cab, her words rang in my ears: "What do you want?" The words shouted in my head.

I looked at Maggie as she checked up the road for a cab. It had been awkward speaking of Euphemia together, yet I felt a warmth toward Maggie and her family, and felt excited to meet the Captain again. I shook my head. *Is it really all over?*

Chapter 23

A Nod's as Good as a Wink

Maggie deftly rolled her hair and pinned her hat again. She looked stunning, and my heart raced a little as I took her soft hand and helped her up into the cab. Soon we were on our way back up the hill to Kingsland, and I braced myself as we climbed the stairs again to the front door. I had no idea how Euphemia would react.

Hector was home reading the paper and looking the most relaxed I had seen him in years. His face lit up as I entered the room. *How good to see him again!*

"Harry, good to see you boy!" We shook hands heartily. "What are you doing up this way?"

"I took your advice. My two brothers and a friend have moved to Coromandel, driving three teams of horses to transport goods into the stampers and the upper town in Kuaotunu. It's a temporary opportunity while we sniff out where best to focus our efforts. How are you going? Maggie said you were waiting for a ship to return from Victoria."

"It's hard to let go, lad. The coal coming from New Castle can't be shipped quick enough. I am filling in for any Master Mariner that needs to take time off or captain a ship that is lying idle. I am far better off doing something than stuck here with the girls fussing over me like I am about to drop dead." He laughed and smiled at Maggie.

"I am sure they are grateful just to have you around."

Euphemia came into the room, with an ink pen in her hand. "Harry, could you please tell him how much we would love to have him, even for two weeks, to sit and relax. Even to read a book, or tend the garden."

I stood transfixed, surprised to see her standing there.

"I am sure he knows just how much he is loved, but a wild stallion is hard to tame."

I walked slowly towards her as she retreated to the kitchen where she had papers scattered over the table, and spoke quietly. "Phee, Maggie and I spoke this morning about your decision. Thank you for your honesty; although it is bittersweet, I understand. It is a difficult time for all of you." She looked directly at me. "You want your independence with many people depending on you."

She put her hand on mine on top of the chair. "I am sorry for my outburst. It was such a shock seeing you with Maggie. I realised in that moment I do not ever want to be tied down. Perhaps one day we may laugh about it all, but for now I have not had time to process exactly how I feel. It is not long since we all lost Barbara, and our livelihood; life has not been the same since then. I hope Maggie told you how she feels?"

"Yes, I think so. I will return tomorrow to the Coromandel. But I will be here again if we get our next break away sometime."

"Do not come on my account, but you are very welcome anytime."

I returned to the sitting room where Hector said, "Harry, I don't know much about what is going on – the girls don't always tell me – but I will be over your way with a delivery into Kuaotunu next month. You may even be unloading our ship, but if not, I will get word to you so perhaps we can have a lunch while the ship is being unloaded. I usually get a few hours while she is beached to avail myself of a little walk about which is good for my knees."

"That would be wonderful. I will keep an eye out for you. I really must be off now but I will see you all soon, I hope."

We shook hands, then he said, "Maggie dear, show him out." We walked to the door together. I went to kiss her on the cheek as she opened the door, but she turned in that same instant and our lips met.

We both stood back, almost as if we had been stung by a bee, a mixture of horror and delight in our eyes as they met. I wanted to kiss her again.

Suddenly, Maggie threw her arms around me and whispered in my ear, "Write to me."

I stared at her in amazement, my heart pounding with excitement. *What does that mean?* I searched her face unsuccessfully for an answer as I walked away.

Oh, Maggie, dare I tell you of my captured heart! Until this moment, I have tamed the desire I feel for you, casting it out like some evil thing, banishing the thoughts aside as things never to be spoken out loud or even imagined in the heart, yet they linger deep inside as friends and not as enemies. Perhaps I am the enemy, the evil thing being unable to choose, a horror you wish to cast aside and never see again for the sake of your sister.

I looked back over my shoulder at her mischievous grin; it imprinted in my mind.

I walked backwards, watching her. "I will," I called out as I walked away down the road. *What did Euphemia mean …'did Maggie tell you how she feels?'*

My heart felt strangely warm again, surprisingly delightful as I made my way along the road until I flagged down a passing cabbie.

A week later, it all seemed like a dream knee-deep in mud, as I returned to the business of hauling goods into the thriving community, my thoughts returning again and again to Euphemia and Maggie as we carried our loads to and fro. *Did Euphemia really love her independence more! What of that accidental kiss at the front door with Maggie … was it a fortunate accident when our lips met so blissfully …? What did she mean by asking me to write?*

It's not long till Christmas when she will be together again with the family. I will send a greeting card and a letter on Sunday; perhaps I can broach the subject.

I called past Thompson's general store; bought a pretty card and a few pieces of scented writing paper. Then we all walked up to the Kuaotunu. It had been a huge 16-hour day for us all as we found our way to the bar for a roast meal; it was standing room only as I stood three deep to order our stagger juice, shouting above the noise of excited voices.

We found a bench and a slab table in one corner that looked out to the street. A fire roared in the grate and big Roy knocked out a tune on the piano, barely heard above the bellows of men in the lounge.

"Harry, where is your squeezebox? I think you should bring it to liven things up down here sometime."

I took out a cigarette, which Rusty lit for me. "Rust, if it were any more lively they would be out dancing in the streets. Anyway, my arms are sore from unloading sacks of grain."

"Probably sore from wrestling. How's it going? I don't often see you buying cards … so what's going on with Euphemia?"

"It's the strangest thing. I told you about Euphemia's outburst and her not wishing to be tied down. What I didn't tell you was, as I was leaving the house, I turned to give Maggie a goodbye kiss on the cheek and she turned to me in the same moment and we kissed, literally."

"On the lips?" Rusty laughed heartily. "What did Phee say?"

"Maggie saw me to the door alone … we just stood there, not quite knowing what to do or say. Rusty, these last few days I cannot get it out of my head. That kiss was warm."

"Sounds like 'A nods as good as a wink' if you know what I

mean … Is that who the scented paper is for?"

"She asked me to write to her. But there's more … When I spoke to Phee, she asked me, '*Did Maggie tell you how she feels?*' I never thought anything of it till we kissed, now I think of nothing else."

Rusty's eyebrows rose. "Now I can see why you've been so distracted. I just assumed it was Euphemia's outburst. This is complicated … What will you do?"

I shook my head. "I admire this family and feel strangely connected to them. Maggie is gorgeous. If I cannot be with Euphemia then I will happily pursue Maggie."

"What if she doesn't feel the same way?"

"Only one way to find out. In the meantime, I will throw myself into training and take my mind off it all."

"Who are you training with? I think I will come by next time to watch you."

I'd been training with two of the lads from Vermont – Foster and Leahy – who were good sportsmen with similar weight – about twelve stone.

"There's about ten of us: Peebles, Casey, Coglan, McLeod, Blumbry, Tuohy, Leehy and, of course, Sutherland, who is one of the best I've seen. There's not much between them, and they all need people to train with for the upcoming tournament. Most of us are exhausted after swinging a pick inside a tunnel. I suppose it gives us a little sanity."

"When is the match?"

"It's a few weeks away yet – 23rd of September – and should bring a packed crowd. It's bad enough when we are training, we could charge bystanders in the hall to watch."

Joe and Johnny had been talking to the lads at the next table and turned to join us again.

"How did you go today, Joe? At one stage I thought you were going to overtake me when you offloaded so quickly at *Try Fluke*;

you were catching up all day."

"I think I might have but, you have the better team and John does not offload as quickly."

"Get out of here, you little runt. Look who's talking!"

"Anyway, where is there room to pass."

"I saw Johnny get held up with the road gang trying to put in another corduroy of Manuka to even out the road."

"Harry, it doesn't seem to matter how much work is done on the road, within a week its back to deep ruts, jarring loads, with wheels sliding sideways into deep ponds of mud."

"Makes you hang on tight, Rusty!"

"John, did you pick up any interesting folk today?

"Only a couple of lads coming home from school. You, Harry?"

"I picked up Jack Sutherland who I have been training with. He paid me two shillings to hitch a ride up the mile to the top settlement. It's the first time we've spoken properly. He's Australian, from Victoria, twenty-six … and comes from a mining family. He studied mining at Ballarat but particularly Metallurgy and Chemistry. He's made good money from both wrestling and mining. He was saying that there is a school of mines about to open up here in the valley, not far from where we live. He urged me to look at opportunities to get into tunnelling for the railways."

"Harry, there's no railways here unless you count our little mine carts. I bet we carry similar loads on the tracks carrying quartz rock from the tunnels."

"John, he said that a team of men had been brought in from America at great expense to help with all the tunnels, bridges and rail traversing through the coast. They wanted to teach skills in tunnelling in all the mining towns so that men were educated, experienced and competent. He said the government cannot get lines laid quick enough with all the coal needed everywhere."

"How could you do that and work?"

"A School of Mines has already opened in Thames. It's on-the-job training, working tunnels during the day with study at night; they meet once a week to have classes. He said the government were just in the process of making it compulsory to have a certificate to be in charge of mining and tunnelling.

Rusty erupted. "About bloody time! Too many men dig a hole then shore it up badly, wondering why they get buried alive, blown to bits with gelignite or poisoned with gas. There's an awful lot to learn from what I can see."

John had just sat down again with beers as I talked about the Certificate of Mines. His face turned visibly sour as he looked at me.

"Harry, I can see by your face you can already see an angle – come on, out with it. I just hope you aren't thinking of doing that on top of us working twelve to fourteen hours a day, and training for your wrestling matches too."

"John, you are right. How long can a man work like this! Have you seen all the 50-year-olds? They look sick; their bodies are spent. The School of Mines is right here, a brilliant opportunity to look for gold, learn the trade, then I could take contracts all over the country laying rails while using the Certificate to be in charge of Tunnel Gangs."

Rusty rolled tobacco into a cigarette paper. Joe looked deep in thought. "Couldn't you just do it without the school? Surely it can't be that hard."

"He told me it's a complex process to learn, with many areas of expertise to master: Mineralogy studying rocks and Metallurgy with steel, practical chemistry for blasting, ventilation and explosives, engineering loads, drainage, land and mine surveying, practical astronomy.

"Practical astronomy? Whatever for?"

"Rust, I think, it is for plotting a course across a set of

mountains if the tunnel is miles in length underground. They also teach mathematics, mechanical drawing, mining and applied mechanics, Physics, pumping, pit works, pneumatic hammers and steam-powered engines with a raft of other things like management, and record keeping.

"I wouldn't mind learning all that … it would be interesting."

"What's to stop us all being certified. We could take on a few other lads to help carry the loads."

"I think I want to be a farmer – I'm dreaming of owning land in Martinborough one day."

Rusty slapped Joe on the back. "Joe, you stick to that dream. I'm with you … Harry, how long does it take?"

"It's a three-year course, but you can work extra hours and shorten it a little. He said he'd put in a word for me to get in now, and be ready for all the lines they propose to run the length of New Zealand."

"I bet there is good money in it, Harry," Joe said.

John had gone quiet and looked less than happy. "It would suit you perfectly being in charge of men, but where does it leave us!?"

"What's on your mind, John? Come on … there are plenty of good men about that would be sick of swinging a pick in the dark to fill your shoes carting goods. I know two men – climbers who scale mighty Kauri trees all day for the gum sap, just to be outdoors. Imagine doing that. Some of those trees are twenty feet to the first branch. They're getting paid half what you make."

John stood and banged his fist on the table. "It's no good you going off half-cocked. I've come up here to support you carting goods when I could have stayed down in Ohinimuri."

"John, it's been a big day. While you're standing, how about cooling off and buying us another round."

"Bahh! Rusty, you don't know him like I do. First he talks about it, then next minute he's up to his armpits in it. It all sounds so wonderful!"

"I'm sure I could still work outside of the mining, carting goods to work in with you guys; it's not like you need me a lot of the time. They need men every day to run one of the three shifts on the stampers. I could do twelve at night till eight in the morning or four in the afternoon to twelve. It wasn't my intention to keep you here, John. If you can make more than ten bob a day in these times, good luck to you … This seems like a real opportunity for me, and I'm going to take it."

"See what I mean, Rusty. *Pahh!*" John stood glaring at me.

"Come and join me then. Get a certificate. It could open doors for a whole career."

"What, and have you in charge of us?! I am only here until I can earn enough money to buy a farm. I'm with Joe, holding onto Father's dream of being a landowner."

John took the empty jugs begrudgingly and headed for the thirsty throng at the bar.

Joe looked admiringly at me. "Good for you, Harry. There's no moss growing between your toes."

Talking to the boys made me more determined than ever. I thought, *I will make inquiries first thing in the morning. Sutherland said to ask the Manager at Mariposa; he would know what was happening in town. I can kill two birds with one stone, using my time here to learn the trade, make some money and get a qualification.* I could not help Jack's words going over in my mind. *'Harry, diversify, be in charge of men, you are born to it.' … Jack, you're exactly right.*

John came back looking salty, but had calmed down a little as he put the jugs down. I filled everyone's glasses and stood holding my beer aloft. "Thanks, John. Here's to having a few wins along the way!"

I gripped his shoulder. He looked at me, but held his words, while I said, "Here's to new opportunities!"

We all shouted, "To new opportunities!"

It wasn't long till that opportunity came my way, as I had to go through to the School of Mines in Thames, Ted at *Mariposa* having asked me to pick up a casting directly from Price Engineering in Thames and deliver it back to the workshop the following day.

When I got there, The School of Mines was only a few streets away from Prices, so I went over there to find Mr Cahill; he told me there was still a place for one more student in the upcoming year and, given that this was a high-level course, places filled fast.

"Can you tell me a little more about it. I have asked around and found out a few things."

"These days, lad, if you want to be in charge of men in this line of work, legislation is pushing that you must be qualified. You will need to send your application immediately if you wanted to be part of the next intake."

So I did just that.

The Friday before the big match, I received a reply in the mail. I ripped open the envelope to find I had been accepted. I was so excited and planned to write to Maggie and send my letter on the outgoing mail boat before the predicted storm hit on the morrow, right when the match would be on. The sky grew darker by the hour as the wind started to lash the coast, throwing huge waves high onto the beach front. By morning, everything was awash with a muddy torrent of water scouring the river bed out, and threatening to burst its banks. I had not managed to write to Maggie.

"Come on, lads, we won't get a place to see the match. If it rains much more, we'll need a boat to get there."

"Luckily, this weather will have stopped hundreds from attending."

We made our way to Loram's Hall at 7pm. The place was already packed, the roads completely blocked by every horse and cart owned on the Coromandel Peninsula.

"Could we have had a worse night? I think they let a dam go in heaven last night," Sutherland shouted.

"It's going to be a great match though between two of the best wrestlers on our doorstep. Foster and Leahy are fairly equal opponents."

By the time 8pm came, the roar of 300 men was deafening. Sawdust and mattresses had been laid out with five different wrestling styles planned and £10 a side with 75% of door takings to the winner. I had literally never seen a more exciting match since we fought in the tug of war with the Cabbies in Wellington. Leahy finally won but threw money down for Foster as a subscription, which everyone added to.

Foster spoke up saying he would not do another match at present as it took too much time and energy to train. The dynamite smoke had wrecked his lungs and he needed to work for his family to live.

The next day, I wondered if anyone in town would get any work done at all as every man looked like a light had been ignited, trying to guess when the next competition would be played in town.

It never took much to be the talk of the town in such a small community. If there was an event to gamble on, men would line up for a flutter. The horse races that Kuaotunu was famed for were one such event.

Chapter 24

In the Nick of Time

Joe and I were sitting on the beach waiting for a ship to bring in its cargo while the other boys went for tobacco. It was one of those pearler days with the sun glistening on the water like diamonds and the waves barely lapping the shore.

"Joe, there are a few men riding the track around the lake to prepare themselves with their horses. It's too exposed, I think we should keep it quiet. It's good to have a slight advantage of surprise. "Nothing around here happens without everyone knowing."

"We could smuggle Black Jack into the valley under the cover of darkness and train him up in the bush."

"Word will still get out."

The biggest problem is that I've not ridden Black Jack; he sounds like a bit of a handful."

"Oh, he's feisty, but he loves the chase. Do you think you are up for it?"

"I am looking forward to it – I have heard so much about this famous horse – and I have had a fair bit of experience on a horse."

"Have you a plan to train because the race meeting is fast approaching."

What do you think our competition is?"

"I am not sure. This is the sort of place the king could drop in with his thoroughbred or a farmer unhitch his colt. I have him registered for the day, hoping not too many would take an interest."

"When do you think he will make it up here?"

"Jack is sending another team with him on the ship. They need to arrive in about two weeks, closer to the time, we will ride him in from Mercury Bay and keep him out of sight for a few days.

"What about if we stay over there for four days or so, there is not going to be much on, being Christmas day. I can ride him out of sight, giving us a few days to bond."

"That sounds even better, then you can ride him into town on the day."

As the days drew closer, we found out from the club secretary, Mr Gribble, that there were going to be seven races. We were entered in two: The Kuaotunu Cup and The Publican's Purse. We all decided to pack up our gear and stay over the hill in Mercury Bay. When the race was over, we would ride back over the hill, and be home for Christmas.

The day arrived as we settled into the Mercury Bay Hotel, and arranged to pick up the horses. Joe took Black Jack out, watered him, led him round the yard, all the while talking to him softly. He brushed him down before he saddled him, gently rode along the beach and then out country a little way. About an hour later, he came in at a colossal speed, with a grin from one ear to the other.

"Harry, he's an absolute beauty! The stories you told of him do not do him justice. We have a real chance for a win, if the competition's not too steep."

"Good boy, Joe. Let's see how we go in a few days' time."

Joe spent the next three days riding Black Jack around Whitianga, putting him through his paces, while we enjoyed the few days to relax after such a monstrous year. Christmas day we kicked back, making the most of time. The next day we went ahead, leading the horses over the hill, leaving Joe to follow for the big race day on the morrow. We were like school boys before a match, full of excitement.

Joe had got away before dawn, and tied up outside in the bush before we woke.

We were all dressed in minutes, and more anticipation filled the air than when the jolly man in red had come only twenty-four hours before. The stampers were silent but the crowds were full of cheer as they gathered around the horses and carefully weighed up their odds. I patted Joe on the back.

"Give 'em hell, Joe!"

We watched the horses line up ready to go, nerves rising as our race would be next. I whispered to Rusty, "Have you ever seen such an unusual group of horses. I don't think there's a thoroughbred amongst them. Here, Rusty, go and put this bet on for us, quickly before they close." I handed him quite a few pound notes.

He grinned and nodded and hurried off.

I hope we come somewhere in the top group. I scanned the stands, looking for familiar faces; waved to a few of the lads.

Soon Rusty returned. "There was quite a queue. I put a sizeable bet on our Black Beauty. Jack has certainly looked after him for us?"

"I think he certainly has a good chance of winning something."

"… but he's not used to running on a track like this, it will be fairly torn up in this race. How do you think Joe will do?"

"I guess we won't have long to find out."

As the first race got away, the crowd erupted with shouts of encouragement as the horses found their way along the back of the beach then turned to head madly round the lake. The judges stood poised watching from their stand as the first horse Volcano flew past the finish line well ahead of the rest.

Next was the Publican's Purse. I had butterflies as Joe sat poised perfectly upright on Black Jack. He always looked fine in a saddle. The crowd quieted, waiting for the gun, then suddenly they were off. Black's coat glistened in the sunlight as his muscles rippled just like that first Saturday I saw him at Jack's. He fought his way up out of the pack of eight, looking good as he rounded the bend coming round for the last stretch. He was neck and neck with Cornish Boy as they headed toward the last leg and past the Judges stand. I couldn't tell who had won from all the shouting as the crowd exploded like a blast of dynamite and blocked my view.

Then I saw Joe heading back toward us with a big smile on his face.

The result announced over the loud hailer: Black Jack had won by a nose. Rusty leapt up and down, shouting "We won! We won!"

"I put all that money you gave me on this race!"

"Where's the ticket, go and see."

I went the opposite way and found Joe. "How was it, Joe? You did well out there!"

"I felt like we would win. It was exhilarating! Black is a champion, his power going forward … it was like riding a traction engine."

"I think it could be another good Christmas for us all. Do you think he'll recover for the next race?"

"He should do. He feels like he has plenty of running left in him."

"Well done, lad."

Rusty's red hair bobbed bright in the sunlight, matching his face as he came toward me through the crowed. Keeping his hands in his pockets, he whispered, "You won £35 and 6 pence – 12 weeks wages! And there is prize money too."

"Well done, boys. How did you go, John?"

"I can't complain." he grinned. "I'll be spending some, let's put it that way."

"What about you, Rusty?" He pulled out his hand and it looked like at least £5."

"Enough for me to go see Ruby for a few days."

I wrapped up £10 and buttoned it down into Joe's pocket. "Thanks, little brother, you did well. One race to go," I said, smiling.

Our next race was the last for the day, then we were heading back over the hill before dark to paddock rest him while we were away.

The horses lined up; this time there were two other horses that would cause a little competition but the jockeys were not nearly as light as Joe. The gun went off and all plunged forward and headed down the straight. Black again had to fight his way through the pack. We watched, our breaths held, and hearts pumping as Black stayed near the lead. They headed up the last leg toward the judge's stand and up when the roar of the crowd. From where I stood it was hard to pick who had made it across the line first.

I sprinted out to meet Joe again, just as it came over the loud hailer "Jessica, first; Black Jack, second." I shook Joe's hand when he'd leapt from the saddle. "Who would have thought … two wins in a day. Congratulations! You rode it well, Joe."

Three people came up and congratulated us.

"Who is the owner of Black Jack? I am from out of town," one asked.

"Harry Bagust and my friend here, Rusty O'Flaherty. Did you have a win?"

He shook my hand vigorously. "Jack McGuiness. I liked the

look of your stallion so I picked him for a win and I am going home a happy man."

"I'm glad you had a good day – we were just as surprised as you."

"You're a bit of a black horse, Harry. I didn't know you had such a fine animal. Race horses and wrestling." He shook his head and wandered away with his companions.

I found Rusty. "Are you ready to head home or are you going back to celebrate?"

"I am having an early night. I took that last ticket in: there's more winnings. I didn't tell you I put £4 on the last race for a place for us. I will save what I've got to take Ruby out in style, otherwise you know what will happen," he said, laughing.

"Rusty, I feel suddenly exhausted. I think the adrenalin that has kept me going for days has just run out. I am really looking forward to getting home."

Rusty bundled up the pound notes and slid them into my pocket. "Thanks for placing those bets. Our boat doesn't leave till tomorrow afternoon so I think I will sleep here the night and get away after breakfast. You will make the boat?"

"I've got these *friends* I bought Scottish whiskey from; it's a special supplier in Kuaotunu. It's good medicine in times like these. Come on, we'll sleep like babies."

Rusty's special medicine had us not knowing what day it was, even at 6am. It therefore took us a while to get going but we packed up, loaded up our horses, and bought a loaf of bread on the way out.

We all fell asleep aboard the steamer almost before she set off. By the time we berthed in Wellington, we were a little revived, even if suffering from a dry mouth.

We must have looked a sorry sight as we arrived because the first thing Ellen did was stoke up the copper to boil all our clothes. "You're not coming into my house smelling like billy goats! Go and clean up."

We woke in the morning to the smell of butter and sugar as Mother had cooked a great slab of fruit cake, which now sat cooling on the table. The kids were all running about playing chasey, except Joe who had suddenly become a man. Not enough though for Lovey to stop chastising her little brother for the hair on his chin. Mother complained bitterly, squeezing Joe in a tight bear hug, that she'd sent away a boy, who'd become a man. I found myself two or three times sitting in the corner of a room, nodding off as I listened to the joyful fragrance of family. Sounds of laughter, playful banter, chopping in the kitchen, smells of a roast in the oven, a woman's voice, then I would come to and wonder where I was again. It was a delight to see the whole family content, even for such a short time.

It was a wild party celebrating with everyone, seeing in the new year. It seemed like we had no sooner arrived in Martinborough than we were on our way home again. Lovey would hardly let Joe go, making him promise to return soon. Mother tried to hold back her tears as she waved us off, but her hanky soon came out of her pinny pocket.

On my return, I launched myself into my new job, juggling between being a student and miner while helping the lads desperate to run loads. The work was going to take time to adjust to, from being out in every weather to being totally inside in total darkness. I had still not managed to write to Maggie as it had been a busy few weeks with all the excitement of wrestling, horse racing and sailing home for Christmas. I finally penned a letter to her, sitting in the candle light one night after the lads had all gone off to bed.

Dear Maggie

How are you and the family?. I know it is not that long since I saw you but it feels like an age.

We have been slogging it out with long hours hauling cargo into Kuaotunu before the festive season arrived. Christmas feels odd this year with only the three boys around although we had a few days home. Most men were displaced from family at this time and the normal festivities of family are rather lacking. The big events around are the horse racing and wrestling, the latter held on the 26th of December. These are one of the only days off that men get to enjoy out here and the stampers shut down. We have a good horse that Jack Lane sent up from Wellington with the last batch of horses for the year. Joe rode like a champion jockey after only a few days to get used to Black Jack, securing two wins, one first and the other second. We left for Martinborough directly after that just for a few days over Christmas as nothing much stops here. There is too much at stake for them to shut everything down and they still need coal.

I have been training long hours wrestling as I met a group of champion wrestlers that are part of the mining crews here. I have a match coming up in March over in Coromandel against a chap about my size.

The church created an atmosphere of cheer around with Christmas carols being sung by a group of folk coming round door to door with lanterns and little parcels of Christmas mince pies. It made me think of your heavenly voice and I wondered if you had been practising to sing in a Christmas service this year.

It will be a particularly tough time for you again,

without Barbara to celebrate with. I only hope the Captain was in time for your Mother's remembrance day.

The children down at the school hall produced a serious Christmas play, which ended up the most hilarious affair. Some of the small boys dressed up as three wise men, Joseph, Mary and wee Baby Jesus in the manger acted by a few others. One of the boys' beards fell off and while the children tried to put it back on, the other boys shepherds crook caught a sheet of the other, which fell off, leaving him in a white singlet. Everyone was in stitches.

I am most excited to tell you, there is an opportunity for me to learn mining up here. It is a course through the School of Mines, studying at night and working during the day. The places were filling fast for the new year, so I sent in my application straight away and received a letter saying I had been accepted. It is a three-year course with the intake starting this month. I think of you often and am spurred on in my work at the thought of seeing you this new year. The thing is, Maggie, when I was leaving your house, Euphemia asked, "Did Maggie tell you how she feels?"… that question has gone over and over in my head. I realised I may not have understood what she meant. Was there more you wished to say? I have layed in bed many nights, wishing I had the chance to ask you again… even though I have had love for Euphemia, I cannot stop thinking of you. I keep seeing your face as I go about my days. I look forward to your reply,

Yours sincerely,

Harry.

Chapter 25

A Little Bird Told Me

Apprehension had set in as it was the last week before my course started: I was about to enter the pay roll for Vermont mining. Joe came past from the beach with sacks of flour and oats loaded high. It was only the previous morning that I had said to him, 'Joe, keep an eye out: Hector could turn up any day'.

"Harry, Captain McQuarrie is asking after you. I told him I was your younger brother. He's delivered a load of horse feed from up north, and Canterbury flour."

"Good lad, I will head down there now."

I arrived in the small settlement near the beach and corralled the horses in a pen. I found Hector with four loaves of bread under his arm from the bakery.

"Captain, it's great to see you." We shook hands heartily.

"Happy New Year, laddie! So this is where you are hiding out."

We headed to the Kuaotunu for lunch and found a table in the back corner.

"I have a letter burning a hole in my pocket from young Maggie," he said as he sat down. "She spoke to me one night about you." He put the letter on the table and I looked at the perfect handwriting.

"Sir, I owe you an apology and an explanation. I have behaved rather foolishly."

He sat there wordlessly, looking at me.

"When Emily fell pregnant," I began, "we were wed in a registry office. When she later lost the child, she fled to Australia. It has been a tumultuous year for us all I feel. I had hoped Phee would forgive my folly but I completely understand her reason for being upset."

"It came as a shock to all of us, lad, as you say in the midst of our many troubles, but I have lived long enough to know life's never perfect. She has strong ideas, our Euphemia; you have got to respect her for that. She has a lot on her plate at present. I am not sure she will ever be the marrying kind, and it'll take a brave man to tame that wild filly."

He stopped for a moment and looked directly at me. "Harry, you must also have been aware of young Maggie's attention?" He tapped his finger on the letter on the table. "I suspect I would not otherwise have taken this letter from her insistent hand when she asked me to deliver it personally to you."

I picked up the letter, which sent my heart immediately into a spin as I imagined her words. "Sir, as I may not see you for many months, should Maggie feel the way I do toward her, do I have your permission to court her? I know I will be away for months at a time – I do not even know yet where this gold mining town will lead me – but I am resourceful enough to provide for her. I admire so many things about her. You have a wonderful family, sir."

"Well, I am keen to see my girls happy … Son, if Maggie's smiling face is anything to go by … I think she might be agreeable, but it is up to her entirely."

"Would you like me to ask Euphemia's permission first?"

"She has already given her blessing. I spoke to her before I left and she said she will not stand in the way of Maggie's happiness."

I looked at him in shock. "How does she know of my feelings for Maggie when even my own heart wrestles with it?"

"I think she saw it even if you did not. She could see how you felt but she also wants Maggie to have a chance for love."

I leant back on my chair as a wave of relief came over me. *Phee is an amazing woman. But I already knew that.*

"Now tell me about this wrestling … how is the competition?"

We chatted then, about wrestling and that the world's greatest athlete, Donald Dinnie, would be there in two months and how wrestling had become popular and that I was training to compete against ten other men. Then we talked about my new venture into mining and gaining the qualifications required. I ended with,

"As it turns out, the top wrestling athletes are right here in Kuaotunu and not only that we are expecting the world's greatest athlete Donald Dinnie here in two months. The wrestling has almost gotten out of control, everyone is talking about it. I am training at present with ten other men that are the elite of New Zealand.

"I saw the posters up everywhere, that is certainly an amazing opportunity. What about this School of Mines, how will you fit it all in."

"We are going to employ another man and still make good money on our contract. I will work one of the mining shifts and then help out where I am needed."

"What sort of qualification would you come out with?"

"It will give me a 'Certificate of Mining' needed to run any rail projects now or be in charge on a mine site. A large number of the pupils are actually studying from the railways, but the part that interests me is the roading, tunnelling and track laying. There are endless opportunities available with the main trunk line rumoured to be started soon. "You were the one who first spoke of working for the railways."

"Well, if that is the case then I am glad I spoke up," Hector replied.

"It's a fine opportunity to learn the trade with a School of Mines right on our doorstep."

"A little bird told me you had a win too?"

"That was a bit of luck really, Joe rode so well. It was nice to have a little money in our pockets for Christmas when we headed home for four days. We ended up winning over £40 on the race right over there on the beach. Our horse Black Jack has been well looked after back in Island Bay."

"Harry, you make me tired. I have worked like you in my life but now, at seventy, my body has given all it can. I am keeping my hand in but Murdoch can do all the leg work now. He is a good lad, and I think it's in his veins like this old sailor.

"I worry for Hannah though. She should have studied at university. I am not sure what she will do. She is quite headstrong, and please don't be offended should you visit next time – she is most disgusted with you. And don't forget, if you need connections there are a number of lodges you may wish to be a part of in Thames; it's good for business, as you never know who you will meet."

We ate a hearty meal but now I could not wait to read the letter that I kept looking at on the table. Murdoch came along the street looking for The Captain. I tapped on the window and he came through the doors.

We shook hands. "I hardly recognised you with those whiskers and strong arms. Sounds like you are enjoying being on the seas."

"It helps to have one of the best captains in the Pacific. He's not easy on me though … has to show the other men he doesn't have a favourite. It's alright though, I know I'm the favourite." We laughed as we rose and walked to the door.

"Look after him. I might see you soon if I am up your way. All the best. Captain, look after those knees!" I shook his hands heartily. "Please give my love to each of your family."

"I will, son. All the best for your upcoming wrestle. Remember, it's not about having the strength of a horse, it is the strength of your heart, character and mind that will sustain you in life. God bless you, son."

I went back into the hotel and sat to read Maggie's letter in that quiet corner alone.

Dear Harry,

Thank you for your letter, it was a most pleasant surprise and I am delighted that you spoke of your thoughts toward me. I have tried to hide my feelings for the sake of Euphemia since I first met you when you came to our house. You have indeed set my heart alight. Tea with you the other day was a great turmoil for me trying desperately to hold fast my admiration. I could not help my feelings for, as much as I tried to quench them, they kept springing up, betraying me. I know part of you will always love Euphemia and her you. On one hand I feel sad for her to miss out on your love, she has a strength of character that I do not. I too regret not speaking up the day you were here which was made more difficult still when we accidentally kissed. When Father said he was coming your way with a shipment, I leapt at the opportunity to send a reply, by Father's hand. I would love to see where you are one day soon as I try to imagine your wee settlement. We are settling into this neighbourhood, which is growing by the day. It is a convenient place to live with easy access to the city and port as we are close to Kingsland's small community.

There are plans well under way to have a tram running, possibly right past our house, perhaps by 1896. It is wonderful that you have found such a great opportunity there. I will be very interested to hear more of your

I sat reading it again, devouring each word like a hungry kitten. It seemed a long while between receiving letters back and forth to Maggie, sitting up late in the candlelight trying not to fall asleep. I would read and reread her letters, remembering many lines by heart. It did not help that I had such long days, mining, studying, lifting weights and exercise. Weeks slipped by unnoticed. I was continuously working, eating and sleeping, so it was a great distraction to head over to the Kuaotunu to catch up with the boys.

"Joe, it's great to see you. How did you go today?"

"Everyone's gone mad talking about Donald Dinnie. Is he really the world's greatest athlete? Do you think you will get to spar with him when he gets here?"

"I doubt it. He is going to wrestle against Sutherland though."

"Is it true he is the champion in sprint, hurdles, pole vault, putting the stone, hammer throw, tossing the caber and wrestling. Did I forget anything?

"Long and high jump."

"Is there anything he can't do?"

"I don't know how he does it. We're an athletic family but I could never lift those 775 pound stones and he carried them five yards, that's not human, and he turns sixty this year."

I slapped Rusty on the arm. "Aren't they in your neck of the woods?"

"The Donald Dinnie Stones … I've seen them alright. I walked across the Potarch Bridge and back where he carried them. He and is Da were stonemasons. Each boulder has an iron ring fixed to it, so that scaffolds could be attached. They would lift them up as counter-balance."

Joes face was lit up like a Christmas tree "No wonder he is considered The Strong Man of the Age. Doesn't he also hold a title for "World Champion Wrestler."

"Aye. It is going to be crowded here in March when the crowds come to his matches."

"It was bad enough in shocking weather three months back. You are so fortunate to be training with Sutherland. What's he like?"

"Slippery as an eel. Just when you think you have him for a fall, you're thrown flat on your back, or flipped on your head. I have had a couple of good bouts with him though. Brother James is a good wrestler too. We used to train together, but he was always a lot stronger than me. I think if he was here, it would be close now."

Chapter 26

Legend in One's Own Lifetime

It was now March 20th '96 and only a week away till the match with the famous Dinnie and Sutherland. Wrestling had become a craze in the Coromandel, especially since the last big match. Sutherland thought I should test myself out on a medal winner and arranged a bout with John Morrison, who was the proprietor of the Royal in Kuaotunu. I had been training every chance I got. The boys were excited on the afternoon of the bout and finished work early. We borrowed a decent cart for the journey, and arrived in the town of Coromandel with plenty of time to relax.

We found a crowded Hotel that was open for dinner. The boys ordered at the bar; I had a piece of dry toast. Already people were gathering in the streets. Foster saw us sitting in the window and came through to wish me the best. "What styles are you wrestling?"

"It'll be Greco, Catch and Cumberland. He's about the same height."

"Take your time; don't be in a rush, and don't forget to have fun out there. You could end up being a legend in your own lifetime!"

"Thanks, William, for the good advice. Great match in September." He waved as he went.

"Harry, he was from the Kuaotunu bout. He looks about your weight. What about Morrison?"

"He's twenty-six and weighs in at eleven stone. He's been a

miner."

"We should have had the bout in Kuaotunu. It's almost impossible for people to get accommodation here. Coromandel has exploded in the last eighteen months. A policeman I met said he even had two lads voluntarily ask for lodgings in the lock up, just to have a roof for the night."

"I heard of a man who rents his boat out on the river."

"John, they wanted to have the match in the Coromandel Town Hall to draw a bigger crowd. We get a percentage of the door sales and £5 a side for a win. We don't have a hall big enough in Kuaotunu. Anyway, it's only two hours by boat from Thames and who doesn't like getting out on a Friday night after being cooped up like a rat in a dark hole."

"I read in the paper that Morrison last year had twice tussled with seven of the most well-known wrestlers in the district – Robertson, Ryan, Gleeson, Quinn, Dickson and McKay – both times coming away with a second-place medal. You might just end up being a legend if you win." Rusty offered me a cigarette.

"No thanks, Rust. I thought I would knock those off for a bit. I find when I'm out running, I've been getting a little wheezy."

"What chance do you think you will have of beating him?"

"I think a reasonable chance, Joe, but he's a fine wrestler. You remember on the Annual Excursion of the Thames Miners Union. It was a spectacular day with thousands crawling out of caves like ants to sugar. Gleeson won and Morrison came second. It's like Hector said to me the other day: it's about mental toughness and skill, not brute strength. I've had to wrestle many times below my weight, but am I mentally tough enough for Morrison? Who knows."

"Harry, that place was like a carnival. I've never seen anything like that in the capital city. It seems like all the best talent is here." Rusty already had a towel around his neck, ready. "All the best athletes pitted themselves against each other in every running, jumping, or throwing event imaginable."

Joe looked sad. "Unfortunately, I had to work that day. The paper said the steamers *Gailoch* and *Rotomahana* had to turn 200 away in Thames or they'd have sunk. They had 500 people on board each one."

Joe said, "The wrestling was the favourite. I had to stand up on my toes to see over the huge crowd."

"It will be a good test of my training. you can only stretch yourself when you pit yourself up against a stronger opponent."

John looked decidedly relaxed. "I get excited crowds like that sometimes at the footy, but that day I think it even drowned out the thumping of the stampers."

"John, you're an excellent athlete, and every second person in the bar knows you." I stood. "Look, hardly a soul knows me! I'm going for a walk to warm up. I'll see you in a few hours. Come early so you can get a seat."

It seemed like every man had crawled from every valley within a hundred miles as I took a brisk walk along the river to warm my muscles before finding my way to the back door of the hall. The excitement was already building within, the voices growing louder as I changed into my shorts and soft shoes in the bathroom and picked up my skipping rope to stay focused.

I checked my watch and took my place in the corner with Rusty. The Referee, Mr Carlisle, came to our corner and asked if we were ready then he brought us together in the ring before introducing us. We wished each other the best as Carlisle reminded us of the rules. Then we faced off for the first bout.

Suddenly we were locked in a classic Cumberland struggle, twisting and throwing from side to side as we measured each other's strength. We entered into a long, impossible contest as we were evenly matched, until I threw him suddenly off balance, catching his foot and throwing him to the floor. The crowd roared with delight. Rusty leapt up excitedly, and waited with water and wet towels till I sat down to catch my breath. *This is the culmination of all this struggle, a chance to burn off frustration.*

Rusty handed me another towel to cool off with before we set about thrashing on the mats for the Grecian Roman bout. "You almost looked like you were having fun out there. It's like Foster said: enjoy it, Harry," he said.

The next struggle was just as intense and at one stage he almost had me pinned as we strained and fought. Then like a voice, Hector's words came to me: "It's not about the strength of a horse!"

Suddenly, I thought of Father stuck in that mental asylum! I braced my back like cast iron. *'This one's for you, Father!* I gripped my opponent tight and in one motion threw him over my head onto his back. Again, the crowd jumped to their feet, elated, till the Master of Ceremonies quieted the crowd once more.

Rusty stood in awe. "Harry, how did you do that? You threw him like a match stick over your head. I've never seen you do anything like that before!"

I shook my head and shrugged. "Rusty, I surprised myself. Let's get this last one over and see what the judges say."

"Give it to 'em, Harry. You've got time. Look after those ribs – he's good at the Catch-as-Catch-can, so take your time."

The crowd now hushed as we faced each other. I was not familiar with his particular skills, but as he gripped my arm, I braced, twisted and threw his leg with lightning speed, throwing him down. Back and forward we fought on the mat, it sounding like the roof would lift off as the thunderous shouts fluctuated in waves. He was over me now, muscles bristling. I could not shake his grip, as we seemed to hold interminably. Then in a split second, his grip faltered, almost imperceptibly, in the dripping sweat. Swiftly, I caught his arm through, and thrust against his shoulders, slamming them to the mat. It was like a shotgun blast as the excited crowd shook the floor. I thought it might collapse under their pounding feet. Rusty came with a towel and couldn't help himself; he picked me up in his arms and lifted me clean off the floor like a child.

Mr Carlisle quieted the crowd, and asked for the judges' verdict.

All I could hear was Rusty shouting, "We won! We won!!"

I shook hands with Morrison, who seemed truly happy.

"Well played, Harry. Come to my bar, I'll shout you a drink sometime."

"I will hold you to that. You are a worthy opponent, Morrison; we must do it again."

Suddenly, we were surrounded by men slapping me on the back and shaking my hand. I looked up to see my brothers' beaming smiles. A moment captured in time, *if only Father was here to see it.*

The next morning, I woke to Bolt licking my face. I gave him a pat and squinted into the sunlight, wondering what time it was. I felt sore all over as I swung my legs out of bed. My trainer had said to take two days to recover, which I did lazing about in the house, reading some manuals I needed to catch up on. I had slept like a baby for the two nights, but was woken the second by shouts coming from outside in the darkness.

David Melkie's son was shouting: *"Fire in town*, come 'n help! *Fire in town*, come 'n help!" I shook the boys awake and we madly dressed and ran for our steel buckets. The sky was lit up like daylight as the fire had already taken hold. Joe jumped on the back of my horse as we rode as fast as we could with our buckets in hand. By the time we arrived, the drapery was already out of control, the fire so hot it was impossible to get near. Men were running from the bend in the river with buckets.

"Quick, Joe, take these two and run. I will speak to Charlie."

Then Rusty arrived at my side. "What can we do?" he shouted.

"The drapery is gone," I told him, "but we might be able to save our hotel. The fire's blowing in that direction so it's only a matter of time. I'll go up on the balcony and soak the decks. We might have a chance. Find a rope!"

A large crowd had gathered, looking distressed and helpless. George Loram stood there like he'd seen a ghost, muttering, "It's happening again, almost exactly a year to the day."

"What is, George?"

"My hotel in the upper township … 30th of March, 1 am… all ashes … no one to help!"

I left George standing there. "John, organise these men together like a chain gang. At this rate, we could lose the whole town."

I heard John asking for buckets as I ran into the hotel. Joe had arrived already with two as others saw what we were trying to achieve; they followed suit. Inside, Charlie frantically tried to save furniture and precious belongings. "If I can get on the balcony, we might be able to douse the timber deck," I said as I ran to the top floor. "Joe, throw the rope! I will start throwing buckets of water around up here."

Down the street, a large team of people outside McShefferys and Petersons tried desperately to carry water. Already the fire was almost too hot for me. Everywhere, hot embers fell on the deck around me, but the greatest danger was from sparks flying up under the eaves into the dry roof space. The fire had transformed a quiet still night into a raging storm. Flames leapt thirty feet into the air, whirling like a tornado, and throwing hot embers into the black sky. The fire brigade frantically worked the huge water pump but it was like throwing a pea at a charging bull.

Finally, I had to give up as the heat became too much. People downstairs carried whatever they could out into the street. The butcher shop next door had been sheltering the hotel a little, but now that was fully alight, and a strong smell of roast meat mixed with scorched woollen fabric wafted on the air. As the fire took hold, the weatherboards on the hotel started to smoke then burst into flames, while everyone still tried to save what they could. Then the roof caught fire and within minutes was burning furiously. Charlie stood with his hands on his hips at the front of the hotel, as if saying goodbye to her.

Next, windows exploded and the fire roared within. He must have realised it was all over and yelled out to the firefighters, who momentarily stopped in their tracks. He screamed out above the crackling, spitting noise, "She's gone, boys. It's all yours now."

It was like switching a light on. Suddenly with renewed strength, the firefighters focused on the bar and started running out with all the precious cases of malt, brandy and barrels otherwise doomed in the ferocious flames.

One of the men handed me a warm beer, which never tasted so good. It was the most surreal moment as I stood catching my breath, hypnotised by the bright orange and blue flames. Our beloved hotel was burning out of control and we could do nothing but gaze in horror.

Then suddenly we turned our attention to my wrestling partner, Morrison's Royal Hotel, and the public Hall immediately opposite on both sides. We ran with buckets to do all we could to douse the buildings with water, our efforts paying off as we saved the Royal with only scorching to the outside of the building and the Town Hall apparent. My body was still bruised and sore from the bout with John Morrison and now here we were together, frantically running around trying to save his hotel. Morrison's face streaked with black soot as he came over to shake my hand. "Harry, I'm indebted to you. Someday I will repay you!" He gripped my hand with both of his in a single shake of respect.

Words couldn't describe the feeling of helplessness I had as I watched half our town burn down, yet I felt privileged to have helped save some of it.

In the cold light of day, piles of ash and twisted steel lay everywhere. Many had not been fully insured. Mr Hennesey's drapery had just been fully furnished with new stock. Fire was always a constant enemy, especially when sparks were free to fly into the air and settle on crisp dry pieces of timber.

Quite a few men did not show up for work that day, choosing instead to help where they could to restore the town to order, making stacks of twisted iron and charred wood. One of the locals had dragged a case of whiskey up into the hills and showed up a week later much the worst for wear. Within days, the Town Hall was set up as a bar where Charlie and his indomitable spirit organised a place for the huge number of men in town to gather and socialise.

The wrestling was forgotten for a few days as another topic of conversation filled the nights, recollections and stories relived in vivid colour and vigorous arm waving. Comical reenactments, like scenes on a stage, of men with buckets, and flames as high as Kauris, and men pitting their strength against the scorching heat.

Within days, the town would again be ablaze with men pitting their strength, but this time it was another wrestling match. Like a soothing balm, the battle of Sutherland versus Donald Dinnie rekindled the town's buoyant spirit of comradeship – the most magnificent event cradled among those illustrious hills. It swept through the Coromandel peninsula like a roaring fire, occupying hearts and minds all the way to Auckland. Sutherland had been training hard but had almost hidden himself away, as he couldn't even buy a loaf of bread without being interrupted. Stories abounded of the world-famous Dinnie's exploits which kept many a man almost disbelieving until the 30th day arrived. The hall was filled and spilled out by the hundreds into the street. The huge crowd outside listened intently as a scout stood shouting like an auctioneer on a soap box, every detail of the fight relayed to the eager listeners who stood mesmerised by what they could not see but fully imagined.

Sutherland had unexpectedly saved seats at the front for us, right amongst the action.

Rusty looked at me, his eyes lit bright with excitement. "Harry, I feel like royalty. It's hard to conceive that this veteran wrestler is still in such fine shape. He doesn't look much older than when I saw him as a boy."

"I would love to be as fit as him at sixty!"

"Harry, do you think Sutherland has any hope of winning a bout?" John asked.

"If it was me, I think I would fight him for nothing just to savour the experience."

"That's good winnings, £25, if he can pull it off."

"Throwing six times in an hour is superhuman, I am not sure I could," I replied.

The referee came forward and motioned the excited crowd to quiet. A few men entered the ring and spoke about the fire and encouraged others to give donations to those who had lost everything. They also entreated the crowd to remain calm as the hall was at bursting capacity. The first warm-up match was between Sutherland and Leahy, whetting the men's appetite for more. Sutherland threw his opponent in a half-arm roll to the crowd's delight, then did it again a few minutes later. Their bout finished by 10 am when Sutherland threw him, this time clear over his head, generating thunderous applause through the town.

After a break in the program, which sent the room into a blast of chatter, the room was quietened again as Dinnie and Sutherland took their places on the mat. Silence reigned as the two worthy opponents rewarded the audience with a brilliant bout. The little hall had never seen so much excitement and a crescendo of clamouring voices threatened to lift the roof, with every glimmer of brilliance the two men showed. Within hours, Dinnie only just defeated Sutherland. The wrestling was over, however, the storytelling had just begun, moments locked away as one of those unique memories brought to life and retold again on special occasions with the recollection of "I was there the day Dinnie and Sutherland fought it out in the little Kuaotunu Hall."

Chapter 27

Dressed to the Nines

As Autumn approached, the deciduous trees turned all shades of red to gold, which meant the winter rains would soon be upon us. I'd been working underground for a few months, starting on a pick and shovel, digging out and laying tracks, studying the quartz rock seams with the science behind the compression of forces to create gold. It opened up a whole new world in the study of geology to suddenly see rocks filled with iron, sediment or basalt. My studies progressed well and the boys appeared to be content. Joe was a master now, driving the horses, negotiating every bump with good sense and careful skill. John's focus remained on saving money to settle down on a farm and at present had not found anything that paid better. Rusty was just out for a good time, which was easy in this friendly community. He was endlessly patient with Bolt, teaching him tricks.

Since the fires, the community had bonded stronger and I knew it would be hard to leave it when the day came. Charlie, within days of his fire, had sent out for quotes to rebuild our local lady, which was rising again at a blistering pace. April seemed a perfect opportunity to take a week off to see Maggie while the days were still clear. I looked forward to it, and stayed busy to make the time go faster as I counted down each day. I had sent a letter ahead, asking Ruby if she could be chaperone so we could go out together. I then sent a telegram the day before I sailed, saying we would arrive in the late afternoon.

As the ship slowly berthed, I could see them both waving happily from the pier, Maggie's white dress glowing in the sunlight. My heart suddenly felt full as I slung my bag over my shoulder, ready to be first down the gangplank.

I linked my arms through theirs. "Honestly, you ladies look more stunning every time I see you. Where am I privileged to escort you both on this glorious day?"

"Harry, your arms are huge, they are like rock," Ruby noted immediately. "Yes, you are looking very dapper, dressed to the nines. And are you even taller?"

We laughed

"It's probably my big head," I said, "from all the fame of being a big fish in a very small town down there. At least, here I won't get stopped in the street."

"Let's head up to the tea house on Queen Street."

We started striding along the path towards Queen Street.

"Tell me, how is John? He is hopeless at writing."

"I have a letter from him in my bag; he is doing well, and always a positive outlook when it's bleak. Rusty wanted to come in a few weeks but sends his warm regards."

"I think it is very fitting you call him Rusty, considering his handsome red hair."

Maggie almost skipped along the road holding my arm tightly. She looked stunning with a deep blue brimmed hat to match her eyes, a bold white ribbon around her chin to match her dress. It was like I was seeing Maggie for the first time. Her sunny face was ruddy with delight as she kept glancing at me in anticipation.

"How is everyone at the house?" I drew her into the conversation.

"Murdoch is doing well. He was happy to see you a few weeks ago. He's nearly finished his apprenticeship down at the port. Father, as you know, is still shipping wherever there is an opportunity, but I fear he must retire soon."

I held the girls' arms tightly as a carriage appeared on Custom Street, its big wheels intimidatingly close. We stood for a moment. "That was close … Now, how is Phee?" We crossed over Custom with Queen Street now directly in front of us.

"Euphemia is busy keeping records, and scheming a way to open her own eatery, perhaps once the twins are finished school. The twins are doing well in their studies … and Hannah! Well … she is a typical young fifteen-year-old."

"How is life down in Kuaotunu? You must tell us of your wrestling bouts."

"Let's just say, it's not an easy life, but a wonderful community to be part of. The only respite we seem to get for our weary bodies in search of that elusive gold is Sunday. I seem to study every night."

"I do not know how you manage to hold down two jobs, study, and train for wrestling. You must spend all your days exhausted."

"I do," I said, smiling down at her. "I find I dream of sleeping in the warm sunlight like our dog Bolt, but then I wake and no-one is patting my head." The girls laughed again. "How far up is it, Ruby?"

"Ahh, not as far as the theatre."

"Your wrestling must be exciting to watch."

"There's not much to entertain folk, so it's a huge craze among the men."

"I have not heard you talk about Bolt?" Maggie this time.

"He is a great companion, gets horribly spoilt by us all. Rusty has trained him mostly, but we got him as a puppy while working at the stables. He's a black Kelpie with a white patch round his eye, very smart and just seems to know if you're having a bad day."

"Where do you live? What is it like where you are?"

"We are in a little miner's cottage up in a valley about three miles from the coast. There are steep hills all around us and thick bush that has mostly been cleared. It looks like giant moles have dug directly into the sides of the hills. We have little trolley train lines coming out of the hills like Cuckoo clocks everywhere, with small mine carts pushed out full of quartz rock from underground tunnels. We are all burrowed deep into the hills searching for that allusive vein with a pick and shovel, leaving networks of random rabbit holes everywhere."

Very few people were on the street as we made our way up on the shady side. Maggie shivered slightly.

"Let's cross over and walk in the sunshine, there's a cold draft under these canopies. Watch out for the horse manure just there." I pointed to a small ball of green dung on one side.

"Oh, that is thoughtful, Harry. My coat is warm, but Maggie's dress is a little light."

A man looked at me like he knew me. "Harry Bagust, the champion wrestler!" He came over and shook my hand. "I'm Harold Hill … nice to meet you."

"Didn't think anyone would recognise me up here."

"Myself and a few of the lads came down for the bout – it was a great show you gave."

Maggie looked up at me smiling, and looked surprised.

"Nice to meet you, I better get off this road."

Ruby rubbed her hands across my chest in a playful way "Oh, Harry, you're on fire!"

We all laughed.

"Talking of fire, Harry … I heard there was a terrible fire in Kuaotunu."

"Yes, in the lower town, down near the beach. We lost the Butcher shop, the Drapery, the General store, two hotels, a broker, guest houses, a bakery and stables, all have burned down."

"We were so concerned for you all, reading about it in the

Auckland Times. You must tell us about it later. I hope you did not suffer burns?"

"All the townsfolk fought bravely late into the night to save her, to no avail. But most businesses are making huge efforts to rebuild as there is a desperate community of over a thousand people now."

"What do you do for meals?"

"I am often studying, so the boys cut me slack. Joe tends to do a great deal of cooking. He's the best cook, often whipping up a hearty meal. Rusty is the most experimental, with John's full repertoire being meat and potatoes in one pot."

Ruby pointed to the little tea shop sign three shops ahead.

"Looks like we are here." I opened the door for them both as Ruby spoke to the lady to arrange a private table to one side of the bright room. It was decorated in all Ruby's favourite bright colours, with exotic Japanese fans, silks and bouquets of bold white lilies.

I carefully pulled out their chairs, sliding them in gently as Ruby waved the lady for service. She ordered tea and three slices of orange cake. The girl nodded and hurried off towards the kitchen.

"The cottage is in a valley close to eight stamping batteries," I continued my response to Maggie. "It's a convenient township which has almost all the same stores and accommodation as the lower. The School of Mines is there too, which is handy for me.

Ruby looked concerned. "It must be really noisy!"

"Each big mining company have their own battery, then there is a public one for the smaller miners. They are dusty and running twenty-four hours a day, except for Sunday. The ground rumbles a little as they vibrate."

"Is there a church you can go to?"

"There are two churches, and a school mid-way up the valley. I have been to church a few times but mostly we are so tired or have only a few hours to catch up with friends that we do it on Sunday."

"Are there many women there?"

"Ruby, there are many families in Kuaotunu with about a hundred children in attendance at the school. It has an interesting population from every corner of the globe, all trying their hand to find a little good fortune. There's a Chinaman and a large group of local Māori who has some fertile land growing good crops for the locals. Most families have two or three cows they milk each day and chooks of course. We just buy ours off a neighbour."

"I could not imagine having a cow in the backyard in Kingsland, but I do hear one every now and then down in Glenmore Valley.

"It must be awful being in the dust all the time. How do you know where to dig?"

"Maggie, that's what's so interesting and we are learning on the job. We know the geology is right but it is really a stroke of luck and knowing what to look for to find a vein. It's a little bit of Mineralogy, science and luck," I said, laughing. "As you dig, it can be like finding a needle in a haystack. The gold is mostly hidden in the rock, showing only when it is crushed to dust in the stampers then treated. It shows up in the fine dust particles mixed with solution."

"So how do you get down into the holes?"

"The hills are steep, so we dig directly into the hillside. Once the hill is breached, we dig sleepers into the tunnel floor where tracks are laid for the little mining carts. Clay fill is flung into the nearest gulley from the carts, while valuable quartz is stockpiled, ready to be carted away for the stamper. Once the quartz rock is crushed into dust, the cyanide is added which clings to the gold allowing it to be processed out of the dust particles."

Ruby and Maggie looked at me with great interest "So that's

how gold is extracted, with cyanide?"

"Ruby, it isn't like the really dangerous cyanide – it's diluted."

"I would be terrified inside a tunnel. Is it scary?" Maggie asked.

"Apart from big Wetas we disturb entering a dark tunnel …". Ruby screwed up her face, shuddering with disgust. "I swear there would have been fifty last week just inside the doorway," I went on. "It's just airy sounds of picks and shovels echoing inside the tunnels, sometimes an Irish tune can be heard reverberating off the sediment walls by some highlander's Celtic voice. When all's silent, the friendly flicker of a carbine head lamp is comfort against the impenetrable darkness should your lamp run out."

Ruby looked scared. "Surely there must be some light from outside."

I laughed. "I imagine it's a little like they describe hell to be. If your light goes out, it's so black, even when your eyes adjust, you can't see the smallest glimmer of light … even if you are looking directly towards the entrance … nothing but darkness!"

Now Maggie screwed up her face, repulsed "Ohh! I hate the darkness but I hate Wetas more. They are worse than a huge spider! It is terrifying to have one caught in your hair, quite impossible to remove!"

"You will have me checking my dress for spiders now, but Wetas do love to hide in a damp, dark corner. I always check when I am clearing leaves at home, it's not uncommon to find a big Weta. Here is our tea coming, I am actually quite hungry. I felt so nervous waiting for you to come, I had not noticed till now."

A young girl set down our cake forks and plates quietly then cleared everything off her tea trolley onto the table. Maggie was delighted and thanked the girl, who was about her age.

"Isn't this lovely! … Harry, please go on. I feel like I can imagine it so much clearer now. I was thinking before, couldn't the tunnel collapse and how do you know which way to dig?"

"Maggie, the shape of the tunnel is critical: it must have a curved roof to prevent collapse, and enough room to stand, but if the rock looks soft, we shore it up with big timbers. We shape them with a slight gradient to allow the water to drain away as water drips constantly, seeping through the roof, wetting your clothes and filling up boots with water. Tunnels branch off at right angles on each side in a grid pattern every twenty feet in the hope of crossing a rich seam. All too often tunnels do collapse, men are buried or fall down a shaft. It is dangerous with poison gas sometimes or a man can be crushed by a loaded runaway cart. It's about being thorough to prop the roof where needed and being careful to keep your wits about you. That's why I am studying, to keep men safe to send them home after a day's work."

"It must be very difficult working in the dark," Ruby said as she delicately sipped her tea.

"You can only see where your lamp is shining from your hat. It is a strange sensation coming out into the light, especially if you lose track of time when it's already dark. If it's sunny, your eyes feel like they have been stabbed – it takes quite a few minutes to adjust to the brightness. That's why some men work into the night as it makes no difference once you're in the tunnel, it's a constant temperature, no wind, only rain coming off the ceiling. And constant dust." I smiled. The cake was just like Mary would make and made me immediately feel homesick. "Oh, this cake is good!"

Ruby gathered her bag and put on her gloves. "Sorry, I lost track of time. Please excuse me, I need to find a scarf for the winter months that will soon be upon us. I hope you don't mind if I do a spot of shopping? I will be back in about an hour or so. Will that suit you both?"

We nodded, staring at her, not quite sure if she was politely creating an opportunity for us both. I stood, waiting for her to gather her umbrella and bag. She winked at me, and I smiled agreeably to her. "Thank you, we will see you in due course."

As she left, I put my hand on Maggie's soft warm hand.

"I am so excited to be here with you today. Can you pinch me – it feels like a dream! It has consumed many of my waking hours and even many of my dreams, imagining this moment … I can't believe it has arrived. I have spoken to The Captain to ask his permission and although I have not spoken to Euphemia, your father assured me, she is agreeable, only as far as you are … Would you allow me to court you?"

Maggie's face flushed and her eyes lit brightly. She put her other hand on top of mine. "Yes! Oh, I have wanted to tell you from the first time I saw you that day with Phee on the footy field.

"When you did not write for those many months to Euphemia, I thought you were lost to another. I had hoped that at least you and Euphemia could be together. I was prepared to hide my love, even move away to another place if need be. It is my dream come true to be able to say yes to you. But there is something I must ask if it is all right to be so forward."

"Yes, of course, please do."

"I want also to say to you straight away, I do not want to be compromised in my Christian values. I do not expect you to believe in God, but I know you are a man of the world and I want to be clear with you now. I will expect you to guard me so that we are not seen to be alone in a place where anything can be misconstrued about our sobriety."

I looked deep into her eyes. "Thank you. Maggie. for being forthright with me. I assure you I will not bring dishonour to your name in this way. I want you to tell me if we are in a situation you are not comfortable with, in case I am not aware of it."

She smiled at me. "Thank you, I will be clear."

"I am all of a sudden quite hungry, even after the cake. Shall we have something more to eat?"

"That would be great!" I said. "I could eat a horse."

We spoke freely then about, family, friends, local street happenings, joys and sorrows. It was effortless to be with her, like I was being warmed in her sunlight.

Chapter 28

Changes in the Wind

By well into winter in Kuaotunu, one by one the new buildings had risen again from the ashes like a Phoenix. The builders showed up in mid-May to rebuild Mr and Mrs Cowan's *Heart of Kuaotunu*. By mid-August, they had fulfilled a promise to finish within ninety days as we were again telling lies over a jug of local ale.

"It's been finished off so beautifully; I see they are starting work expanding the Royal."

"Did you hear Mrs Cowan nearly drowned when they were travelling back from Mercury Bay, crossing Brown's Creek at the beach the other day. The tide was up so the horses started to swim. When Charlie looked back, his wife was disappearing into the water. He rushed to her and just managed to save her, as she went under for the third time."

"It's horrid. Imagine being nearly ready to open the new hotel and your wife drowns. Harry, by the way, you've been playing well. Your little squeeze-box has livened things up."

"It's your Irish jigs that have had the boys' spirits lifted, Rusty!"

Rusty had broken up with Ruby who felt he could not keep her to the lifestyle she was accustomed to, which made him long for home a little.

I found a moment, which was well overdue, to send a letter to Maggie.

My Dearest Maggie

How are you? I hope it will not be long till we can be together again.

I am still wrestling regularly which helps keep my hand in. It has been a great way to meet friends outside the hotel and stay in condition.

Do you remember Sutherland who we practiced with? He went on tour travelling all over New Zealand wrestling Donald Dinnie for show. They made good money touting for £25 - £50 offered to throw Sutherland three times in thirty minutes. Sometimes he beat him and other times he couldn't, but they also offered classes for a fee after each show, for people to learn some of their wrestling moves.

Donald Dinnie's daughter, Little Elvie, performed Scottish highland dancing each time, gracefully wooing the crowds.

Sadly, again there was a fire in town, starting in the Public Hall where Naylors had a novelty shop. This time it burned down the sea side of the town, narrowly missing our brand new Kuaotunu Hotel. It burned down Tamerage's Store, McSheffrrey's private dwellings, and Hennesey's stables.

Mrs McCormick opened a brand-new guest house with ten rooms, and by November Mr Thompson will have a new store. New houses line the street where ash piles had lay less than eight months before. Mr Hennesey's had a great deal to recover from with the drapery under insured, however, he has just pegged out where the new building is to go and loads of timber have been delivered.

The hungry monsters still crush night and day with

steady improvements to the crushers and methods. We had trained up four good men to run the transport, which I still have some income from. I renegotiated the cartage rates and sent Jack his fee.

I'm continuing to learn a great deal, soaking up like a sponge all the experience from the many miners who have come from everywhere. In this way, I've learned new methods and techniques of blasting, cutting tunnels and laying tracks. They've just put me in charge of a large group of men at the Vermont. Sadly, two men died on other sites, one wood cutter, falling down a Winze and the other buried by a rock fall. It worries me to see so many injuries, and many fingers lost being blown off with caps or dynamite as men become over confident using them every day.

Our horse races are still the hot favourite and Black Jack is definitely a hit with the townsfolk.

John has made a name for himself playing footy all over the country and is sought after to play for anyone in the Thames region – Paeroa, Coromandel, Karangahake and Ohinimuri. He decided to move to the big city of Thames nearer to a bigger pool of players and opportunities, which was probably well over due.

Joe was missing the family, wanting a change of scenery so reluctantly we have let him go back to Martinborough. He wants to run his own coach service and work on a farm for a local family, which he will succeed in.

I am sad for you, Maggie, as you just missed out voting on the 4th of December. I can't believe Seddon got back in again with only 54% of the vote. The Government elections took up far too much hot air in the evenings at our local

I had made the journey a number of times to visit Maggie and, as it was coming up to Christmas, I decided to stay for Kuaotunu's big race day event. Rusty put a bet on for us again, and did well – enough to enjoy a week off over the festive season. I said goodbye to Rusty and headed away, excited to be spend time with the McQuarrie family. I would miss seeing my own family but I would get down in a few months' time.

I arrived in New North Road with butterflies in my stomach, feeling like a child the night before Christmas, which it actually was. I had a few small presents under my arms for the family which made it a struggle to knock on the iron knocker.

As the door opened, I could hear running footsteps on the wooden floor, and sure enough, as the door opened wider, a rush of blood filled my heart as Maggie ran to greet me. She threw her arms around my neck and hugged me tightly.

"Maggie!" I lifted her off her feet and spun her around on the porch.

"Harry, I must have heard every footstep going past the door today, and every time I heard the door go with one of the children's friends visiting, I thought it was you. How are you? Was your sailing calm? You look well! Let me take your coat. Oh, listen to me … you cannot get a word in … come inside, please."

I took my presents into the lounge where a large fir tree in a steel bucket stood in the corner. It was so tall it nearly touched the 12-foot ceiling.

"What a beautiful tree!"

"What are you doing tonight?"

"I have nearly everything ready for Christmas Day tomorrow, what did you have in mind."

"You'll find out. Where would you like me to put my things?"

"I have you over the road at number 11 as the neighbours have gone away for Christmas and said we are very welcome to use their house."

"That is great. I will just put my bag there for now."

"Maggie, you have your home looking so lovely," I said as she helped me stow the gifts under the tree, "somehow it just smells like home. Our place is quite damp and cold, being in the bush at the bottom of the hill, and it's been a very wet winter. We had such a horrific storm a few weeks ago, two of the sheets of iron came off the roof."

She smiled that I was pleased. "It's a big job, Harry, keeping everything tidy with everyone coming and going. Euphemia is finishing early today to help me prepare the food. She is such a good cook. She really must start her own Cookery – she is wasted doing bookwork for people. But I shouldn't complain – everyone's little bit keeps us going."

"It will be nice to see her. It's been so different for me in Kuaotunu the last few weeks, not having the boys around. I miss Joe the most, he's a great lad and always cheerful, and very particular about everything, like you. He makes a good job of everything he does and will be very successful one day. He's the one out of us all that seems to save his money, squirrelling it away. He will have his own farm soon enough, having already leased a small plot."

"I have about two hours before Phee gets home, would you

like to do something now?"

"Good idea. I will drop my bag off at the neighbours on the way."

Heading out onto New North Road, I looked up and down the hill. There were plenty of people around, but no cabs.

Maggie showed me to her neighbours' spare room next door and, as we were coming out, a cab came over the rise with an older lady passenger. I waved at the cabbie, who slowed enough for me to call out

"Can we share a ride?"

The cabbie hesitated.

"Sure, that would be lovely," the lady called back as the cab came to a halt. I helped Maggie up.

"Good evening. I am Harry Bagust, and this is Maggie McQuarrie. It's not easy to hail a cab this time of year."

"Lovely to meet you both. I am Gweneth. Please sit; we might have to squeeze up a little but it is Christmas. He looks good in that suit, doesn't he, dear. Where are you two young folk off to all dressed up?"

"He won't tell me where." Maggie raised an eyebrow and smiled.

"Oww, that is exciting. Well, you picked a lovely evening to be out. Are you from the Parnell McQuarries?"

"Yes. My father is Captain Hector and my Uncle John lives there as well.

"I think it might have been your uncle's once – a grand house."

"Have you got family over for Christmas, Gweneth?" I asked.

"My brother has come up from Whanganui, staying for a week. My next stop is here. You have a lovely evening. You make a delightful-looking couple. Merry Christmas."

"Thank you, and to you too."

The cabbie stopped outside a fine two-storey house, waited

till Gweneth safely alighted then moved away again.

"Where to, folks?"

"Queen Street, thank you …"

I sat a little closer to shelter Maggie from the afternoon breeze.

The lights of New Market were warm and inviting, as we pulled up in the Main Street and as we walked along looking in the shop windows I had the idea to pretend we were extremely wealthy, imagining what lovely things we could buy. We tried on hats and fur coats; imagined wearing beautiful clothes, pointed out exquisite jewellery and fine shoes.

"Oh, Harry, those crocodile shoes would look incredible on you!"

"Wouldn't they, but imagine me wearing those in Kuaotunu, they'd be covered in mud in five minutes." We laughed at the thought of being in such finery there.

I pointed through the jeweller's window. "I like that beautiful watch – the one with sturdy gold chain and brilliant white face. Shall we go in to take a closer look?"

She smiled and nodded. "I have never thought of doing this. I like that hat pin there with the little butterfly."

"It is lovely. I like those cufflinks too. Excuse me, can I look at that watch and those cufflinks."

"It is a lovely watch, isn't it, sir. Is it for you?" the shop assistant asked.

"We are really just window shopping for now, but I do like them. The watch has a beautiful pressed gold case … Maggie, what have you seen?"

Delight lit her eyes. "I love that fine gold rose brooch with the matching earrings, a gold ring with a rose and a tiny diamond."

"Would you like to try them on, miss?"

"Oh no!" she said, giggling.

"Try them. It's just a little fun. You can look in the mirror over there." I beckoned the assistant, winking at her. She looked about Maggie's age and responded immediately. "Yes, that would be lovely, miss …"

"Maggie, I thought we might go to the tearooms after this – it's only two doors down."

Maggie looked up while the assistant fitted the brooch, earrings and matching ring. "Oh yes, that would be nice. I think we have about an hour before we must head back."

"These look lovely on you, and the ring fits you perfectly, miss. It is always a little hard to fit rings – everyone's a slightly different size. Look in the mirror here."

Maggie's eyes lit up brighter as she held her hand out to see the ring.

"We won't be too long then… Oh, turn around. Ah, yes they are beautiful!" I discreetly placed my wallet on the edge of the counter.

"Maggie took them off, and gently gave them back. "Thank you, they are exquisite. One day, when we are wealthy, we can return."

I walked towards the door, draping Maggie's shawl over her shoulders. It was ten past three and the street bustled with children running about.

We passed the shoe shop again and spied a vacant table in the front window of the tea rooms and headed for it. I beckoned the waitress over, ordered two teas and cakes, and patted my coat for my wallet. "Oh-oh. I took out my wallet out at the last shop. It must still be there. I will just pop back."

I hurried back to the jeweller, where the assistant stood holding up my wallet.

"Actually, Miss I will take the matching hat pin, the brooch, earrings and ring, but you must do it quickly as I am trying to surprise my lady friend. Leave the hat pin out, thanks."

"Sounds like change could be in the wind for someone?" she said as she quickly wrapped the items in cotton wool and set them into a little wooden gift box. She handed me the hat pin. That will be £10/6."

I handed over the pounds and coins and casually walked back into the tea shop. The waitress was just making up our tray, so I took the moment to take Maggie's hand and place the hat pin gently into it. "I want you to have this … I couldn't resist it."

"Oh, Harry, it is *so* pretty." Her hand closed over mine. "Thank you so much. What a lovely afternoon it has been. I will treasure this to remind me of that young couple you described farewelling each other on the ship." She took it carefully and fitted it into her hat. "There, what does it look like?"

"Exquisite, Maggie …. Whatever you wear, you would look beautiful."

"You clearly have not seen me in the garden with Father's smelly old coat and galoshes."

Chapter 29

Sealed with a Kiss

We returned to the house ten minutes ahead of Euphemia. I went to give her a greeting kiss on the cheek but she threw her arms around me and hugged me warmly.

"How are you, Harry? You look very handsome in that suit. I hear you are on your own with Rusty now."

I nodded. "Yes, and we now have to take turns more often with the cooking as Joe's returned home now. I've been so looking forward to seeing you all again."

"And you will. Murdoch and Father are working at the shipyard at present, but will be home around 5 pm. Hannah is at a friend's place, due back anytime, and the twins could be anywhere. I asked them to stock up the wood bin but look it's empty again."

"I'll fill it."

I shucked my jacket and did whatever I could to assist: fetching the wood, plucking the turkey, and pulling fresh potatoes and carrots from the garden. It seemed good to be in a home with happy banter from the girls, just like home, as they debated about the best herbs to put into the turkey stuffing, and what coins to hide in the Christmas pudding.

On Christmas morning, I woke at 4 am, to absolute silence. I'd been living for so long with the drone and vibration of the stampers, I kept waking through the night unaccustomed to the quiet. Now I could even hear the faint clip-clopping of horses' hooves.

I put the kettle on as the curtains were still closed at the Captain's house across the road, and took out the jewellery; held up the little ring with its intricate gold rose. *This is it. I want to be with her. First the Miner's certificate as my commitment to provide for her – it means waiting another year … Her mother's remembrance is the perfect moment, it's a very special day for her.*

A while later, I looked outside again. Chimney smoke had just started rising in the pre-dawn light. I shaved, dressed up and crossed the normally bustling main road, and knocked on the door.

A bleary-eyed Hannah opened the door. "I hoped it was you," she said, giving me a little hug. "Merry Christmas, Harry. And thank you for the stocking. I love the little sewing kit, thimble with cottons … How did you know?"

I grinned. "I asked Maggie. Merry Christmas, Hannah! Gee, you are nearly as tall as Phee. Has it been that long since I saw you last? It must be six months at least."

"Yes, at least. I was at school in Kaurihohore and missed your last visit. And you've changed too – you're looking very strong, Harry. Will you be staying long this time?"

"I only get a few days off but I will have the new year with you all. It is lovely to be staying so close."

"Mr and Mrs Green are quite elderly, and are talking about moving closer to their daughter in New Plymouth at some time. You should ask about renting it." She laughed

Just then, Maggie poked her head into the hall. "I thought I could hear voices. Come through, Harry, and have some breakfast."

I walked through to find the men at the table. "Good morning, Captain. Boys … Merry Christmas!" We each shook hands.

"Happy Christmas, lad; it's good to have you with us! Did you sleep well?"

"Strangely, no. I am so used to the stampers thumping … but within a few days I'll be right."

Euphemia came through rubbing her face and looking half asleep; she kissed Hector on his bald head. "I am here, even though I didn't get to sleep till 2 am. Merry Christmas, Harry!"

"Merry Christmas to you, Phee."

Maggie filled the table with beautiful food: fried bread, tomatoes, bacon, eggs and fried potato cakes.

"And thank you, Harry, for the gifts. That was really sweet."

The boys chorused a thank you for the little toys I had bought from the new store."

"My brush set is very much appreciated, lad," Hector added. "I am getting incredibly efficient doing my hair these days as I have less and less of it to comb." Everyone laughed. "If everyone is settled, let me give thanks to the Father." Hector bowed his head, and everyone took each other's hands as he said Grace.

A relaxed few days followed, with everyone making the most of the rest, especially Murdoch and Hector. We all went walking together, twice with Maggie. I walked with Euphemia to the park where we met up with Ruby. I played catch with the boys; sat talking to Murdoch about his experiences at sea. Then the 29th arrived and the girls were running around making preparations for Annie's remembrance day celebration.

Hector sat in the sitting room alone reading a book when I took him in a cup of tea and cake. "Can I interrupt you for a minute, sir?"

"Certainly, Harry what is it?"

I stood facing him, feeling slightly nervous as the last time I did this was with Emily's father. "Sir, I have a request. Could I have your daughter's hand in marriage?"

Hector took out his eyeglass and shut his book. He stood.

"Well, son, I have not had the pleasure of being asked before and a little at a loss as to how I should reply. Firstly, I should clarify which of my daughters you wish to marry," he said with a glint in his eye.

"Yes, I had not been specific." We both laughed. "Maggie, sir!"

"I think it is traditional for me to ask if you can keep her and what your prospects are for the future. However, I have already witnessed your character both in your work ethic, bond with family and choices you have made, both good ones and bad. I measure you as a strong man, with enough character to be true. Where had you hoped to live and how long would your betrothal be?"

"I would like to get my Miner's Certificate first which I should have by this time next year. I would imagine we could live in Auckland but if Maggie wanted to come to Kuaotunu or wherever the mining takes us, that is something to talk about."

"When did you have in mind to ask her?"

"With your permission, tonight at the Green's house. I was going to ask you if it would be alright to do it today, as it is such a special day for Maggie and all the family. I thought you could come over after dinner for sweets?"

Hector looked me straight in the eyes; held his chin in contemplation. "You do know what this day means to me!"

"Yes, sir."

He walked away with his head down, deep in thought. Then he said, "These are my little girls who are extremely dear to me. As a family, this is Annie's special day, but I cannot think of a lovelier way for her to be remembered than on this day." He walked back to me. "If Maggie agrees, I am more than happy to give my blessing on your union." He took my hand in both of his, and shook it heartily. "Well done, lad. Best of luck."

I had thought so many times about how I would propose to Maggie, and then it came to me.

I found Euphemia in the kitchen by herself and, taking her quietly aside, held her hand. "Phee, I would like us all to have dessert at the Green's place tonight. I want to ask Maggie to marry me."

She pulled her hand away and looked at me in horror. "What!" She turned her face away.

I had dreaded this day but knew it must come. She took a step backwards, folding her arms across herself. "I'm sorry you caught me off guard. I thought this was going to be easier." Her voice raised a little. "*Damn you* for what you did with Emily! I would still be with you." She stood, her head bowed as tears touched her eyes. "It's alright …" She put out her hand to stop my approach. "I am just tired from all the late nights."

She turned and we stared at each other, tears rolling down her face. "Harry, the truth is I still love you!" She came closer and placed her hand gently on my chest. "I want you and cannot have you. I swear I will never love another! What do I do now? I have to stand by and watch … I know you love me too and cannot say … we are both damned… What do I do with these feelings?"

She turned away and looked out the window. "I want Maggie to be happy too," she said softly, "and I cannot wish her married to anyone better. I cannot stop you … I can't win either way.

"Of course, you should ask her, and what better day than today." She came back to me; held me. "It's a lovely idea." She took my face gently in her hands; kissed me passionately on the lips. I tried not to kiss her back but she was right: part of me loved her. Then she turned and walked away.

I collapsed into the chair. *Is this really happening? I thought I repulsed her! It's not possible surely to love two people at once!?*

I walked out of the house and along the road, trying to make sense of it all. Sitting looking down over the valley of Glenmore, guilt poured through me. *I should not have kissed her like that, but she is my first true love. What if I was still with Euphemia? I doubt it would ever work, she is so stubborn. Isn't it better this way, she wants her independence? She does not want to be tied down … what other choices do I have? She is right, we are damned.*

I lay on the bench seat; looked at the bright silver clouds rushing past overhead. *Harry, this is your silver lining. You should be pleased that all this is revealed today and not a year from now. Our feelings will fade just like these clouds, breaking and forming into something new. We will both look back on this day and wonder what it was we saw in each other. I do not have another choice.*

Do I want to be with Maggie? Yes of course, There are so many things I love about her., I feel like I am home when I am with her. I have strong feelings for her. Then this is it. No more second-guessing. This is what I want … I will tell her tonight.

I found the Gramophone in the lounge at the Greens and set it up on the back porch overlooking the yard. I placed candles on two little tables, and threw rose petals from the front garden onto the back lawn, then I hurried back down to Maggie's house.

The boys had set the table with the silver cutlery and the food was steaming hot. A large candelabra had candles throwing light onto everyone's smiling faces. One after another, they spoke excitedly about their many beautiful memories of Annie. There were tears and laughter. Every now and then, Phee watched me with a look of resignation.

Then Hector said, "Now for dessert. We are going over to the Green's but we will bring everything over. I think we all know Harry and Maggie have not had many chances to have time together, so you two go ahead and we will bring the dessert in an hour's time. Put the kettle on, stoke the fire and we'll see you soon."

Maggie looked confused. "What? What's this about? You are

acting rather odd, Father."

I took Maggie's hand and led her over the road, walking through the gate over the rose petals, up the steps and out to the back porch.

"You have candles burning already," she said, turning as I held out a beautiful bunch of summer roses.

"These are for you"

"Harry, these are lovely, thank you, but what is all this about? You should be saving your money. I will put them in a vase and get the fire on for everyone."

I quickly wound up the gramophone and placed the needle, letting soft piano music play.

"Harry, that is lovely music."

I took her hand; danced with her slowly in the evening light.

"Harry, you have gone to a lot of trouble – this is wonderful, but I will need to improve my dance steps.

Looking deep into her eyes and amongst the red petals, I knelt down; took out the little box and, opening it slowly, showed her the gold ring. "Maggie McQuarrie, would you make me the happiest man in the world and marry me?"

"Oh my! Oh my! What? *Yes! Yes*, of course!" She squealed in delight and bounced on her toes. She took the ring; held it delicately in her fingers, then allowed me to slip it on her finger. She looked into my eyes and whispered, "This is why all the petals and Father being strange?" She threw her arms around me in delight and I held her tightly.

Then she sat on my lap so we were eye to eye as she surveyed my face. Kissing me gently for the second time, I knew this time was on purpose. It took me into oblivion. All the hope of a future together, *sealed with a kiss.*

"Harry, I had no idea you could be so cunning. Did you really plan this all out, hoping I would try on a ring in the shop the night before Christmas?"

"I wanted to ask you today as it is so special to you. I didn't know how to get your ring size or how to buy something that you would really like."

"When did you ask Father?"

"Today. He was in the lounge by himself. He said if you agreed, he would be delighted."

"I have all these things running through my mind like …" She took my hand. "Does Phee know?"

"I asked her if it would be alright tonight. She was upset at first but agreed it would be perfect."

"She will accept it in time … How exciting I am going to marry … when?"

"How about a year from now?"

"Do you mean on the 29th, because that would be so lovely? … but it seems such a long time to wait."

"Well, I had not wanted to steal your mother's special day, but if it is alright with all the other family, that would be lovely. I want to get my Miners Certificate first. You could come to live with me or perhaps we can rent this house of the Greens if it's available."

"How do you know about that?"

"Hannah said they might move in the next year or so."

"You seem to have it all planned out already … it's a good plan."

We were interrupted by the family coming through with peach and apple pie and whipped cream. Hannah ran in first.

"Can I see your ring? Oh, it's so pretty. Is that a diamond in the middle?"

Phee came over and, glancing at me, smiled.

She stood in front of us both and, with a genuine smile, said, "I wish you both every happiness. Oh, this is so pretty."

She hugged us both warmly, as did the rest of the family. The fire and laughter warmed the house, and what better way to celebrate. Maggie, Phee and Hannah broke out in a song and each of the family recited a poem or a tune on the piano till late in the evening.

Chapter 30

Strike While the Iron's Hot

The year flew by in Kuaotunu as I kept busy at work managing loads of quartz at the stamper to keep production up. On a beautiful clear afternoon with a terrific blue sky, the sun shining low on the horizon, I looked up, aware of a figure standing in silhouette. As I squinted through the glare, my heart nearly stopped. There, in a bright blue dress, was Maggie. I had to pinch myself but was she here, *with bad news perhaps. Is everything alright?*

She was shouting to me, but the crashing of the stamper drowned out all other sound. I ran through the sheds and out to her, shouting, "Maggie, what are you doing here? Is everything alright?"

"No. I am fine, but I just needed to see you. It has been too long … Hannah is with me too. " *Oh, sweet relief.*

"Let me inform them that I am finishing for the day and I will come." I ran down to the men working at the crusher and told them I was finishing up. "You've done alright, Harry. Who's in the dress?"

"She's my sister, so keep your eyes in their sockets. Jim, can I borrow your cart?"

"Sure. I will get a ride with one of the lads."

I took Jim's cart, and hitched it to the horse. "Come on, let's get out of here. Have you got a place to stay?"

"Yes. I booked into the guest house opposite the hotel." She took my arm, and stared at me with a huge smile. "It is wonderful

"

to finally see you. I think of you all day and try to keep busy. It was Father who said to come, so I thought I'd strike while the iron is hot and be impulsive for once."

"I think of you constantly too. I can't wait for your letters to arrive. I read them again and again … thank you, I am sure I have not sent half as many as you.

"Don't worry, I know you are grafting long days, at least we are together now. I cannot believe the noise coming off that machine – doesn't it make you deaf by the end of the day? I had to come and see for myself. It's all starting to make sense now."

"What? I can't hear you?"

She punched me on the shoulder. Then threw her arms around me. We embraced; held each other, not wanting to let go. "Sorry, I must be smelly and dirty, but you've made my week, and to be honest, all the other men on site too," I said laughing.

"The dust is like a cloud coming off that thing, blowing over everything. No wonder you said the horses are the colour of mud."

"Come on, I'll take you to our wee cottage so I can get changed. Will Hannah be alright? How long have you got?"

"Euphemia offered to work from home for a week and Hannah has come down to keep me company while you are at work."

"It's Friday tomorrow. I will ask for the days off; I can always work a different shift. I swear you get more beautiful every time I see you."

We pulled up outside the little white cottage to Bolt barking excitedly.

"Oh, you are a lovely boy." She crouched on the front step and patted him. "What a great dog. He must be great company now the other boys are away."

I invited her in. "Yes, but sometimes he waits all day for us to take him out, if one of us can't take him with us. Sorry for the mess, we are mostly here to eat and sleep."

"It's quite tidy really, considering I surprised you. Where does Rusty sleep?"

"These are the bedrooms back here. Rusty snores over there, and at present we have one spare. It's too complicated to get someone in, so we leave it empty. This is our little lounge with separate kitchen, the bathroom, copper and toilet are outside. It's a humble place but all we need. Give me a minute, I'll throw some water over me and get changed. There are some newspapers from our local correspondent there if you want to read about our local community while you wait. I'll only be a minute."

I went out to wash, coming back in a towel.

Maggie looked up, and her eyes widened in surprise. "I don't think I've ever seen you like this," she said; she strolled over to me, stroked my bare chest and lay her head against me. "I can't wait for us to be together as husband and wife. I dream of us being together all night, every night."

"Let me get dressed. I'm feeling a little uncomfortable here," I said, taking her hands in mine. "Believe me, I try *not* to think about us together every night. It will happen soon enough."

Maggie sat back down and read the local news. "Oh, this is awful."

"What is it?"

"Last week, a poor guy – W. Young – got his thumb and two fingers blown off with dynamite, and suffered bad lacerations to the right hand. His friend Casey had to ride over shocking roads to Coromandel hospital."

"Yes, that was bad. The poor guy had to sail to Auckland Hospital after that. I can't imagine losing three fingers."

"You look good," she said as I came back into the room, "but your collar's sticking up." She deftly flicked it, and straightened my tie. "I've done this for Father constantly." It was delicious to have her nibble fingers smooth my shirt. "There, that's better. Nothing a good iron couldn't fix."

"One thing we do not possess," I said, laughing. "Shall we go? Do you want to eat at the guest house or should we go to one of the hotels?"

"It might be nice to eat at Mrs McCormick's. It will be quieter to talk, and you can see Hannah too."

"Sounds good: it's probably too much for you to meet any of my friends from the Kuaotunu yet. The men at work only saw you for a minute and asked who you were. I told them you were my sister."

"Does your sister do this?!" She kissed me on the lips. "I'm sorry … that was impulsive too."

My two hands almost completely wrapped around her waist as we held each other to talk.

"It's just … I want to be near you … I want to talk to you about our future. We really must prepare our wedding plans. I have two sisters that are determined that if Mother is not there then they will step in on her behalf. You know what Father is like: he does not like to get involved. Aunt Christine is very excited, even Uncle John, who we rarely see, congratulated me on the street last week. He wished us all the best, hoping he would be invited. Aunt Sarah is lovely, offering to help as much as we need, even to use their house."

"I'm sorry that my work has been so busy. Let's sit down to plan a few things after we've caught up a little. Perhaps tomorrow."

"That would be wonderful. Phee has already made a list. She is happy to do the catering, then have people to help on the day so she can be released to unwind a little."

The cart lurched about as the sea of mud was in front of us.

"Hold on, I will go slow but this is the bumpy, muddy part, it can throw you right off if you hit the wrong spot, which happens often in the dark." We suddenly lurched sideways throwing Maggie hard against my ribs. "That was a lucky one. Are you alright?"

"Yes, I am fine."

"The men on the roads make hundreds of bundles of Manuka, strapping them together then burying them in the deep mud. It's called a corduroy, as they are stacked against one another in rows. The loads of coal are so heavy that it only takes a week or so for them to break through, leaving a hole that a wheel can drop into, throwing the cart violently to one side."

The church steeple was in silhouette ahead of us.

"That's the undenominational church on that side and the school up there with the Master's house above. They get the best view of the valley. There's also a library if you need and of course the Catholic church there.

"It's a lot bigger than I thought. Where do you practice wrestling?"

"Mostly down here in the hall, depending what events are on. We had the circus come to town earlier this summer. Sometimes an opera will come, or a visiting theatre group.

"How is Hector? I always worry about his knees, and how much longer he can keep that up, being thrown about the deck of a ship."

"He is not sailing much at all but likes to keep in touch with some of the men in the yard. Everything is changing though with steamships almost taking over the shipping industry. I think it's sad but he is all for innovation and progress. Now they are building with steel ribs and steel hulls. Many shipwrights have given up as there is not as many yards working in timber."

"Maggie, he has done well to last this long, although, perhaps it has kept him fit and healthy… Almost there … oh there is Hannah now. She must have spotted your blue dress."

As I helped her down, Hannah came up excitedly and gave

me a hug. "Welcome to Kuaotunu, Hannah. Did you make it onto the cart in the ocean with dry feet?"

"It was fun. I took my shoes off, and felt like a puppy when they carried me ashore. This is a nice little town, and Mrs McCormick is sweet. Are you coming in?"

"Yes. Just let me tie up the horse."

Over the next four days, we took little excursions into many corners of the peninsula – spending a day in Mercury Bay with a picnic – tramping to the top of Black Ridge. We took a boat round to Hot Water beach and sat in the hot thermal water with the freezing sea washing over us. Maggie was impressed, though she found the stampers a big adjustment; she looked exhausted after a few days without sleep. She was delighted to meet the many people I had made friends with since I arrived, even coming into our local to meet the lads. She said it would not be too difficult to imagine living here. The day came for her to return, and we stayed up the entire night talking, not wanting to bid each other farewell.

"Have you got all your bags? Perhaps, Hannah, you could check. Maggie, it has been incredible having these days together, the time has gone like lightning. It's a funny thing that, when you want time to go quickly, it seems to take forever, when you treasure it, wishing it to slow down, it passes in a blur."

"Thank you for going over our wedding plans, Harry. I know Phee will be happy as we can now tick things off as we organise them. Will you get Rusty's suit jacket made here?"

"Yes, we have a fine drapery. I will get him measured in the next few weeks. This reminds me of cabbie work – I haven't lifted a trunk in a long time. Can you manage that leather bag, Hannah?"

"I might look thin but I am stronger than you might think."

I whispered to Maggie, "Sixteen and determined! A trait a few of you McQuarrie girls possess."

"I heard that!" Hannah poked out her tongue at me.

"Maggie, we have less than six months to go, I will try and come up in six or eight weeks and will send a wire to let you know when. I know the time will go quickly as you prepare for our big day, especially celebrating only days after Christmas. It will be perfect if we can get Hector there and not stuck at sea."

I wrapped my arms around her tightly, holding her. "Thank you for coming; it has been such a precious time, of course, except having Hannah."

"Hannah came over and kicked me in the shins. Nice to see you too, Harry."

"Come here, you little scallywag." I gave her a big hug, and whispered to her, "Thanks for coming. It was fun having you around, even to boss us about. Take care getting home." I kissed her on the forehead. She glanced up at me with a beaming grin, and gave me a little wave.

"Give Bolt a hug from me."

The months went by quickly as I went back and forward, and letters arrived regularly. Getting a letter then saving it till I was home to linger on each word was the happiest part of my week.

The Greens had gone away to their family in New Plymouth again for Christmas, generously leaving their home for Rusty and members of my family from the north to come for the wedding. Christmas dinner was relaxing as we sat around the big table again. Everyone busily prepared everything for the wedding. The weather grew overcast but appeared like it might stay fine. I had my trousers, suit, tie and silk shirt all laid out, neatly pressed by Mother. Mary was in the kitchen as I came out.

"Morning, brother. This is it! How do you feel, though you've already done this once?"

"Not like this. I feel nervous! …actually, marrying Emily was more like a contract signed in the registry office. This is different: I really love Maggie; I want to be with her."

Mary came near and looked into my face. "Oh, brother, I am so happy for you! From the little time we spent together yesterday, she is a delight. I can see why you get on so well."

"She makes me feel like I want to be a better person."

"Well, let's start getting ready so you can put that ring on her finger."

"Where is that little brother of ours?"

Mary burst through his door. "Come on, brother, it's time! Hurry up and get dressed." She stood by Joe's bed then jumped up, sitting on him. "Joe, come on! It's time to get up!" She bounced up and down until he flipped her off.

"I'm awake. I was hoping if I looked asleep you would leave me be."

"You too, Rusty. I'm not too shy to jump on your bed either. I am off to make tea for Mother. Would you like one?"

"How long have we got?"

"It's quarter to eight, so about an hour. You boys have gotten lazy."

I shut the door. "Sisters! They are annoying, Rusty, but I think you only have brothers?"

"Yeah, two brothers … always thought I would love to have a sister."

Joe and John sat up. "Why don't you adopt one of ours. You have choice of five!" Joe said.

"You might meet a girl at the wedding. How long are you up?"

"I'm heading back to Kuaotunu in the morning on an early boat."

"It seems surreal to be back in the same room with you two. We had such fun in Kuaotunu. Good memories. But I don't miss being told what to do."

We arrived early at the church, and made our way to one side of the stage. Rusty looked more nervous than I; Joe smiled at me as I stood next to Johnny…

Adorned in all their summer finery, everyone gathered and took their seat inside the huge chapel, while the organ played soft music. Footsteps echoed off the glorious high wooden roof, and light shone through the stained-glass window. I whispered to Rusty, "Have you got the rings?"

He looked surprised, "No, I thought you had them!"

My heart started thumping as I looked at his serious face, then I noticed his eyes sparkling. "Rusty, that's not funny!"

I looked about at the familiar faces: Hector sat next to Mother who gave a little excited wave, then sat Mary, and then the three boys.

Suddenly the music stopped, and the excited crowd became hushed. The Minister came forward, motioning for everyone to stand.

Chapter 31

A Woman After My Own Heart

The wedding music played as Hannah slowly stepped down the aisle followed by Euphemia, and lastly my Angel. She took my breath away in her glorious dress that flowed along the floor, its slim waist, lacey sleeves, and the intricate veil Mother had crocheted. *What a mystery it is for me to be here today. How did I get here after all that has happened in the last three years? She is surely a woman after my own heart.*

"We are here today to celebrate the marriage between Margaret McQuarrie and Henry Thomas Bagust, to be united today in the house of God, before family and friends. Thank you all for coming. Please be seated. I am glad the weather held off this morning; it will be a lovely afternoon celebration for the family being held at the family home, in Kingsland. Margaret and Harry have been waiting for the past year to be joined in holy matrimony as they were waiting for this special Remembrance Day today of Annie McQuarrie, who passed nine years ago today. It is lovely to have Harry's mother, Anne Bagust, up from Wellington today, who also represents her husband.

"Who is it that gives this woman to be wed today?"

Hector came to the front, his serious face tinged with delight. "I do, and also on behalf of my Annie."

"Thank you, sir. Well, what a beautiful couple; it is my joy to have watched Maggie for many years come to this very stage and sing like a bird. My charge today is to you, Harry. In scripture, the church is considered the followers of God, a symbol of Jesus's bride that he longs to be with again one day, when he returns, to find her without blemish. Therefore, this union is not to be entered into lightly for, as the good book says, "We must love our wives as Christ loved the church and sacrificed himself for her.

"This is particularly interesting in light of the fact Jesus did not only die for her but washed the disciples' feet, saying "I have come to serve, and **not** to be served but to give my life a ransom for many.

"Harry and Maggie, in this way I challenge you today, if you are both giving to each other, you will both receive. Love each other as you do today and don't forget the little things you did when you first met.

"Well, now is the part that we all look forward to, your vows, spoken to each other as witnessed by everyone here today. Who has the rings today?"

Rusty nervously checked his pockets, then smiling, produced them. "I do!" Everyone laughed.

"Good. Now, your turn, Harry. Here is the ring, just when you are ready."

"I, Henry Thomas Bagust, do take you, Margaret McQuarrie to be my lawful wedded wife, to have and to hold, for better or worse, whether rich or poor, in sickness and in health, even until death do us part."

"Good. Maggie, here is your ring. When you are ready."

"I, Margaret McQuarrie, do take you, Henry Thomas Bagust, to be my lawful wedded husband, to have and to hold, for better or worse, whether rich or poor, in sickness and in health, until death do us part."

Maggie's eyes were locked with mine, but I could not help glancing for a split second at Euphemia. She stood stern-faced, staring back at me. Maggie flicked a glance to see where I was looking and my skin chilled. I smiled reassuringly at her and squeezed her hand and refocused on the reverend's bible.

"Well, it is my pleasure today in the house of God, before family and friends to announce you, Harry and Maggie, to be husband and wife."

Euphemia carefully lifted the veil, her gaze catching mine for a second.

"You may kiss the bride!"

I took Maggie's face in my hands, and felt her tremble slightly as I kissed her warm lips. Shouts of delight rose from friends and family.

As we proceeded down the aisle, Rusty and Joe shook my hand heartily. Phee and Hannah kissed me on the cheek. Then Hector came forward. "Congratulations, son. Good to have you as part of our clan."

Mother took my arm. "My boy, that was beautiful – you can still cause me to shed tears. Congratulations to you both … Maggie welcome to our family … Mrs Bagust."

"Oh, thank you; this is exciting, isn't it? And yes, I am, aren't I. Please stay for a few days so we can share time together. We are only having one night away, so we can spend a little time with you all before you go."

As we came through the doors and stepped into sunshine, people cheered, and rice cascaded over us.

In true tradition, Maggie looked at me then holding her bouquet high in the air for a minute called out, "Are you ready girls?"

Excited squeals filled the air as girls jostled for a good position then Maggie tossed it up. Euphemia lunged for it competitively, caught the stem then, with a look of horror, tossed it to Hannah who stood right next to her, amid shouts of laughter.

Maggie whispered to me, "It probably means nothing at all, but I hope Hannah finds a fine young man soon as it's definitely too late for Phee."

The rest of the day was a bit of a blur as we shook hands and spoke to old friends and extended family. A camera was set up in one corner of the chapel for photographs to be taken, then we slowly travelled back to New North Road. Phee rushed ahead to arrange the afternoon tea. while we waved to folk cheering along the streets. They had noticed the white ribbons draped across the front of our open carriage but Rusty had painted a rough wooden sign on the back of the carriage, announcing to everyone our nuptials.

We felt like royalty.

Arriving home, I enjoyed catching up with Joe and John, before Hector stood and tapped a glass for attention.

"I would just like to say a few words. Firstly, Harry, welcome to you, your mother and the Bagust family. It has already been a few years that you have been involved in our lives and I consider you a son. We look forward to getting to know you better. I would just like to remember the family that could not be here today: my wife Annie and Barbara, who we sorely miss. I was delighted that Harry and Maggie chose this day to celebrate as this was the day nine years ago she passed away and I would hope they have many years as happy as we were together. Please raise a glass to toast the happy couple Mr and Mrs Bagust."

Everyone cheered, Euphemia glanced my way and winked.

"Stay around. There is plenty of food. I understand Rusty must get away soon, and Murdoch has to return to work too. Harry tells me he and Maggie will be away overnight, but will be back tomorrow so they can spend a little time before family sail home.

The party went on into the night with speeches, cake and toasts until I quietly took Maggie's hand, and whispered, "Now? What do you say?"

"Good idea. I will quickly change and bring my purse." I went about quietly thanking folk, excusing ourselves, then we slipped away. Rusty drove us down to the Imperial Hotel for the night where we had shared our hearts that wonderful yet intense morning last year when it suddenly dawned on me how strong my feelings for Maggie were. Rusty had already checked us in and organised a key to the Honeymoon Suite. We held hands as excitedly we found our way to our door. We could hardly contain ourselves as I unlocked it, and kissed her in the hallway. I kissed her neck as I drew her close, then scooped her into my arms and carried her through the doorway. She smiled coyly as I placed her on the bed and locked the door behind us.

We wished we didn't have to end our time together as we played and talked until the early hours of the morning. Maggie had almost never been anywhere alone, and longed to hide away for at least another week. But the family were expecting us back in the Green's house for New Years, so we packed and caught a cab to Kingsland, arriving the afternoon of the 31st December to help with the festivities.

What a magnificent way to celebrate the coming of 1898, with a beautiful bride at my side in Kuaotunu. She joined us, not wanting to be apart again, as we had been the year before.

Quartz crushing had started to decline and all the mines were slowly laying off men, making a tougher year for Maggie than we had experienced before. I heard of opportunities on the Westland Railway expansion project down south, so sent off applications for a Foreman's job.

Maggie met me after work one day, and waited till I was washed and settled. She sat calmly at the table with her hands folded like she had something to say.

"What is it? Is everything alright?" I asked.

"It's good news! I think I am pregnant! I feel different these last few weeks and I am late!"

I could not help it but my brain took me straight back to that moment Emily announced she was pregnant. That was so full of dread, but this was joy!

"Really!" I rose and hugged her tightly. "When do you think you are due?"

"I don't know for sure, but I met the midwife shopping in town today and she said it could be due about October."

Just then Rusty walked in, and picking up on the conversation.

"Did I hear right ... a new bairn!" We both stood smiling at him. "No! You never said!" He thrust out his hand, and gave me a hearty congratulations then kissed Maggie. "Harry, that's fine news. A blessing on you both! We must celebrate!"

"We've only just found out, so you are the first to know." Then the future crossed my mind. "I don't want you having a baby here – the mud is impassable. Perhaps you could go back with your sisters for support."

"I will see. I do not want to be away from you, and Bolt will keep an eye on me, won't you, boy." He wagged his tail vigorously.

As the rains began in late April, Maggie found it more difficult to get about, especially in muddy, wet conditions. She did her best but, by the end of the month, I insisted she head back up to Kingsland. It all seemed to work out perfectly as we received word from Phee that the Greens were about to head down to their daughter's again, leaving their house vacant for us to rent at an affordable price. Maggie, however was extremely reluctant to move back to Auckland, not wanting to be separated. The next day, as she was wrapping up some meat, she glanced at a news article in the Times dated the week prior.

She squealed and ran to us, holding the paper up awkwardly in wet hands, then read the article aloud.

"Harry, Rusty, look at this article I found. It's from last week. They are looking for good men with mining certificates to help with the railway overpass between Greymouth and Christchurch. It says here:

> *Although the project to complete a line through from Greymouth and Christchurch started back in 1887, it is far from completion. For some time, a legal battle has ensued between the London office of the Westland Railway Company and the Government. The public works department has taken over the project and work is now ready to resume at an accelerated pace. Many good men are needed as there is considerably rough country to pass through with up to 24 tunnels proposed and many viaduct bridges needing to be built.*

"Harry, this sounds like us! It goes on to say that once they have the rail through to Greymouth, they plan to run it through to Nelson. They already have eighty miles of track laid on the Westland side, but in Canterbury, they have only managed to build a bridge over the Kowai River with a short stretch to a place called Otarama."

Rusty looked excited. "So let's get down there! This is what we've been waiting for, isn't it? A chance to use our skills, be part of a huge project. They'll have work for the next twenty years."

"This certainly is what we've been holding out for. What do you think, Maggie?"

"The timing is perfect. With you with your mining certificate, we are free to look for other work, and it's starting to get really cold here this time of year. I insist we have a nice house to live in though. I am sure we will find another small community to be part of. But what will we do with all our belongings?"

"We will pack up our gear, and sell whatever we can't carry."

Maggie looked at Rusty. "What do you say?"

"I'm in. Let's not delay! We may be able to secure reasonable lodgings and work … hopefully before they are all filled."

"I'll write a letter tonight to the Westland Railway asking for appointments and what accommodation they would provide."

"It will be heart-wrenching to bid farewell to our friends here, but it is time and I can feel greater opportunities await."

Even Maggie felt sad as the ship sailed away. In many ways, our experiences here had shaped our lives. We'd had many adventures we would hold dear for many years.

After spending a few days with the family up in Auckland, we took the long journey to Lyttleton in Christchurch, with letters of recommendation from management in my hands. Before we signed up to the public works though, we investigated what we were getting ourselves into. Leaving Maggie in the hotel, Rusty and I took the rough track up over the ranges on horseback into the Waimakariri River and trekked all the way to Black River.

"Look at the tents set up. Are we really contemplating living in a tent up here in the snow-covered hills? I met a Scot on the boat that said the coldest part of the year up here is like being back in the Highlands."

"Rusty, they plan to build a railway station here."

"Up here? Whatever for!"

"The train will initially only run to here, but first there's something like sixteen tunnels to forge. They think the passengers will get off and take a stagecoach through to Otira until the rest of the tunnels are completed. At Otira, they will catch another train that will take them on to Greymouth."

"How are they going to cut a rail from here to Otira."

"Rusty, I've seen the maps. They are talking of cutting a tunnel through these hills that's eight miles long, underground, on a steep slope!"

"If you were ever looking for a challenge, Harry, this is it.

How are they ever going to cross these four huge gorges? It can't be done!"

"I'm excited! What a project! They are saying they have to build massive viaducts to span those two valleys. That's 240 feet high, and there are four of them, not to mention rail bridges."

"It'll take a lifetime!"

"Ten years, they say."

"Harry, do you realise how cold it is today? It's only the first week in July."

"We will need to find a cottage for Maggie down the bottom of the hill in Springfield or Sheffield. They looked like nice little communities as we passed by."

Within months we were settled in Canterbury, where, as the paper reported, men were needed in every field of work. Rusty and I gained good-paying jobs and we found a cottage for Maggie we could come home to on the weekends. They laid out an ambitious plan to cut a railway line from Greymouth, through to Otira Valley then over the southern plains to Christchurch.

I travelled back to Auckland the first week of October, to be around for the birth of our first child. Little Euphemia was born on 23 October 1898. We named her according to tradition – after Hector's mother – Euphemia McCullum and Maggie's sister, Phee, who'd been like a mother to Maggie.

Phem was such a delight to behold and immediately stole our hearts. I had been around many babies but she was so different!

Being near the family, even for a short time, was joyful. They spoilt Phem immediately, and it was a sight to see Hector, the gruff, weathered, old sea captain, cradling this wee girl, quietly singing Scottish tunes to her.

Rusty started work on the little cottage while I was in Auckland, so by the time I returned to Springfield, the lion's share was almost done. With Maggie coming down after

Christmas, we used every spare moment to tidy up the cottage.

As Jack Lane predicted, I was indeed in charge of men. It was truly an impossible task to conceive the laying of a train line through rocky gorges that even a goat would find impossible to traverse. Yet rain, hail and snow, we blasted, shovelled, levered with crow bars and swung picks to drive this impossible task forward.

By the August of '99, we were thrilled – Maggie was expecting again. She had settled well into the small community but missed her sisters dearly.

Back in Martinborough, James worked alongside Joe on the farm and they had become close, but they had also become fierce competitors in the sheep dog trials … in a brotherly way. This was the biggest event of the year in farming communities. In one competition, they excitedly read that J. Bagust was one of ten finalists from the Wellington district. Both were convinced it was them, and argued the point with the judges, who reluctantly relented, allowing eleven in the final competition.

Neither won the war but, as the year passed, it seemed like another war might break out in the South African Republic. The British Empire was preparing to send in a strong force to quash 400,000 rebel Boers. British troops were being called up, one of which was James, as he'd done a stint for the NSW mounted Rifle Division. When James received his letter, Joe was determined to be part of the action, wanted to enlist and defend the Motherland.

James scolded him, and refused to let him go – he was too young. Finally, though, on Joe's firm insistence he agreed, but only if he accompanied him. James then ran into a problem: he had debtors who were after him, and he'd served time: it would all be on his record. Joe was also under age, so they decided to change their name to Baghurst, and gave our parents different professions. It worked. They enlisted, putting their ages as thirty-two and thirty-one years of age; they sailed in February 1900, taking two fine horses gifted by the Martin family with them.

Chapter 32

Fools Rush in Where Angels Fear to Tread

Quote: *NZ is a peculiar country. You cannot get over its geographical configuration. You cannot bring together the two ends nearer than they are. There will always be a certain amount of isolation in different parts until the iron horse (railway) runs through the two islands.*

Our little cottage in Kowhai Bush, four miles from Springfield, was a great community, having been established when the rail was run over the plains from Christchurch a few years before.

Hector finally gave up sailing ships after a fall in which he hurt his hip, and Phee would not let him go again.

Euphemia and Hannah came to stay for a few weeks before Christmas. We met them in Greymouth, where we booked two rooms in the Gilmer Hotel overlooking the Grey River.

I needed a rest and looked forward to staying near the beach for a week, while Maggie spent some lovely time with her much-missed sisters. They had not seen six months old Hector since he was born. I'd not been back to civilisation for months and looked forward to spending some time alone with Maggie and with the children.

It seemed so long since I had seen Euphemia; she looked confident and carefree.

"How are you, Harry? It was a brilliant idea to meet here."

I nodded and smiled. "How is the captain?"

"He has a walking stick now, but he gets around alright. The government recently introduced old age pensions and announced thirteen lucky recipients in the newspaper. Father was one of them … fancy that, being one of the first few in New Zealand to receive £18 a year. He really feels less of a burden to us all, and now he is seventy, it is time for him to relax."

"You care for him well. I want to thank you too for caring for Maggie when she returned to Auckland to have the baby. She was struggling and you helped her get through those last few months."

She smiled. "He is such a handsome wee fella."

"We are both thrilled to have a son." I puffed out my chest. "Hector Henry Bagust, born 17th of May, 1900."

"He's certainly a healthy boy. Now he's responsible for carrying both your grandfather's and great-grandfather's names."

"Well, it's one way to honour them both."

She turned and looked out over the river. "Harry, it's strange the way the sun goes down in the middle of the night here."

I drew in deeply of the warm night air, loving the long summer nights in Greymouth; they were like sweet medicine after the bitter cold of the 5,000 feet high mountains near us in Waimak. "Mmm," I agreed. "The sun usually goes down after nine because we are that much further south. If you went to the south pole, it can be dark all day and in the opposite season, it's daylight all night. When we've been stuck working in some of those deep gorges over the last few years, sometimes we only have a few hours of sunshine, so it's very similar."

"That's incredible." She softly breathed in the warm night air as we stood together on the balcony. "It is certainly a splendid sight standing here looking out to sea. Look how the orange light reflects off the Grey River over there."

We both enjoyed the view. Then she randomly said, "How is Joe? Isn't he in the Boer war?"

I nodded. "He *and* James are there. We had word from

Mother that Joe is returning from South Africa in late November with two other soldiers injured in battle. Apart from nearly dying of malaria, he is otherwise uninjured, and will arrive in Wellington to a jubilant welcome as the Major of Wellington is holding a celebration lunch for them as a 'Welcome Home'. I'm extremely proud of him.".

"Each leg of their journey was published in the newspapers, you know. He is quite the hero." Then she turned and looked directly at me, our eyes meeting and holding for a brief moment. Then she drew another long breath in and let it out. "I must go and help Maggie with the children," she said.

I stood looking out over the river for a while longer, then washed and dressed, and headed out. Phee saw me pass by her room.

"Harry, where are you off to?"

"I'm going to catch up with Rusty and the lads downstairs to celebrate Joe's return."

"Wait! I'll come too! I've read what they achieved up there – I think he's a very brave lad."

I turned back to the girls. "Would you ladies like to come too?" But Maggie had her hands full with the two little ones and was enjoying having time with Hannah.

The bar was crowded so Rusty had gained us a table in a sitting room to one side. I held up my glass "To Joe and James, here's to you both, brothers. You took the courage to go and fight for our country. You're bloody fine fellows!"

Everyone raised their glasses. "To James and Joe!"

"Harry, I read it's been a tough time up there: the Guerrilla warfare is not conventional, and our boys have had to learn a whole new strategy to fighting."

"Joe's lucky to make it back with all the random bombings they've had. They never knew when someone would sneak in and plant a bomb in their camp."

"He's a courageous little bugger, your brother. Tenacious though."

"Mother said they called him Inspector Bagust up there. They say one of his outfit received a Victoria Cross for bravery."

"Harry, why did you not go to war?" Phee asked.

"I wanted to … but, damn it, the government said they needed me here to get the line through to Christchurch for the coal. It was desperately needed for steam ships and every other industry … and to keep the home fires burning, I suppose."

We all laughed.

"Harry, I am so pleased you didn't go! What if you'd been killed?"

"Guess we'll never know! I could get killed any day working where we are. That Waimak River is frightening. There are so many accidents that never get reported. I could fall into the river and freeze to death."

We all laughed at that too, though it wasn't far from the truth, and it make Rusty look serious. He said, "Come on, let's have another round. I want to celebrate what we have right here. No bombs, no war."

We lost count of the tally but we finally called it a night, staggered out of the bar and said goodnight to Rusty. The sun was just setting at 9:30.

Phee linked her arm through mine. "Look at that sky; it hardly feels real. Let's go and sit on the riverbank."

Indeed, the clouds and reflections on the water were stunning.

"We'll watch the sun disappear into the ocean," she added.

The last rays were breathtaking, the clouds suddenly looking like they were on fire.

"Harry, I can't remember a more spectacular sight!" she said, laying back on the grass so she could look up and take in the whole sky. "Come, look at the sky with me!"

"I need to get back soon … I'm feeling rather tired – probably a mixture of exhaustion and alcohol." Nevertheless, we lay next to each other on the grass, mesmerised by the magical sunset, the faint pastels rainbow colours sweeping across the horizon.

"Harry, Rusty's such a good friend. You're so lucky."

I almost laughed. "I think he was keen on you back there. And I remember you two got along well at the wedding a few years back."

"No way! Ohh, all those whiskers … you have to be joking."

We turned to look at each other. "Come on, Phee, you must have met someone you admire."

"Harry, when have I had opportunity to meet anyone with all that is going on in our house. I am thirty this year; I will never meet someone now. Besides I have only ever loved one man, and I regret the day I let him slip away." She looked into my eyes as if searching for something. "Imagine if we had been together, I wonder sometimes how it could have been."

I looked away. "Phee, it is something we cannot change now – you cannot turn back the clock."

She put her arm around me and pressed her cheek to mine. "I have not stopped loving you, Harry Bagust. I look at you with Maggie and I can't help thinking … it should have been *me*. I have never known a man. All this wasted!" She ran a hand expressively up and down her body. "I want to be loved and have a family. How do I do that now – I'm considered an old maid!" She leant on one elbow and said up close, "It was the biggest mistake of my life to let you go." She looked me in the eyes again. "You're right, I cannot turn back the clock, but sometimes I still find myself at night thinking of being with you."

"Phee, I don't understand. You are such a beautiful woman; any man would be crazy not to fall in love with you. Perhaps they are scared of you because you have strong ideas," I said, smiling.

She slapped my arm. "Be honest with me, Harry. Are you

scared of me?"

"Honest! Be honest! If I was being honest, I would say all the things that I have never dared. But I'm not about to start, I've had too much to drink."

She held my face with one hand, her breath now hot in my face. "Then tell me the truth … you were silent that day I poured out my heart to you, those years ago in the kitchen! I want to know! I could tell you wanted to express something. Tell me now, when will we ever have the chance again."

"Euphemia, too much water has gone under the bridge to dig those feelings up like old bones … after all these years. I think I'd better go."

"Harry, to me it still feels like yesterday. I have relived those moments a thousand times. They are not dry bones to me. There is no one to hear them." She lay against me, her hot breasts on my chest.

"Phee, there have been times when I've seen you from the other side of the room, and have to force myself to look away. My body is always charged with desire for you. I still love you now and feel aroused by you! My mind says it could never work, but my desire wants … … well, I have dreamed of it many times."

She silently held my gaze. "I could have lost you in the war, but instead I lost you … I want to be lost *with* you." Then she whispered in my ear, "Is it so wrong for us to be lost in love … turn back the clock … don't you want me!"

She started unbuttoning her blouse. "Harry, I do not want to be with another when all I have dreamed of is being with you. What are you waiting for."

She kissed me on the lips, passionately, and gently slid my hand inside her top. I tried to reason: Maggie had known of my love for her. Did I have to choose just this once.

I had not been with Maggie in months as she was now four

months pregnant and tired much of the time. I felt little will to fight it. I kissed her in return, just as passionately, and she wrestled off her blouse and chemise and lay topless on the grass. The orange of sunset reflected across her chest. Waves of suppressed desire now exploded within me, crashed in rhythmic motion like the ocean hitting the beach. All the years of emotion I felt toward her flooded in like it was yesterday, a torrent of bright orange passion ignited by years of dreaming, anguish, repentance, till we lay on our backs gasping for breath. My body felt like aflame, mirroring the fiery passion we'd felt that had been hidden for so long …

As we gathered ourselves, taking in each other's gaze, neither of us had any illusions that this fire could be destructive if it again burned out of control.

We finally sat up in the semi darkness, looking at each other in silence … staring at one another, saying nothing and yet everything all at once.

I slowly walked her back to the hotel, where she took my hand and looked at me contentedly. "I will go ahead … see you tomorrow."

I let her hand go and sat quietly, part of me feeling horror while the other part felt contented, relieved. I smoked a cigarette then went back, and slipped into bed. I lay wide awake for hours, staring at the ceiling, wondering what had just happened before sleep finally claimed me.

The next morning after breakfast, I had morning tea with Hannah while little Phem ran around on the hotel balcony.

"You were out late," she said. "I heard the door close. Did you have a good night?"

I felt shame after last night, and wanted to confess to Maggie, but how to tell her. What if Hannah knew?

"I caught up with a few men and had a drink to Joe," I said briefly. It wasn't a lie, just not the whole truth.

Hannah was nearly twenty, and a good soul to be around. She had been a great deal of help with her auntie's children when staying in Kaurihohore, now with our two little ones, who loved her dearly.

She always spoke her mind, and had a good grasp on what was happening in the world.

"You are so good with the children, Hannah, but what would you like to do if you really had a choice?" I changed the subject.

"I would like to go to university and study or even learn tailoring. I love learning new things and reading interesting books about creative people. I have been making some wonderful creations at home now there is a spare work room in the house. Father bought us a treadle sewing machine."

"You are lucky to have a father like him."

"We know," she said, "but we are fearful. Father is suffering with his knees more these days." She shook her head. "I have never thought of him as old, but the other day, I saw him coming along the road without his hat and saw a little old man. It shocked me."

Euphemia came out into the warm sunshine, holding little Hector, and sat with us on the balcony. With her so close, I felt confused and angry at myself for letting this get out of control.

She held Hector up, speaking to him, "He's going to have big shoes to fill, to be like Granddad … What an adorable wee chap."

"Oh, it's such a beautiful day. I can't believe we must go back in four days. I don't feel the least bit like leaving."

Euphemia glanced into my eyes nervously.

Little Phee held her pants.

"You want to go toilet…?" Hannah said, picking up little Phem and whisking her off to the bathroom. It was the opportunity I needed; I whispered, "Phee, I feel terrible! This can never happen again. I am sorry I let things get out of hand.

I truly do not know what to say."

"Harry, I think we probably both feel a sense of relief."

"*Relief!* … What if Maggie finds out?"

"How long have I wanted to be honest with you. I do not regret it for a moment."

"I do not want to hurt her. We must never speak of this again. Can you promise me!"

"Of course! Who am I going to tell … I might tell myself sometimes."

It was now late November, four days before the girls sailed for home. Maggie had enjoyed having them around, and was sad for days, not knowing when she would see them again. I threw myself back into work, nervously waiting for weeks, hoping Euphemia was not pregnant. Just when I thought I could brush the whole experience under the rug and breathe a sigh of relief, Maggie received a letter saying Phee had been sick for months. *What do I do? It is going to come out! The saying is true: Only fools rush in where angels fear to tread.*

One night as I prepared for bed, Maggie came into the room. "Did you know Euphemia is pregnant?" she said straight out. "She is well on the way. I need to ask: do you know anything about it?"

My skin felt suddenly cold and my stomach tightened. "Maggie, I didn't know how to tell you. When we went that night to celebrate Joe's return, we drank heavily and things got out of hand. We casually went to watch the last of the sunset. She brought up our relationship all those years ago, asking me how I really felt. I tried to tell her, it was water under the bridge, but she told me how she loved me still. I was not aware I still had these deep unresolved feelings and before long we kissed."

Maggie picked up her wedding rings off the tall dresser and hurled them at my head. "She is my sister! … How could you do this?! I thought for sure you would deny it, not dreaming you could do such a thing. You are a bastard, Harry Bagust! Don't tell me you still love her!"

"I think a part of my heart has always loved her. I was shocked at my feelings, as it had been so long. But I love you. I did not mean to hurt you like this!"

I moved towards her but she pounded on my chest with her fists.

"This was my beautiful chest all those years ago, mine alone! Have you been with her before?"

"No, only you."

"Me and Emily, and who knows who else. How can I trust you now."

"There has been no one else."

"I don't know what to say … what will happen to the child?"

"I do not know. Perhaps it could be adopted out."

I don't want to see you tonight! And you're not sleeping in here anymore."

I tried to make it up to Maggie but she was already pregnant with our third child and would not let me even touch her, and our situation was not helped by the long days at work.

Little Margaret was born on the 14th of April 1901, then five months later, Euphemia also had a little girl – Annie on the 10th of September. Maggie took the children up to help Phee adjust for two months. They seemed to bond together again, although I do not know how, and decided to keep it secret that we were living separate lives.

Christmas 1902 was a happier time in our lives as I booked us in for our wedding anniversary to Hanmer Springs. A sports carnival was held so I entered many of the events, and won a prize. The children had a wonderful time and, on the 29th, I dressed up to spend a special evening with Maggie. She kissed me then pushed me away again, saying she was afraid to get pregnant again, and that she still needed time.

The next two winters were bitter but Maggie enjoyed the warmth of the summer days in Kowhai Bush with the children.

The tough conditions at work became harder as we climbed higher and deeper into the steep valleys and gorges. We dug out then poured colossal concrete abutments and foundations to erect massive steel structures for the viaducts. We used tons of dynamite, carried mostly on horseback into the steep terrain.

The government had brought in men from Europe to help with the building of the four steel structures 240 feet high that seemed completely daunting, an almost impossible task given the remoteness and freezing conditions.

We made good progress over the last four years building a new station at Broken River. Like a prehistoric snake, the Waimakariri River wound its way in the shadows of the enormous Torlesse mountains. Even Kowhai Bush, which seemed to be on the flat was 1,300 feet above sea level, which meant the trains running back to Christchurch from the top were actually carrying coal downhill.

One day we received word that Joe had been chosen as one of three New Zealand soldiers from the British colony to represent us at the King's coronation on the 26 June 1902. Some said he was chosen because he looked so handsome sitting perfectly straight and upright in a saddle. The family suggested it was perhaps because he had also been in a group of twelve men who broke through the enemy in South Africa, one receiving a Victoria cross for his efforts.

Hector became ill and did not look good, so Maggie went north with the children to spend time nursing him. We were all devastated when Hector passed away in his sleep on the 12th August,1903. The funeral was huge with folk coming from every corner of New Zealand with words of condolence. He'd been a giant in our eyes and was sorely missed. He left six children and four grandchildren – he had outlived two wives and six children.

That year, the government tried to push a rail project along in Karangahake and, wanting to be nearer to Maggie and the children in the Auckland district, I took a foreman's role there for the new tunnel shaft.

I packed up again and moved to Karangahake, but the conditions were so appalling in Ohinimuri we decided Maggie should stay in Auckland where little Phem could start school.

I was glad for the opportunity to be closer to Maggie as I could go up on some weekends. Maggie had also decided to stay on for a while in Auckland as the weather was lovely and the children had grown so well together. She also enjoyed having time with Phee, and the two babies were so close in age they seemed like twins. Between them, they decided that Marg and Annie could be brought up together as sisters, so Maggie took on looking after the four children while Euphemia went off to work in the tea house.

With Christmas around the corner, we decided to get together with all the Auckland family and everyone gathered in the two houses for our annual Christmas celebration.

Chapter 33

Off the Rails ...

Christmas eve was a warm balmy evening, and we sat out on the front porch. The house had been a hive of activity preparing for Christmas with such a big family get-together at our house, but we all knew it would not be the same without Hector's fine stories around the fire in the evenings. The turkey had been plucked and cleaned ready for the long slow cook on Christmas day. Joe had joined us for the festive season so we made a small bed up on the front porch for him. Phem and Hec loved to have him over as he happily played with them for hours. Maggie realised she did not have a present for him so headed out late to Kingsland shops to buy him a gift to place under the tree. I sat in the lounge chair, which felt like laying on a cloud after the hard wooden stools we'd had in the workers' railway huts at the camp. I glanced at the mantel clock. *Half seven. She should be back by now.* I must have dozed off, fatigued after travelling up from Karangahake to Auckland and spending a long day on a crowded ship. I was suddenly awakened by distressed voices coming from outside, then Joe rushed in shouting: "People are coming out onto the street as there has just been a huge explosion. They think it could be a tram as it went past only minutes ago. It may have come off the rails."

I jumped up, quickly pulled on my boots at the door and followed Joe out, a deep sick feeling hitting deep in my stomach.

"Quick, run over and tell Phee. Ask Hannah to come and

mind the children."

I ran as fast as I could, scanning the way ahead. I could already hear a woman screaming in pain, and terrible moans from seriously injured people all around. As I drew nearer, I saw that bodies were strewn about the road, some motionless, others in a dazed state. They must have been jumping off to escape the impending doom. The scene was utter chaos. Suddenly a dark shadow appeared in the middle of the road with one dim gas lamp still eerily flickering at the rear. I could just make out two trams, a double decker and the single combination that had passed only minutes before. They were now melded a quarter of the way into the other, creating a long mass of tangled wreckage. My heart thumped like a hammer. The rear car was stuck up in the air so men, still bloodied, were helping lift passengers down out of the tram windows. My legs were suddenly gripped with fear. *What if Maggie is in there?* A mother, sobbing, held her frightened children. A stunned man, hobbling on one foot, winced in pain, holding what looked like a broken hand. Horrified neighbours from surrounding houses stood stunned, while passers-by immediately comforted those who by now were stumbling away from the disaster. Hysterical woman thrust their screaming children through the broken windows, begging someone to help save their babies. An older woman with two crushed lower legs cried out in agony as two men carefully carried her toward a nearby house.

I could not bear to think of Maggie trapped inside that mess. Frantically, I searched the many dazed and agonised faces of people climbing down out of the tram, but I could not see her. A small child suddenly clung to my legs, crying for her mother. I lifted her up in her blood-stained dress and held her close; carried her to an older, kindly looking lady. Two seats lay on the road, thrown by the force from the upper deck. I stood them up, motioning to two men carrying a lifeless body to place her there.

A man with a lantern was on the top deck trying to help people down. A lady lay still, sprawled across a bench seat and a man's arm hung over the side in the dim light.

Soon a huge crowd of people gathered to help. In the half-light, people staggered along the road. Some were helped along by others, blood on their faces and hands. A man in front of me was coming to his senses, trying desperately to get up, not realising his leg was broken at right angles behind him – he'd obviously leapt off the top deck at the last minute. I rushed to him, grabbing a hat on the road to put under his head. "Sir, sir, lie still; your leg is broken."

"Where am I?"

"You must have leapt from the tram and banged your head. Here, put your head on this hat and try and stay still. I have just heard doctors and staff are coming from the hospital – they will be here soon."

Just then Euphemia was at my side. "Phee, keep this man still. I need to find Maggie."

I searched every face, every shape in silhouette, for the familiar curve of Maggie's body, all the while praying *Dear God don't let her be suffering.*

"Go! I will make him comfortable and see who else needs help. … Sir, please stop trying to get up, your leg is broken."

I stood on the rear of the tram, searching the darkness for Maggie's face. I desperately tried to recall what she was wearing, but could not see her anywhere.

It was like a war zone; so much sticky blood; people shouting everywhere. Screams came from the twisted mass of metal and timber as I drew near to look inside the tram. A man yelled out, there are people trapped between the cars! I followed the voice and could see a man's face white with fright.

"How many are trapped?"

"I think it's a man and a woman; they are crying out for help."

"Please help me – anyone!" came the voice as I peered into the dark, and willed my eyes to adjust to the light. I rushed along to where she was trapped, just making out the lady's face. "Are you badly injured, Ma'am?"

"My legs are pinned by some timber. I can't move or feel my feet," she wailed. "There's a man over there … said his name was Benjamin but he's stopped calling out now."

"Ben, are you alright? *Ben!* … Has anyone got a lantern?" I shouted into the street. Ben did not respond from the darkness.

"Do you have family nearby that we can fetch for you. What is your name? Where do you live?"

"Cassie," she said faintly. "Cassie Hill. … 15 George Street."

By now two or three people had brought portable gas lanterns and, as the light shone on the wreckage, the carnage became clear. It looked more like stories of a bomb blast, splatters and trails of blood, smashed glass, splinters and mangled steel. We could see the woman's face clearly. She was now barely conscious, with blood running off her chin from a wooden splinter buried deep into her cheek. Her white dress was completely soaked in blood from her crushed legs and upper thighs.

I leapt back onto the siding, shouting out into the gathering crowd. "Are there any men available – there are people pinned between the carriages. Come quickly, together we may be able to separate the cars." A chorus of men's voices came from all around, shouting, "Tell us what to do!"

I haven't a clue, I thought, *but at least we can do something.* Out the corner of my eye I saw a young lad nearby and caught his attention. "Hey, laddie!" I called out.

He ran over, looking at me intently.

"This lady needs her family immediately! Run up that hill as fast as you can to 15 George Street and fetch her family." I pointed north. "Can you do that?"

"Yes, sir. 15 George Street!" He sprinted off into the half light of the street lamp. One man came over holding a lamp high and I could now see a large number of bright concerned faces, all eyes to help.

I shouted out into the crowd. "In a few minutes we are going to try and pull the carriages apart. They may not move but we must try. I need you to secure yourself a good grip on Number 32; she is the lighter of the two and pray for a miracle. Hopefully, we can pull her off the double decker to free these folk. It's a slim chance, we must do something."

Suddenly Euphemia was beside me. "How can I help?" she whispered. "And how do you know what to do?"

"I am so glad you're here. I've seen plenty of accidents with men crushed between mining carts," I said, moving away from the injured woman. "I've just sent a lad to fetch this young woman's family. Once her family has had a chance to say their goodbyes, we'll try and get these wretched cars apart."

Euphemia frowned. "You don't think she will survive this?"

"I've seen men crushed before. They appear responsive until the cart is removed … when the blood rushes in to their injuries, it can kill them due to the pain."

Euphemia turned to the young lady. "Cassie, my name is Phee; try and remain awake …"

"I feel cold … is my father there!"

"We have called for your family and we have a large group of men and women who are going to try and free you. Your family will be here any moment; we will wait for you to see them first."

Just then the lad arrived back, puffing. "They are coming right away."

I stepped down just as Mr Hill rushed into the light, his face gaunt with horror.

"Sir, your daughter is pinned between the carriages. We sent for you because we are going to try and separate them.

Sometimes when this happens, it can cause worse injuries, so you have a few minutes to make speak with her before we start. Here is a lamp so you can see her."

He climbed up on the siding with the lamp, his hand shaking.

"Oh, my dear, dear girl., I am so sorry, I wish so much it was me pinned there instead of you. All I want now is for you to be alive and hold you in my arms again; that would be the greatest Christmas gift of all.

"Daddy, I am sorry. I wanted everything to be perfect for the family visiting … Daddy, don't leave, I feel so scared!"

"I am not leaving; I will stay right here."

"I can't feel my legs! Please, tell Mother and the others I love them."

He reached out to gently touch her face but she was too far away, and she winced as she lifted her arm to reach him.

"Be brave, my lovely girl. Be brave. Everyone is doing all they can to get you out!"

I jumped down and shouted to the men and women who had found a place to pull. The crowd looked large enough to lift it right off the tracks. "Righto, lads and ladies, on the count of three … this is the tug of war of your lives. Each time I yell pull, let's give it all we've got! One. Two. Three. *Pull!* … *Pull!* … *Pull!* … *Pull!!!*"

The carriage creaked a little, and shards of glass dropped onto the road, but the cars were stuck fast.

Cassie screamed, a blood-curdling sound.

A runner burst in, trying to catch his breath. "There's another tram … on the way … coming up from Eden Terrace … she'll be here in about ten minutes."

"Good, lad!"

I shouted again. "If you're in the dark and can help us pull, come and lend a hand. Let's give it *everything*, one more time!

"*Ready?* One. Two. Three … *Pull! Pull! Pull!* There was a small shudder, but it was like the cars were now one. I looked up at Cassie, who had slumped forward. I tapped Mr Hill on the arm. "I am sorry, sir; they are just too wedged together. There is a tram on the way from the city, we will try to free her with chains."

I spoke again to the desperate faces. "Thank you, everyone. We will wait for the tram and perhaps we can help lend some extra force in a few minutes."

Mr Hill looked distraught. "Please, hurry. She has gone quiet."

I took the lantern and shone it on her head which was now bent forward, her breathing laboured. The man on the other side of the tram had not been responsive either.

"Phee, please stay with Cassie. She might wake. I cannot imagine where Maggie is at all. Where do you suppose she is?"

"Harry, don't worry. She is probably enjoying the celebrations in the city; she will be on her way home soon. She'll arrive any minute in a cab, you'll see. When we have done all we can here, I will help you check she is not about."

Chapter 34

A Sight for Sore Eyes

I constantly checked every face for Maggie as the lamp swung round to and fro. Euphemia jumped off the tram and helped a lady bandage a man's head just as the two lights of the incoming tram slowly made its way down the steep incline where only an hour before the fully loaded double-decker had plummeted at tremendous speed. As its lights shone on the scene, it looked like half the city had turned out.

I looked at the agonised faces of the new helpers as the tram slid to a halt; they were transfixed by the scene unfolding before their eyes.

"It's a relief to see the doctors finally arriving," Phee said.

Every few minutes, carriages from every corner of the city had been arriving. It didn't take long to hook the chain up and prepare to pull the big combination apart. We loaded men into the tram to give it extra traction as the conductor swung the power lever, slowly pulling back till the chain was tight. Cassie had not come to her senses again, but as the tram car tightened the chain, her scream rent the air, along with a tremendous noise of ripping timber and squealing steel. Phee ran in as the tram dragged the battered car away up the road. Doctors rushed forward to help Cassie, who had fallen to the road, screaming in agony. I felt relieved to see her being lifted gently onto a stretcher. They set to work straight away with torniquets, bandages and chloroform to dull her pain as her father stood holding his mouth.

Again, my mind went to Maggie. *Where was she?*

I could not let it rest, and started asking people who may have been on the carriage.

Phee came and stood next to me as I asked a man standing near, looking like a lost child. He had lost his hat but had blood on his face and down one arm. "Sir, were you on the tram car tonight. I am looking for my wife?"

"Yes, I was. What did she look like? Our tram must have had at least seventy people on board. I pray it was not the young woman that was hit by the overhead trolley arm."

We both stood, preparing ourselves for the worst news as my heart thumped in my chest with dread. "Maggie is twenty-six and has darkish hair," I said. "She may have been wearing a light blue dress with a matching hat."

"Yes, Harry, she was. I remember waving to her as she went out your front door."

The man looked back and forward at us. "I can't be sure if it was her – it all happened so fast – but I remember a man with a young woman in blue, giving up his seat, insisting she lay down just before the crash. She was terribly frightened and so he stayed to hold her hand, telling her it would be alright.

"Terror fell on the whole car as soon as all the lights went out and suddenly someone cried out, "There's a tram coming up … we are going to crash!" The man's eyes widened as he relived it. "The second tram car didn't seem to have seen us, as our lights had all gone out when the trolley pole came off the wire. By this time, our tram was hurtling towards them down the steep hill." He was prattling now, back in the midst of it. "Extreme panic overtook many people, and they screamed and shouted. 'We are going to die!' Some people fell to their knee's praying; others just threw themselves over the side onto the road below. I shouted out 'Get down! Stay on board,' then told them to lie down and brace themselves against the seats. But that young man tried to hold her hand, holding on to the rail. He was ripped away, flung clear over the side still holding her hand as it crashed."

"Oh, my God. The poor man. I wonder if he survived? Dear Maggie, how must she have felt."

"Do you think she was hurt?"

"She lay low to protect herself as she was right behind the two people killed by the end of the trolley pole that flailed about. See … it all started as we pulled into the loop to wait for the next tram. You could hear the ratchet brake being applied, but it did not grip. Firstly, we heard Fred Humphrey, the conductor, shout 'Move aside' as he went running down the stairs for the rear brake lever down below. By this time the car was gathering speed and we felt sure they would throw the main brake or reverse the thrust. But the trolley was still gathering momentum, going at a terrific speed. Suddenly, the trolley arm doubled over, and wrenched off the wire. There were more screams as we were plunged into darkness, but the greatest danger was coming. It was horrifying, because by then we were already out of control." Tears now streamed down the man's face. He was still right there in the moment.

"Not only were we gathering speed down the incline with so much weight on board, but in the darkness the trolley pole lashed out, smashing the first young lady in the head – I think she died instantly. She fell backwards over her seat, only inches from what could be your wife's face. Blood spurted out over her. I'm sure your wife would have tried to run if she could, as she just screamed and screamed. It was more horrendous because of the dark. Then a second man next to her was hit in the head as he tried to protect the other passengers. In fact, now I think of it, that couple may have been friends, as your wife had been chatting away excitedly like they were off for the evening together.

"Two older men tried to grab the arm with their walking sticks, but it kept crashing down every time it flew up, flicking off another cross wire. He too had injuries to his head and was sent flying, nearly over the front of the tram."

"The car was obviously out of control and now started from side to side like a ship. We thought the whole thing was going over, and held on for our lives in case she went over. The first we heard of the second tram was the screams from below. We looked up and could clearly see the lights in the distance. Next minute, we hit the first bend. Two young fellows hanging onto the side were trying to climb off but were flung straight over the side.

"It felt like an eternity as we lay, knowing at any second we may be dead. The crash was like a horrendous bomb exploding, everything suddenly going into slow motion. I saw people, luggage and bench seats fly over my head. I thought my legs would snap as I braced against the bolted seat. Those moans will keep me up at night … you've no idea the horror … I can't believe I'm actually alive … it seems like the most terrible nightmare.

"Did you see Maggie get off?"

"Oh yes, she was probably the first to jump up, completely hysterical by now to find the young man that had been flung from her grip. I grabbed her arm, as it looked like she was about to throw herself over the side after him. She was quite out of her mind. I suggested she climb down onto the window sill below and I helped her climb over the side and held her as best I could. Poor lass, her eyes were wide with terror."

"Come," Euphemia said, gripping my hand firmly. "We must get home. It sounds like Maggie needs us."

It was the first time I had felt her warm hand since we

touched that night.

"Harry, perhaps she has calmed down a little by now. Thank you so much for your help." Euphemia hugged the man. "God bless you for being so caring."

I shook the man's good hand warmly. "Yes, I am so sorry. By the way, I'm Harry Bagust. This is Euphemia McQuarrie."

"I'm John," he replied.

"I wish you all God's blessing in finding your wife."

We pushed our way through the crowd. A man stopped me on the way through and thanked me for my efforts to help.

It seemed to take an age to run back along the tram line to our little house at Number 11 on New North Road. We searched the faces for any glimmer of Maggie's face or a blue dress. We met Joe out the front of the house holding the kid's hands. "Joe, is Maggie here?"

"No. I thought she was with you. Was she not on that tram?"

"We think she was, but we're not sure. We met a man who described her exactly, saying that she was one of the first to get off the double-decker, by climbing over the side. Keep an eye out for her – if it is her, she could be quite delusional. I'm going to check some of the houses along the street near the accident."

"I'll come too," said Phee. "We can cover more houses that way."

We almost marched up the road, back to the site, going from one house to another. Even though it was late, most people were out watching the commotion, so it was easy to call out, "Have you seen a young lady in a blue dress?"

One person said they had, but then described her as perhaps a school girl. As we made our way along each side of the street, I was surprised how many people had taken in passengers from the tram and given them soup or hot sugary tea for the shock.

"Have you seen a young woman in a blue dress?"

"No, I haven't, but I was over at my friend's place along the road earlier. They have a woman with them from the accident – no injuries, but she's a mute."

My heart started beating like a drum against my ribs *Could this be her!? … Surely she can speak.* "Can you take us to her!"

I looked over the road for Phee; she was just coming off the front porch of a house.

"Phee!" I shouted. She looked up and ran across the road.

"This lady has a friend who has taken in someone that might be Maggie."

The elderly lady fetched her bonnet and street shoes, and threw a shawl round her shoulders. "Follow me, dear. It's not far down the hill. My friend found her in a daze sitting on their front porch when she arrived home."

We followed the lady along the road and down the hill a little way, then in through a small picket gate.

"Yoo-hoo! Nellie!" She knocked on the door. "Oh, I thought you said you were off to bed."

"I couldn't with worrying over this poor girl, and the noise in the street will go on for hours yet."

"Nell, these folk are searching for a woman in a blue dress. Could they see if it's his wife?"

"Come right in. I think she is sleeping now, but we can sneak in for a moment. Let me fetch my lamp."

We crept into the hallway and she quietly opened the door; lifted the lamp enough for the light to cast across the back of her blood-soaked head. Phee gasped at the sight, still unsure if it was really her. Part of me was hoping it was not her and that somehow she was still out celebrating in the city. The rest of me was desperate to hold her and unlock this strange mystery. I was not sure as she was turned away to the wall with blood all in her hair and clothes, but Phee saw a hat sitting on the chair and gave an involuntary shout. "Oh God, it's her!"

Then she whispered, "It's her … I know it is. She got that hat only weeks ago ready for the Christmas church renditions. What should we do? It would be terrible to wake her, but what if she woke in a strange house, after all she has suffered."

We crept back out. I suddenly felt I was about to vomit, as the realisation hit me, and closed my eyes for a minute and breathed in deeply.

When I opened my eyes, Nell was pointing a finger at me. "You are the man helping on the tram, trying to pull the cars apart. Your friend's a hero for getting in there to help, knowing his wife was out there somewhere! You must stay with her."

Phee spoke up as I was struggling to comprehend all that had transpired. Part of me felt relief at finding her; another part was becoming overwhelmed by the whole night.

"Maggie was just going to the city to buy a present. We searched everywhere for her, finally thinking she might have gone home as she has three little children waiting for her."

"Well, dear, me and Katherine went up the road after hearing BOOM to see the unbelievable carnage. We watched in horror as they carried away perhaps a hundred people. Of all nights for it to happen, there could not have been more folk on those tram cars. I must admit, I have wanted to try that new double-decker myself … anyway when we returned, we swung open our little gate and there was your wife on the front porch, sitting in the rocking chair. I got a terrible fright as she looked dead. She has hardly spoken a word since we found her, just stares blankly into space. We assumed she was either mute or in terrible shock. I could see the blood all over her face and dress, and worried that she had injuries, so I checked her over. Being a retired nurse, I soon realised she didn't have no injuries so we prised her hat out of her hands, carefully washed her face with a warm cloth, and put her to bed. They'll be real busy at the hospital right now so it was better for us to look after her till things settle down. She has not spoken except when I straightened her hair. She said,

"Thank you, Mother'."

"That's all? She did not speak other than that?"

Phee put her head down and quietly sobbed. "Mother passed nine years ago."

"I'm so sorry, dear." She gently put her crippled, arthritic hand on Phee's head. "I have seen this before, dear, in war time. A person can be so traumatised that they just shut down with anguish and shock.

"Harry, I think I will stay here tonight, if it's alright with Nellie. I can sit beside her bed in case she wakes. You look exhausted, I think the best thing you can do is go home and have a good night's sleep to be ready to face whatever happens tomorrow. We will need to be strong to make it through this."

"Yes, dear, that is a good idea," Nellie said. "I don't think it would be wise to move her tonight. Let's see how she is in the morning. These things can take time to heal; she may be weeks like this but she is young, she will bounce back."

I took a deep breath. *I need a cigarette. I need to breathe.* "Phee, can I get you anything from home?"

"You could check on the twins and make sure they are alright. I will be alright sitting with her tonight."

"If you young people need anything, just knock on my door."

"Thank you, Nellie. We are so grateful. I will check on her then get away home."

Phee sat in a wicker armchair next to Maggie's bed, and I relaxed on the floor next to her, listening to Maggie's breathing. Suddenly, exhaustion hit, like the day's horrific events had caught up with me, even the adrenaline was gone. I leaned back on Phee's legs and she stroked my head. I must have dropped off to sleep at some point as I woke to Maggie's screaming, *"Oh God, it's going to crash! It's going to crash!"*

She was in a sweat, Phee comforting her and stroking her brow with a wet flannel. Maggie seemed to come to for a few minutes, then slept again.

"Will you be alright, Phee? I could stay with you," I whispered.

"It will be a long night, but no one knows her better than me. I am concerned that she still might have injuries."

"I think if she did, she would become conscious with pain. Keep an eye on her, I will come back early."

I hugged her and walked out, quietly closed the door behind me. Phee waved through the window from her chair as I walked up the street towards home. I felt drowsy but my mind rattled with a hundred things. I stopped to light a cigarette, and pulled out my watch. 12:15. *Oh it is already Christmas morn.*

My mind bounced like a ball between *'God, how could you let this happen,'* to *'It could have been so much worse'* but the only thing I could control this night was making sure all the families were cared for and ready for tomorrow. I would try to keep this quiet for tonight and see what tomorrow brought.

I carefully opened the front door, trying not to let it squeak. A candle was burning and Joe was sitting up with a book.

"Did you find her? She hasn't come home, and I could not sleep. Hannah was so upset, she cried and cried. I made food for the children and sent them all off to bed, saying that 'Maggie has just been out at the Christmas festivities, you will see her in the morning'."

"Joe, I am so glad you were here! Don't tell the children but Maggie was found on a lady's front porch a few streets from the accident. She's not injured, but she's in terrible shock. Phee is sitting with her at the lady's house till morning. Go and get some sleep, we will need to put on our happy faces for the children."

Chapter 35

Like Birds Set Free

The Kingsland community was devastated by the tragic disaster. Every family in the community had been affected in one way or another, and we were no exception.

I could not sleep that night worrying about Maggie and lay in the dark, telling myself I could do nothing till morning. When daylight came, I was already down at Nellie's sitting on the front doorstep of the house, smoking to calm my nerves. A dog barked next door but finally settled as I sat quietly taking stock of the situation and trying to plan a way to get through this chaos.

We would start today as usual with presents, then breakfast. We'd tell the children that Mummy was away sleeping ... at least for their sake. I asked Joe to tell only Murdoch, the twins and Hannah how we found her.

I took a gift with Christmas mince pies that Euphemia had made to Nellie, and we carefully roused Maggie out of bed and took her home. We changed her into her night clothes, and put her to bed. As we did, we noticed she had a small wound on one leg. Everywhere else she had black bruises and dried blood on her legs and arms. Though the children had woken early and excitedly came into the lounge to see the presents under the tree, they had not noticed us slip past.

Hannah and the twins came in early, making little games with five-year-old Phem, Hector jnr and two-year-olds, Marg and Annie. Joe and Phee tried to keep busy, moving about the kitchen to make a luxurious late breakfast for everyone.

We did our best to be cheery amid strong feelings of loss, after losing Annie, Mary and Barbara, and now Hector only months ago. Hannah twice excused herself from the table and returned sometime later with red eyes. "I feel helpless. What can I do to help her recover? What if she never recovers?"

"Hannah, Maggie is very sick, but we are confident she will recover. This week we will take her to a doctor and see what they say."

"I think she needs to stay in Auckland instead of that cold dreary weather of Karangahake. She can be near the hospital or a specialist up here."

"Are you going to be around for the next few weeks?"

"Phee, I am here to help with the children or whatever else you need," she said.

We took Maggie to many doctors and specialists before one said he had seen this before diagnosing her with Galloping diabetes which they say was brought on by the shock. She stayed in bed, mostly with Hannah nursing her and caring for the children.

In the new year, in Karangahake, the pressure mounted as they were pushing it along, determined to open before Christmas 1904. They desperately needed the tunnel to get the gold out of Waihi Mine and the coal in to fuel the stamping batteries and machines.

We were working night and day to get it finished in time so there was not much chance to get away back to Auckland. The first chance I got was on the 18th of July, as Euphemia was urgently wanting me to go over the court documents for Maggie's hearing in August.

Maggie had gone downhill and was now in bed most of the time. She was also very weak and her legs and ankles were swollen. The doctor said her kidneys were failing and tried different medicines to help, and recommended that she go into hospital if she deteriorated further.

Through Phee, Maggie had made a claim for damages of £550 against the tram company, the case being heard on August 27th.

"Phee, where are you?" I said walking through the quiet house when I arrived. I found her in her bedroom. "There you are. My, you've lost weight … are you alright?"

She looked up. I immediately noted the frailty in her face. "Not really," she said. "I don't know why I am feeling so flat but honestly, Harry, it is all I can do to get out of bed in the morning. I feel overwhelmed by it all."

"You look pale. When was the last time you sat in the sun?"

She glared at me. "You must be joking!" she said, raising her voice. "The three boys are upset and have said to me, there must be more that can be done. Hannah is only just managing with looking after four children that are not hers with one at school, needing lunches, school supplies and delivering her to school each day. She looks after Maggie day and night and it is often sitting by her bed for hours or reading her a story and hasn't had a break except when I take over for a few days to let her sleep.

"We are both watching our beautiful songbird fade away till she is unrecognisable. I am sure the doctors do not know how to treat her and despite their best efforts she is getting worse by the day."

I put my hand on her shoulder. "Phee, could we ask someone to come in and help?"

"We do not have anyone we could ask for help as a lot of our friends cut us off years ago when we got Tuberculosis or one of the scandals Father suffered. I have not been able to go to work as there has been so many other things to organise with doctors visiting, picking up medicine and this court case coming up. I am utterly exhausted.

"Harry, it is like all the loss in my life, even before Mother's death, my sweet sister Mary, Barbara, Father, and all the friends and family we have lost has finally caught up with me. Now, looking at these papers spread all over the floor has taken me straight back to that witch Madame Vines defamation case on Father. That was the last nail in Father's coffin. He never got over that."

I listened attentively as she spoke of the bond she and Maggie had shared through the years, with all the nursing of sick family, shunning of friends because of tuberculosis, shipping scandals and bankruptcies the family had suffered through. My heart felt torn apart just trying to imagine the massive load Euphemia had carried on her shoulders to support her family. Now it seemed she had reached the last straw.

"Maggie is dying, Harry. She is never going to see these three beautiful children grow up, fall in love, get married! I am faced with that every time I pick up one of your children."

"I am here now. I will do whatever you need to help for a few days at least."

"Harry, I can't believe how much it means to talk to you about this. Hannah and I are too young to lose both our parents. It is so hard when there is no other adult to have a conversation with. You know me so well; I have always been able to talk to you. When surrounded by children all day, I have forgotten how normal it is to share troubles together. So many times when I feel vulnerable I wish for the strong arms of a man."

Her voice broke, as all the grief and sorrow she had held back for years, and all her attempts to be strong and not showing weakness, were released in a giant flood. Nothing was going to hold it in. As tears streamed down her cheeks, I held her in my arms and let the waves of loss pour out. I felt her pain; watched helplessly, hopelessly. My own eyes moistened. Would we ever wake from this never-ending nightmare. I too needed her support, as seven years of my love for my singing angel was about to be gone forever. The one person who had remained stoic, who really knew my dread, was in my arms. She looked into my eyes and then, without a word, we kissed, and felt again our souls knit together in this strange yet familiar outpouring of passion and release. A dormant bond I had tried so hard to suppress, bubbled up again, and spilled over as our clothes were thrown about the legal papers strewn on the floor. The cage door opened and we were again like birds set free.

I spent the next few days visiting Maggie but work was desperate to push this tunnel through. Part of me could not bear to see my wife looking weak, and wanted to spend every moment at her bedside. The other part wanted to run away, leave, pretend it was not inevitable. It was ironic that I spent my days in dark tunnels and here we were in the darkest tunnel of all together, that one day soon we would never escape from.

I threw myself again into my work but found it hard to concentrate as poor Maggie filled my mind. The hearing was now only days away. Would she be able to attend? She had said if the tram company paid out, she would love to see the money go toward a beautiful farm somewhere.

On Sunday, I caught up with John and Joe in Ohinimuri.

"How did the hearing go, Harry? Did they get a victory?"

"Yes. I have just found out they have awarded her £550. She is determined to have a legacy for the children's future. So I am going to put some feelers out to see what is around."

"How is Maggie doing?"

"John, she is very ill. I don't know what is going to happen. She is going downhill fast. I feel for Hannah who is looking after all the children and Maggie while I am here. We need me to work, but I just want to take care of her. I think she will need to be moved to Waikato Hospital if she gets any worse."

"Oh well, she will come right eventually… Did you hear that we are playing this week against Paeroa again? It should be a good match as we have Cameron back from his injury!"

"John, thanks … but I think I will get away. I have a few things to catch up on. See you boys tomorrow."

I could not believe them. They were both in their own world They didn't understand the pressures of family life or the love that I had for Maggie. John was a household name with the footy, and among the local druids, but they were caught up in single life. John hoped one day to be married but for now he was saving every penny to put towards an investment.

I found Rusty who had asked around about a decent farm. "Harry, one of the men said he had heard of a glorious 600-acre property for sale in Kirikiriroa. I looked into it and found out, Mr John Kenny, a well-respected local, has tended the farm for forty years but he's become sick and is desperate to sell. He does not have a family to leave his farm to, so reluctantly is selling everything, including the furniture, to move up to Auckland. It is a bargain at £820."

"Well done, Rusty, that sounds perfect. Does it include any stock?"

"Twelve horses, farming equipment and livestock."

"We don't have enough on our own. Perhaps John could lend us £200. In the six years Maggie and I had been away working on the Westland Rail line in Black River Station, he's probably made enough to help us out. We could also sell some of the equipment and livestock we don't need to recoup some of the money."

The next day I found John for a drink and asked for his help, he was a little hesitant at first, wanting to know when he could get his money out again and what he would get in return. We decided to go in together to purchase it, with our share being the bigger portion. We signed to make it official on the 6th of September, 1904. Maggie was still very weak but insisted on coming to visit. Hannah nursed her as she sailed to Raglan on the 26th and we made up a room for her on the sunny side, looking out over the green farmland. It was good to have her home. We thought the fresh air would do her good, that and finally realising our dream. I got back every second week, but she was still going downhill and on October 15th she went back to see a specialist. He said she needed to be cared for in hospital and so we admitted her into Waikato so she could be near the children.

We were working night and day to complete the tunnel before Christmas and I found it harder and harder to get away. The job was now well behind schedule and, with the prime minister scheduled to cut the ribbon, they wanted nothing to cause the company to lose face. Finally, we were nearing completion and they had organised a huge grand opening for the 13th of December. I was in agony as I knew Maggie was not at all well but decided to leave immediately after the celebration and head straight to see her, to spend our last Christmas season together.

At 5am on the 12th of December, a young man knocked on my door to hand me a note. It said: Call Hannah immediately at the hospital. I suspected the worst.

I ran to the hotel and woke up the proprietor and telephoned the hospital, who put Hannah on.

"Hannah, is that you? You sound awful!"

"We've been up all night. Maggie passed away in the early hours of this morning, Harry. She seemed fine so we did not want to disturb you as we knew the grand opening is today and you would be here immediately after your speech."

"Oh Hannah…" I stood fixed to the ground, my legs suddenly turning to jelly! "How! … I do not understand! I didn't realise she was so near! I should have just left days ago, I kept thinking we would get to enjoy a little of Christmas on the farm together.”

“They said there were complications.”

“I will pack my bags straight away and come up.”

“But haven’t you got the Prime Minister’s speech and cutting the ribbon at 10 am?”

“Richard Seddon does not need me to stay … if not for their bloody schedule, I would be there now!”

“Harry, she is peaceful now. There is nothing a few hours is going to change. See it through and then come.”

I held the telephone in silence, thinking about it reluctantly. “I suppose it is only a few extra hours. I will pack up now and stay for the cutting of the ribbon, then bugger them, I will come immediately after. How are you?” She burst out crying, sobbing from the depths of her soul. “Hannah, I am so sorry, I will be there as soon as I can.”

“Harry, we have had so much grief in our lives … it brings it all back again!

“I will be there as soon as I can get away, just leave it all for me to organise. I will see you later tonight.”

It hit me as I started to think about it all… *Hannah must be distraught. She has looked after the children and Maggie almost full time over the last year.* I was in shock as I thought of my lovely Angel … *I never got to say goodbye! The children will never grow up knowing their mother’*…

Danny, the proprietor, had been watching my face. “Are you alright, cobber? Looks like you’ve seen a ghost?”

“My wife just died … she’s twenty-nine … three children!” I gripped hard to my hat and stared at the floor as it all sunk in.

“Harry! I am so sorry … can I pour you a whiskey? You’ve got a huge day ahead.” He took a glass and poured it half full.

“I didn’t get to say goodbye!” I wanted to cry, but I just felt numb. "We've just bought this lovely farm … she never got to enjoy it."

"Why don't you just go, Harry – I'm sure everyone will understand."

"As soon as the ribbon is cut and the officiating complete, I'll be gone."

I travelled through the afternoon directly to the hospital. Hannah was there while Phee looked after the children at home. I held Hannah as she sobbed and sobbed. There was nothing to say, it was all just too painful. I slowly walked into Maggie's room and closed the door behind me. I could not believe it was Maggie's lifeless body lying there, she looked like she was sleeping. I knelt down and kissed her cold hand affectionately; whispered, "Maggie, my song bird … That damn tram! How could this happen to us? … You had so many more songs to sing. Who will sing to our children now!?"

I could not leave her, but eventually Hannah knocked quietly on the door. "Harry, I think we must go. It's nearly dark and we must get home on the roads."

I laid Maggie's hand gently on her chest.

"Hannah, her eyes are so sunken. Did she suffer? … though I suppose she is at peace now." I kissed her lips and stroked her head for the last time; looked back as we walked away.

Euphemia came with me the next day to help do the official paperwork. She was amazing, having dealt with so many funerals in her own family. It was a blur as we worked together.

Within a week, the funeral was behind us: Maggie had been transported back up to Auckland and laid to rest beside her father and family in Symonds Street.

Over the next week, I comforted Hannah often.

"Harry, it is so hard! … little Phem and Hec do not understand where Mummy went. I told them 'She has gone to be with Jesus in heaven.'

"Hannah, it is hard knowing what to say. I would not know what to say either."

"Yesterday they said 'Will she be here for Christmas? Mummy always sings to me in bed. I want Mummy. I said, 'She is singing in Heaven with the Angels now and having Christmas with Jesus'… I can sing to you!"

"It's a very hard time for us all. How do any of us make sense of it."

I sat down with her. "Hannah, I have not told you how much I admire the way you have loved and cared for our children and Maggie especially. I could not have gone to work if it was not for you holding the fort here. You are an incredible woman."

"Harry, I have struggled … It is so hard! Every time the children ask for Maggie it is like I am reliving her death all over again.

"I was excited today and wanted to tell Maggie about something I saw down the street, then I remembered she's gone."

"As you know, it takes a long time … How you and Phee cope, having lost Hector only months ago."

"I did not believe she would die. I really thought we would find someone who could help her recover."

I put my arms around Hannah. "We cannot make sense of these things, but while these little ones are still alive, she is still with us. Who knows why God allows these things to happen." I heaved a deep sigh. "Would you like me to get someone in to take over looking after the children?"

"I am happy to look after them for now. Let's talk about it once things settle down a little. I know their routines but let's share the responsibility until you feel like you can manage on your own. It makes good sense to have Annie with the other children over here, but I know I will find it hard expecting any minute for Maggie to be right there."

"Hannah, I am already dreading the thought of the tram accident anniversary coming up in the next two weeks."

"I am not sure I could face it either, being there for Christmas with the tram accident memorial, Father's death, now with Maggie gone, it will only get worse. All the flowers and well-wishers on the street will remind me of it every day.

"Harry, the neighbours have been so kind giving us flowers, gifts, hugs, and wishes of condolence, but I need to get away."

"Why don't we all stay for Christmas at the farm, it would be amazing for the children. I am sure Murdoch and the twins would love it! Maggie would have dreamed of it."

"That's a good idea. It will be good to get away for a few weeks."

"How long before you have to go back, Harry?"

I pulled a dour face. "I am free at present, but they are asking me to head back to the Westland Rail job. I should be excited as they are now ready to start on the big tunnel. It's one of two of the longest tunnels in the world and they want me to be the shift boss.

"What you will do?"

"I'm not even going to think about it until after Christmas, Hannah. I need a break. It's been exhausting work and with all that you have all suffered, I want to give you a break too!"

Chapter 36

Two Bomb Shells

"Euphemia, all these years I had dreamed of owning land, and here we are living on this beautiful farm forged over forty years, that has risen out of the virgin bush due to John Kenny's bare hands. This grand house, shaped out of this land, pit-sawn weatherboards, four big chimneys with hand-fired bricks, and wide verandas on two sides ..." I stood pointing to all the things out around me. "The oak furniture matches the beautiful tongue and groove dado-panelling running around that loungeroom wall. Comfortable sitting chairs in the study and a formal lounge overlooking the front yard. The huge Kauri table with its twelve chairs beside the kitchen is enough to fit everyone."

In every direction on the lower side, luscious green grass ran down to a river. Elsewhere, fruit trees stood like soldiers guarding the vegetable garden and a beautiful stand of bush rose up further over. The children ran about, not knowing what to do with all the space, then settled for playing on the front lawn.

"I've never seen them so happy, but damn it, Phee ..." I smashed my fist down on the table. "I'd give it all up just to have my songbird back. I feel like there's never going to be another song!"

"This is a beautiful farm, Harry, and I can't believe that Maggie is not here to enjoy it, but the children are so happy here."

I let out a deep breath that had locked inside from my anger.

"It's like a dream come true, but as much as I'm trying, it is like you say, bittersweet. Phee, no matter what mind games I play, I will always know it was purchased with Maggie's life. She will never be here to enjoy it. How do I get past that?"

I had not seen Euphemia so relaxed for such a long time. She looked radiant and did not have to go back to work until the second week after Christmas. She came to me and held my hands.

"Harry, you must remember how she was able to have four weeks here before she went into hospital. Even though she could hardly walk, she knew this would bring you all so much joy. Her spirit is here! If Maggie could see the children running around now...."

"They are so content. Have you noticed how quickly they drop off to sleep each night?"

"Whose are those cows over there?" Her gaze went further afield.

"We leased out 180 acres over on that side for grazing to help pay for the farm. The neighbour drops off fresh cream sometimes after milking."

"I love having fresh cream and eggs to make Madeira cake. You will have to plant wheat next. What part does your brother John have in it?"

"It was a bargain as Mr Kenny had no son to leave it to, but it was still more than the tram company's compensation. John had squirrelled money away from working in the mines and with some persuasion lent us the rest."

"Hannah said you had been offered work down in Greymouth back with the Public Works for Westland Rail!"

"I don't know. It's the job I've been working towards all my life, but now that Maggie's gone, I don't even care. I feel like ... what is the point?"

"What would you do instead?"

"This is a big farm – plenty to do with all the livestock. I could work the farm alongside John."

"Harry, I know it has been a dream come true for you to have a farm one day, but firstly you must know, you will never be a farmer! You are always looking for a better opportunity. This farm would suit you for about three months until, like an itch, you would launch into something new."

I looked at her, totally surprised by her comment.

"I have watched you for years now. You love the chase of a new thing. You love managing people but you are not good at day-to-day maintenance. Maggie did that."

I sat in a chair and lit a cigarette. *By God she's right.*

"The second thing is … you have never really got along with John that well – you are both so competitive, full of strong ideas and determination. Can you imagine working on the same farm with him? You would blow up the first time you had a great idea that he didn't like – which would be often as he is jealous."

I looked further stunned, as if I was suddenly walking around naked. "How did we not end up together, Phee, when you know me better than I know myself. We have a child together – we both love one another … have you ever thought about it?"

Euphemia lowered her voice as there was an open window in the homestead off the sun porch. "Not just one child!"

"What do you mean? Surely not!"

"The night you came back and I poured out my heart."

"How far along are you?"

"Well, I tried to remember, I think it was about mid-July."

"Don't we have even more reason now! …We have no excuse!"

"Harry, are you asking me to marry you?"

"I'm not ready for that conversation just yet … Let's call this a healthy discussion … My Marg and our Annie are virtually like twins. If we have another child, I will need a wife to look after them and your other nieces and nephew. You even said in the past, '*I wish I had never let you go!*'"

"It sounds rather convenient – someone to manage your house!"

I tried to whisper but felt angry. "Phee, you know that is not the case! I have loved you all these years, I slept with you because I have strong feelings for you! Now we have the chance to be together and you don't want to take it?"

"Calm down, Harry. It is not like I haven't thought about it!"

"What will happen to this child if it does not have a father?"

"Harry, who says my child needs a father for it to be happy?"

"*Our* child."

"I know I said that about not letting you go. I was drunk and it was two years ago, things have changed!"

My voice rose. "Alright, Phee, here is an honest observation from me! You are a free spirit. You love the idea of being passionately in love but really you would not last five minutes in a relationship because it is too much commitment for you … It is you who need your child looked after as you are far too busy with all the exciting things you want to achieve … running a business where there is no place for your own children."

Euphemia looked around as if someone might have overheard us and rose to her feet

"What? Harry, that's not fair! …I can do commitment. Look how I have looked after the house all these years! … I *do* want to have a life and not be stuck washing clothes and looking after a husband! … Maybe you are right, it would be nice to have Annie looked after in a family instead of alone with me … the thought of being passionate with you gets me excited but it could never work … look at us … we are too much alike. We would be tearing one another apart in five minutes … or less."

"This is the wrong time to be discussing all this. Everything is still so raw." *Oh, this woman … is so infuriating.* "Where does that leave *me* then!? Are you really serious, you would choose not to be with me! You would adopt this child out?"

"Harry, I think most of the time you are gorgeous. I would gladly sleep with you, but I do not want to marry you!" She stood in the open doorway looking out over the farm.

I wanted to break something. *How can she be so obstinate and stubborn!* I puffed furiously on my cigarette; sat back in the chair, flabbergasted. *I thought when Maggie died, one thing she might have condoned would be the two of us finally joining together in marriage … after all this time. After already having a fling or two…* I lit another cigarette.

As Phee walked away, she called back, "Hannah will marry you!"

It was like two bombshells dropped into the middle of my heart … "Hannah?" I shouted after her.

Hannah popped her head around the corner. "Did you want me?"

"Oh … we were just discussing what to do for Christmas. Shall we do something completely different and go camping down in the bush by the stream at the back of the farm?

"That sounds like fun. Have we got a tent?"

I tried to shake Phee's comment from my head. "Yes. Yes. The boys can help me erect it. We could cook out in the open for a few days, under the stars."

"We have three days away to organise everything, and the weather looks like it could be good for a few days."

"Good. I will ask Murdoch and the boys to come and help get things ready. We will load the big wagon and then if anyone does not want to sleep on the ground they can sleep in there."

As the weeks went by and the Christmas season passed, I couldn't help but notice Hannah after Phee's comment. I had not seen her as anything but a young girl, but suddenly I started noticing things about her. She was devoted to the children; often had a mischievous glint in her eye towards me. Although she was twenty-four, I loved the way she was so interested in so many things, and she could hold a great conversation. I really liked being around her.

January came and I received in the mail word that they needed me on the Otira tunnel as the company contracted to start there was having trouble.

If I am not cut out to run a farm, what am I going to do?

The prospects and the money were great in Otira, but how could I juggle family life with work being so far away? I would need a carer, or a wife. I wanted to ask Hannah how she felt about making a commitment to me, but it felt awkward as it was obvious – I really needed a wife.

Euphemia and the other family members had left a few weeks earlier, leaving just Hannah to look after the four children. I still felt angry with Phee, especially as she'd pointed out I would never be a farmer. As much as I wanted to prove her wrong, it annoyed me knowing she was damn right. I felt disquieted for days thinking about the big tunnel, and the opportunity I must not let pass. I kept putting off asking Hannah, but knew I must!

The opportunity arose as we relaxed one evening. Hannah sat sewing when she suddenly lifted her head and looked me straight in the face. "Go on, ask me!" she said.

I looked up from my paper. "Beg your pardon?"

"I know you have been skulking around for weeks wanting to ask, so do it." She carried on sewing.

"Alright, Hannah. All these months I have not asked you why you have so graciously looked after the children. I do not know what Maggie or I would have done had you not stepped in when you did and looked after Maggie and all the children all this time."

"Haven't you considered I didn't do it for you! … It has been one of the most trying experiences of my life to watch Maggie go downhill and die … every day I felt so powerless and sad for the children. The night she died she kept asking for you over and over. I hate you for that.”

“What? Why did you not tell me that before?”

“Harry, there has been so much going on. When would have been the right time? We did not know how to reach you as the exchange was shut that night. In the finish, she said to me, ‘I was hoping to have Harry here, to ask you both together before I die, but in case I do not see him again will you promise me, Hannah, that you will look after my children and bring them up? Euphemia is too independent even though she and Harry are in love. He is a good man, if he asks you to marry him, you will be happy.”

I threw the paper down on the floor and went over and sat beside her, watched her face for sincerity.

“I did not say anything because I did not know how to tell you.”

I stood again; walked about the room; lit a cigarette. “Hannah, that was a huge thing for her to ask you.” I stood looking at her, stunned. “I am so sorry I was not here. Damn that bloody tunnel!” I pulled a chair over and sat in front of her.

“I can never make it up to you, the sacrifice you’ve made. How do *you* feel about all this?”

She kept sewing automatedly. “I have watched you with the children and our family since I was a little girl. I know about your love for Euphemia, that you’ve slept with her a number of times … that you need someone to look after the children. I also overheard you talking to Phee on the front porch. She is probably right: it would never work with you two; you want different things in life; you would fight like cats and dogs.”

“It is painful to know how right she is … I just can’t believe that Maggie said all that to you! She was the most intuitive, lovely woman.”

“I also already knew Phee was pregnant. She has been sick for weeks now and her mood has changed?"

"Hannah, the night I came from Karangahake, we were compiling all the paperwork for the tram case. She poured out her heart and the pain we felt together. I comforted her. With all we have been through, it just happened."

"I do not condone it, but I am not surprised. Phee has carried much of the burden of this family over the past few years. She has been overwhelmed at times with no one to confide in. To answer your question, I adored my sister but I am not sure exactly how to fulfil Maggie's earnest appeal. I cannot imagine how it could work for me to care for the children … but I made a promise to her. What else was I to say – No, sorry I want to have a life of my own?"

I looked at her serious face. "Would you consider a union?"

Her face remained serious. "Don't tell me you're asking me to marry you!?"

"I have watched you since that night when Phee spoke of your admiration. To be honest, I hadn't really seen you as the beautiful, intelligent woman you are till Phee's outburst that night … to me, you were a young schoolgirl … but I have seen your deep love for our children and the way you nursed Maggie tirelessly. You have even taken on Annie for Euphemia as one of your own. I would love to have the opportunity to court you, if you would allow me."

She put her sewing down, stood and walked behind the settee then leant forward with her elbows out.

"I am twenty-four … you are asking me to commit my whole life! If I say yes to our courtship, I am potentially saying 'I will marry you."

"What is it that you want?"

"What do I want? Do you really care, or are you looking for a contract? I want to go to university and get an education; I want to fall passionately in love with a man while I am still young and have a family of my own.”

“What about the children?”

“Really, Harry! These are my nieces and nephew but they are not *my* children. These children are your responsibility! I am free to walk out that door whenever I choose.”

“Is there a way we can make an arrangement?”

She came over to me and spoke sternly. “I know that you are someone who is used to ordering people about and getting what you want with your charm. I’ve seen it for years. It seems to me, you might need to find yourself a governess to sign a contract, not a lover to share your life with. I think it is all too easy for you. I may just walk off one day and leave you to it. What have you ever given me?”

“I am sorry, Hannah. You are right. I have assumed too much of you. I know I have put you on the spot.”

“You are damn right you have expected too much! Do you know what *I* have sacrificed so you could go to work. I’ve been caring for Maggie and your children for a year now.”

“I did not think … I have been a selfish fool.”

“I know you will take the work at Otira that you spoke of. So what of the children? If I do go, they will be with someone who will not love them the way I do. I will be miserable knowing I had betrayed my own sister?”

“It is too complex and too hard to fathom tonight … Yes, I will probably take the job. I think we could make a new start. Is it alright to speak about this another time when we have had time to think and calm down a little?”

“Yes, I am off to bed now. Good night, Harry.”

She was still annoyed as she walked away without looking back.

I was again left speechless. How could I have taken her for granted … expected so much. And what could I do now?

Chapter 37

Keen as Mustard

Hannah found me in the shed the next day, "Harry, I am sorry for what I said last night; it has been incredibly hard processing everything. I couldn't sleep last night. We are all grieving. Anyone would be overwhelmed at the thought of a huge commitment and looking after four children. Let's just give it some time." She turned to walk away.

"Wait!" I walked closer to her. "Hannah, I have never respected you more than I did last night. I have been a stupid fool and you have every right to say what you did. You need to do whatever you have in your heart to do. If you wish to go to university, I would be more than happy to pay for you to study. If you *are* going to leave, could you give me time to find someone to care for the children?".

She looked at me coolly. "I will let you know when I am ready to leave." And she walked off.

I decided to do as she said and take a little time to show my appreciation even if she left. She needed to rest and recuperate a little. I spent time with the children playing games, milking the cows each day, feeding the chooks, cutting wood and making myself busy. The best way for us both was to get to know each other a little better. She had always been the little sister who I threw on my shoulders when she was eight years old; now she was a strong, beautiful woman.

I rose early, made the fire for her each morning before she

rose, made tea and boiled eggs on a tray which I took in to her. While she was getting the children ready, I cleaned out the wood box, filled up the baskets and made the children's breakfast and school lunch. I brought in the washing and folded it; picked up the children from school. In the afternoon, I took the children for a walk around the farm to give her time to prepare a meal. After dinner, I would read to the children, which became my favourite thing. Every now and then I caught her glancing my way from the kitchen. She never said much, curling up in front of the fire with a book while I caught up with the newspaper.

It was strange not going off to work each day, and I found myself one day laughing over something Hannah had said, realising I had not laughed in so long. I had started to play the piano accordion again while Hannah joined in with a song or two on the piano. She had a sharp mind and recited poems or literature in a fine voice. I found myself starting to look forward to the children going off to bed.

Three weeks passed and one night, after the children had been tucked into bed, I filled a glass of wine and found a pack of cards. I looked over at her reading, her face shining in the lamp light.

"Would you like a game of cards?"

She looked up, held her place with one finger on the page "Alright. What shall we play?"

"Any good at poker?"

"Not really but are we playing for money? You're not competitive, are you?"

"No, not at all!" We both laughed heartily.

"Hannah, I used to think of you as spoilt."

"Oh, I am sure I was! It has not been that easy over the past few years with Father. I do not think you have made it easy with some of the places you have taken Maggie and the children for work."

She came to the table and I dealt her a hand; arranged my cards and looked at her over them. "The problem with my work is that the railways are often in some valley in the middle of nowhere where there is no proper road, no towns, just rows of tents and poor facilities, full of grumpy men who are living away from their families.

"That is why you are putting the rail through."

"Yes. Most of the working men's camps are shocking conditions."

"Can I make an observation?"

"Please do."

"It has been lovely to see you relaxing with the children over this time and getting to know them better, but I think you are too tough on the children. You have spent so much time away from them you have never really got to know them."

I felt offended. "What do you mean, tough?"

"They are children – they are not meant to be perfect."

"I lost my father at nine. I have tried my best to be a good father but I haven't got a clue really. Hector has been the closest example of a father I have witnessed, and I am truly sorry we have lost him."

"You have come alive in the last week. I have not seen you like this."

"It's one of the nicest fun times I've had in years to truly relax. I have really enjoyed your company. I watch the way you care for the children … you are very kind. And I am trying … I will never forget the way you nursed Maggie with such compassion.

"Harry, it is no small thing you are asking of me. I want a lover, but I want to see if we are suited first. For now, the answer is not what you are searching for but I will see."

"Oh, so there is hope then?" I said in jest. She just smiled and focused back on her cards.

Another night I spoke up while making the fire. She was engrossed in a book, mindlessly sipping her hot tea "I have thought a lot about what you said the other night. I am sorry, many times I am rough round the edges as I spend all day telling men what to do. Sometimes it can be like managing children, sorting problems and disputes. Mostly, they are the roughest toughest men alive who are working in horrific conditions. Some of these men are being poisoned by gas through poor ventilation or have fingers blown off or crushed. They get paid badly; it is hard work no matter what you do. When I come home, I am often tired and grumpy. It is so foreign. You are tender, kind, caring. You make me want to try harder."

"Grumpy and impatient! Yes!" she said, smiling.

I went over and sat next to her. "Thank you. I have room for improvement." We laughed.

"Oh, I met the neighbour's daughter today," she said. "She was coming over to invite us to church this Sunday."

"How old is she? I have an idea."

"What? … she is about seventeen, the oldest of five children … You can't ask her to marry you!"

We both laughed again.

"What's your idea?"

"You'll see."

On Sunday, it was surprising how friendly everyone was and Hannah had not yet worked out what I was up to, until I came back one afternoon from fetching Charlotte in the buggy.

"Please come in. You have already met the children … and Hannah!"

"Oh, I love this beautiful home. I would sometimes come and cook with Mrs Kenny in her big kitchen."

"It's lovely to see you again. It appears by the sneaky look on Harry's face, he is up to something." Hannah was in her sewing apron, having come from the sitting room. "I want to take you to town."

Her eyebrows rose. "What should I wear?"

"You look lovely as you are. Perhaps change your shoes and bring a cardigan. I thought we could go for lunch."

Hannah's face lit up.

We made our way to town and soon we had eaten a sumptuous lunch in a fine dining parlour. I took her to a women's dress shop and told her to buy whatever she liked.

"Oh, Harry, can we afford this?"

"Hannah, anytime is a good time for some lovely new clothes."

"I do declare, Harry Bagust, you love clothes almost as much as me."

She did not take much convincing as she came out time and again in a new outfit; it was such fun. She smiled with delight at all the latest colours and styles.

"Harry, I feel guilty. The children all need new outfits. Could we go to the drapers and get fabric perhaps."

She took time looking through fabrics, picking out the perfect colours. Then we visited the shoe store, and returned home with two hat boxes, a dress and three lengths of fabric to cut out three dresses for the girls and a summer blouse for herself.

We arrived home to a lovely meal that Charlotte had cooked, and sat by the fire with a fine bottle of wine. I took Charlotte home in the last of the evening light and pressed four shillings into her palm. It was a glorious evening with a bright orange sunset as Hannah and I sat on the porch with a glass of red wine.

"Red sky at night, shepherds' delight. I don't know if I am the shepherd but, Hannah, these many weeks have been a thrill for me. I feel like I have got to know you for the first time."

"Me too. I must say, Harry, you have surprised me." She put her glass down and flicked me a sneaky grin. "Give me a minute!"

She slipped inside and came back ten minutes later in her glorious pink dress with tiny little white flowers on it and white shoes. Like a ballerina, she twirled around across the wide porch.

"Stunning!" I jumped to my feet and caught her slim waist in one hand, and twirled her on the spot. "Hannah, you are such a beautiful woman. I love this dress, it's alluring … in fact, wait."

I went through to the lounge and threw open the double-hung windows that opened to the porch, stoked up the fire, wound the gramophone and carefully placed the needle. I returned to her; pushed the chairs aside to clear a space. Then I took her hand, and we danced along the huge porch as the dusk lit up the horizon and the heavens came alive with one or two bright stars. We danced as one, her face beaming in the flickering fire light. She was light on her feet, like a feather, as we held each other close. We both looked at one another as if trying to measure the joy on each other's face. She stopped and, releasing her hair, tossed the ribbon over a chair, kicked off her shoes and took my hand again.

"Come on, Bagust, let's see what you've got!" she said with a cheeky grin.

I was suddenly captivated by her slim body and vibrant face as I took her by the waist and gently kissed her for the first time.

"Harry, that was not horrible – who knows, this might work yet," she said laughing.

We danced again, back and forth, transported to another world as our bodies melded in one movement of time and place. My passion and desire rising, I kissed her again. Her returning kisses were like a feather caressing my lips. She stood still then, looking at me with a serious face, measuring mine in return.

"Harry, this has been one of the loveliest days of my life … this was a test to see if you had it in you … today I have seen a man as keen as mustard to go the extra mile. I am prepared to commit my love to you. Your kisses are like sweet honey, unhinging all my resolve not to sleep with you …" She took my hand. "I have never been with a man, be gentle with me."

Without another word, she led me to her room where she sat on the edge of her bed. "Harry, this is the answer to your question I think you might like to ask, if I gave you the chance. The answer is … yes!

Chapter 38

Turn Up for the Books

On April 20th, Hannah and I sat across the table together discussing the sale of the farm when the children ran in with the mail. Hannah opened a letter from Euphemia saying it was time for her to come now as she was only about a week away from having the baby.

"She has obviously worked up until the last minute," I said. "You can leave the children here and we will manage while you are gone."

She poured me a fresh cup of tea, and handed me a biscuit. "Harry, there are so many things to organise for us going away. You will never get anything done looking after the children! I will take them with me. Besides, Phee will enjoy having a little life about the house again. Annie is her daughter, even though we have not told Annie that."

"There is a lot to get done but I could wait till you come back. How long do you think you'll be away?"

"Phee is almost due so I will stay for ten days after the baby is born to help out, then I will be back. Aunt Sarah or Aunt Christine will call on her after that."

"Alright then, I will pack, get all the repairs done and paint around the property to get it ready for sale. We have a house full of belongings and furniture, much of which we won't have room for in a small cottage.”

“Perhaps we can sell it with the house. I just hope we do not have to live in a work camp, otherwise we might as well take four suitcases, and pack a few boxes to go on the ship to Otira.”

“I am not sure yet but I think it would be good for us to have a house in Greymouth. I will stay in the work camp during the week then take the rail back in the weekend.”

“How long do you think the tunnel is likely to take to complete?”

“It could take ten years depending on the type of rock we find. They are saying it’s eight and a half miles through.”

“That’s an awful lot of dynamite, worn-out picks and shovels. Doesn’t that scare you a little, Harry?”

“I’m excited by the challenge – it will be a steep learning curve, but I think I’m up for it. How do *you* feel about it?”

“It’s certainly a turn up for the books for me. I have struggled with taking on four children, now I am relocating to somewhere I have only visited for a few days.”

“It is a bustling modern city with all the gold and coal industries; you could just get involved in something. Phem and Hec will be in school so it won’t take long to meet other mothers and settle in. Or you could come and live closer to Otira. We will basically have a small town set up – you might even find it nicer in a small community. I am told there is a school there too.”

“What will we do about the farm? Can we lease it out if it doesn’t sell!?”

“Bloody John, I told him the other day about us possibly going to the Westland project; he said he wants his money out because he has already found a farm that he wants to buy … Euphemia was right: I should never have borrowed the money from him!”

“Don’t get upset, Harry. Perhaps he has other reasons – he might have met a girl and wants a place of his own. It could be a good thing in the long run."

"My brother has always had a chip on his shoulder as if somehow he was hard done by. There's nothing for it but to sell."

"Did you happen to notice how frustrated you get when you come under pressure? You have been so relaxed all these months. You don't have to be in a rush." She came and sat on my lap, "I will miss you for a few weeks."

"Hannah, you won't even have time to think of me, looking after your demanding sister."

We kissed passionately before she got up and started packing the things she would take with her. It always surprised me how many trunks and boxes were needed for four children. I sent word that we would come down to Greymouth early next year as we prepared the farm. I placed an advertisement in the paper for the 26th April listing all the stock for sale. I began selling farm equipment we did not need, filling cases and trunks with the rest of our possessions ready to be shipped south.

The days went by quickly with much to do, then on the 8th of May I received a letter from Hannah saying Mary had come into the world on the 6th. Hannah would be home in the next two weeks. I thought, *I now have four girls. Hec might need a brother!*

I readied the farm for sale, making sure everything was repaired and painted. Hannah arrived in the late afternoon of the 20th, and all the children came running out to greet me, as I welcomed them home.

"Harry, the place looks so lovely; it makes me want to stay now that everything looks so finished. It is such a shame to be leaving here. Look at those rows of oaks: they are turning orange with the autumn. It looks like you have most things packed … the house looks so bare."

"Well, I realised we needed to get a lot of this on the ship so it's ready and waiting for us when we arrive. Besides, I missed your company, and the children's, so I kept busy. I could not bear the silence and did not know there were birds around here till you left."

"Thomas Bagust!" She started chasing me round the room, smiling, while flicking me with her gloves. I caught her waist and kissed her passionately.

"You look radiant. City life has done you good.

She kissed me again, and whispered, "It's not that … I'm late… feeling sick …" She smiled, hoping I would catch on.

"Oh, Hannah, really! When did you know? I was just telling myself I have four girls; perhaps it's time to give Hec a baby brother!"

"I thought I would surprise you. When I went aboard the *Talune* up to Auckland, I was unusually sick all the way. I thought maybe I had caught a bug off someone, because I am never sick on a ship. I spent a few days feeling very off and told Phee I was sick even after meals. She said, 'Did you have your monthly? Then I realised I was late. Phee just laughed at me saying, 'I know what you've been up to! Maggie would be delighted for you. You could have waited, mind you. I thought 'isn't that the pot calling the kettle black?'"

Hannah faced me and gripped my shoulders. "You know what this means, don't you?" She fixed her gaze on me.

I changed the subject. "How is little Mary?"

"She is doing well and growing by the day; she has your nose. She's a delight, and sleeping through already!"

"Is Phee going to keep her?"

"She is talking of adopting her out. I offered for us to somehow take her on, but Phee said it's too much with a baby on the way, and us moving down south. She has spoken to a McLeod cousin who is keen to adopt her. So that might work out alright after all."

"Can you get off. My knees have gone to sleep."

"Cheeky thing! … Phee is still talking of opening a restaurant."

I did not know what to say. Part of me felt angry that Euphemia did not want to marry me and give little Annie and Mary a chance to be with their own parents. On the other hand, we already have our hands full. At least we would be able to see her grow up, knowing she had close family that loved her. I carried all the luggage in and settled the children.

The next day I made a special trip into the jeweller in Hamilton to look for an engagement ring. I dressed up that night and helped get the children into bed.

"Where are you going with that red tie, Harry?"

I poured her a drink then dropped down on one knee and took out the ring from my waistcoat pocket.

"Oh my! You are serious! If you want to make an honest woman of me, it's too late," she said, laughing.

I took her hand; held up the ring.

"It was not till you went away that I realised how much I have looked forward to sitting talking with you in the evenings when the children are asleep. I love sitting peacefully knowing you are in the room. I want to be with you. You are amazing, Hannah. Will you marry me?"

"Oh, I don't know … Give me one good reason?"

"Hannah, truly, this has been one of the best six months of my life. Maggie was right when she said we would be happy together."

"What prospects do you have … You have not asked my father yet? …" She looked at me with a cheeky grin.

"You just love to see me on my knees and wouldn't I just love to ask him … if only I could. What would he say?"

"Thomas Henry Bagust, I will only say yes just so you don't have to be on your knees any longer … And he would say …" She pointed her chin and said in a gruff voice, "Now what are your prospects, young Harry? Do you come from good stock?"

I laughed at her theatrics and stood up to hug her. "You are such a witty, beautiful woman … I would love to have asked Hector for your hand in marriage. Would he have given his blessing?" I held her hands; looked directly into her eyes.

"Father loved you, Harry. I am sure, given the turn of events, he would have been overjoyed."

"I think he might have been shocked that Euphemia said no!"

"Harry, he might be shocked that he has five grandchildren and another on the way. I am sure after all his troubles and Madame Divine's scandal nothing would have surprised him."

"Thank goodness he did not live long enough to see Maggie die the way she did. I can't believe it has been six months already."

"How should we celebrate?" Hannah changed the subject. "We could have a wedding and invite the family. It's probably too late to have it here, but we could have a celebration in Auckland!"

"I would love to do something, but with Phee having sleepless nights with little Mary, the farm selling and us moving to the South Island, we should just register in the local office."

"You are probably right. We have many things to organise. Let's have a family celebration in Martinborough on the way down.

"Good idea. Hopefully we'll have money then too." She laughed.

"Let's aim for the 1st of June. We will need two witnesses."

"How exciting. Even if it's in the registry office, I am still going to dress up!"

"I will too then … you know, we do not need to be in a rush, so why don't we travel south and stay for a few months with my family. I know my sisters would be thrilled to meet you and get to know you a little. Otira can wait. They have not met all the little ones yet either, it would be a great chance to spend time together."

"Where would we live?"

"There's plenty of space at Mary's. Perhaps we could even stay till our little one is born, then go south. That way we can celebrate Christmas together. I will write and ask if that is alright with them – I do not want to presume."

"Tell them we would come as soon as the house has been sold."

We dressed up on the first of June and signed our names on the marriage certificate to make it all official. Charlotte came over one last time to look after the house and the children for a few days while I took Hannah to a luxurious hotel for a few nights.

It did not take too long to secure a buyer, as the farm looked magnificent. It was painful to be leaving our dream that Maggie and I had worked hard for, but we would put the money into a new investment of some sort. Phee was right: I was not born to be a farmer. Perhaps the family gene was not passed on to me.

I had read many times in the world news section, of our farming cousins in Australia … Grandfather's brother George, whose sons Henry and John Bagust bred the perfect Australian farm dog, a Blue Heeler. They either loved their dogs or loved farming, perhaps it was a bit of both.

Joe loved farming. It was really in his blood to be working with animals. He was a champion with his sheep dog, giving the locals in Martinborough some stiff competition.

Within months, we were settled into Mary's and relaxing, as I didn't need to work straight away having received a great price for the farm, and had paid John his share. I sat with her on the porch one morning having tea while Ellen and Hannah prepared to go and pick raspberries for jam.

Mary went past, then stood with her hands on her hips. "You know, Harry, I don't ever remember seeing you so content. Martinborough is looking more like our family seat than Timaru ever did with all our grown-up families here."

I nodded. "Hannah is really enjoying time with you all. It helps her cope as I know she misses her sisters, but the children are having fun getting to know their cousins. We will miss you all when we move south."

"We absolutely love Hannah! … Don't go," she said with a laugh. "Will you work while you are here?"

"I'd better, or you, Mother, El and Hannah will find me work to keep me occupied twenty-four hours a day. Joe has found me work on the farm he is employed at. Last week I joined him as part of his footy team. He boasted about my wrestling skills to some of the lads, so I trained in a few bouts with the local boys last week. Right now, I'm feeling very sore. Come and sit; I feel I haven't caught up with you properly."

She took a seat next to the washing pile.

"Here help me fold some of these." She tossed a pile of clothes on my head.

"We are lucky to have you here even for a few months. Do you like being back in our wee community? There are plenty of things for the children to be involved in … even if you can't sneeze without someone knowing about it?"

I started to make a stack of clothes on the table. "I saw Annie Linders a few days ago. She looks very old. Do you ever wonder where Emily could be?"

"Harry, wherever she is, I wish her well. Wouldn't she be laughing at you, with a handful of children. It's turned out for the best, don't you think?"

"Who would have thought, hey? This little town reminds me of being in Kuaotunu, although they were telling me at the bar how there is this bizarre rivalry still going on between the Harris family and the Martins."

"Joe told me about young Sarah Harris, a girl he has seen a few times up in the grand Harris mansion. I think it could be an infatuation, but he is too shy to approach her."

"Mother did say we should marry into them." I grinned. "Good for him."

"They are both a little young yet, but who knows? Do you think James will come down for Christmas?"

"I think Mother sent a letter asking him to come and celebrate Christmas with us all. Hopefully, he will bring Marg and Ernest with him. He's doing a slaughterman's job in Pukerino out towards Taranaki at present."

"I think he has changed since he returned from War. He said how it has made him appreciate what he has, living in peace."

We sat in silence for a moment. Then Mary said, "Hannah is getting big. The baby is due in January, isn't it?"

I nodded. "Mid-January. She's already hot and uncomfortable so by the time January comes, she will be more than ready to have it. At least it will be cooler in Greymouth through the summer months. We have decided to call it Kenneth after Hannah's brother if it's a boy, and Gladys if it's a girl. It's always a process picking names together, isn't it!"

"Harry, we will miss you when you go. Are you really looking forward to digging tunnels again?"

"I'm looking forward to getting my teeth into another challenge. It will be a very long project, the Otira tunnel, just breaking through is an incredible feat of engineering and calculations. We will dig in from each end, with a steep gradient uphill. If our calculations are out by a tiny amount, in a distance of eight and a half miles, we could miss each other completely."

She threw a bunch of socks at me. "This is what you studied hard for, but you might be sad to be inside a tunnel instead of out in a sheep paddock!"

"Sheep farming does not have the same appeal for me. Imagine carving a world-record-long tunnel through an enormous mountain ... an almost impossible task. I've got to be a part of that."

"Oh, the glory, Harry."

"I don't know about that, but the achievement compared to farming can't be matched!" I held my hands up with my palms open. "Anyway, the work is hard but it's constant and you know you are most likely to be paid."

"Don't you miss the farm in Kirikiriroa though; it sounded like a beautiful property."

"It was hard to sell it, considering it was one of the last things Maggie and I dreamed of together. I miss her, Mary, she was my sweet Angel. It's different with Hannah, she is a delight, but somehow different."

"You have probably not had time to grieve yet! It sneaks up on you. It's not been long since you lost her."

I leant forward, spoke a little softer. "My grieving was also over Phee not marrying me. I really don't understand women sometimes. How could she adopt out our child, when she could have been with me!"

"Perhaps it was not meant to be. She was the first woman to vote in New Zealand as a suffragette, it takes someone with an iron will to make that choice and to remain single. She obviously considers her independence more important! ... In a strange way, I admire her."

"An iron will is right ... Marg and Annie will start school next year, but Phee wants Annie held back so that Annie thinks she is Maggie's child and not hers. Can you imagine her growing up thinking her mother is dead and Phee is her aunt ... little Mary never knowing her mother at all ..."

"Perhaps it is better they never know. How would they feel knowing Phee did not want to be their mother?"

"I hadn't thought of it that way."

Hannah came in then. "What are you two talking about?"

Epilogue

I have 500 gold sovereigns in my hand, the price of selling the saloon. But I'm getting ahead of myself.

Otira crouched in a wet cold valley, with a road over it that resembled a massive snake winding its way up the steep gorge to the top of the alpine range. Only the sturdiest team of horses or desperate man dared the journey that connected the east coast to the west, passing over the rugged inner core of the South Island. If we could get this rail line in, it would save days sailing through perilous waters in the treacherous Southern Ocean. I'm sure in many years to come if this tunnel was complete, folk would still be enthralled by the grandeur travelling over snow-covered alps, viaducts spanning deep ravines and sixteen bloody tunnels.

Gazing out the windows still caused the hardiest soul trepidation, horror and amazement, wondering at our grit, courage and determination to traverse these impassable gorges. Such feats of engineering over these precipitous mountains could only be conceived with a touch of insanity. To connect the two pieces together an eight-and-a-half-mile uphill tunnel would need constructing. The two ends, cut toward each other, should only be out by the thickness of a steel bar. This tunnel would need an engine the size that has possibly not been invented yet. An engine capable of superhuman strength to even conceive pulling such massive loads of coal up through these alpine mountains and out onto the plains to Christchurch.

I felt excited by the possibilities ahead of us and, at the end of this contract, we would find a place to settle down where opportunities abound.